Amelia Calver

Everyday biography

Containing a collection of brief biographies arranged for every day in the year

Amelia Calver

Everyday biography
Containing a collection of brief biographies arranged for every day in the year
ISBN/EAN: 9783337271022

Printed in Europe, USA, Canada, Australia, Japan

Cover: Foto ©Raphael Reischuk / pixelio.de

More available books at **www.hansebooks.com**

EVERY-DAY BIOGRAPHY.

CONTAINING A COLLECTION

OF

BRIEF BIOGRAPHIES ARRANGED FOR EVERY DAY IN THE YEAR,
AS A BOOK OF REFERENCE FOR THE TEACHER,
STUDENT, CHAUTAUQUAN AND
HOME CIRCLES.

BY

AMELIA J. CALVER

NEW YORK:
FOWLER & WELLS CO.,
775 BROADWAY.
1889.

PREFACE.

On a pleasant September afternoon as I strolled along the seashore, I was attracted by the number, variety, and beauty of the colored pebbles which adorned the lips of the sea. With an eagerness of interest, I soon selected as many as I could carry away; but as I brought my pleasant search to a close, I cast one glance at my gathered treasures, and a longing gaze at the infinite stretch of glittering shore that I must leave, and the thought of the yet scattered beauties haunted me.

But when again in my mountain home, and I found in my collection such a variety, from the large symmetrical stone of milky whiteness, through every shade of color to the crystallized dew-drop, representatives of as many elements of the geological world, I appreciated my pebbles none the less, that on the wave-washed shore there were still myriads of pebbles whose number would be increasing through all time.

Similar to this seaside incident has been the experience of gathering the material for this little book, now offered to the public. In duties as teacher, in studies as Chautauquan, I have for several years past been collecting and arranging names in the order here found, as an easy reference for " Author's Days " in school, and " Memorial Days " in the Chautauqua home circle, until it was suggested by friends, that the work might be of profit to other schools and other home circles.

This little book makes no pretensions to a Cyclopedia, embracing every name of note in history, but represents some of those who by word or work, leave a distinct color on the shore of time, and have become conspicuous as my pebbles were upon that sparkling seashore.

Although many of the "grand old masters," the epoch-making names, are prominent, it has been an object also to present the "humbler poets," who sing the "simple heartfelt lays" that guide and gladden these common every-day lives of ours, where it is to be hoped this little volume will be especially useful. In compiling this work, I have regarded conciseness a necessity, and accuracy a duty, and have therefore aimed to consult the best authorities; and if it shall find a welcome on the desk of both teacher and student, and in the home library, where more costly references are wanting, I shall feel repaid for the time and care devoted to it   A. J. C.

Every-Day Biography.

January 1.

EDMUND BURKE, an illustrious British orator, lawyer, statesman and philanthropist, born in Dublin, Ireand, Jan. 1, 1730. Died July 9, 1797. His name will ever be remembered as a friend to the American colonies during their oppression by King George III. and by his memorable speech during the trial of Warren Hastings, which, though it did not convict Hastings, condemned his crimes in India, and saved the name of England.

PAUL REVERE, an American patriot of the Revolution, and one of the earliest American engravers, born at Boston, Mass., Jan. 1, 1735. Died in 1818. He was one of the noted Boston " tea party," and is famous for his " midnight-ride," through the county of Middlesex, to give notice of the intended attack of Gen. Gage. The town of North Chelsea, Mass., was named Revere in his honor in 1871.

ANTHONY WAYNE, "Mad Anthony," an American general during the Revolution, born in Chester County, Pa., Jan. 1, 1745. Died at Presque Isle (now Erie), Pa., Dec. 1796. His most brilliant achievements were his capture of Stony Point on the Hudson, July 15, 1779, and his complete victory over the Indians in Ohio.

Maria Edgeworth, a popular English authoress, born near Reading, Eng., Jan. 1, 1767. Died in May, 1849. Her writings for the young were particularly beneficial.

Arthur Hugh Clough, an English poet, born at Liverpool, Eng., Jan. 1, 1819. Died at Florence, Italy, Nov. 13, 1861. He was a favorite pupil of the famous Dr. Arnold of Rugby, and h's career was watched with sanguine hope. Emerson said of him in 1848, that "Tennyson would have to look well to his laurels."

Paul Hamilton Hayne, sometimes called "the Southern poet laureate," born at Charleston, S. C., Jan. 1, 1831. Died, 1886. He was editor of the "Southern Literary Messenger," and an author of rare talent.

James Ryder Randall, a Southern poet and editor, born in Baltimore, Md., Jan. 1, 1839.

He was author of "Maryland, my Maryland," the spirited confederate national song, published at the opening of the civil war.

January 2.

James Wolfe, a celebrated English general, born in Kent, England, Jan. 2, 1720. He was the hero of the capture of Quebec, during the French and Indian war, and died on the battle field, at the moment of victory, Sept. 13, 1759.

Hugh Swinton Legare, an American statesman, scholar and journalist, born in Charleston, S. C., Jan. 2, 1797. While editor-in-chief of the "Southern Quarterly Review," he elevated it to the first rank as a publication. Died suddenly at Boston, Mass., June 16, 1843, where he had gone with President Tyler to attend the celebration of the Bunker Hill monument.

John Romeyn Brodhead, an American historian, born in Philadelphia, Jan. 2, 1814. Died May 6, 1873. His eighty volumes of information, gathered in Holland, London and Paris, with which he returned in 1844, after a three years' search, was the greatest addition which the colonial history of New York ever received.

William Vincent Wells, captain, engineer, traveler, and a great-grandson of Samuel Adams, born at Boston, Mass., Jan. 2, 1826.

He built and commanded the first steamboat seen on the interior waters of California.

January 3.

Marcus Tullius Cicero, an illustrious Roman orator, philosopher and statesman, born at Arpino, Italy, Jan. 3, 106, b. c. He was killed by the soldiers of Mark Antony, near his villa, Dec. 7, 43 b. c. No greater master of composition and of the music of speech, has ever appeared among men. About eight hundred of his letters on politics, literature, domestic affairs, etc., and fifty of his orations, are extant.

Lucretia Mott, an American Quakeress, a noted reformer and philanthropist, born on the Island of Nantucket, Jan. 3, 1793. Died Nov. 11, 1880. She was an earnest and eloquent advocate of anti-slavery, and a trusted leader in the cause of woman's suffrage.

Douglas William Jerrold, celebrated as a humorist, journalist, a dramatical and satirical writer, born in London, Jan. 3, 1803. Died   1857. "Black-eyed Susan," one of the most popular dramas ever acted on the English stage, and "Mrs. Caudle's Curtain Lectures," are among his many writings.

Larkin Goldsmith Mead, a noted American sculptor, born at Chesterfield, N. H., Jan. 3, 1835.

He executed the celebrated "Recording Angel," the colossal statue of "Vermont" placed over the dome of the state-house at Montpelier, and other statues, prominent among which is the monument placed over Lincoln's tomb at Springfield, Ill., Oct. 15, 1874.

January 4.

AARON BURR, sen., father of Vice-President Burr, born in Fairfield, Conn., Jan. 4, 1716. Died in 1757. He was both a scholar and an eloquent man. His marriage with Esther, daughter of Jonathan Edwards, caused a name infamous in American history, to be connected with that eminent divine.

PAUL LOUIS COURIER, an ingenious and popular French author and pamphleteer, born in Paris, Jan. 4, 1772. He was assassinated in Touraine in 1825. His "Pamphlet des Pamphlets" has been pronounced "the most finished work in respect to taste, and the most wonderful in respect to art, in the language."

JAKOB LUDWIG GRIMM (the eldest of the noted Grimm brothers), an eminent German jurist and philologist, born at Hanau, Jan. 4, 1785. Died in Berlin, Sept., 1863. He was author of many works of the antiquities, language, and mythology of Germany, which are considered standard. His "Tales" are especially valuable in preserving the "folk-lore" of the country.

BENJAMIN LUNDY, an American philanthropist, born in Sussex Co., N. J., Jan. 4, 1789. Died in 1839. As early as 1815, he founded an anti-slavery association called the "Union Humane Society."

ISAAC PITMAN, inventor of the modern system of phonography, born at Trowbridge, Wiltshire, Eng., Jan. 4, 1813.

His brother, BENJ. PITMAN, also a phonographer, was a reporter of the treason-trials, and the trials of the assassins of President Lincoln.

January 5.

STEPHEN DECATUR, a celebrated American commodore, born at Sinnepuxent, Md., Jan. 5, 1779. He was famous for being at two different periods (1804, 1815), victorious over the pirates of the Barbary States in Africa; bringing them to terms, and extracting payment for injuries done to the American commerce. He was killed in a duel near Bladensburg, Md., by Com. James Barron, March, 1820.

ZEBULON MONTGOMERY PIKE, an American officer and traveler, born at Lamberton, N. J., Jan. 5, 1779. He was a surveyor of the newly acquired territory of Louisiana in 1805, and discovered that lofty peak of the Rocky Mountains in Colorado which bears his name. He commanded the expedition sent against York (now Toronto), Canada, and was killed in the assault, April 27, 1813.

ROGER CHARLES TICHBORNE, the real owner of the Tichborne estate, born in England, January 5, 1829. He is supposed to have been lost at sea, as the vessel in which he sailed April, 1854, was never heard from; and his estate being claimed by the impostor Arthur Orton, alias Thomas Castro, was the cause of the noted "Tichborne Trial."

January 6.

JOAN OF ARC, "Maid of Orleans," one of the most noted heroines of history, born in Lorraine, Jan. 6, 1411. In April, 1429, she led the Orleanists against the Burgundians and their English allies, and was so victorious that in three months Charles VII. was crowned at Rheims, and France was liberated, according to the prediction of her "voices." She now wished to return home, but was retained by the king ; and was shortly after captured by the Burgundians, delivered to the English, who burned her May 31, 1431. Her death stamped infamy on all parties connected with the war.

THOMAS CHITTENDEN, an American statesman, born at East Guilford, Conn., Jan. 6, 1730. Died 1797. He was one of the principal founders of Vermont, and was chosen first governor of that State.

CHARLES SUMNER, an American statesman, orator and lawyer, born in Boston, Mass., Jan. 6, 1811. Died March 11, 1874. He was distinguished for his strong anti-slavery principles, and was a confidential adviser of President Lincoln throughout his administration. Among his important services rendered to the government, were the "Resolutions on Foreign Mediation," and the "Freedman's Bureau" bill.

PAUL GUSTAVE DORE, a noted French engraver and designer, born in Strasburg, Jan. 6, 1832. Died Jan. 23, 1883. He is considered one of the most prolific designers which art has known, and the Doré Gallery has long been open in London for the purpose of exhibiting his designs.

SAVORGNAN DE BRAZZA, the French explorer of Africa, born at Rome, Jan. 6, 1842.

He has opened to the French a new, short, and easy road to the center of Africa by constructing a road from the French settlement at Gaboon to a tributary of the Congo, seventy miles from its mouth, thus overcoming the obstacles of the cataracts by which its mouth is blocked.

January 7.

ISRAEL PUTNAM, a celebrated American general of the Revolution, born at Salem, Mass., Jan. 7, 1718. Died in 1790. He distinguished himself during the French and Indian war by his reckless courage, and was particularly noted for his bravery at the battle of Bunker Hill.

MILLARD FILLMORE, the thirteenth President of the United States, born in Cayuga county, N. Y., Jan. 7, 1800. Died March, 1874. He was elevated to the office of President by the death of President Taylor, July 9, 1850.

MOSES YALE BEACH, an American mechanic and inventor, born in Wallingford, Conn., Jan. 7, 1800. Died 1863. He invented the rag-cutting machines now used in paper mills. In 1835 he became proprietor of the New York "Sun," said to be the first penny paper published in this country.

ALBERT BIERSTADT, an eminent landscape painter, born at Dusseldorf, Germany, Jan. 7, 1830.

He is famous for his magnificent pictures of scenes in the Rocky Mountains, where he spent several months sketching in company with Gen. Lander's expedition to that region.

THOMAS DE WITT TALMAGE, D.D., a celebrated American divine, born in New Jersey, Jan. 7, 1832.

He edited the "Christian at Work" for several years, and by his lectures and writings has attained a national reputation. He is pastor of the "Brooklyn Tabernacle," the largest Protestant church building in America.

January 8.

NICHOLAS BIDDLE, an American financier, born in

Philadelphia, Jan. 8, 1786. Died Feb., 1844. He was director and president of the United States bank in Philadelphia, which in Jackson's administration, was *the* political question of the day, the vetoing of which was one of the causes of the financial crisis of 1837. Mr. Biddle was the man entrusted with the fund for the establishment of Girard College, and to his exertion is due one of the most beautiful structures of modern times, the plan of which he proposed and caused to be reared, in the face of wild political excitement and opposition.

LOWELL MASON, the first musician who received the degree of "doctor of music" in America, born in Medford, Mass., Jan. 8, 1792. Died Aug. 11, 1872. He was author and compiler of many collections of choice music, and to him Massachusetts is indebted for introducing music into the public schools. "Bethany" alone would have rendered his name immortal.

JAMES D. WILLIAMS, an American statesman, widely known by his sobriquet, "Blue Jean," born in Packaway County, Ohio, Jan. 8, 1808. Died 1880. He was a member of Congress, and his election to the office of Governor of Indiana was one of the severest contests in the political history of the U. S.

GEORGE LUTHER STEARNS, a merchant of Boston, born at Medford, Mass., Jan. 8, 1809. Died there April 9, 1867. He was a prominent member of anti-slavery organizations, was a firm friend of John Brown during his campaign. He founded the "Commonwealth" and "Right Way" newspapers.

ALFRED R. WALLACE, an English scientist, traveler and explorer, born in Monmouthshire, Eng., Jan. 8, 1822.

He arrived at the theory of natural selection independent of Darwin's researches, and for his vast collection of natural specimens, and additions to natural history, he has received medals from two societies in France.

January 9.

ARMAND JEAN DE RANCE, a French abbé, born at Paris, France, Jan. 9, 1626. Died Oct. 27, 1700. He is noted as the founder of the order of "Trappists" of La Trappe, a class of monks who subject themselves to the practice of great austerities, and the endurance of extreme privations.

LEMUEL SHAW, LL.D., an eminent American jurist, born at Barnstable, Mass., Jan. 9, 1781. Died at Boston, March 30, 1861. He drafted the charter of the city of Boston, and for twenty-seven years was one of the corporation of Harvard College.

EDWARD JARVIS, M.D., a noted author of medical works, born at Concord, Mass., Jan. 9, 1803.

He has added valuable contributions to the science of medicine, and in 1852, was made president of the American Statistical Association.

EDWIN F. HATFIELD, D.D., an American editor, author, and divine, born in Elizabethtown, N. J., Jan. 9, 1807. Died 1883. He has contributed many valuable works to religious literature.

January 10.

ETHAN ALLEN, an officer of the Revolutionary war, born at Litchfield, Conn., Jan. 10, 1737. Died near Burlington, Vt., Feb. 12, 1789. He was leader of the famous "Green Mountain Boys," of Vermont, and hero of the capture of forts Ticonderoga and Crown Point, May 10, 1775.

MICHEL NEY, a famous French marshal, styled by Napoleon Bonaparte the " Bravest of the Brave," born at Sarre-Louis, Jan. 10, 1769. After the battle of Waterloo he was tried for treason by some of the factions of France, and shot Dec. 7, 1815. His death was a useless, cruel sacrifice, which has ever been a blot on French history.

DANIEL WISE, D.D., a Methodist divine, born at Portsmouth, Eng., Jan. 10, 1813.

He has edited several religious and Sunday School papers, and is author of more than thirty noted religious works for the young. He came to the U. S. in 1823.

January 11.

ALEXANDER HAMILTON, an illustrious American statesman, orator, and general, born on the island of Nevis, one of the West India Islands, Jan. 11, 1757. He was the first Secretary of the Treasury, after the adoption of the Constitution, and to him belongs the credit of placing the finances of the infant nation on a firm basis. Said Webster : " He smote the rock of the national resources, and abundant streams of revenue burst forth. He touched the corpse of public credit, and it sprang upon its feet." He died a victim of Aaron Burr's barbarous duel, July 12, 1804.

EZRA CORNELL, founder of the Cornell University at Ithaca, N. Y., born at Westchester Landing, N. Y., Jan. 11, 1807. Died at Ithaca, Dec. 9, 1874. He was father of Alonzo B. Cornell, a public man of New York, and for three years its governor.

BAYARD TAYLOR, a distinguished American traveler, author and poet, born in Chester Co., Pa., Jan. 11, 1825. Besides being author of many noted books of travel, he regularly contributed to "The Literary World" and the "Tribune," and was for a time assistant-editor of the latter paper. In 1878, he was appointed Minister to Germany, and died in Berlin, Dec. 19, the same year.

January 12.

JOHN WINTHROP, founder and first governor of Boston, born at Groton, Suffolk Co., England, Jan. 12, 1588. Died at Boston, March 26, 1649. He is said to have been eminent for wisdom, magnanimity, and other virtues.

SAMUEL HARRIS, the "apostle of Virginia," born in Hanover, Va., Jan. 12, 1724. Death unknown. He was a colonel of the militia and a Baptist divine, and was ordained an apostle by the general association, 1774.

JOHN HANCOCK, an American statesman and patriot, born in Quincy, Mass., Jan. 12, 1737. Died Oct.　,1793, He was chosen president of the Continental Congress in 1775, and was the first signer to the "Declaration of Independence," July 4, 1776. Was governor of Massachusetts from 1780, with the exception of two years, until his death.

JOHANN HEINRICH PESTALOZZI, a Swiss teacher and educational reformer of great merit, born at Zurich, Jan. 12, 1745. Died Feb. 27, 1827. He is considered the "Socrates of modern education," and the improved methods of teaching to-day are the outgrowth of the "new departure" inaugurated by him.

ALFRED TENNYSON, D.C.L., the celebrated poet laureate of England since 1852, born at Somerby in Lincolnshire, Jan. 12, 1809.

Among his many short poems, "The May Queen" and "Enoch Arden" are the most popular. "In Memoriam," a touching tribute to his friend, Arthur H. Hallam is his sweetest.

His place of residence for several years has been on the Isle of Wight.

January 13.

HUGH ORR, a manufacturer and inventor, of Bridgewater, Mass., born at Lochwinoch, Scotland, Jan., 1717. Died Dec. 6, 1798. His muskets made for the State of Massachusetts are said to have been the first manufactured in New England. He also invented machines for cleaning flaxseed, and manufacturing cotton.

SAMUEL WOODWORTH, an American journalist and poet, born in Scituate, Mass., Jan. 13, 1785. Died in 1842. He, in company with George P. Morris, founded "The New York Mirror" in 1823. Among his many lyrics, is the popular poem, "The Old Oaken Bucket."

SAMUEL PORTLAND CHASE, an eminent American statesman, born at Concord, N. H., Jan. 13, 1808. Died May 7, 1873. He was Secretary of the Treasury during Lincoln's first term, at which time he introduced "greenbacks." In Oct., 1864, he was appointed Chief Justice of the Supreme Court, which place he held until his death.

WILLIAM HENRY WELLS, an English editor and author, born at Plymouth, Eng., Jan. 13, 1810. Died 1885. He was one of the original editors of "Punch."

CHESTER SMITH LYMAN, an eminent American astronomer and scholar, born at Manchester, Conn., Jan. 13, 1814.

Going to the Sandwich Islands for his health, he taught the Royal School there, having as pupils four of the recent occupants of the Hawaiian throne.

When surveyor of California he sent to the Eastern States one of the earliest authentic accounts of the discovery of gold. He was also one of the revisers of Webster's Dictionary for the edition of 1864.

HORATIO ALGER, a popular American author, born at North Chelsea (now Revere), Mass., Jan. 13, 1834. His forte lies in describing juvenile life in New York city, which his "Ragged Dick" series plainly attests.

January 14.

WILLIAM WHIPPLE, statesman, general, judge, and "signer" to the "Declaration of Independence," born in Kittery, Me., Jan. 14, 1730. Died at Portsmouth, N. H., Nov. 28, 1786.

January 15.

PHILIP THE BOLD, Duke of Burgundy, born Jan. 15, 1342. Died in 1404. He was one of the most powerful French princes during the minority of Charles VI., and was the rival of the Duke of Orleans.

PHILIP LIVINGSTON, a "signer" to the "Declaration of Independence," born at Albany, N. Y., Jan. 15, 1716. Died 1778. He was one of the founders of the Chamber of Commerce, and greatly assisted Yale and Columbia Colleges.

January 16.

MOLIERE, whose real name was Jean Baptiste Poquelin, was born in Paris, Jan. 16, 1622. Died 1673. He was a celebrated French comic actor and author, to whom the most eminent critics have awarded the prize for the best written comedies. "The Misanthrope" is esteemed one of his masterpieces.

CHARLES HENRY DAVIS, an American naval officer, born in Boston, Mass., Jan. 16, 1807. Died 1877. To his efforts the American "Nautical Almanac" owes its present foundation.

January 17.

LEONHARD VON FUCHS, a German botanist, born at Wemdingon, Swabia, Jan. 17, 1501. Died May 10, 1566. As a botanist he corrected many current errors in the nomenclature of plants. That beautiful plant, the fuchsia, bears his name.

BENJAMIN FRANKLIN, one of the most eminent of Americans, a philosopher, statesman and author, born at Boston, Mass., Jan. 17, 1706. Died in Philadelphia, April 17, 1790. As a philosopher we find his discovery that lightning and electricity are identical, to be among his successes in that line. As a statesman he was one of the five chosen to prepare the "Declaration of Independence," and one of its "signers." Was sent to England, and also to France, as ambassador in behalf of the colonies. As an author his "Autobiography," and "Poor Richard's Almanac," were popular. His worth to the world is immortalized by Turgot's famous words: "He wrested the thunderbolt from heaven, and the scepter from tyrants."

THOMAS ALLEN, an American divine and patriot, born at Northampton, Mass., Jan. 17, 1743. Died Feb. 11, 1810. He was the first minister of Pittsfield, Mass., where he was ordained in 1764. His son William is the well-known D.D. and author, who for nineteen years was president of Bowdoin College.

CHARLES BROCKDEN BROWN, the first American novelist of any note, born at Philadelphia, Jan. 17, 1771. Died Feb. 22, 1810. He was editor of the "Monthly

Magazine, and American Review," and in 1803 founded "The Literary Magazine and American Register," which he edited for five years.

FELIX ROBERTSON, M.D., born at Nashville, Tenn., Jan. 17, 1780. Died there Sept. 10, 1865. He is thoroughly identified with the city of Nashville, being the first male child born in the city, practised medicine there forty years, was twice mayor, also long a president of the Bank of Tennessee, and a presiding officer of the University of Nashville.

CALEB CUSHING, a distinguished American jurist, politician and scholar, born in Essex Co., Mass., Jan. 17, 1800. Died 1879. He was appointed commissioner to China, and in 1844, negotiated the first treaty of the United States with that government.

HENRY INMAN, an American portrait painter of note, born at Utica, N. Y., Jan. 17, 1801. Died 1846. He was commissioned by Congress to adorn the National Capitol with historic paintings, but died before he had completed his work.

January 18.

BARON MONTESQUIEU, a brilliant, original and popular French author, born near Bordeaux, France, Jan. 18, 1689. Died in Paris, Feb. , 1755. He acquired a sudden celebrity by his "Persian Letters," in 1721 ; but his greatest work was "The Spirit of Laws," to which he devoted fourteen years. In eighteen months it ran through twenty-two editions.

JOSEPH TUCKERMAN, D.D., an American Unitarian divine, born at Boston, Mass., Jan. 18, 1778. Died 1840. He was one of the founders of the "American Seaman's

Friend Society," as well as many other philanthropic institutions.

DANIEL WEBSTER, a celebrated American statesman, jurist and orator, born at Salisbury, N. H., Jan. 18, 1792. Died at Mansfield, Mass., Oct. 24, 1852. He is considered "the greatest orator that has ever lived in the Western Hemisphere." One of the most remarkable speeches ever made in the American Congress was his reply to his opponent, Hayne, of South Carolina, who had strongly advocated "State Rights," and which terminated in those noted words, sacred to every true American : " Liberty and Union, now and forever, one and inseparable."

January 19.

JAMES WATT, a Scottish engineer, philosopher and inventor, born at Greenock on the Clyde in Scotland, Jan. 19, 1736. Died near Birmingham, Eng., Aug., 1819. He is distinguished for his important improvements on steam-engines, for his discovery that water when converted into steam, is expanded into eighteen times its bulk ; and by some writers it is claimed that he made the great chemical discovery—the composition of water—instead of Cavendish.

BERNARDIN ST. PIERRE, a celebrated French writer, born at Havre, France, Jan. 19, 1737. Died in Jan., 1814. He is regarded as one of the best prose writers of France, and his noted book " Paul and Virginia," is considered one of the finest works of French literature.

SAMUEL LORENZO KNAPP, an American editor and biographical author, born at Newburyport, Mass., Jan. 19, 1784. Died 1838.

HOWARD MALCOM, D.D., a Baptist divine, born at Philadelphia, Jan. 19, 1799. Died March 25, 1875. He was one of the founders of the "American Tract Society," and of the "Sunday School Union," also a missionary to China and India.

ROBERT EDMUND LEE, a celebrated Confederate general of the civil war, born at Stratford, Westmoreland Co., Va., Jan. 19, 1806. Died Oct. 12, 1870. He was son of General Henry Lee, of the Revolution, often called "Light-Horse Harry," and married the daughter of the adopted son of General Washington. After an arduous struggle as major-general of the Confederate forces—which as a Virginian he felt bound to lead—he surrendered to Grant, April 9, 1865, and thus closed the war.

EDGAR ALLEN POE, a distinguished American editor and poet, born at Baltimore, Md., Jan. 19, 1811. Died in 1849, of delirium tremens, that sad curse of humanity, which has engulfed so much literary genius. His "Raven" and "The Bells" will, of his short poems, longest live to perpetuate his memory.

January 20.

SUSANNAH WESLEY, the mother of the noted Methodist divines, born in England, Jan. 20, 1669. Died July 23, 1742. She is said to have been a model mother, and her sons owed much to her wise counsels. Her last request was: "Children, as soon as I am released, sing a psalm of praise to God."

RICHARD HENRY LEE, an American patriot, statesman and orator, born in Westmoreland Co., Va., Jan. 20, 1732. Died June 19, 1794. During the summer session of Congress, 1776, he it was who introduced the measure, "The United Colonies are, and ought to be, free and independent;" and two days later was "signer" to the "Declaration of Independence."

Robert Morris, a distinguished American statesman and financier, born in Lancashire, Eng., Jan. 20, 1734. Died in Philadelphia, 1806. He was a "signer" to the "Declaration of Independence," and it is said that "to Washington as general, Franklin as negotiator, and Morris as financier, American Independence owes its success." He pledged his private fortune to assist the soldiers, and yet in his old age he was imprisoned for debt!

Nathaniel Parker Willis, a distinguished American poet and miscellaneous writer, born at Portland, Me., Jan. 20, 1807. Died at his home, "Idlewild," Jan. 21, 1867. He founded in 1828 the "American Monthly Magazine," subsequently merged in the "New York Mirror," and in 1846 became associated with G. P. Morris as editor of the "Home Journal." His "Scriptorial Poems" are particularly beautiful.

David Wilmot, an eminent American legislator, born at Bethany, Wayne county, Pa., Jan. 20, 1814. Died at Towanda, Pa., March 16, 1868. He was distinguished as an opponent of slavery, and was author of the "Wilmot Proviso," a bill prohibiting slavery in the territory acquired from Mexico after the war of 1848. This, though a failure, created great excitement.

January 21.

John Fitch, an American inventor, born in Windsor, Conn., Jan. 21, 1743. Died in Kentucky, 1798. He is said by authorities to be the originator of running vessels by steam as early as 1785. He plied a boat on the Delaware at the rate of seven miles an hour, in 1790, but he gained no profit by it, and was considered an insane projector.

Francis Elias Spinner, an American military officer and politician, born in Herkimer county, N. Y., Jan. 21, 1802.

In 1861 he was appointed treasurer of the United States by Lincoln, which office he held until 1875, and his curious signature on the "greenbacks" during that period became more familiar than the autograph of any living man.

John Charles Fremont, the "Pathfinder" of the Rocky Mountains, an American explorer and general, born in Savannah, Ga., Jan. 21, 1813.

He was appointed by the government, in 1842, to open an overland route through the "Rockies" to the Pacific, at which time he ascended the peak which now bears his name. His subsequent expeditions among the savage tribes and inhospitable deserts have hardly been surpassed in the records of human adventure. He was sent as one of the first United States Senators from California in 1850, and in 1856 was nominated for President on the Republican ticket.

Horace Wells, M.D., an American dentist, born at Hartford, Union county, Vt., Jan. 21, 1815. He was the first to employ "laughing gas" to destroy pain during dental operations, which he caused to be used on himself successfully, Dec. 11, 1844. He died in a fit of mental aberration, on account of losing his patent, Jan. 14, 1848.

John C. Breckenridge, an American statesman and general, born near Lexington, Ky., Jan. 21, 1821. Died May, 1875. He was elected Vice-President with Buchanan in 1856, and nominated for President on the Democratic ticket in 1860. He occupied the position of Confederate general during the civil war, and in January, 1865, was appointed Secretary of War of the Confederacy.

THOMAS JONATHAN JACKSON, "Stonewall Jackson," a noted general of the Confederate army during the civil war, born at Clarksburg, Harrison county, W. Va., Jan. 21, 1824. Died of a wound received by mistake from his own forces during the battle of Chancellorsville, May 10, 1863. The advantages which the Confederates gained in that battle were dearly purchased by the loss of their noble leader.

January 22.

FRANCIS BACON, commonly called "Lord Bacon," one of the most illustrious philosophers of modern times, born in London, Eng., Jan. 22, 1561. Died April 19, 1625. He is more praiseworthy as a philosopher and a man of genius, than as a politician.

CHARLES O'CONOR, an eminent American lawyer, born in New York, Jan. 22, 1804. Died in Nantucket, 12, 1884. Though he had for some time previous retired from business, he was undoubtedly the greatest lawyer of the country, which with the stainless purity of his life, will make his name one long to be remembered.

JENNIE FOWLER WILLING, an eminent educational and temperance pioneer, born in Burford, Canada, Jan. 22, 1834. As an educator she was appointed Prof. of English Language and Literature at the Illinois Wesleyan Unversity; and as a pioneer in the temperance cause, was one of the first crusaders; and elected first

President of the National Woman's Christian Temperance Union, and became first editor of its organ, " Our Union."

January 23.

GEORGE GORDON NOEL BYRON—Lord Byron—an English poet of rare genius, born in London, Jan. 23, 1788. Died at Missolonghi, Italy, April 19, 1824. The sudden success of his most remarkable publication, " Childe Harold," gave rise to his noted expression: " I awoke one morning and found myself famous." He contracted his last illness during his efforts in the cause of Grecian freedom.

WILLIAM PAGE, an American artist of great merit, born in Albany, N. Y., Jan. 23, 1811. Died 1885. He was at one time president of the National Academy, and some of his copies from the old masters have been mistaken for originals.

LORENZO NILES FOWLER, one of the founders of the firm of " Fowler & Wells," born Jan. 23, 1811. He is author of several works on phrenology, and has lectured extensively in the United States and Great Britain in the interest of that science. His wife, Dr. Lydia Folger, was among the first female graduates of a medical college in this country. She died in London, Jan. 26, 1879.

January 24.

FREDERIC II., of Prussia, surnamed " The Great," born Jan. 24, 1712. Died Aug. 17, 1786. He was king from 1740 to 1786, and he left to his nephew and successor a powerful and well organized kingdom, one-half larger in area than it had been at his own accession.

JOHN MASON NEALE, an English theologian and historical writer, born in London, Jan. 24, 1818. Died at East Grinstead, Aug., 1866. He was founder of the sisterhood of St. Margaret, and a writer of many popular hymns, among which is "Jerusalem the Golden."

HENRY JARVIS RAYMOND, LL.D., an able American journalist, orator and statesman, born at Lima, N. Y., Jan. 24, 1820. Died in New York city, June 18, 1869. In 1851 he founded the "New York Times," which he continued to edit with success until his death.

JOHN MACGREGOR, "Rob Roy," a modern traveler, born at Gravesend, Eng., Jan. 24, 1825. He is author of the "Rob Roy" Series, which was the name of the canoe in which he explored the Danube, Nile, Jordan, etc.

January 25.

EZEKIEL CHEEVER, an eminent teacher in early colonial times, born in London, Eng., Jan. 25, 1615. Died Aug. 21, 1708. He was one of the founders of the New Haven colony, and having received a superior classical education in England, he devoted his time to teaching in the different colonies for seventy years.

JOSEPH LOUIS LAGRANGE, one of the most eminent geometers of modern times, born at Turin, Jan. 25, 1736. Died in April, 1813. His valuable discoveries in the general principles of mathematics and astronomy are considered second only to Newton's. "After Newton's discovery of the elliptic orbits of the plants," says Playfair, "Lagrange's discovery of their periodical inequalities is the noblest truth in physical astronomy."

ROBERT BURNS, the national bard of Scotland, born near the town of Ayr, Scotland, Jan. 25, 1759. Died

July 21, 1796. His peculiar fitful genius never led him to attempt any lengthy work, but his "Tam O'Shanter" proves that he was capable of placing something among the world-renowned productions equal to Goethe's "Faust" or Cervante's "Don Quixote." Had his brilliant life extended into thoughtful and sobered age, his probably would have been a leading name among poets.

JAMES HOGG, "the Ettrick shepherd," a British author, born in Ettrick, Selkirkshire, Scotland, Jan. 25, 1772. Died Nov. 21, 1835. In 1813 he gave to the public the "Queen's Wake," which, says Prof. Wilson, "is a garland of fair forest-flowers, bound with a band of rushes from the moor," and procured him a high reputation as a poet.

GOUVERNEUR KEMBLE, born in New York city, Jan. 25, 1786. Died Sept. 16, 1875. He established the West Point Foundry, at Cold Spring, in 1817 ; was one of the first and most active advocates of the Hudson River Railroad, and one of the last survivors of the "Tontine Association."

JOEL PARKER, LL.D., a distinguished American jurist and author, born at Jaffrey, N. H., Jan. 25, 1795. Died at Cambridge, Aug. 17, 1875.

January 26.

CORNELIUS P. VAN NESS, LL.D., an American lawyer and statesman, born in Vermont, Jan. 26, 1781. Died in Philadelphia,   1852. He was appointed commissioner in 1818 to settle the boundaries between the United States and Great Britain.

THOMAS NOON TALFOURD, an English dramatist, essayist and biographical author, born in Doxey, a suburb of Stafford, Jan. 26, 1795. Died   1854. He was biographer of nearly all the prominent authors of his day, and was the first to recognize publicly the genius of Wordsworth.

JULIA DENT GRANT, wife of the honored general and president Grant, born in St. Louis, Mo., Jan. 26, 1826.

When America called Grant to the presidential chair, she stood with dignity at his side, and commanded the respect of all who beheld her ; and this respect has been enhanced by her continued dignity through the trials and sufferings of Grant's last days.

January 27.

THOMAS WILLIS, M.D., F.R.S., an eminent English anatomist and physician, born at Great Bedwin, Wiltshire, England, Jan. 27, 1621. Died in 1675. He was one of the founders of the " Royal Society " and for many years was considered " the most famous physician of his time."

WOLFGANG AMADEUS MOZART, one of the greatest musicians and musical composers of the world, born at Salzburg, Jan. 27, 1756. His masterpiece is the opera " Don Giovanni " or " Don Juan ;" but his " Requiem," composed with the presentiment of his death, is considered his most sublime work. The jealousy of contemporary musicians marred and shortened his life. He died Dec.   , 1791, and went to his grave unfollowed by a friend, with fifteen other dead, to the common burying ground of the poor, and his grave is unknown.

FRIEDRICH WILHELM JOSEPH SCHELLING, one of the four chief metaphysical philosophers of Germany, born near Stuttgart, Jan. 27, 1775. Died at Ragaz, Switzerland, Aug., 1854. In 1826 he was appointed to the chair of philosophy in the University of Munich, where his celebrity as a lecturer attracted multitudes of students from various countries of Europe. On his succeeding Hegel as professor of philosophy at Berlin in 1841, he was hailed as one destined to deliver Philosophy from the logic of Pantheism, and lead her back to Christ. Schelling is distinguished from the other great philosophers of Germany, by his combining with rare intellectual powers, poetic gifts of a high order.

DAVID F. STRAUSS, an eminent German author and theological critic, born in Ludwigsburg, Germany, Jan. 27, 1808. Died at his native place, Feb. 9, 1874. His " Old Faith and the New " is one of his best known works.

January 28.

RICHARD DE BEAUCHAMP, twelfth Earl of Warwick, born in Worcestershire, Jan. 28, 1381. Died at Rouen, 1439. He was called by the Emperor Sigismund, the "father of courtesy;" and also gained the title of "the good earl." He was the father of Richard Neville, known as "the king-maker."

JAMES TALLMADGE, LL.D., an American lawyer and statesman, born at Stamford, N. Y., Jan. 28, 1778. Died in New York city, Sept. 29, 1853. He was one of the founders of the University of New York, and for nineteen years was president of the American Institute.

WILLIAM TUDOR, an American scholar and author, born at Boston, Jan. 28, 1779. Died at Rio Janeiro, March 9, 1830. He was one of the founders of the Boston Athenæum, first editor of the " North American Review " and originator of the Bunker Hill Monument.

January 29.

EMANUEL SWEDENBORG, founder of the "Sweden-borgians," sometimes called the "New Jerusalem Church," born in Stockholm, Sweden, Jan. 29, 1688. Died March 20, 1772. Besides his many theological writings he published many scientific and philosophical works, and had the friendship and confidence of the sovereigns of Sweden until his death.

THOMAS PAINE, the noted deistical author, born in Thetford, England, Jan. 29, 1737. Died in New York, 1809. His work "Common Sense," did much to arouse the Americans to the necessity of an independent republican government. A portion of his "Age of Reason" was written while imprisoned in France, in 1795.

GEN. HENRY LEE, "Light-Horse Harry," a general of the Revolution, born in Westmoreland Co., Va., Jan. 29, 1756. Died March 25, 1816, of injuries sustained while trying to defend the house of Alexander C. Hanson, an editor, from a mob. In his celebrated eulogy on Washington occurs the words: "First in war, first in peace, and first in the hearts of his countrymen."

ALBERT GALLATIN, an eminent American statesman, born at Geneva, Switzerland, Jan. 29, 1761. Died Aug. 12, 1849. He was a great oracle and leader of the Republican party; was one of the signers to the treaty of Ghent, in 1814, in company with Adams and Clay.

January 30.

WALTER SAVAGE LANDOR, an eminent English author and poet, born at Ipsley Court, Warwickshire. Eng., Jan. 30, 1775. Died at Florence, Sept. , 1864.

Nathaniel Prentiss Banks, an American statesman and general, born at Waltham, Mass., Jan. 30, 1816. He was an able general of the Federal army during the civil war, previous to which he was governor of Massachusetts at three elections. He was at one time Speaker of the House, and served as chairman in the Fortieth and Forty-first Congress.

January 31.

Anthony Benezet, an eminent philanthropist, born in France, Jan. 31, 1713. Died in 1784. He was a zealous opponent of the slave trade, and his tracts written on the subject after he emigrated to America, are said to have first drawn the attention of Clarkson and Wilberforce to that subject.

Gouverneur Morris, a distinguished statesman of New York, born at Morrisania, Westchester Co., N. Y., Jan. 31, 1752. Died in his native town, Nov. 6, 1816. He assisted in drafting the State constitution of New York, and was one of the committee which drafted the Federal Constitution of 1787. He was also one of the originators of the New York canal system, and of the coinage of the United States.

Bernard Barton, known as the "Quaker poet," born in London, Jan. 31, 1784. Died Feb. 19, 1849. He was a member of the Society of Friends, and his works are noted for their pious sentiment and tenderness.

Franz Schubert, an eminent German composer, born at Vienna, Jan. 31, 1797. Died there, Nov. 19, 1828. He exercised himself in almost every species of musical composition, but is best known by his songs and ballads, more than fifty of which still live, and are ranked among the most exquisite productions of the kind.

JOHN SUMMERFIELD, a Methodist divine and distinguished pulpit orator, born at Preston, England, Jan. 31, 1798. Died in New York, June 13, 1825. He was one of the founders of the "American Tract Society," and his rare eloquence attracted large crowds in the cities of America.

JAMES G. BLAINE, an American statesman, born in Washington Co., Pa., Jan. 31, 1830. He was elected to the Thirty-eighth, Thirty-ninth, Fortieth, Forty-first, Forty-second, and Forty-third Congresses, serving in the three last named as Speaker. He was appointed Secretary of State in Garfield's Cabinet, but resigned on the death of the latter. He was the defeated Republican candidate for President in 1884.

February 1.

SIR EDWARD COKE, an eminent English judge and jurist, born at Milcham, Norfolk, England, Feb. 1, 1552. Died Sept. 3, 1633. He was the principal framer of the "Bill of Rights" and carried it through Parliament, and was author of legal works which are still standards of law in England.

CHARLES MINER, "John Harwood," an American journalist and author, born at Norwich, Conn., Feb. 1, 1780. Died at Wilkesbarre, Penn., Oct. 26, 1865. By his writings he introduced and popularized silk culture in the United States.

RICHARD WHATELY, Archbishop of Dublin, a noted English thinker and writer, born in London, England, Feb. 1, 1787. Died at Dublin, Ireland, Oct.   , 1863. He was one of the founders of the "Broad Church" party, and is justly considered to have been one of the most profound and original thinkers of his time.

February 2.

SIR WILLIAM PHIPPS, a prominent American in early colonial times, born in Woolwich, Eng., Feb. 2, 1651. Died in London, February 18, 1695. He was an ignorant shepherd, knighted for successfully obtaining $1,000,000 worth of treasure from a sunken Spanish ship off the coast of the Bahamas. He served in the colonial army against the French in 1690, and in 1692 became the first royal governor of Massachusetts.

HANNAH MORE, a noted English teacher, poet and authoress, born at Stapleton, England, Feb. 2, 1745. Died Sept. 7, 1833. "The Shepherd of Salisbury Plain" is one among her many works. At her death she left a fortune of £30,000, one-third of which was bequeathed to charitable purposes.

JOHN C. DALTON, a distinguished American physiologist, born at Chelmsford, Mass., Feb. 2, 1825.

His many valuable works have given him a wide reputation, and placed him in the first rank of American physiologists.

February 3.

JOSEPH C. NEAL, an American journalist and humorous writer, born in Greenland, N. H., Feb. 3, 1807. Died in 1848. In 1831 he became editor of "The Pennsylvanian;" in 1844 founded the popular "Neal's Saturday Gazette." "Charcoal Sketches," his best known production, was published 1837.

FELIX MENDELSSOHN, an eminent German composer, born at Hamburg, Feb. 3, 1809. Died Nov. 4, 1847.

His "Elijah," an oratorio, caused a greater sensation in the musical world than had been known since the days of Handel. He was aided in his musical entertainments by his talented sister Fanny, to whom he was devoted, and her death gave him a sorrow from which he never recovered.

HORACE GREELEY, a distinguished American journalist, born in Amherst, N. H., Feb. 3, 1811. He was founder or editor successively of the "Morning Post," "New Yorker," "The Jeffersonian," and "The Log Cabin;" but in 1841 his journalistic talents culminated in "The Daily Tribune," which, through his influence, became an earnest advocate of temperance, woman's rights, the abolition of slavery, and other reforms. He was an unsuccessful candidate for the Presidency in 1872, which, with the loss of his wife, caused his death Nov. 29 of the same year.

AMELIA B. WELBY, an American authoress, born at St. Michael's, Md., Feb. 3, 1819. Died at Louisville, Ky., May 3, 1852.

ELISHA KENT KANE, M.D., a distinguished American explorer, born in Philadelphia, Feb. 3, 1820. Died at Havana, Feb. 16, 1857. The purpose of his Arctic expeditions—to find Sir John Franklin—was a failure; but his well written account of his voyage, together with his knowledge of the existence of an open Polar sea, made of them a grand success.

February 4.

ANNE, Queen of Great Britain, and last reigning sovereign of the house of Stuart, born in Twickenham, near London, Feb. 4, 1664. Died 1714. She was the second daughter of James II. and succeeded to the throne in 1702. One of the most celebrated events of her reign was the union of England and Scotland, 1707. As a period of literature, her reign compares well with the Augustan age of Rome. Newton, Addison, Pope, Bolingbroke, Swift, De Foe, and Arbuthnot, were celebrated men of the times. Anne's seventeen children all died before she became Queen.

Josiah Quincy, LL. D., an American statesman and author, born at Boston, Feb. 4, 1772. Died at Quincy, Mass., July 1, 1864. He was the second Mayor of Boston, and for sixteen years was president of the Harvard University. "King Josiah the First" was a title given him while he was leader of the Federal party in the National Congress.

Lucy Hooper, an American authoress and poet of great promise, born in Newburyport, Mass., Feb. 4, 1816. Died August 1, 1841. Whittier wrote a beautiful poem to her memory.

February 5.

John Witherspoon, D.D., LL.D., a distinguished American divine and scholar, born in Haddington, Scotland, Feb. 5, 1722. Died Nov. 15, 1794. He was a father of the Presbyterian church in America, and a "signer" of the "Declaration of Independence." He identified himself so thoroughly with the interests of his adopted country, that to perpetuate his memory, his colossal statue was erected and unveiled in Fairmount Park, Philadelphia, 1876.

James Otis, a celebrated American patriot and orator, born at West Barnstable, Mass., Feb. 5, 1725. So ardent was he in the cause of American oppression, that he was considered by the English government one of the three unpardonable rebels of the colonies, John Hancock and Samuel Adams, being the other two. He was killed by lightning, May, 1783.

SIR ROBERT PEEL, called by his opponents "Orange Peel," in allusion to his hostility to Catholics, a celebrated English statesman, born in Lancashire, England, Feb. 5, 1788. He was universally respected for honesty, truth and ability. He filled many eminent positions in the government, and influenced important reforms. Died in consequence of a fall from his horse, July 2, 1850.

JOHN LINDLEY, LL. D., F. R. S., botanist and author, born in Catton, Norfolk, Eng., Feb. 5, 1799. Died near London, Nov. 1, 1865. He was one of the most eminent botanists of the present century ; was professor of botany in University College, London, and his writings on that science are of first importance.

OLE BORNEMANN BULL, a celebrated Norwegian violinist, born at Bergen, Feb. 5, 1810. Died August 18, 1880. Having met with brilliant success in the principal capitals of Europe, he came to America in 1845, purchased 120,000 acres of land in Pennsylvania, and planted the Swedish colony of Oleona ; but it proved a failure.

DWIGHT LYMAN MOODY, an eminent American evangelist, born in Northfield, Franklin county, Mass., Feb. 5, 1837.

His success as an evangelist, plain and unassuming as he is, proves the fact that religion is of the heart, not the head ; and a direct, forcible appeal will reach the heart, while the elegant and flowery discourse loses its way in the intricacies of the brain.

February 6.

AARON BURR, an American soldier and statesman, born at Newark, N. J., Feb. 6, 1756. Died Sept. 14, 1836. He was Vice-President of the United States during Jefferson's term, but after the ill-fated duel in which Alexander Hamilton lost his life, he became unpopular. His attempts to work against the government in Mexico and the adjacent territories, caused his arrest for treason, but though tried, he was acquitted.

DAVID REED, an American scholar and philanthropist, born at Easton, Mass., Feb. 6, 1790. Died at Boston, June 7, 1870. He founded the "Christian Register" in Boston, 1821, and was one of the founders of the American Anti-Slavery Society in 1828.

WILLIAM MAXWELL EVARTS, an eminent American lawyer and statesman, born in Boston, Mass., Feb. 6, 1818.

He was the leading counsel for the defense of President Johnson during his trial in 1868, and was one of the three lawyers appointed by President Grant, in 1871, to defend the interests of the citizens of the United States during the Geneva arbitration, which met to settle the "Alabama Claims."

February 7.

SIR THOMAS MORE, an eminent English wit, philosopher, author, and statesman, born in London, Feb. 7, 1480. In 1516 he produced his famous Platonic fiction, "Utopia." He was appointed Lord Chancellor, in place of Cardinal Wolsey, which position he resigned, because his conscience refused to sanction the divorce of Queen Catherine from Henry VIII. He was pronounced guilty of treason for denying the king's supremacy as head of the church, and was executed July 6, 1535.

Sydney E. Morse, an eminent author and journalist, born at Charlestown, Mass., Feb. 7, 1794. Died in New York, Dec. 23, 1871. In 1815 he founded the "Boston Recorder," the first religious newspaper of the country, and in 1823, with his brother, R. C. Morse, founded the "New York Observer," the oldest weekly newspaper in New York. Bought out and published the noted Morse's Atlas and geographies. He was brother of S. F. B. Morse.

Charles Dickens, one of the most popular of English novelists, born at Landport, Portsmouth, Feb. 7, 1812. Died June 9, 1870. Of his works so well known, "David Copperfield" (in which, it is said, incidents of his own life are introduced), is regarded by many as the best; while the peculiar vein of humor in the "Pickwick Papers" has never been equaled in English literature. He was a noted reader, as well as writer, and gave his last reading on the 5th of March, 1870.

February 8.

Samuel Butler, a witty English poet, born in Worcestershire, England, Feb. 8, 1612. Died Sept. 25, 1680. He was hostile to the Puritans, and satirized them in his noted poem "Hudibras."

James W. Webb, an American journalist, born at Claverack, N. Y., Feb. 8, 1802.

He was for thirty-four years sole editor and proprietor of "The Morning Courier" and "New York Enquirer," which two papers he united in one.

Jules Verne, a modern French writer, born at Nantes, France, Feb. 8, 1828.

His peculiar fanciful works, commencing with "Around the World in Eighty Days," have become very popular.

February 9.

William Henry Harrison, ninth President of the United States, born at Berkley, Charles county, Va., Feb. 9, 1773. Gaining the battle of Tippecanoe, at a time when the settling of Indian affairs in the "Northwest" was of importance, won for him a popularity which at last led him to the Presidency. But he lived only one month afterward, and died April 4, 1841.

Samuel J. Tilden, an eminent American lawyer and statesman, born in New Lebanon, Columbia county, N. Y., Feb. 9, 1814. Died at Gramercy Park, New York, Aug. 7, 1886. He was governor of New York in 1874, and an unsuccessful candidate for the Presidency in 1876.

Samuel Bowles, an American journalist, born in Springfield, Mass., Feb. 9, 1826. Died in 1878. He was for many years editor-in-chief of the "Springfield Republican," one of the most successful journals in the United States.

William D. Whitney, a noted American scholar, born at Northampton, Mass., Feb. 9, 1827.

He was the first President of the American Philological Association, and a leading Orientalist and Sanskrit scholar.

February 10.

Samuel Wesley, eldest brother of Charles and 

John Wesley, the founders of Methodism, born in London, Feb. 10, 1690. Died Nov. 6, 1739. Like his distinguished brothers, he was greatly gifted in poetry, and will be known to posterity by his contributions to the Methodist hymn book. He was one of the founders of the first Infirmary at Westminster, now St. George's Hospital.

ALBERT G. GREENE, an American judge and scholar, born at Providence, R. I., Feb. 10, 1802. Died at Cleveland, Ohio, Jan. 3, 1868. He was for many years president of the Rhode Island Historical Society. He will be long remembered by his popular lyric "Old Grimes is dead."

JOHN RUSKIN, an English artist and eloquent writer on art and nature, born in London, Feb 10, 1819.

Among his many eloquent works, "The Seven Lamps of Architecture" and "The Stones of Venice," are particularly noted for their efforts to introduce a loftier conception of the significance of domestic architecture.

February 11.

DANIEL BOONE, a famous American pioneer and hunter, born in Bucks County, Pa., Feb. 11, 1735. Died Sept. 20, 1820. His name is always associated with the settlement of Kentucky, whose wilds he was the first white man to penetrate.

LOUISA CATHERINE ADAMS, wife of John Quincy Adams, born in London, England, Feb. 11, 1775. Died in 1852. "With her closed the list of the ladies of the Revolution."

LYDIA MARIA CHILD, a noted American writer, born at Medford, Mass., Feb. 11, 1802. Died at Wayland Center, Mass., Oct. 20, 1880. She was one of the earliest writers of the anti-slavery agitation in America, and her works on that subject are esteemed among the best of their kind. Many think that in writing her " Progress of Religious Ideas " she wandered from her true work in life; her genial, kindly spirit fitted her better for the imaginative and philanthropic.

ALEXANDER H. STEPHENS, LL.D., an American statesman, born near Crawfordville, Ga., Feb. 11, 1812. Died March 3, 1883. He was Vice-President of the Confederacy during the civil war; and in 1870 published "A Constitutional View of the War between the States."

THOMAS ALVA EDISON, Ph.D., Chevalier of the Legion of Honor, the great American inventor, born in Milan, Erie County, Ohio, Feb. 11, 1847.

While his name is intimately associated with the electric light, telephone and phonograph, his other useful inventions multiply rapidly in his extensive laboratory in Menlo Park, N. J., and really the " Wizard of Menlo Park " will soon lead the van of the world's inventors.

February 12.

COTTON MATHER, a celebrated American theologian and writer, born at Boston, Mass, Feb. 12, 1663. Died there Feb. 13, 1728. Of his many works his " Magnalia Christi Americana" is the most noted. His connection with the Salem witchcraft is said to be more the fault of the age than the man, as his philanthropy was rare for that age.

THADDEUS KOSCIUSKO, an illustrious Polish patriot and general, born in Lithuania, Feb. 12, 1746. Died in Switzerland, Oct. 16, 1817. He assisted the Americans during their Revolutionary struggle, and at the close returned to Poland, and vainly fought for its independence.

NAHUM MITCHEL, an American statesman and judge, born at East Bridgewater, Mass., Feb. 12, 1769. Died there Aug. 1, 1853. Judge Mitchel is chiefly remembered as the author of the first extended town history published in America—the history of Bridgewater.

PETER COOPER, an eminent American manufacturer, inventor and philanthropist, born in the city of New York, Feb. 12, 1791. Died April 4, 1883.

His immense wealth was always devoted to the advancement of art and science, and the cherished object of his life was fully realized by the building of Cooper Institute in New York, "to be forever devoted to the union of art and science in their applications to the useful purposes of life." He was one of the six capitalists who formed the first Atlantic Telegraph Company in 1854.

ABRAHAM LINCOLN, sixteenth President of the United States, born in Larue County, Ky., Feb. 12, 1809. Died April 15, 1865. He was President during the terrible crisis of the civil war, and fully executed the object of his administration—the freedom of the slaves and the restoration of the authority of the government, but just in the hour of triumph he was cut off by the hand of an assassin, John Wilkes Booth, who shot him in Ford's Theater, Washington, D. C., April 14, 1865. "The name of Lincoln," says the historian Merle d'Aubigne, "will remain one of the greatest that history has to inscribe on its annals."

CHARLES ROBERT DARWIN, F.R.S., an eminent English naturalist and author, born at Shrewsbury, England, Feb. 12, 1809. Died Aug. 20, 1882. Among his many works, his "Origin of Species" has rendered his name immortal, and his "Journal of

Researches," written after his voyage as a naturalist to South America, is said to be the most entertaining book of genuine travels ever written.

BENSON JOHN LOSSING, an American historian and engraver, born in Dutchess County, N. Y., Feb. 12, 1813.

Most of his works have enjoyed a great and worthy popularity.

GEORGE H. PREBLE, U. S. N., an American naval officer, born in Maine, Feb. 12, 1816. Died   1885. He passed through the entire line of officers in the navy during the Mexican and civil wars, and as an author has made valuable contributions to history. He is the author of "Our Flag."

CHARLES MAURICE TALLEYRAND, an eminent French diplomatist and wit, born in Paris, Feb. 13, 1754. Died there, May   , 1838. His was a checkered life of good and ill—now a favorite and now an enemy of royalty.

DAVID DUDLEY FIELD, an American jurist, born at Haddam, Conn., Feb. 13, 1805.

He is eldest brother of Cyrus W. Field, and gained distinction by his writings on law reforms.

JOHN A. RAWLINS, a distinguished American general, born at East Galena, Ill., Feb. 13, 1831. He was associated with General Grant in all his campaigns and battles during the civil war, and rose to the rank of major-general. He was appointed Secretary of War in Grant's administration, but died soon after, Sept. 6, 1869.

February 14.

GALILEO GALILEI, an illustrious Italian mathematician and philosopher, born at Pisa, Feb. 14, 1564. Died Jan.   , 1642. While officiating as professor of mathematics in the University at Pisa, he discovered the law by which the velocity of falling bodies is accelerated; and during this period he invented a thermometer. In 1609 he constructed a telescope, the first one used for astronomical purposes, although he conceived the idea from a toy spy-glass made by Jansen, a Dutch optician. He invented the clock pendulum, which idea he obtained from the swinging of a lamp suspended in a church; but his most important discovery was that of Jupiter's satellites, which afforded the first good method of determining longitude.

JOHANN CHRISTOPH VON GLUCK, an eminent German composer, born near Newmarket, Feb. 14, 1714. Died in Vienna, Nov., 1787. During his popularity a violent musical contest was carried on between Gluck and the French composers. The queen of France, Maria Antoinette, supported the former, who had been her teacher in music. He is considered the father of the modern opera and "the Michael Angelo of music." His "Iphigenia in Taurus" is considered his masterpiece.

SAMUEL OSGOOD, an American statesman, born at Andover, Mass., Feb. 14, 1748. Died 1813. He was appointed commissioner of the Treasury' in 1785, and in 1789 first postmaster-general.

JAMES APPLETON, an American general, born at Ipswich, Mass., Feb. 14, 1815. Died Aug. 25, 1882. He was an energetic champion of total abstinence, and the first expounder of the principle underlying the Maine law.

HENRY GRINNELL, an American merchant, born at New Bedford, Mass., Feb. 14, 1797. Died June ,1874. He was the first president of the American Geographical Society, and fitted out two expeditions in search of Sir John Franklin. Grinnell Land, in the Arctic seas, is named in his honor.

CYRUS H. McCORMICK, a noted American inventor, born in Rockbridge County, Va., Feb. 14, 1809. Died in Chicago, May 13, 1883. By his invention of the noted reaper which bears his name, he has done more than any one man to make America the center of the grain trade of the world.

WINFIELD SCOTT HANCOCK, a noted general of the civil war, born in Montgomery County, Pa., Feb. 14, 1824. Died Feb. 9, 1886. He was an unsuccessful candidate for the Presidency in 1880.

February 15.

JEREMY BENTHAM, a celebrated English jurist and utilitarian philosopher and author, born in London, Feb. 15, 1748. Died at Westminster, June 6, 1832. He was the greatest critic of legislation and government in his day ; and the doctrine of utility, his leading principle, "the greatest happiness of the greatest number," though coined by Priestley, grew out of the theory of his life work.

RUFUS WILMOT GRISWOLD, an American author and publisher, born at Benson, Vt., Feb. 15, 1815. Died in New York, Aug. 27, 1857. He was publisher of the first edition of Milton's prose in America ; and among his works is "Washington and his Generals."

SUSAN BROWNELL ANTHONY, an eminent advocate of woman's suffrage, temperance and anti-slavery causes, born in South Adams, Mass., Feb. 15, 1820.

She was manager of the International Council of Women held in Washington, D. C., during the month of March, 1888.

WILLIAM FRANKLIN PHELPS, an American educator and author of note, born at Auburn, N. Y., Feb. 15, 1845. He was president of the National Association for the Centennial year, and author of valuable books for school teachers.

MARCELLA SEMBRICH, or more properly Mrs. Stengel, one of the foremost soprani in the world, born in Galicia, Feb. 15, 1858.

She has sung in most of the principal cities of Europe, and as one of Mr. Abbey's large and excellent troupe won great fame in America.

February 16.

PHILIP MELANCTHON, one of the great Protestant reformers, born at Bretten, in the Palatinate of the Rhine, Feb. 16, 1497. Died at Wittenberg, April 19, 1560. He was a valuable co-worker with Martin Luther, and though they varied in some of their views, their intimate friendship was never broken. He wrote his most important work, the "Augsburg Confession," in 1530.

HENRY WILSON, the "Natick cobbler," an American statesman, born in Farrington, N. H., Feb. 16, 1812. He was an energetic laborer in the anti-slavery cause, and for many years was a member of the National Senate. In 1872 he was elected Vice-President of the United States and died in the Capitol at Washington, Nov. 22, 1875.

JULIA COLEMAN, one of the leading philanthropists and temperance reformers of to-day, born in Fulton County, N. Y., Feb. 16,

For upward of twenty years she has studied the subject of alcohol in all its phases, and is at the front in the scientific educational temperance work, being author of leading scientific text books for both old and young. Her conferences, conducted in connection with grove camp meetings, are very largely attended and exert a wide influence. With her test apparatus she exposes the sly spirit of alcohol in many of the innocent nostrums sold in the form of tonic bitters.

February 17.

JOHANN TOBIAS MAYER, one of the most celebrated astronomers of the eighteenth century, born at Marbach, Wurtemberg, Feb. 17, 1723. Died Feb. 20, 1762. Mayer was the author of many able works, and of some ingenious inventions, among them the repeating circle.

JOHN PICKERING, LL.D., an American jurist and scholar, born at Salem, Mass., Feb. 17, 1777. Died at Boston, May 5, 1846.

He is considered chief founder of American comparative philology, founder and first president of the American Oriental Society, and for many years was a correspondent of the noted Wilhelm von Humboldt.

ROSE TERRY COOK, an American writer and poetess, born in Hartford, Conn., Feb. 17, 1827.

Her contributions to the periodicals of the day are hailed with delight.

February 18.

MARY I., Queen of England, 1553–1558, born at Greenwich Castle, Feb. 18, 1516. Died Nov. 17, 1558.

She was the daughter of Henry VIII. and Catherine of Aragon, and will always be remembered by her persecution of the Protestants, which branded her with the title of " Bloody Mary."

JEAN MARIE ROLAND, an eminent French statesman and author, born in France, Feb. 18, 1734.   He was the husband of the famous Madame Roland, and during the French Revolution they were both imprisoned.   Roland escaped, but on hearing of the execution of his wife, he stabbed himself, Nov.15, 1793.

CHARLES LAMB, a popular English essayist and humorist, born in London, Feb. 18, 1775.   Died at Edmonton, Dec. 27, 1834. His reputation is founded chiefly on his prose works, especially the " Essays of Elia." He was tenderly attached to his sister Mary, and was assisted by her in some of his works, particularly in his " Tales from Shakespere."   She survived him thirteen years.

GEORGE PEABODY, an eminent and philanthropic banker of London, born in South Danvers (now Peabody), Mass., Feb. 18, 1795.

He is said to have given more than $2,000,000 to the founding of colleges, schools and scientific institutions, and $300,000 for the benefit of the working classes of London.   He died in London, Nov. 4, 1869, and his funeral services were performed in Westminster Abbey, but his body was brought home to his native town for interment.

WILLIAM TECUMSEH SHERMAN, an eminent American general during the civil war, born in Lancaster, Ohio, Feb. 18, 1820.

He was second only to Grant in prominence through success, and his famous " march to the sea " will remain in bold relief as long as history is written.

February 19.

NICHOLAS COPERNICUS, the celebrated astronomer, born at Thorn, in Prussia, Feb. 19, 1473. Died June 11, 1543. By his great discovery that the planets move around the sun, he is author of the "Copernican System," which entirely remodeled all previous systems. His great work, "The Revolutions of the Celestial Orbs," was only printed in time to be placed in his hands the day he died.

GEN. THEODORE LYMAN, an American author and politician, born in Boston, Mass., Feb. 19, 1792. Died at Boston, July 17, 1849. He was author of many works, and founder of the State Reform School at Westborough.

SIDNEY RIGDON, a Mormon leader, born in St. Clair, Allegheny County, Pa., Feb. 19, 1793.

It is said that Rigdon was the printer who first made public (in connection with Joseph Smith), "The Book of Mormon," a manuscript given him to be printed by one Spaulding, its author. He was one of the presidents of the Mormon Church, but refusing to acknowledge Young, after the death of Smith was excommunicated, and died at Friendship, N. Y., July 14, 1876.

REV. LEONARD BACON, an American divine and author, born at Detroit, Mich., Feb. 19, 1802. Died Dec. 24, 1881. He was author of many theological works, and a distinguished adherent of the Congregational Church. In 1850 he became one of the editors of the "Independent."

WILLIAM WETMORE STORY, LL.D., an American lawyer, sculptor and author, born in Salem, Mass.. Feb. 19, 1819.

He has spent many years in Rome, and is better known as an artist in Europe than in America.

February 20.

FRANCOIS MARIE VOLTAIRE, the most remarkable name in the history of French literature, born at Chatenay, France, Feb. 20, 1694. Died May 30, 1778.

He was an intimate friend of "Frederic the Great" of Prussia, and "ruled the kingdom of letters with regal sway during the eighteenth century," and is supposed to have contributed more to the subsequent Revolution in France, and the temporary overthrow of religion in his native land, than any one man.

DAVID GARRICK, a famous English actor, born in Hereford, Feb. 20, 1716. As an author he exercised his talents with success in writing numerous comedies, etc., but as an actor, Pope said, "he never had his equal, and never will." He died in London, Jan. 20, 1779, and was buried with great pomp at Westminster Abbey beside the tomb of Shakespere.

WILLIAM PRESCOTT, an American officer of the Revolution, born in Groton, Mass., Feb. 20, 1726. Died Oct. 13, 1795. He fought with distinguished bravery at the battle of Bunker Hill, where he was one of the chief commanders.

ANGELINA GRIMKE WELD, an American philanthropist, born at Charleston, S. C., Feb. 20, 1805. Died 1879. She, with her sister, Sarah Moore Grimke, liberated their slaves and delivered public addresses against slavery, as early as 1836, when it was rather a novelty in the United States.

WILLIAM ALLEN BUTLER, an American lawyer, born in Albany, N. Y., Feb. 20, 1825.

He is the author of the noted poem "Nothing to Wear," which has obtained great popularity both in Europe and America, and by which he will be known as long as city life and fashion exist.

JOSEPH JEFFERSON, an American comedian, born in Philadelphia, Feb. 20, 1829.

He has won his reputation by his remarkable performance of the part of Rip Van Winkle, in the play of that name written by Dion Boucicault, from Washington Irving's exquisite romance.

February 21.

NATHANIEL ROCHESTER, Major-General during the Revolution, born in Westmoreland County, Va., Feb. 21, 1752. Died May 17, 1831. In 1818 he purchased large tracts of land in the Genesee valley and settled in Rochester, which had been named after him.

SANTA ANA, a Mexican president and general, born at Jalapa, Mexico, Feb. 21, 1798. Died June 20, 1876. He was defeated by both Scott and Taylor in the Mexican war and went into exile. His subsequent life was one of many triumphs, defeats and changes, incident to the revolutionary character of the Mexicans.

ELIZABETH R. THOMPSON, a noted American philanthropist, born in Lyndon, Vt., Feb. 21, 1821.

She is the great granddaughter of the brave Hannah Dustan, and a relative on the maternal side of Pocahontas, the Indian princess. Inheriting an income from her husband has enabled her to carry into practice schemes of noble philanthropy, for which trait she has been distinguished from early life. Through her efforts, students have been educated to posts of honor and trust, schools have been founded, colleges endowed, the weak and infirm have been provided for and the erring reclaimed. Some years ago she bought three thousand acres at the foot of the Rocky Mountains, near Denver, where, by erecting public buildings, she formed a nucleus for a flourishing settlement. It is said that she has given more than fifteen farms to persons worthy of her gifts, for with philanthropy she also possesses that discrimination which is the needed balance. She lost much property in the great Boston fire of 1872, and before ascertaining her own losses, telegraphed to her trustee, "Are my tenants suffering ? if so, provide for them."

WOLCOTT GIBBS, M.D., LL.D., a noted scientist and author, born in New York City, Feb. 21, 1822.

He is author of many valuable researches, and one of the editors of the " American Journal of Science and Arts."

ALICE E. FREEMAN, Ph.D., an eminent pioneer of female education, born in Colesville, Broome County, N. Y., Feb. 21, 1855.

To her is due a notable share of the great success attending the hazardous undertaking of co-education. She was one of the pioneers when the University of Michigan opened its doors to women. In 1882 she became president of Wellesley College.

February 22.

GEORGE WASHINGTON, the first President of the United States, born in Westmoreland County, Va., Feb. 22, 1732. Died Dec. 14, 1799.

As a Revolutionary patriot, soldier, general, statesman and " father of his country," his name will always live ; " but," said Garfield, " eternity alone will reveal to the human race its debt of gratitude to the peerless and immortal name of Washington."

Joseph Meacham, the leading agent in organizing the so-called Shaker Church and its system of community of interests, born in Enfield, Conn., Feb. 22, 1742. Died at New Lebanon, Aug. 16, 1796. He was a gifted Baptist minister, previous to his conversion to the doctrines taught by Ann Lee, and was appointed by her to lead the believers in her testimony and organize their church relation.

Josiah Quincy, Jr., an American orator and patriot, born in Massachusetts, Feb. 22, 1744. To promote the public welfare, and the cause of liberty, he made a voyage to England, October, 1774, and after conferring with Dr. Franklin and other friends of America, hastened to return with plans and counsels, which it was not prudent to commit to writing; but before the end of his voyage, he died at sea, April, 1775.

James Russell Lowell, LL.D., an eminent American poet, author, editor, and humorist, born at Cambridge, Mass., Feb. 22, 1819.

His many works, too popular to need mention, are among the treasures of the household library. The "Vision of Sir Launfal" is considered his most ambitious poem. He has lately returned from the court of St. James.

February 23.

Samuel Pepys, F.R.S., an English gentleman, and connoisseur, born in London, Feb. 23, 1633. Died there May 25, 1703. He was founder of the Pepysean Library at Cambridge; but his reputation is founded on his short-hand "Diary," written 1660–1669, though not published until 1825, which has given a clear insight into the every-day life of the times of the later Stuarts.

GEORGE FREDERIC HANDEL, one of the most excellent, profound and original of musical composers, born at Halle, Saxony, Feb. 23, 1685. Died in London, April 14, 1759. In early life his musical studies were severe and his compositions many; but it was not until he was fifty-five that he gave himself entirely to oratorio, his true work. The people of Dublin, for whom he wrote his greatest work, "The Messiah," were the first to appreciate his full worth. Mozart and Beethoven reverenced him as a superior, acknowledging that he excelled all other composers in the colossal effects of his choruses.

EMMA C. HART WILLARD, a pioneer in the cause of female education, born in Berlin, Conn., Feb. 23, 1787. Died at Troy, N. Y., April 15, 1870. Besides her many valuable works as author, she was founder in 1821, and principal of the Troy seminary for girls.

JOHN H. VINCENT, D.D., LL.D., "The Apostle of Sunday Schools," editor and author, born at Tuscaloosa, Ala., Feb. 23, 1832.

He was the chief founder of the Normal and International Sunday-School Lesson System; but his latest beneficence to mankind is the Chautauqua series of educational institutions of which he was the chief organizer. In May, 1888, he was ordained a Bishop of the Methodist Episcopal Church.

February 24.

EPHRAIM WILLIAMS, an American officer during the French and Indian war, born at Newton, Mass., Feb. 24, 1715. Possessing a grant of land in the present township of Williamstown, Mass., he bequeathed his property to found a free school there, which afterward became Williams College.   He was killed while leading a regiment to the invasion of Canada, Sept. 8, 1755.

Theophilus Parsons, an eminent American jurist, born in Essex County, Mass., Feb. 24, 1750.   Died in 1813.   He was a member of the convention which, in 1779, framed the State Constitution of Massachusetts ; also a member of the convention called to ratify the Constitution of the United States in 1787.   As a lawyer he had few equals in the United States.

William H. Crawford, an American statesman, born in Amherst County, Va., Feb. 24, 1772.   Died Sept. 15, 1834.   He was elected to the United States Senate in 1807; minister to France, 1813 ; became Secretary of War, 1815 ; and Secretary of the Treasury, 1816.   In 1824 he was nominated for the Presidency with three others, Jackson, J. Q. Adams, and Henry Clay.

George William Curtis, a popular American author, orator and journalist, born in Providence, R. I, Feb. 24, 1824.

Besides his many noted works, prominent among which are "Lotus Eating," "The Potiphar Papers," "Prue and I," etc., he has been an editor of "Harper's Weekly," and of the "Easy Chair" in "Harper's Monthly."

Homer Winslow, an American painter of note, born in Boston, Mass., Feb. 24, 1836.

His "Prisoners to the Front," exhibited in the Paris Exposition, was one of the few American pictures which French artists would recognize, and made his name famous.

February 25.

Charles Cotesworth Pinckney, an American

statesman and patriot, born at Charleston, S. C., Feb. 25, 1746. Died there Aug. 16, 1825. He was aide-de-camp to Washington in some of his memorable battles, and a member of the convention which framed the Constitution of the United States in 1787. But his name is rendered immortal by his reply to the French Government, when it demanded tribute of the United States: "Millions for defense, but not one cent for tribute."

JOHN G. SIMCOE, an English officer during the American Revolution, born in Essex, England, Feb. 25, 1752. Died in England, Oct. 26, 1806. He commanded the battalion of Tories, known as the "Queen's Rangers," and was with Cornwallis at Yorktown. Lake Simcoe in Ontario was named for him.

BENJAMIN TALMADGE, an American officer of the Revolution, born on Long Island, Feb. 25, 1754. Died at Litchfield, March 7, 1835. He was one of the last survivors of the Revolutionary war who had attained celebrity.

IDA LEWIS, "the Grace Darling of America," born in Newport, R. I., Feb. 25, 1842.

Her father, the keeper of Lime Rock Lighthouse, becoming paralytic, Ida was obliged to use the oars herself in providing for the family, which made her so expert that at the early age of sixteen she was numbered with the brave, by rescuing drowning people. Eleven lives were saved by her in as many years; but the last brave deed of March 29, 1869, when she rescued two soldiers from Fort Adams, whose boat had capsized, gave her national popularity.

February 26.

DOMINIQUE FRANCOIS ARAGO, a celebrated French

astronomer and natural philosopher, born at Estagel near the Pyrenees, Feb. 26, 1786. Died Oct. 2, 1853. He made several discoveries in the science of electro-magnetism, for which he received the Copley medal of the Royal Society of London, in 1825. He was a strong republican, and though he opposed the election of Louis Napoleon, and refused to take the oath of allegiance, his eminent services were so recognized by the emperor, that he was excepted from the enforcement of the law on this point.

Victor Marie Hugo, a celebrated French lyric poet and novelist, born at Besançon, Feb. 26, 1802. Died May 22, 1885. Like Arago he was a strong republican, and like him refused to take the oath of allegiance to Louis Napoleon in December,1851, but unlike him he was banished, and retired to the Isle of Guernsey. Of his many noted novels, ''Les Miserables'' is perhaps the best known.

February 27.

Martha Whiting, one of the pioneers of female education in America, born in Hingham, Mass., Feb. 27, 1795. Died there August 22, 1853. She founded the Charleston Female Seminary, where some of the noted women of America have been finely educated, prominent among whom are Mary A. Livermore and Abbie R. Knight.

Henry W. Longfellow, an eminent American poet and scholar, born at Portland, Me., Feb. 27, 1807. Died at the '' Craig House,'' in Cambridge, his home, March 24, 1882. He was a descendant, by his mother, of '' Priscilla, the Puritan Maiden,'' whose adventures he describes in his '' Miles Standish ;'' while his father was one of the early members of the House of

Representatives. For eighteen years he was professor of modern languages in Harvard College, and during this time many of his noted works appeared. His first collection of poems, " Voices of the Night," raised him at once to the first rank among American poets. " Evangeline " is one of his most admired, and held to be his greatest, production. " Hiawatha " is the most original and popular, and said to have the largest sale. The simple and direct appeal to those sentiments common to all mankind, has given him the endearing epithet of " the sweet poet of human nature," but best of all "his life was his greatest poem."

HOWARD CROSBY, D.D., LL.D., an eminent scholar and divine, born in New York City, Feb. 27, 1826.

As a professor, pastor and author he is equally popular ; also noted as one of the scholarly " revisors " of the Old Testament.

February 28.

MICHEL MONTAIGNE, a celebrated French philosopher, and essayist, born at the chateau de Montaigne, in Périgord, Feb. 28, 1533. Died Sept. 1592. Although he was the author of many works, yet he is best known by his " Essays," one hundred and seven in number, divided into three books, and embracing a variety of topics. These " Essays " have enjoyed an unparalleled popularity. " No prose writer of the sixteenth century, has been so generally read nor probably given so much delight as Montaigne."

RENE ANTOINE REAUMUR, a celebrated French natural philosopher, born at Rochelle, France, Feb. 28, 1683. Died Oct. 18, 1757. He was an enthusiast in the studies of natural history and mathematics, and by his writings first made his countrymen acquainted with the art of making steel from iron. Reaumer's porcelain is employed in many purposes.

MARY LYON, an eminent educator, born in Buckland, Mass., Feb. 28, 1797. Died at South Hadley, March 5, 1849. She was founder of Mount Holyoke Seminary of which she was principal, 1837–1849; and it is an abiding monument to her energy, and sublime faith.

BERTHOLD AUERBACH, a popular German author, born at Nordstetten in Wurtemberg, Feb. 28, 1812, Died Feb. 8, 1882. Among his many works is "Spinoza," a historical romance; but his reputation rests chiefly on his " Village Tales of the Black Forest."

ELIZABETH RACHEL FELIX, commonly known as " Rachel," a celebrated French actress of Jewish parentage, born at Munf, Switzerland, Feb. 28, 1820. Died at Cannes, Jan. 3, 1858. As a tragic actress she has probably never been equaled.

February 29.

EDWARD CAVE, an English printer, born at Newton, England, Feb. 29, 1691. Died 1754. He is memorable as the founder of " The Gentleman's Magazine," issued n 1731, which he published successfully until his death; and it still flourishes.

ANN LEE, the founder of the religion of the so-called " Shakers," born in Manchester, England, Feb. 29, 1736. Died at Watervliet near Albany, N. Y., Sept. 8, 1784. Suffering much persecution in England, in 1774 Ann and a few of her followers came to America. The radical principles of faith of the "Shakers" are duality of deity, virgin purity, equality of the sexes, community of goods, consecration of life, labor and treasures, to God.

GIOACCHIMO ROSSINI, the greatest composer of the present century for the Italian lyrical stage, born in Pesaro, Feb. 29, 1792. Died in Paris, Nov., 1868. The original and incomparable opera of "William Tell" was pronounced by all musicians the most beautiful of his works.

March 1.

WARREN COLBURN, an American mathematician, born at Dedham, Mass., March 1, 1793. Died at Lowell, Mass., Sept. 13, 1833. His "Mental Arithmetic," published in 1821, had an extensive circulation in Europe as well as the United States, and has never yet been equaled.

WILLIAM J. WORTH, an American general, born at Hudson, N. Y., March 1, 1794. Died at San Antonio, Texas, May 7, 1849. He was prominent during the war of 1812, and the Indian wars succeeding, and for his valuable services in the Mexican war was advanced to major-general. His remains rest at the junction of Broadway and Fifth Avenue, New York, over which the city has erected a monument.

JOHN J. PIATT, an American poet, born at Milton, Ind., March 1, 1835.

He was joint author with W. D. Howells of "Poems by Two Friends." His wife, Sarah M. B. Piatt, is also distinguished as a writer.

WILLIAM D. HOWELLS, a popular American editor and author, born at Martinsville, Belmont County, Ohio, March 1, 1837.

He was United States consul at Venice, 1861–65, and is at present considered the most successful dramatic writer of America, as well as one of the greatest living novelists.

March 2.

JUVENAL, one of the most celebrated of the Latin satirical poets, born in Aquinum, March 2, A.D. 40. Died in Egypt, A.D. 125. None of the productions of Juvenal were given to the public until he had passed the age of sixty. Sixteen of his satires have been preserved.

ROBERT II., of Scotland, founder of the Stuart dynasty, born in Scotland, March 2, 1316. Died at Dundonal Castle, May 13, 1390. He was a descendant of Robert Bruce, and the family were the high stewards of Scotland, hence their surname.

ANDREW MARVELL, an eminent English patriot and satirical writer, born at Winstead, Yorkshire, Eng., March 2, 1621. Died in London, Aug. 17, 1678. He has been called "the British Aristides;" was a friend and assistant of Milton, when the latter was Latin secretary to Cromwell.

SIR WILLIAM HOWE, an English general during the Revolutionary war, born in England, March 2, 1729. Died 1814. He was prominent at the battles of Bunker Hill, Long Island, White Plains, Fort Washington, and Brandywine. He is said to have been deficient in all the qualifications of a general, which Franklin knew when he wittily remarked, on hearing that Gen. Howe had taken Philadelphia, "Howe has not taken Philadelphia, so much as Philadelphia has taken Howe," and so it proved.

DEWITT CLINTON, an eminent American statesman, born at Little Britain, Orange County, N. Y., March 2, 1769. Died Feb. 11, 1828. He held several offices in the gift of the government, such as mayor of New York city, United States senator, governor of the State of New York, and candidate for the presidency as competitor with James Madison.   New York State is indebted to him for the construction of the Erie Canal, and he lived to witness the prosperity it produced.

CARL SCHURZ, a German orator and general, born near Cologne, March 2, 1829.

His liberal views caused him to settle in the United States, 1852, and he soon interested himself in the government of his adopted country ; was a general in the civil war, and senator from Missouri, 1869.

ORESTES CLEVELAND, first vice-president of the United States Centennial Commission, born at Schenectady, N. Y., March 2, 1829.

He bought out and developed the Dixon Crucible Co. to the largest and most successful establishment of the kind in the world.

March 3.

EDMUND WALLER, an eminent English poet, born at Coleshill, in Hertfordshire, March 3, 1605. Died in 1687. He was an intimate friend of Sir Philip Sidney and Edmund Spenser, and it was to a sister of the former that he addresses his " Saccharissa."

WILLIAM CHARLES MACREADY, a popular English tragic actor, born in London, March 3, 1793. Died at Cheltenham, 1873. He was the last of the great Shakespearean actors.

DIO LEWIS, D. D., an American reformer of the essentials requisite to the health of women, born at Auburn, N. Y., March 3, 1823. Died May 21, 1886. He was an inculcator of the idea that proper physical and healthful exercise would replace the use of drugs. He founded a school in Boston for teaching gymnastics and calisthenics as a regime for the public schools.

March 4.

Count Casinir Pulaski, the Polish patriot, who assisted the Americans in the Revolutionary war, born in Lithuania, March 4, 1747. Through his endeavors to liberate Poland and seize the king, he was outlawed and fled from his country. Meeting Franklin in Paris, he joined himself to the American cause. He was mortally wounded in the assault on Savannah, and died Oct. 11, 1780. When the Polish king heard of his death he remarked " Always brave, but always the enemy of kings."

Percy Bolingbroke St. John, an English traveler and author, born at Plymouth, England, March 4, 1821.

He is a valued contributor to magazines and literary periodicals.

March 5.

Gerard Mercator, a celebrated Flemish geographer and mathematician, born in East Flanders, March 5, 1512. Died in 1594. He is best known by the two superb globes he made for the emperor Charles V., and the method of geographical projection called by his name.

Salem Town, LL.D., author, and for forty years a teacher in the State of New York, born at Belchertown, Mass., March 5, 1779. Died at Greencastle, Ind., Feb. 24, 1864. His series of school readers, spellers and definers, were sold by the million.

Frederic S. Cozzens, an American writer, born in New York, March 5, 1818. Died Dec. 23, 1869. He is best known as the author of " Sparrowgrass Papers," originally written for " Putnam's Magazine."

Isaac I. Hayes, M.D., surgeon to the Grinnell Expedition under Dr. Kane, born in Chester County, Pa., March 5, 1832. Died Dec. 17, 1881. He participated in two other Arctic expeditions, and received gold medals from the Geographical Societies of both London and Paris. He is the author of several volumes of interesting Arctic journeys.

March 6.

MICHAEL ANGELO, a celebrated Italian painter, sculptor and architect, born near Florence, Italy, March 6, 1475. Died Feb. 18, 1564. Being employed by Pope Julius to build his mausoleum it was suggested by San Gallo, an architect, that a new chapel should be erected expressly for so superb a monument, and this idea was the cause of the erection of " St. Peter's," the most magnificent church in the world. Forty years afterward when the church was actually begun, Michael Angelo was appointed the architect, and he devoted the remainder of his life chiefly to that grand fabric; and although he lived to the age of ninety he did not see it completed. He drew until he could no longer hold a pencil, and carved as long as he could guide a tool. In painting, the great work on which his fame rests, is the ceiling of the Sistine Chapel.

GERRIT SMITH, a distinguished American philanthropist, born in Utica, N. Y., March 6, 1797. Died in New York City, Dec. 28, 1874. He was one of the leaders of the Anti-Slavery Society, and was noted for his philanthropy. Having inherited one of the largest landed estates in the country, he distributed nearly two hundred thousand acres of it among the poor.

PHILIP H. SHERIDAN, " Little Phil," one among the noted generals of the civil war, born in Somerset, Perry County, Ohio, March 6, 1831. Died August 4, 1888.

His "Turn, boys, we're going back!" which decided the battle of Cedar Creek, are among the noted words of noted generals.

March 7.

GOOLD BROWN, an American teacher and grammarian, born in Providence, R. I., March 7, 1791. Died March 31, 1857. His works on grammar have probably had the most extensive circulation of any of the kind.

STEPHEN H. TYNG, SEN., D.D., an American divine of note, born at Newburyport, Mass., March 7, 1800.

He has been pastor for many years, and a leader of the evangelical party, author of several valuable works, and editor of religious periodicals.

EDWARD PAYSON ROE, an American minister and novelist, born in Newburg, N. Y., March 7, 1838. Died at Cornwall, N. Y., July 20, 1888. He served during the war as chaplain, after which he became a Presbyterian minister at Highland Falls, near West Point. He began his literary career with "Barriers Burned Away," in 1872, an imaginary episode of the Chicago fire. "Opening a Chestnut Burr," "Near to Nature's Heart," and many other volumes followed, and he is considered the first religious novelist of our time. His work on "Fruit and Fruit Culture" is considered an authority.

March 8.

SIMON CAMERON, an American politician, born in Lancaster, Pa., March 8, 1799.

Was four times chosen Senator of the United States; appointed Secretary of War, and was afterward minister to Russia.

ALVAN CLARK, an American optician, born in Ashfield, Mass., March 8, 1804. Died in Cambridge, Mass., August 19, 1887. In 1844 he became interested in the manufacture of telescopes, and was the first person in the United States to make achromatic lenses, and the most important modern telescopes have been constructed in his factory at Cambridgeport.

EVANGELINUS A. SOPHOCLES, LL.D., born in Greece, March 8, 1807. Died 1883. He emigrated to the United States, entered Amherst College, was for several years tutor, and afterwards professor of languages in Harvard College.

CHRISTOPHER P. CRANCH, an American artist and poet, born at Alexandria, Va., March 8, 1813.

Many of his finest poems appeared in the " Dial."

EDWIN PERCY WHIPPLE, a distinguished American critic and essayist, born at Gloucester, Mass., March 8, 1819. Died 1886. He has been a contributor to several of the leading periodicals of America, and as a lecturer has acquired a high reputation.

JAMES SHERIDAN MUSPRATT, Ph.D., M.D., a British chemist, and author of scientific works, born in Dublin, Ireland, March 8, 1821. Died at West Derby, Feb. 3, 1871. He founded the Liverpool College of Chemistry and became a professor there.

March 9.

AMERICUS VESPUCIUS, after whom the American continent was named, born at Florence, Italy, March 9, 1451. Died at Seville, February 22, 1512. A German named Müller, who published Vespucius' account of his voyage to the new world, was the one who applied the name.

Honoré G. R. Mirabeau, a famous French orator and statesman, born at Bignon near Nemours, March 9, 1749. By establishing the "States General," as the dominant power of France, he started the French Revolution of 1790. But the storm which he tried at first to quell, was too terrific for his strength. He suddenly broke down and died April 2, 1791.

Franz Joseph Gall, M.D., a German physician, born at Tiefenbrum, in Baden, March 9, 1758. Died near Paris, August 22, 1828. He is distinguished as the founder of the system of phrenology, and was assisted in his great work on the subject by his pupil and coadjutor, Dr. Spurzheim.

William Cobbett, a popular and vigorous political writer, born at Farnham, England, March 9, 1762. Died June 18, 1835. Emigrating to America in 1792, he became editor of "Peter Porcupine's Gazette" in Philadelphia. He returned to England in 1800, where he continued a successful author and editor for over thirty years.

Isaac Hull, an American commodore, born in Derby, Conn., March 9, 1775. Died Feb. 13, 1843. He is distinguished as the commander of the American frigate "Constitution," which captured the British frigate Guerriere, the first naval action of the war of 1812, and for which he received a gold medal from Congress.

Edwin Forrest, a popular American actor, born in Philadelphia, March 9, 1806. Died Dec. 12, 1872. He has been one of the most successful of American actors.

March 10.

Ferdinand V., King of Castile and Aragon, surnamed "The Catholic," born at Sos, Spain, March 10, 1452.

Died Jan. 23, 1516. His name will live in the annals of history, in consequence of the three noted events of his life : his connection with Columbus in the discovery of America, the expulsion of the Moors from the beautiful kingdom of Granada, and by the indelible stain of the Inquisition, which by his consent was introduced into Spain.

KARL WILHELM SCHLEGEL, an eminent German scholar and critic, born at Hanover, March 10, 1772. Died at Dresden in 1829. He with his brother August, are considered founders and leaders of the romantic school in German literature.

ALEXANDER III., the present emperor of Russia, born March 10, 1845.

He ascended the throne after the assassination of his father, March 13, 1881.

March 11.

TORQUATO TASSO, a celebrated Italian epic poet, born at Sorrento, March 11, 1514. Died April 25, 1595. He was the son of Benardo Tasso, whose fame as a poet he eclipsed. His epic poem, "Jerusalem," is considered the great epic of modern times.

JOHN MACLEAN, an American statesman and jurist, born in Morris County, N. J., March 11, 1785. Died April 4, 1861. His name was thrice brought before conventions as a candidate for the Presidency.

FRANCIS WAYLAND, D.D., LL.D., an eminent American divine, scholar and author, born in New York city, March 11, 1796. Died at Providence, R. I., Sept. 26, 1865. His works on "Moral Science" are looked upon as among the great guiding monuments of human thought, in the department to which they belong.

March 12.

GEORGE BERKELEY, an English bishop and metaphysical philosopher of great merit, born near Thomastown, Ireland, March 12, 1684. Died in Oxford, England, Jan.   , 1753. He removed to Rhode Island in 1728, and during his two years' stay in America, wrote the poem which immortalizes his name, containing the line, "Westward the course of empire takes its way."

MARIA LOUISA, daughter of Francis I. of Germany, born at Vienna, March 12, 1791. Died there Dec. 18, 1847. She was married to Napoleon I. after his divorce from the Empress Josephine in 1810.

THOMAS BUCHANAN READ, a distinguished American poet and artist, born in Chester County, Pa., March 12, 1822. Died in New York, May 11, 1872. As an author he is best known by his poem "Sheridan's Ride." His "Closing Scene" was considered by the "Westminster Review," one of the best American poems ever published. "Longfellow's Children" is esteemed one of his best pictures.

COMMODORE JOHN L. WORDEN, an American naval officer, born in Westchester County, N. Y., March 12, 1818. Died 1886. He was commander of the "Yankee cheese box," the "Monitor," in her famous fight with the iron-clad "Merrimac," March 9, 1862, the first battle between iron-clad ships in the world's history.

March 13.

GEORGE B. WOOD, M.D., LL.D., an eminent American physician and medical writer, born in Greenwich, Cumberland County, N. J., March 13, 1797. Died March 30, 1879. As a professor in the University of Pennsylvania he did more than any other man of his time to advance its interests. As an author, his medical works have been adopted as text books for medical students; and of his "United States Dispensatory" more than 120,000 copies were sold soon after its publication.

JAMES VETCH, F.R.S., a British engineer, born at Haddington, Scotland, March 13, 1789.

He made important suggestions utilized by DeLesseps in regard to the ship canal across the isthmus of Suez.

March 14.

ROBERT OWEN, a socialist and philanthropist, born in Newton, Wales, March 14, 1771. Died Nov. 19, 1858. He endeavored to embody his social reform principles in a community, three times, the last at New Harmony, Ind., but they were all unsuccessful. His followers bore the name of "Owenites," from which sprang the English "Chartists."

JAMES BOGARDUS, an inventor and engineer, born at Catskill, N. Y., March 14, 1800. Died April 13, 1874. He made important improvements in cotton spinning, invented many useful mechanical instruments, and in 1847 he built in New York city the first iron building in the United States.

JOHANN STRAUSS, a celebrated German composer, born at Vienna, March 14, 1804. Died there Sept. 24, 1849. He did much to elevate the social music of Vienna, his works being principally waltzes and lively airs, in which department of music he has never been surpassed.

SAMUEL T. SPEAR, D.D., author and for many years editor of the "Independent," born at Ballston Spa, N. Y., March 14, 1812.

VICTOR EMANUEL II. (of Sardinia), the first King of United Italy, born at Turin, March 14, 1820. Died Jan. 9, 1878. He succeeded to the throne of Sardinia by the abdication of his father in 1849. In 1859 Lombardy was added to his kingdom, and soon followed Tuscany, Parma and Modena, and in 1861 all Italy had gathered to his standard with the exception of Venetia, still claimed by Austria, and a small part of the Papal States adjacent to Rome, still held by the Pope, and protected by French soldiers. In 1866, Venetia was taken from Austria, and when in 1870, Napoleon III. withdrew his army from Rome the temporal power of the Pope, which had existed ever since early in the ninth century, was broken, and Italy for the first time in its history was a nation, and a united kingdom.

March 15.

ANDREW JACKSON, seventh President of the United States, born at the Waxhaw settlement, Union County, N. C., March 15, 1767. Died June 8, 1845. He won his place in the nation's regard and popularity, by the capture of New Orleans, Jan. 8, 1815, which was considered one of the most brilliant and decisive battles ever gained by the American army. Among the principal events of his term was the establishment of "rotation in office," he having made more removals in one year than all the other Presidents in forty years before. His veto of the bill which granted a new charter to the Bank of the United States, July, 1832, was the issue which divided him and the opponents to his second term. His famous toast "Our Union : it must be preserved," was given at a banquet, April, 1830.

WILLIAM LAMB MELBOURNE, viscount, a popular English statesman, born at Melbourne House, Derbyshire, England, March 15, 1779. Died at Brocton Hall, Nov. 24, 1848. He was the responsible head of the British government at the accession of Queen Victoria.

March 16. 

CAROLINE L. HERSCHEL, sister of Sir William Herschel, born in Hanover, March 16, 1750. Died in 1848. She lived with her brother until his death, and shared his daily toils and nightly vigils, thus inscribing her name in luminous characters on the records of astronomy.

JAMES MADISON, fourth President of the United States, born in King George County, Va., March 16, 1751. Died at Montpelier, Va., June 28, 1836. As a statesman and philosopher he secured the highest consideration of the nation, and his writings on the Constitution were second only to those of Hamilton. The principal event of his administration was the war of 1812.

CHARLES A. WASHBURN, an American author and inventor, born at Livermore, Me., March 16, 1822.

He was United States minister to Paraguay during the terrible revolution of that country and wrote an interesting account of his troublesome residence in that country. He is also the inventor of the typograph, and other ingenious machinery.

March 17.

SAINT PATRICK, the apostle and patron saint of Ireland, born at Bannavan, a small village of Tabernia, in Scotland, 372. He is supposed to have been one of the earliest teachers of Christianity in Ireland, and so careful and consistent was he in promulgating his doctrines, that he won the entire population without serious opposition. Why the 17th of March is kept in his honor is uncertain. Some claim it be on account of the disputed date of his birth, the 8th and 9th of March, which the

Pope, the little, added together and called it the 17th.
Others say he died on that day in 454.

THOMAS MACKEAN, an American patriot, and
"signer to the Declaration of Independence," born in
Chester County, Pa., March 17, 1734.   Died 1817.
He was governor of Pennsylvania, 1797–1808, and a
political friend of Jefferson.

MADAME ROLAND, one of the most noted and highly
gifted women of France, born in Paris, March 17, 1754.
Taking part with the Girondists in the French Revolution, when that party fell, she was executed Nov. 9,
1793.   Her last words were : "O Liberty ! what
crimes are committed in thy name."

ROGER B. TANEY, a distinguished American jurist,
born in Calvert County, Md., March 17, 1777.
Died in Washington, D. C., Oct. 12, 1864.   He was
the fifth Chief-Justice of the United States, which place
he occupied 1836–1864.   His strange and unjust decision
in the "Dred Scott" suit, 1857, removed the last barrier
to the extension of slavery, and fastened reproach to a
name that could have commanded the respect of the
nation on any other subject but slavery.

THOMAS CHALMERS, the most eminent Scottish divine
of the present century, born in Fifeshire, March 17,
1780.   Died May 30, 1847.   He was an eloquent and
powerful pulpit orator, and a leader in theological dis-
cussions.   He was the principal chief of the "Evangelical" party of 470 other clergymen who seceded from the
Established Church, and organized what is known as the
"Free Church."

March 18.

JOHN C. CALHOUN, an eminent American statesman,
born in Abbeville district, S. C., March 18, 1782.

Died March 31, 1850. He was sent to Congress in 1811, and from that time until his death, his political career was one of the most marked in American history. He served as Senator, Secretary of War, Secretary of State, Vice-President, was candidate for the Presidency. He, with Webster and Clay, formed "The Great Trio."

FRANCIS LEIBER, an eminent German historical and political writer, born at Berlin, March 18, 1800. Died Oct. 2, 1872. Being too liberal in his political opinions for his own country, he came to the United States, where he was an invaluable aid to the government. His motto, "No rights without its duties, no duty without its rights," was the keynote of his political writings.

GROVER CLEVELAND, twenty-second President of the United States, born in Caldwell, Essex County, N. J., March 18, 1837.

He was inaugurated President in 1885, resigning the governorship of New York for the national office.

March 19.

ELIAS HICKS, a noted preacher of the Society of Friends or Quakers, born in Hempstead, Queens County, Long Island, March 19, 1748. Died Feb. 27, 1830. For many years he was an approved minister in the Society, but early in the present century he began to promulgate views different from those held by a majority of the Quakers. The result was a schism, and the two parties were known as the "Orthodox" and the "Hicksites," although the anti-orthodox division of the Society do not acknowledge the name of "Hicksites."

CHARLES KNIGHT, an eminent English editor and author, born at Windsor, England, March 19, 1791.

Died March 9, 1873. He was founder of the system of the generalization of useful knowledge, which is illustrated by his " Penny Magazine," " Penny Cyclopædia," " British Almanac" and many other works.

David Livingstone, M.D., LL.D., a Scottish missionary, distinguished as an African explorer, born near Glasgow, Scotland, March 19, 1813. Died at Ulalla, Africa, May 1, 1873. In 1849 he crossed the continent of South Africa, from the Zambesi to the Congo, discovering Lake Ngami and other waters, and from this time forth his life was spent in and for Africa. He was several times reported dead, and when at length he was missing for some time, Henry Stanley pushed his way into the interior to Ujiji and found him alive, but in great destitution. His "Missionary Travels and Researches in South Africa" is a work of great interest and value.

Seth Green, an American pisciculturist, born in Rochester, N. Y., March 19, 1817. Died August 20, 1888. By the application of the results of his close observation, he has done more than any scholar to advance the science of fish culture.

March 20.

Ovid, a popular Roman poet, born at Sulmo, ninety miles east of Rome, March 20, 43 B.C. Died at Tomi, a small town at the Delta of the Danube, 18 A.D. As a poet he is celebrated for his " Metamorphoses," which Hawthorne has dealt so pleasantly with in his " Wonder Book" and "Tanglewood Tales."

Neal Dow, an American general and philanthropist, born in Portland, Me., March, 20, 1805. He is the " father of the Maine Liquor Law," the passage of which he secured while a member of the legislature of Maine.

CARDINAL JOHN McCLOSKEY, a Catholic bishop, born in Brooklyn, N. Y., March 20, 1810. Died Oct. 10, 1885. Upon the death of Archbishop Hughes, in 1864, McCloskey was chosen his successor. In 1875 he was appointed Cardinal by Pope Pius IX.

NAPOLEON II., the only son of Napoleon I., born in Paris, March 20, 1811. Died of consumption in Vienna, June 22, 1832. Although he never actually occupied the throne of France, he is generally reckoned among the French sovereigns. In 1814 Napoleon I. abdicated the throne in favor of his son, but Louis XVIII. was preferred by the Senate and the young Napoleon was taken to Austria by his mother, Maria Louisa.

March 21.

ROBERT BRUCE, the heroic and famous "King of Scots," born March 21, 1274. He defeated the English at London Hill and Bannockburn, but in the internum of the two battles had made himself master of nearly the whole of Scotland. He died June, 1329, just one year after the English king, Edward II., had recognized the independence of Scotland.

JEAN PAUL RICHTER, a popular, quaint, and original German author, born in Wunsiedel, Bavaria, March 21, 1763. Died in Beyruth, November 14, 1825. He is known as the writer of " gems;" no writer having made such brilliant remarks, and no ten, as many. "Titan" is generally considered his masterpiece.

HENRY KIRK WHITE, an English author and poet, born at Nottingham, England, March 21, 1785, and died at Cambridge, Oct. 19, 1806.

Benito Pablo Juarez, a president of Mexico, born near Oaxaca, Mexico, March 21, 1806. Died July 18, 1872. He was president when the archduke Maximilian was made Emperor of Mexico by the French in 1864. After the downfall of Maximilian in 1867, he was re-elected to the presidency.

March 22.

Anthony Vandyke, a celebrated Flemish painter, born at Antwerp, March 22, 1599. Died in London, Dec. 9, 1641. He was Rubens' most illustrious pupil, and achieved his fame as a portrait painter, of which about three hundred still exist. His "Crucifixion" is considered one of the finest (or first) pictures in the world, and gives the highest idea of Vandyke's powers.

William I., King of Prussia, and since 1871, Emperor of Germany, born March 22, 1797. Died March 9, 1888. He ascended the throne in 1861, and became head of the Northern German Confederation, and after the war of 1870–71 was proclaimed Emperor of Germany in the palace of the French kings at Versailles.

Joseph Saxton, a noted American inventor, born in Huntington County, Penn., March 22, 1799. Died in Washington, D. C., Oct., 1873. He made the clock which still marks the time from the belfry of Independence Hall in Philadelphia, when he was but eighteen, and subsequently added many ingenious devices to science. He was one of the original corporators of the National Academy of Science.

Stephen Pearl Andrews, an American author and philologist, born in Massachusetts, March 22, 1812. Died May 21, 1886. He devoted many years to the invention of a universal language called Alwato, which perhaps centuries may mature.

Rosa Bonheur, a celebrated French painter of animals, born at Bordeaux, March 22, 1822.

Her "Nivernais Ploughing," which is esteemed her finest picture, has obtained a place in the gallery of the Luxembourg. During the siege of Paris, 1870–71, her studio and residence at Fontainebleau were spared and respected by special order of the Crown Prince of Prussia.

March 23.

William Smith, known as "the father of English geology," born at Churchill, Oxfordshire, England, March 23, 1769. Died at Northampton, August 28, 1839. He was author of several geological works, and published the first "Geological Map of England."

Pierre Simon Laplace, one of the greatest astronomers and mathematicians of any age or country, born in France, March 23, 1749. Died in 1827. Among his great discoveries are the theory of Jupiter's satellites, and the causes of the grand inequality of Jupiter and Saturn, and of the acceleration of the moon's mean motion. He shared the honor with Lagrange of proving the stability of the planetary system. One of his last expressions was, "What we know is but little, that which we know not is immense."

Don Carlos Buel, an American officer, born near Marietta, Ohio, March 23, 1818.

He was an officer of note in the Florida, Mexican and Civil wars. After the last he was made president of the Green River, Ky., iron works.

Schuyler Colfax, an American statesman, born in

the city of New York, March 23, 1823.   Died 1885.
He was grandson of General W. Colfax, who commanded
Washington's life-guards.   Chosen Speaker of the House
of Representatives in 1863–65–67, he gained a high rep-
utation as a presiding officer, and was the most popular
Speaker of the House since Henry Clay.   He was chosen
Vice President with Grant in 1868.

RICHARD ANTHONY PROCTOR, a distinguished English
scholar and astronomer, born at Chelsea, England,
March 23, 1837.   Died in New York, Sept. 12,
1888, of yellow fever, which fatal disease he contracted
in Florida.   He early took to geometrical study, and on
entering King's College, London, 1855, succeeded in
taking first place in seven subjects.   His first literary
effort, an article on "Double Stars," appeared in 1863,
since which time he has won a world-wide reputation as
a scientific writer, lecturer and astronomer.   He was
eminently an instructor of the people.   His best known
works are, "Handbook of the Stars," "Constellation
Seasons," "Some Views of the Earth," "Other Worlds
than Ours," and "Light Science for Leisure Hours."
He has made several lecture tours in Australia and
America, and in April, 1887, took up his residence in
Oakland, Fla., where he had been at work on his "Old
and New Astronomy," a work that has been in preparation for twenty years.   Thus though his star is removed
from our firmament,

> "The light he leaves behind him, lies
> Upon the paths of men."

March 24.

THOMAS CUSHING, an American patriot, born in Boston, Mass., March 24, 1725.   Died February 28, 1788.

He was so prominent a member of the Colonial Congress that he was regarded in Great Britain as one of the leaders of sedition.

Joseph Priestly, LL.D., an eminent English philosopher, chemist and theologian, born near Leeds, England, March 24, 1733. As a chemist the talents of Priestly were considered of the first order, and his researches and writings have added much to the progress of the science. He discovered oxygen, August 1, 1774, which is now considered the "birthday of chemistry." This discovery was followed by the identification of other gases. He died at Northumberland, Penn., Feb. 6, 1804, whither he had emigrated with his family to escape the public odium which his liberal opinions as a minister incurred.

Joel Barlow, an American patriot and poet, born at Reading, Conn., March 24, 1755. Died near Cracow, December, 1812, while a foreign ambassador. As an author he belonged to the first class of his time in America, and was one of the celebrated "Hartford Wits." His "Vision of Columbus," a poem in imitation of Milton, obtained great popularity, and "Hasty Pudding," a humorous poem dedicated to Martha Washington, was much admired. His most elaborate work "Columbiad," an epic poem, is considered by critics to be a failure.

March 25.

Francis Lewis, one of the "signers to the Declaration of Independence," born in Wales, March 25, 1713. Died in New York, Dec. 30, 1803. He emigrated to New York in 1735, and was elected to the Continental Congress, 1775.

Joachim Murat, a celebrated marshal of the French

empire, born near Cahors, France, March 25, 1771. Napoleon pronounced him "the best cavalry officer in Europe," but he was unstable in his purposes, now fighting for, and now against Napoleon; but after the emperor's fall in 1815, while attempting to recover Naples, he was captured and shot for treason, Oct. 13, 1815.

March 26.

BENJAMIN THOMPSON, "Count Rumford," a celebrated natural philosopher and economist, born at Woburn, Mass., March 26, 1753. Died Aug. 21, 1814. Being disaffected with his country in the Revolutionary times, he went to Europe, and for his political services and scientific researches, was made Count, to which he added Rumford, the name of the town in New Hampshire (now Concord), where he once resided. He gave to science many endowments, both in discoveries and wealth; and it is a matter of national pride that the two men, Benjamin Franklin and Benjamin Thompson, who first demonstrated the capital propositions of pure science, in regard to lightning and electricity, were Americans by birth and by education.

THOMAS CLARKSON, an English philanthropist, born at Wisbeach, Cambridge, Eng., March 26, 1760. Died Sept. 26, 1846. He was one of the first anti-slavery committee that succeeded, after much opposition, in abolishing the slave trade by an act of Parliament in 1807.

NATHANIEL BOWDITCH, LL.D., F.R.S., an eminent American mathematician and scholar, born at Salem, Mass., March 26, 1773. Died March 16, 1838. He learned Greek and Latin, without a teacher, and his scholarly attainments won for him a membership in many of the learned societies of both England and America.

William C. Redfield, an American geologist and meteorologist, born in Middletown, Conn., March 26, 1789. Died in Feb. 1857. He conceived the fundamental idea of his famous "law of storms" as early as 1821, and promulgated his theory in 1831. He was first president of the "American Association for the Advancement of Science."

March 27.

Michael Bruce, a Scottish poet, born at Kinneswood, Scotland, March 27, 1746. Died July 5, 1767. His productions were characterized by a singular pathos and beauty. After his death his "friend" John Logan, published a volume of poems which he claimed as his own, but it afterwards proved that he had perpetrated a base literary piracy, and they belonged to Bruce.

March 28.

Saint Theresa, a Carmelite nun, born at Avila, Spain, March 28, 1515. Died at Alba, Oct. 4, 1582. Her religious treatises are accounted among the Spanish classics. She was canonized by Pope Gregory XV. in 1621.

William Tudor, an American general and statesman in the early days of the Republic, born at Boston, March 28, 1750. Died July 8, 1819. He was one of the founders of the Massachusetts Historical Society.

Henry Rowe Schoolcraft, a distinguished American traveler, ethnologist, and scientific writer, born near Albany, N. Y., March 28, 1793. Died at Washington, D.C., Dec. 10, 1864. He was at the head of the expedition which, in 1832, explored, for the first time, Lake Itasca and the sources of the Mississippi river. "His scientific writings," says R. W. Griswold, "are among the important contributions to the literature of this country, and will be read when the greater portion of the popular literature of the day is forgotten."

ORVILLE DEWEY, D.D., LL.D., a distinguished Unitarian divine, born in Sheffield, Mass., March 28, 1794. Died   , 1882.   He was at one time an assistant of Dr. Channing, was also minister of the New South Church, Boston.   As an original thinker and author, his productions are eminently able and profound.

March 29.

JOHN TYLER, tenth President of the United States, born in Charles City Co., Va., March 29, 1790.   Died in Richmond, Va., Jan. 17, 1862.   He became President, April 4, 1841, on the death of Harrison, with whom he stood as Vice-President.   At the opening of the civil war he went over to the South, and was a member of the Confederate Congress when he died.

CHARLES MOORE, an American editor and author, born in Boston, March 29, 1801.

He founded "Zion's Herald" in 1823.

March 30.

SIR HENRY WOTTON, an English diplomatist and writer, born in Kent, Eng., March 30, 1568.   Died at Eton, Dec.   , 1630.   He was ambassador to several countries and is author of the oft-quoted witticism : "An ambassador is an honest man, sent abroad to lie for the good of his country."

INNIS N. PALMER, an American general, born at Buffalo, N. Y., March 30, 1824.

He was brigadier-general in the Union army at Fair Oaks and Malvern Hill.

March 31.

FRANZ JOSEPH HAYDEN, one of the sweetest musicians the world ever produced, born near Vienna, March 31, 1732. Died May 26, 1809. Mozart's love for his " papa Hayden," proved that Hayden possessed a virtue rare in great musicians, he appreciated and recognized the talent of others. His noble master-piece, the oratorio of "The Creation," was performed in Vienna in 1798, and procured his admission into the French Institute.

JOHN P. HALE, an American statesman, born at Rochester, Stafford Co., N. H., March 31, 1806. Died Nov. 19, 1873. He was elected U. S. Senator of New Hampshire, in 1847, and for several years stood almost alone in the Senate on the question of slavery, and maintained a position independent of party.

ROBERT WILHELM BUNSEN, a distinguished German chemist, born at Gottingen, March 31, 1811.

He has invented several important pieces of apparatus which bear his name. Among his brilliant discoveries was that of spectrum analysis, which established a new era in astronomy.

WILLIAM MORRIS HUNT, an American artist, born in Brattleboro, Vt., March 31, 1824. Died Sept. 9, 1879. He was one of the first to introduce the French school of art into America, and many of his well-known pictures have been reproduced in lithographs.

April 1.

WILLIAM HARVEY, an English anatomist, celebrated for his discovery of the circulation of the blood, born at Folkestone, Kent, Eng., April 1, 1578. Died June,

1657. He was physician to James I. and Charles I., and followed the fortunes of the latter during the civil war. He promulgated his important theory in London in 1619, after three years' study upon it; but it was not published until 1628.

Thomas F. Buxton, an eminent English philanthropist, born in Essex, April 1, 1786. Died Feb. 19, 1845. He was a member of Parliament many years; an eminent advocate of the abolition of slavery, and a leader in other humanitarian measures.

Prince Otto von Bismarck, a celebrated Prussian statesman, the Prime Minister of Germany, born at Brandenburg, April 1, 1815.

In 1847 he was chosen a member of the United Diet, since which time, his public life has rendered him a star of the first magnitude in the political galaxy of the world. He was appointed chancellor of the North German Confederacy in July, 1867.

April 2.

Hans Christian Anderson, an eminent Danish poet and novelist, born on the island of Funan, April 2, 1805. Died Aug., , 1875. He has published many noted works, but his original genius is conspicuous in fairy tales, which are characterized by a quaint humor, and have been translated into most of the European languages.

Erastus Dow Palmer, a distinguished American sculptor, born at Pompey, Onondaga Co., N. Y., April 2, 1817.

"The Landing of the Pilgrims" and "The White Captive" are among his principal works.

Moses Wight, an American painter, born at Boston, April 2, 1827.

" The Sleeping Beauty " is one of his ideal pictures.

Laura Elizabeth B. Lyman, "Kate Hunnibee" of the "Hearth and Home," was born at Kent's Hill, Me., April 2, 1831. She was long an editor of "Home Interests" in the "New York Tribune" and since editor of the "Dining-Room Magazine," and contributor to several periodicals.

Leon Gambetta, one of the greatest and most conspicuous of Frenchmen, born at Cohors, France, April 2, 1838. Died Dec. 31, 1882. It was not until 1868 that his name came prominently before the public, as counsel for defendants in political prosecutions, yet so popular had he become, that his death produced a profound sensation throughout France, and his funeral was the greatest that has occurred in Paris since the body of the First Napoleon was taken to the Invalides.

April 3.

George Herbert, "Holy Herbert," an English poet, born at Montgomery Castle, April 3, 1593. Died Feb., 1633. He was a man of profound learning, sincere piety, refined taste and extraordinary wisdom ; and his poetry includes some of the finest lyrics in our language.

Washington Irving, LL.D., a distinguished American author and humorist, born in the city of New-York, April 3, 1783. Died Nov. 28, 1859. " The Sketch-Book " raised Irving to the highest rank of American authors ; and his " Life of Columbus " is considered by critics to be as nearly perfect as a work can be. His residence in Spain as American Minister, gave him an opportunity for writing his " Conquest of Gran ada," "The Alhambra," etc., while by his "Rip Van Winkle," "Sleepy Hollow," etc., he has given a legendary charm to the Hudson river and its vicinity, which will last as long as that noble stream laps the foot of the Catskills.

EDWARD EVERETT HALE, A.M., a noted American author and Unitarian divine, born in Boston, April 3, 1822.

He stands in the foremost rank of American writers, and is one of the counselors to the Chautauqua Literary Scientific Circle.

HENRY MARTYN FIELD, D.D., an American editor and author, born at Stockbridge, Mass., April 3, 1822.

He is a brother of Cyrus W. Field, and a writer of rare abilities. To read his "History of the Atlantic Telegraph," compensates one for not being an eye-witness to the grand undertaking.

WILLIAM M. TWEED, "Boss Tweed," born in New York city, April 3, 1823. He was leader of the famous Tammany Ring and obtained almost unlimited influence in the politics of the state and city. In 1872 he was imprisoned for forgery and larceny; escaped in 1875, was captured and returned to prison where he died in 1878.

HARRIET ELIZABETH PRESCOTT SPOFFORD, an able American writer of to-day, born in Calais, Me., April 3, 1835.

JOHN BURROUGHS, an American author, born in Roxbury, N. Y., April 3, 1837.

He has contributed largely to periodicals, mainly on rural themes, besides being author of many volumes.

April 4.

NICHOLAS BROWN, a distinguished American merchant, born at Providence, R. I., April 4, 1769. Died Oct. 27, 1841. By his liberal endowment to the Rhode Island College of Providence, R. I., it took the name of Brown University in his honor in 1804.

THADDEUS STEVENS, an eminent American legislator, born at Peacham, Vt., April 4, 1793. Died at Washington, D. C., Aug. 11, 1868. He was distinguished as an opponent of slavery, and at the end of the civil war was the most prominent and influential member of the House of Representatives, and was one of the most active managers in the impeachment trial of President Johnson.

DOROTHEA L. DIX, the American "Elizabeth Fry," also known as "the prisoner's friend," born at Worcester, Mass., April 4, 1794. Died July 28, 1887. She early became interested in the condition of criminals, lunatics and paupers, and in their interest visited nearly every State in the Union.

JAMES FREEMAN CLARK, D.D., an eminent American Unitarian preacher, born at Hanover, N. H., April 4, 1810. Died June 8, 1888. He has distinguished himself as an opponent of slavery, and is also an author and poet.

SAMUEL R. WELLS, of the firm of Fowler & Wells, New York City, was born at Hartford, Conn., April 4, 1820. Died in New York, April 13, 1875. He was an author and extensive traveler in the interest of phrenology, and for twenty-five years was editor of different phrenological magazines, one of which was the "Phrenological Journal."

April 5.

THOMAS HOBBS, a famous English philosopher and

author, born at Malmesbury, April 5, 1588. Died Dec., 1679. "A permanent foundation of his fame," says Mackintosh, "consists in his admirable style, which seems to be the very perfection of didactic language." His little tract on "Human Nature" has scarcely an ambiguous or needless word. He was intimate with Bacon, Ben Jonson, Galileo, Dr. Harvey, and other noted men of his day. He was tutor to Charles II.

SIR HENRY HAVELOCK, a distinguished British general, born in Durham, England, April 5, 1795. Died in India, Nov., 1857. To Sir Henry is given the honor of the celebrated "Relief of Lucknow," in India, Sept. 25, 1857, during the Sepoy rebellion, when a small garrison of British soldiers was besieged by a large army of Sepoys.

VICENZO GIOBERTI, a remarkable Italian philosopher and statesman of modern times, born at Turin, April 5, 1801. Died at Paris in 1853. He was the prophet of the uprising of Italy, and wrote many works, which roused the Italians to a longing for a united Italy.

LOUISA CHANDLER MOULTON, an American author, born April 5, 1835.

She began literary life under the name of "Ellen Louisa" at the age of fifteen, and at nineteen published her first book, which was very successful. She was long the Boston correspondent on literary topics of the "N. Y. Tribune," and is one of America's popular writers.

ALGERNON CHARLES SWINBURNE, an English author and dramatist, born near London, April 5, 1837.

Some of his most successful dramas are constructed after the Greek models, in which he first manifested his peculiar powers.

April 6.

RAPHAEL, the "prince of painters," born at Urbino, Italy, April 6, 1483. Died April 6, 1520. He was made architect-in-chief of the church of St. Peter, in 1514, by papal power, and for twelve years was engaged in decorating the Vatican. His last work, and his master-piece, the "Transfiguration," was left unfinished at his death.

JEAN BAPTISTE ROUSSEAU, a French lyric poet of great eminence, born in Paris, April 6, 1670. Died at Brussels, March 17, 1741. He is considered the greatest lyric poet of France.

JOHN PIERPONT an American poet and Unitarian divine, born in Litchfield, Conn., April 6, 1785. Died at Medford, Mass., Aug. 27, 1866. He was a prominent advocate of temperance, anti-slavery, and other reforms ; and as a poet, has produced many hymns, odes, and brief poems remarkably spirited and melodious.

MRS. META HEUSSER, the sweetest female song-writer in the German language, born in the canton of Zurich, Switzerland, April 6, 1797. Died Jan. 2, 1876. Her rare genius, sanctified by deep piety, has made her the most eminent and noble among the female poets of our Evangelical Church.

CALVIN E. STOWE, D.D., an American divine and scholar, born in Natick, Mass., April 6, 1802. Died in 1886. He was the husband of the noted Harriet Beecher Stowe, and from early life was eminent as a scholar, author and translator.

April 7.

SAINT FRANCIS XAVIER, a celebrated Jesuit mission-ary, called "the Apostle of the Indies," born in the kingdom of Navarre, near the foot of the Pyrenees, April 7, 1506. Died on an island near the Chinese coast, Dec., 1552. He visited the East Indies as a missionary in 1541, and during the eleven remaining years of his life, founded several missions, and converted thousands of idolators to the Christian faith. He was canonized in 1622.

WILLIAM WORDSWORTH, an illustrious English poet, born in Cockermouth, Cumberland Co., Eng., April 7, 1770. Died April 23, 1850. Wordsworth, Coleridge and Southey were designated as the "Lake Poets," because they resided in the lake district of Cumberland, and described the scenery of that beautiful region. He succeeded Southey as poet-laureate, in 1843, which niche of honor he filled until his death.

WILLIAM ELLERY CHANNING, D.D., a distinguished Unitarian divine, and one of the most eloquent writers America has produced, born at Newport, R. I., April 7, 1780. Died Oct. 2, 1842. "One of the most beautiful and admirable traits in Dr. Channing's character was his determination not to allow the spirit of controversy, or pride of opinion, to hinder in any way the reception of new truth ;" and as a minister he desired "not that people should adopt his thoughts and convictions, but be true to their own." His last discourse was in commemoration of the abolition of slavery in the British West Indies. He was buried at Mount Auburn, where his grave is marked by a monument designed by his friend Washington Allston.

April 8.

DAVID RITTENHOUSE, F.R.S., LL.D., an American astronomer and mathematician, born at Germantown, near Philadelphia, April 8, 1732. Died June 26, 1796. He was employed with Mason and Dixon to determine the boundary line between Pennsylvania and Delaware, Maryland, and Virginia, in 1763. He was appointed president of the American Philosophical Society on the death of Franklin, to whom, in point of scientific merit, he is considered next in rank.

SIR NATHANIEL W. WRAXALL, an English statesman and historical writer, born at Bristol, Eng., April 8, 1751. Died Nov. 7, 1831. He was an extensive traveler, and many of his works are accounts of the tours he made.

April 9.

RUFUS PUTNAM, an American general of the Revolution, born in Sutton, Mass., April 9, 1738. He formed the Ohio Company which, in 1788, purchased large tracts in that State, and founded the city of Marietta, the first permanent settlement in Ohio, and died there May 4, 1824.

FISHER AMES, a celebrated American orator and statesman, born in Dedham, Mass., April 9, 1758. Died July 4, 1808. He was the leader of the Federal party in the House of Representatives during the administration of Washington, and was reverenced for his eloquence, learning, sound judgment, and for the purity of his character.

JOHN L. SULLIVAN, M.D., an American engineer and physician, born in Saco, Me., April 9, 1777. Died in Boston, Feb. 9, 1865. He was appointed engineer of the first canal in the United States, between Boston harbor and the Merrimac river, and in 1814 received a patent for the first steam tow-boat.

Isambard K. Brunel, an eminent British engineer and Naval architect, born in Portsmouth, Eng., April 9, 1806. Died in 1859. He was assistant engineer with his father in the construction of the Thames Tunnel, and was the chief architect and designer of the "Great Eastern," the largest vessel ever built.

Adelina Maria Clorinda Patti, a popular operatic singer of Italian extraction, born at Madrid, April 9, 1843.

She sang at an early age in New York, and appeared in London in 1861, since which time she has been considered one of the first singers of the day. In 1870, she received the Order of Merit from the emperor of Russia.

April 10.

Samuel Christian Freidrich Hahnemann, a celebrated German physician, born in Saxony, April 10, 1775. Died in Paris, July 2, 1843. He was the founder of the system of medicine known as homeopathy.

Edward Robinson, D.D., LL.D., an eminent American biblical scholar, born in Southington, Conn., April 10, 1794. Died Jan. 27, 1863. His greatest work, "Biblical Researches," written after traveling and studying in Palestine, is considered the best work that has been published on that subject, and one of the most learned works of the century, and for it he received the gold medal of the Royal Geographical Society of London.

William Hazlitt, an eminent English critic and miscellaneous author, born at Maidstone, Eng., April 10, 1778. Died Sept. 18, 1830. Among his principal works are "The Round Table," "Table Talk," "Spirit of the Age," etc.

Maria S. Cummins, a popular American novelist,

born at Salem, Mass., April 10, 1827. Died Oct. 1, 1866. One of her most successful novels, "The Lamplighter," had a sale of 70,000 copies in a single year.

GEN. LEWIS WALLACE, an American general, lawyer, and author, born at Brookville, Franklin Co., Ind., April 10, 1827. He commanded in several important positions during the civil war, and was especially noted for saving the National Capital by the battle of Monocacy, Md., which though it resulted in Wallace's defeat, gave Grant time to reinforce the capital. Among his works as author are "The Fair God," a romantic story of the Aztec civilization in Mexico, and "Ben Hur," a work depicting the life and times of the Saviour. He was seven years in completing this latter work, and at the time is said to have owned one of the best oriental libraries of books and charts in the world. President Garfield pronounced "Ben Hur" one of the greatest literary and critical studies produced in this country; and an eminent lawyer of the United States declares it to be one of the milestones of the nineteenth century.

April 11.

GEORGE CANNING, an eminent English statesman, orator and wit, born in London, April 11, 1770. Died Aug. 8, 1827. He and Lord Brougham were at one time considered the most powerful orators in the House of Commons. He made an important change in the foreign policy of England, in consequence of which that country ceased to be subservient to the designs of the Holy Alliance.

EDWARD EVERETT, a distinguished American orator, scholar and statesman, born in Dorchester, Mass., April 11, 1794. Died Jan. 15, 1865. He was an ordained minister before he was quite twenty-one; and his celebrated oration at Cambridge in the presence of Lafayette, in 1824, won for him the name of orator, which will outlast all his other titles. His last speech, "The Relief of Savannah" was delivered only six days before his death.

April 12.

HENRY CLAY, an eminent American statesman and orator, born near "The Slashes," in Hanover Co., Va., April 12, 1777. Died June 29, 1852. He was sent to the Senate from Kentucky in 1806, and from that date, his life, time and talents were interwoven with the political welfare of his country. He was thrice a candidate for the Presidency, but his adherence to principle instead of party lost for him the unanimous vote. When warned by his friends that his "Compromise Bill" would lessen his chances for the Presidency, he gave his ever-remembered reply: "I would rather be right than President." John C. Breckenridge, his political adversary but personal admirer, gave the keystone to his character, in his proposed inscription for Clay's tombstone: "Here lies a man who was in public service for fifty years, and never attempted to deceive his countrymen."

April 13.

THOMAS WENTWORTH, Earl of Stafford, born in London, April 13, 1593. For his harsh and despotic treatment during his rule in Ireland, he acquired the title of "the bad earl." He was impeached by the famous "Long Parliament" and beheaded on Tower Hill, May 12, 1647.

JEANNE MARIA BOUVIER DE LA MOTTE GUYON, "Madame Guyon," a French lady celebrated for her talents and piety, born at Montargis, France, April 13, 1648. Died June 9, 1717. She suffered much persecution on account of her religious opinions and writings, and at one time was imprisoned in the Bastile.

FREDERICK NORTH, "Lord North," an English statesman, born April 13, 1733. Died Aug. 5, 1792. He was Prime Minister of Great Britain during the American Revolution, and upon receiving news of the surrender of Cornwallis, exclaimed again and again: "O God! it is all over," and soon after resigned his place in the government. The American war is the great blot on his name.

THOMAS JEFFERSON, third President of the United States, born in Shadwell, Albemarle Co., Va., April 13, 1743. Died July 4, 1826, the fiftieth anniversary of American Independence. That immortal document, the "Declaration of Independence" was, with the exception of a few words, entirely his work. He received a classical education, and for his scholarly attainments was styled "The Sage of Monticello." As author of the "Declaration of Independence," and founder of the Republican (now the Democratic) party, Jefferson has exerted a greater influence on the institutions of this country than any other American except Washington. Near the close of his life he founded the University of Virginia.

April 14.

CHRISTIAN HUGGENS, a celebrated Dutch astronomer, and geometer, born at the Hague, April 14, 1629. Died, 1695. As the discoverer of Saturn's rings, inventor of the spiral spring used to regulate the balance of watches, and the first to apply the pendulum to the measurement of time, he stands pre-eminent among contemporary philosophers of all nations.

GEORGE ROSS, an American patriot and signer of the Declaration of Independence, born at New Castle, Del., April 14, 1730. Died at Lancaster July, 1779.

WILLIAM WILLIAMS, one of the founders of the Norwich Free Academy, born at Norwich, Conn., April 14, 1788. Died there Oct. 28, 1870.

HORACE BUSHNELL, D.D., an eminent American divine, born in Litchfield Co., Conn., April 14, 1802. Died Feb. 17, 1876. He was for some time literary editor of the New York "Journal of Commerce" and author of several philosophical and theological works.

April 15.

SIR JAMES CLARK ROSS, F.R.S., an eminent English Arctic navigator, born in London, April 15, 1800. Died in 1862. He served in Arctic expeditions under his uncle, Sir John Ross, also Captain E. Parry. In 1839 he commanded an expedition to the Antarctic regions and discovered Victoria Land.

JOHN LOTHROP MOTLEY, an eminent American historian, born at Dorchester, Mass., April 15, 1814. Died May 29, 1877. His "Rise of the Dutch Republic" has been translated into German, French, Dutch and Danish, and is considered an honor to any literature in the world. In 1861, he was appointed minister to Austria, and in 1869, was sent as ambassador to England.

April 16.

WILLIAM OF NASSAU, Prince of Orange, "William the Silent," the illustrious founder of the Dutch Republic, born at Dillenburg, in Nassau, April 16, 1533. He was assassinated by Balthazer Gerard, a fanatical Catholic, in 1584. Motley says he earned the name of "The Silent" not from being taciturn, but from the instance of his silently receiving communications from Henry II. of France, in regard to plots laid against the Protestants, without revealing to the monarch, by word or look, that he was a Protestant and a great blunder had been committed. To William the Silent is due the honor of being the first among the European states, to practically apply the principle of religious toleration.

EDWARD RAWSON, an early colonial author, born in Gillingham, Dorsetshire, Eng., April 16, 1615. Died at Boston, Aug., 1693. He was one of the first secretaries of the General Court of Massachusetts Colony. His daughter Rebecca was the heroine of one of Whittier's romantic episodes.

SIR JOHN FRANKLIN, F.R.S., the lost Arctic explorer, born at Spilsby, Lincolnshire, Eng., April 16, 1786. He was governor of Tasmania for several years, and in 1845 started on his last polar expedition, in command of the Erebus and Terror. It is believed by all conclusive evidence that he died near Lancaster Sound, June, 1847.

LOUIS ADOLPHE THIERS, an eminent French historian and statesman, born at Marseilles, April 16, 1797. Died Sept. 3, 1877. His "History of the French Revolution" is one of the greatest historical works of the age. After the capitulation of Paris in 1870, he was chosen by the Assembly to be head of the Provisional Government. In 1871, having crushed the Commune and restored order, he became "President of the French Republic," which office he held until 1873, when he resigned to give place to Marshal MacMahon.

April 17.

WILLIAM GILMORE SIMMS, an American novelist and voluminous writer, born in Charleston, S. C., April 17, 1806. Died there June 11, 1870. He was the most successful Southern author, and as a novelist, contested the palm with Cooper. His "Atalantis" is considered his finest poem.

GEORGE B. CHEEVER, D.D., an American divine and author, born at Hallowell, Me., April 17, 1807.

As an author he was contemporary with Longfellow and Hawthorne, and has particularly distinguished himself as an earnest advocate of temperance, and an opponent of slavery.

April 18.

WILLIAM WILLIAMS, a signer of the "Declaration of Independence," born at Lebanon, Conn., April 18, 1731. Died 1811. He was an active patriot, and contributed both by brains and estate to his country. His "last mite" was lent to the Continental treasury during the Revolution.

GEORGE HENRY LEWES (husband of "George Eliot.") a popular English author, born in London, April 18, 1817. Died Nov. 30, 1878. He was distinguished for his learning and versatility, and was largely engaged in literary, historical, scientific and philosophical researches.

April 19.

ROGER SHERMAN, an eminent American statesman during the Revolution, born at Newton, Mass., April 19, 1721. Died in New Haven, July 23, 1793. He signed the "Declaration of Independence," and was a member of the Convention which framed the Constitution of the United States in 1787.

Amos Whittemore, an American mechanician, born at Cambridge, Mass., April 19, 1759. Died at West Cambridge, March 27, 1828. He invented a machine for puncturing the leather and setting the wires of cotton and wool cards, which patent he sold for $150,000. The leading features of the invention were suggested by a dream.

Mary L. Booth, an American author and editor, born in Yaphank, N. Y., April 19, 1831.

Not only as the popular editor of "Harper's Bazaar" has her name become familiar to the literary world, but she has distinguished herself as an historian and translator. Her brain and pen are ever busy.

April 20.

Mohammed, the founder of Islam, or the prophet of Moslem, born at Mecca, April 20, 571. Died at Medina on his birthday, 632. His famous flight from Mecca to Medina, called the Hegira, occurred Sept. 20, 622. The intellectual powers of Mohammed were of a very high order, and as a poet he ranks far above all others who have ever written in the Arabic tongue.

William H. Turner, an American divine and author, born in Boston, April 20, 1802.

In 1825 he became pastor of the First Unitarian Congregational Church in Philadelphia. His translations of Schiller are among the best.

James David Forbes, F.R.S., a British physical philosopher, born near Edinburgh, Scotland, April 20. 1809. Died Dec. 31, 1868. He was the first, after severe attempts, to discover the law of glacial motion, and for this and other scientific discoveries, he received the Rumford medal, and that of the Royal Society of London.

Henry Theodore Tuckerman, an American author, born in Boston, April 20, 1813. Died in New York, Dec. 17, 1871. He occupied a high rank among the art critics of America.

April 21.

Frederich Froebel, German teacher, founder of the "Kindergarten," born at Oberweisebach, in Thuringia, April 21, 1782. Died at Rudolstadt, June 21, 1852. The educational reform begun by Rousseau, carried on by Fichter, Pestalozzi and Diersterurg, finally culminated in Froebel's gospel to childhood, as the "Kindergarten" is called. His first school was founded at Brandenburg in 1840.

Samuel J. Mills, an American divine, born at Torringford, Conn., April 21, 1783. As the "father of foreign missions" he organized the first society in America to contemplate foreign missions in 1808, and in 1817 visited Africa in company with the Rev. E. Burgess, to select a site for a colony, and died on his way home, June 16, 1818.

James Martineau, LL.D., a Unitarian divine, whom Thackeray called "the greatest theologian in England," born in Norwich, Eng., April 21, 1805.

A firm scholar, a penetrating thinker, having a massive, luminous mind, his position is that of the boldest thinker within the Christian limits.

Charlotte Bronte, "Currer Bell," a popular English novelist, born at Thornton in Yorkshire, Eng., April 21, 1816. Died March 31, 1855. Her first successful work, "Jane Eyre," has always retained its popularity. Her sister Emily, "Acton Bell," was like herself a successful novelist, and died May, 1849.

April 22.

Isabella I., "The Catholic," the patron of Columbus in his American discovery, born in Madrigal, Old Castile, April 22, 1451. Died Nov. 26, 1504. Her reign, like that of her consort Ferdinand, is noted for the establishment of the Inquisition in Castile, and the Moorish wars. She was mother of Catharine of Aragon, the unfortunate queen of Henry VIII. of England.

Henry Fielding, an English dramatist and novelist, born at Sharpham Park, Somersetshire, Eng., April 22, 1707. Died in Lisbon, Oct. 8, 1784. His first novel published in 1742, "The Adventures of Joseph Andrews and his friend, Abraham Adams," was regarded as the best work of fiction produced up to that time in the English language. He was a cousin of Lady Montague.

Lindley Murray, a distinguished American grammarian and educational writer, born near Lancaster, Pa., April 22, 1745. Died near York, Eng., Feb. 16, 1826. His name will long be remembered as one intimately connected with the grammar of the English language, as one of its most successful pioneers. Soon after the Revolutionary war he purchased an estate in England, the climate being beneficial to his health, and here he published his "Grammar of the English Language" in 1795, which was followed by briefer works for schools. He was also compiler of the famed "English Reader" and "Introduction" of our ancestors, which contains selections from the best literature of the eighteenth century.

James Freeman, D.D., the first in the United States to call himself a Unitarian clergyman, born in Charlestown, Mass., April 22, 1759. Died Nov. 14, 1835. By his influence "King's Chapel," in Boston, the oldest Episcopal church in New England, became the first Unitarian church in America. He was one of the founders of the Massachusetts Historical Society.

Anna Louise Germain De Stael-Holstein, "Madame De Stael," a French lady of great genius, born in Paris, April 22, 1766. Died July 14, 1817. She was considered the most celebrated authoress of modern times. Her greatest work "Corinne," which was translated into all the European languages, gave such a vivid description of Italy, its country and its people, that from that day, European painters ceased to copy the old masters, and began to portray living Italian peasants.

April 23.

William Shakespeare, the greatest dramatic genius that ever lived, born at Stratford-on-Avon, April 23, 1564. Died on his birthday, 1616. His works so noted need no comment, but it may not be a repetition to say, that of his tragedies, "Macbeth," "King Lear," "Othello," "Hamlet," and "Romeo and Juliet," are the most powerful. His best comic pieces are "Twelfth Night," "Much Ado about Nothing," "Midsummer Night's Dream," "Merry Wives of Windsor," and "Taming of the Shrew;" but the character of Falstaff in "Henry the Fourth," is considered superior to anything in the range of comedy, ancient or modern. While of his dramas, not classed as either tragedy or comedy, "The Merchant of Venice," "The Tempest," and "As You Like It," were the most admirable. It has been said by students of Shakespeare, that for every instance in human experience, an apt quotation can be found in his writings.

JOSEPH M. W. TURNER, an eminent English landscape painter, born in London, Eng., April 23, 1775. Died at Chelsea, Dec. 17, 1851. He left most of his paintings to the nation by will, upon condition that they have a suitable gallery provided for them. They now occupy the "Turner Room" of the National Gallery.

JAMES BUCHANAN, the fifteenth President of the United States, born in Franklin Co., Pa., April 23, 1791. Died June 1, 1868. He was elected a member of Congress in 1820, and from that time until the close of his Presidential term in 1861, with the exception of four years, he filled some government office. When his administration closed, the fearful conflict of the civil war was close at hand.

JAMES ANTHONY FROUDE, an eminent English historian and editor, born in Devonshire, Eng., April 23, 1818.

His greatest work is a "History of England from the Fall of Wolsey to the Death of Elizabeth." He was an intimate friend of Carlyle, and since the latter's death, his biographer.

April 24.

JOHN TRUMBULL, LL.D., an American satirical poet and lawyer, born at Waterbury, Conn., April 24, 1770. Died at Detroit, May, 1831. He was one of the group of Connecticut literati, called the "Hartford Wits." His "McFingal," modeled upon Butler's "Hudibras," was the most popular poem of the Revolution and was serviceable to the cause of liberty.   It still remains one of the best American political satires.

WILLIAM MILLER, founder of the sect of "Millerites," born in Pittsfield, Mass., April 24, 1781.   Died at Low Hampton, Washington Co., N. Y., in 1849.   In 1833 he began to predict that the end of the world would come in 1843, when the faithful would be translated.   His followers, who are said to have numbered nearly fifty thousand, greatly decreased after his death.

April 25.

OLIVER CROMWELL, Lord Protector of England, and one of the most extraordinary men that ever lived, born at Huntington, Eng., April 25, 1599.   Died Sept. 3, 1658. He was member of the Parliament in 1628 which, after passing the " Petition of Rights," was dissolved, and through the arbitrary measure of Charles I. never met again in eleven years.   In 1647, the disturbance had increased to an open rupture, which terminated in the execution of Charles, Jan. 30, 1649, after which Cromwell was " Protector of the Commonwealth " until his death.

MARK I. BRUNEL, F.R.S., a celebrated engineer, born near Rouen, France, April 25, 1769.   Died Dec. 12, 1849.   His most important work is the Thames Tunnel, which is considered one of the greatest triumh of engineering skill in the world.

JAMES MILLER, an American officer during the war of 1812, born at Petersborough, N. H., April 25, 1776. Died July 7, 1851. His reply " I'll try, sir," when asked by his commander if he could take a certain battery at the battle of Lundy's Lane, in 1814, is one of the bas-reliefs of history.

JOHN KEBLE, an English divine and poet of high

reputation, born at Fairford, Gloucestershire, Eng., April 25, 1792. Died March, 1866. His fame rests chiefly upon "The Christian Year." It is said, popularity is a weak word to express the cherished place which this book has among the best people in every organization in our time.

April 26.

DAVID HUME, an eminent English historian and philosopher, born in Edinburgh, April 26, 1711. Died Aug. 25, 1776. His most celebrated work, the "History of England," began to appear in 1754. His sympathy for Charles I. and the Earl of Strafford caused dissatisfaction, and his first volume was unpopular, but the subsequent volumes were better appreciated and raised the author to affluence.

ALICE CARY, a talented American authoress, born near Cincinnati, Ohio, April 26, 1820. Died in New York, Feb. 12, 1871. She first attracted attention by her contributions to the "National Era," under the title of "Patty Lee." Her sketches of western life, entitled "Clovernook," have obtained extensive popularity both in Europe and America.

FREDERICK LAW OLMSTED, an American agricultural writer and architect, born at Hartford, Conn., April 26, 1822.

In 1857, he was appointed chief engineer and architect of the Central Park, New York, also superintended the reconstruction of the Capitol grounds in Washington, D. C. He is also author of many works of agriculture and travel.

CHARLES FARRAR BROWNE, "Artemus Ward," an American humorist, born at Waterford, Me., April 26,

1834. Died at Southampton, Eng., March 6, 1867. In 1860 he became a contributor to "Vanity Fair," a New York comic newspaper, and being invited to lecture soon became very popular.

JOHN CLARK RIDPATH, LL.D., an American author and educator, born in Putnam Co., Ind., April 26, 1840.

His "Popular History of the U. S."—1876—one of his many works, reached the extraordinary sale of 265,-000 copies.

April 27.

EDWARD GIBBON, one of the most distinguished of English historians, born at Putnam, Surrey, Eng., April 27, 1737. Died in London, Jan. 16, 1794. His "Decline and Fall of the Roman Empire," placed by common consent in the very highest rank of English classics, is considered the greatest historical work in existence, and its fame can perish only with the civilization of the world.

SAMUEL F. B. MORSE, a distinguished American inventor and artist, born in Charlestown, Mass., April 27, 1791. Died in New York, April 2, 1872. He founded the "National Academy of Design" in New York, and was its annually elected president for many years. His most wonderful invention, the recording electric telegraph, has been called "the greatest triumph which human genius has obtained over space and time." The first telegraphic message, "What hath God wrought," was sent over the wires May 24, 1844, and was dictated by Anna G. Ellis, daughter of the Commissioner of Patents, who came early in the morning to inform him of the appropriation from Congress of $30,000 for the construction of his first telegraphic line between Baltimore and Washington.

Louis Kossuth, an eminent Hungarian orator, statesman and patriot, born at Monok, Hungary, April 27, 1802.

Seeking to secure a representative Hungarian ministry in the Austrian government in 1848, started disturbances with that country which with alternate triumphs and defeats, terminated in the exile and imprisonment of Kossuth. But through the intervention of England and the United States, he was released in August, 1851, after which he visited both countries, where he was warmly received, but failed to secure aid from them in behalf of his country.

Herbert Spencer, a distinguished philosopher and author, born in Derby, Eng., April 27, 1820.

He is to ethics and politics, what Lyell has been to geology, and Darwin to the development of organic forms. He visited America in 1882, and was considered one of the most distinguished guests the country ever received.

Ulysses S. Grant, the eighteenth President of the United States, and hero of the greatest civil war on record, born at Point Pleasant, Clermont Co., Ohio, April 27, 1822. Died at Mt. McGregor, N. Y., July 23, 1885. He was President two terms, 1869–77, and was elected to his second term by a larger vote, and a larger majority than any other candidate had ever received since the United States had become a nation. The Centennial Exposition at Philadelphia was open during the last year of his second term, and it was a fitting tribute to the nation's hero, that he should stand at its head during its prosperous Centennial year.

April 28.

Franz Karl Achard, a distinguished German

chemist, born at Berlin, April 28, 1753. Died April 20, 1821. He was the pioneer of the extraction of sugar from the beet-root, which, by his studies and writings, he succeeded in introducing into France.

JAMES MONROE, the fifth President of the United States, born in Westmoreland Co., Va., April 28, 1758. Died in the city of New York, July 4, 1831. His administration, 1817–25, was at the beginning of the prosperous time in the United States history known as the "era of good feeling." He asserted the important principle of foreign policy which forms the celebrated "Monroe Doctrine."

DR. EZRA ABBOT, D.D., one of the greatest scholars of the age, born in Maine, April 28, 1819. Died March 21, 1884. No American scholar was his equal, and scarcely a European scholar his superior in the knowledge of the Greek Testament, ancient manuscripts, etc.

ROBERT BONNER, an American journalist, born in the north of Ireland, April 28, 1824.

Since 1844 proprietor of the "N. Y. Ledger."

April 29.

OLIVER ELLSWORTH, the second Chief Justice of the United States, born in Winsor, Conn., April 29, 1745. Died Nov. 26, 1807. He was a chosen delegate to the Continental Congress in 1777, a member of the Convention which formed the Federal Constitution in 1787, elected Senator in 1789, and appointed Chief Justice by Washington in 1796. Adams admits him to be "the firmest pillar of Washington's administration" in the Federal party.

MATHEW VASSAR, founder of Vassar College, born in

East Denham, Norfolk Co., England, April 29, 1792. Died at Poughkeepsie, June 23, 1868. Emigrating to America, he amassed a fortune, and in 1861 he appropriated $408,000 to found the Vassar Female College in Poughkeepsie, and by his will this sum was increased to $800,000.

HOMER V. M. MILLER, a Southern doctor and statesman, born in Pendleton Co., S. C., April 29, 1814.

His eloquence in the Presidential canvasses of 1840–44, won for him the title of "Demosthenes of the Mountains."

ALEXANDER II., Emperor of Russia, born April 29, 1818. Among the important measures of his reign was the gradual emancipation of more than 20,000,000 serfs, which was decreed in March, 1861, and just twenty years from that date, March, 1881, he was assassinated by dynamite. Thus Lincoln and Alexander, who have given freedom to 25,000,000 of the population of the globe, both fell by the hand of an assassin.

April 30.

MARY II., of England, joint sovereign with William III., born April 30, 1662. Died of small-pox Dec. 28, 1694. William survived her as sole sovereign, until 1702.

HOSEA BALLOU, an eminent American preacher, born at Richmond, N. H., April 30, 1771. Died June 7, 1852. He is the author or founder of "Universalism," in the general acceptation of this term, and established the first newspaper devoted to this doctrine, the "Universalist Magazine," in 1819.

ABBA G. WOOLSON, an American author, poet and lecturer, born at Windham, Me., April 30, 1838.

May 1.

RUDOLPH, of Hapsburg, Emperor of Germany and founder of the Austrian Empire, born May 1, 1218. Died Sept. 30, 1291. He succeeded his father on the throne in 1240, and by his courage and love of justice, secured and enlarged his kingdom, and instituted many important reforms in the government.

JOHN WOODWARD, M.D., F.R.S., an eminent English geologist, born in Derbyshire, Eng., May 1, 1665. Died in London, April 25, 1722.

JOSEPH ADDISON, an English author pre-eminent as an essayist, humorist and moralist, born at Milston, in Wiltshire, May 1, 1672. Died June 17, 1719. He was originally designed for the church, but was drawn into literature, by the friendship of Dryden, and by commemorating in verse the battle of Blenheim, in 1709, thus securing royal patronage. Addison's fame rests chiefly on the " Spectator," a daily periodical, edited by himself and Steele, and the most famous that ever appeared in England. Dr. Johnson, the celebrated critic, said, " Whoever wishes to attain an English style, familiar but not coarse, elegant but not ostentatious, must study Addison."

NATHANIEL EMMONS, D.D., an eminent American theologian, born at East Haddam, Conn., May 1, 1767. Died Sept. 23, 1840. Many young men afterwards eminent, were trained by him for the ministry.

ARTHUR WELLESLEY, first Duke of Wellington, a celebrated British general and statesman, born at Dangan Castle, Ireland, May 1, 1769. Died Sept. 22, 1852. He received his first commission in the army in 1787, as ensign in the seventy-third regiment of foot, and gradually rose until, by his victory over Napoleon Bonaparte, June 18, 1815, he stood on the pinnacle of fame. His invincible resolution and capacity for enduring fatigue, gave him his familiar title of the " Iron Duke."

Junius Brutus Booth, a popular English tragedian, born in London, May 1, 1796. He visited America in 1821, where he was very successful. He was pre-eminent in the character of Richard III. Died on a Mississippi River steamboat when returning from California, Nov. 3, 1852.

May 2.

Elias Boudinot, LL.D., an American patriot and philanthropist, born in Philadelphia, May 2, 1740. Died Oct. 24, 1821. He was a zealous advocate of the patriotic cause in the Revolution; was director of the mint at Philadelphia, 1796–1805, and in 1816 was chosen first president of the American Bible Society.

John Gorham Palfry, D.D., LL.D., an American divine, historian and politician, born in Boston, Mass., May 2, 1796. Died April 25, 1881. He succeeded Edward Everett as minister of Brattle Square Church in Boston, in 1818, was an able ally of Sumner and Adams, on the anti-slavery question, and one of the creators of the Republican party.

Bernard B. Woodward, F.R.S., an English historian and scholar, born at Norwich, Eng., May 2, 1816. Died in London, Oct. 12, 1869. He was a valued literary assistant of Queen Victoria and Prince Albert, and his " Encyclopedia of Chronology, Historical and Biographical," is a work of the highest accuracy and value.

Albion W. Tourgee, a popular American author and judge, born at Williamsfield, Ohio, May 2, 1838.

He served in the United States army during the civil war, and subsequently settling in North Carolina as a lawyer and afterwards as judge of the Supreme Court, gave him authority for the subjects of his noted books. The popularity of " The Fool's Errand " exceeded that of any book which had appeared since "Uncle Tom's Cabin."

May 3.

HUMPHREY PRIDEAUX, D.D., an English scholar and author, born at Padstow, Cornwall, Eng., May 3, 1648. Died at Norwich, Eng., Nov. 1, 1724. His " Connection of the History of the Old and New Testaments," is still useful.

WILLIAM WINDHAM, an eminent English orator and statesman, born in London, May 3, 1750. Died there June 3, 1810. He was elected to Parliament in 1783, and in 1787 was appointed one of the managers of the impeachment of Warren Hastings. He was a brilliant orator, and was regarded as the model of an Englishman; though his love of paradox, fastened upon him the name of " Weathercock."

PIERRE PREVOST, a Swiss natural philosopher, born at Geneva, May 3, 1751. Died there April 8, 1839. He was the inventor of the theory relating to radiant heat, called " Prevost's Theory of Exchanges."

GEORGE R. PERKINS, LL.D., an American mathematician and astronomer, born in Otsego county, May 3, 1812. Died Aug. 22, 1876. He is author of the valuable series of arithmetics which bear his name; was professor of mathematics, and principal of the " State Normal School " in Albany, and superintended the erection of the Dudley Observatory of that city.

Montgomery C. Meigs, an American general, born in Georgia, May 3, 1816.

As first lieutenant of engineers, he has been engaged in the construction of several prominent forts of the U. S., also the Delaware Breakwater, and the great work of supplying the National capital with water from the Potomac river.

May 4.

John James Audubon, a celebrated American naturalist, born in Louisiana, May 4, 1780. Died in New York, Jan. 27, 1851. His admirable work "The Birds of America," now in the Astor Library, sold for $1,000 a copy, and was pronounced by Cuvier to be the most magnificent monument that art ever raised to ornithology.

William H. Prescott, an eminent American historian, born in Salem, Mass., May 4, 1796. Died at Boston, Mass., Jan. 28, 1859. His relations with Irving and Motley, as authors, where there might have been a possible competition, are among the pleasant things to remember. Irving abandoned in Prescott's favor, a projected history of the Conquest of Mexico, and Motley received from Prescott encouragement to prosecute his "Rise of the Dutch Republic." Prescott was afflicted from early manhood with defective sight caused by the throwing of a crust of bread by a fellow-student while in college, which shut out the light of day from his left eye forever. Yet with th's serious drawback, his "History of Ferdinand and Isabella," placed him in the foremost rank of contemporary historians.

Horace Mann, LL. D., an eminent American educationalist, born in Franklin, Norfolk county, Mass., May 4, 1796. To his influence is due the fact that Massachusetts is a pioneer in the educational reforms so much needed in the public schools. He died at Yellow Springs, Ohio, Aug. 2, 1859, on account of overwork at the Antioch College commencement, of which he was president.

THOMAS HENRY HUXLEY, F.R.S., an eminent English physiologist and naturalist, born at Ealing, Middlesex, May 4, 1825.

He is a popular lecturer on natural science, and for many years one of the most laborious workers in geological science. He favors the Darwinian theory.

JOHN HANNING SPEKE, an English officer, distinguished as an African explorer, born at Jordans, Somerset, Eng., May 4, 1827. He discovered Lake Victoria Nyanza in 1858, and the source of the Nile, in 1862, by tracing that river to Lake Nyanza. He accidentally shot himself, Sept. 15, 1864.

May 5.

NATHAN SARGENT, "Oliver Old School," an American author, born at Putney, Vt., May 5, 1794. Died in Washington, D. C., Feb. 2, 1875. He was for several years a government officer connected with Congress and the Treasury.

HUBERT HOWE BANCROFT, the historian of the Pacific States, born at Gransville, Ohio, May 5, 1832.

He has impressed himself upon the literature of his time by a work which may be called colossal, his "History of the Pacific States, from Alaska to Central America, from the arrival of the Europeans to the present time." His work will contain in all twenty-eight volumes.

JOHN WILLIAM DRAPER, M.D., LL.D., a distinguished chemist and physiologist, born in Liverpool, England, May 5, 1811. Died Jan. 4, 18?2. He came to America in 1833, and took a prominent part in establishing the medical department of the New York University in 1841. Draper is said to have taken the first human face by the daguerrotype process, and the sitter was subjected to the action of the instrument for thirty minutes.

May 6.

MAXIMILIEN MARIE ISIDORE ROBESPIERRE, a French demagogue and Jacobin, born at Arras, May 6, 1758. As an enemy of the Girondists, he was a leader in the French Revolution, and when that party fell he was the dictator of France. But justice, sometimes tardy, was now prompt, and in a few months after the fall of his rival, Danton, he died on the guillotine, July 28, 1794.

WILLIAM EMERSON, D.D., an American minister, born at Concord, Mass., May 6, 1769. Died May 12, 1811. He was the first minister of Harvard, Mass. Was an accomplished writer, and one of the best orators of his day.

PHEBE A. HANAFORD, an American minister, author and reformer, born on Nantucket Island, May 6, 1829.

She was the first woman regularly ordained as minister in Massachusetts or New England. She has been a pioneer in several stations in life which are now open to women.

May 7.

EMANUEL, surnamed "The Great," King of Portugal, born at Alconcheta, May 7, 1469. Died in 1521. During his reign the glory and power of Portugal attained their greatest height by the discoveries and expeditions of Vasco de Gama, Almeida and other famous captains, who maintained the ascendancy of the Portuguese arms in India and Brazil, from 1497 to 1520.

CHARLES WILLIAM WELLS, M.D., F.R.S., born in Charleston, S. C., May 7, 1757. Died in 1817. Although American, he was educated in Europe, and always remained a loyalist. Going with the King's troops to St. Augustine, Fla., 1782, he published the first weekly newspaper in that province. He received the gold and silver Rumford medals from the Royal Society in 1816 for the celebrated "Essay on Dew," which is his greatest work.

May 8.

GEORGE POPHAM, an early English colonist to America, born in Somersetshire, England, May 8, 1550. Died 1608. He sailed from England, May 31, 1607, in company with a nephew of Sir Walter Raleigh, and landed at the mouth of the Kennebec, where they planted the first English colony in New England ; but Popham dying the next year, the colony was abandoned. The Maine Historical Society has several times celebrated the anniversary of the foundation of the "Popham Colony."

JAMES HAMILTON HAMMOND, a Southern politician and legislator, born in the Newberry district, S. C., May 8, 1807. Died in 1861. He was elected to Congress in 1835, chosen Governor of South Carolina in 1843, and in 1857, became a U. S. Senator. In a speech delivered by him in the Senate, March 4, 1858, occurs the noted personification, "Cotton is King."

May 9.

WILLIAM SLADE, an American governor, author and

editor, born in Cornwall, Vt., May 9, 1786. Died at Middlebury, Vt., Jan. 18, 1859. He rendered great service to the educational cause by annually sending a number of competent teachers to the Western States. He served in Congress from 1831–43, and distinguished himself by his opposition to slavery.

JOHN BROWN, of Ossawatomie, a distinguished champion of anti-slavery, born in Torrington, Conn., May 9, 1800. In 1855 he emigrated to Kansas, where he took an active part in the contest of that State, caused by the passage of the Kansas-Nebraska Bill, advocating "squatter sovereignty." In 1859 he formed the bold plan of freeing the slaves in Virginia, and on the night of Oct. 16 he surprised Harper's Ferry, seized the arsenal and armory, and took forty prisoners. But his small band was soon overpowered and captured. He was tried in November, and hanged Dec. 2, 1859.

May 10.

WILLIAM LADD, an American philanthropist, born at Exeter, N. H., May 10, 1778. Died at Portsmouth, April 9, 1841. He was one of the originators of the "American Peace Society," and was for many years its president. He edited the "Friend of Peace," "Harbinger of Peace," and published many other writings on the same subject.

JARED SPARKS, a distinguished American historian and biographer, born at Wellington, Conn., May 10, 1789. Died in 1866. He was editor of the "North American Review," and later of "The Library of American Biography," for which he wrote the biography of many noted Americans. "His great merits," says Griswold, "are reverence for truth, soundness of judgment in regard to evidence, and exhausting fulness of detail and illustration."

MONTGOMERY BLAIR, an American officer, politician and statesman, born in Franklin Co., Ky., May 10, 1813.

He was appointed postmaster-general in Lincoln's first term. Was brother of F. P. Blair.

May 11.

JANE PORTER, an English novelist, born at Durham, Eng., May 11, 1776. Died at Bristol, May 24, 1850. "Thaddeus of Warsaw" and "The Scottish Chiefs" are her best known works.

ROBERT C. SANDS, a distinguished American journalist and scholar, born at Flatbush, L. I., May 11, 1799. Died at Hoboken, N. J., Dec. 17, 1832. He was editor, or assistant editor, of several magazines, and with the poet Bryant and Mr. G. C. Verplanck, wrote "The Talisman," a literary annual of high character.

May 12.

CHARLES LINNÆUS, a celebrated Swedish botanist and the most influential naturalist of the eighteenth century, born at Rashult, Smaland, May 12, 1709. Died Jan. 10, 1778. In 1730, he conceived the idea of a reform in botanical method and nomenclature, and by travel and long and severe study, produced the great "Philosophic Botanica," "which," says Cuvier, "exhibits on every page proofs of the rarest ingenuity, and the most surprising profoundness of observation."

JUSTUS VON LIEBIG, one of the greatest chemists of the present century, born at Darmstadt, Germany, May 12, 1803. Died April 18, 1873. He founded in the University of Giessen the first model laboratory of

Germany. Great in every department of chemical science, yet he owes his celebrity chiefly to his discoveries of organic chemistry. He received the title of "Baron" in 1845, and accepted the chair of chemistry at Munich in 1852.

ROBERT C. WINTHROP, an American statesman, author and orator, born in Boston, Mass., May 12, 1809. He was a descendant of Governors Winthrop and Bowdoin, of colonial days. Elected to Congress in 1840, he continued there ten years, and was appointed in 1850 to fill out the unexpired term of Daniel Webster. He was the chosen orator on several noted occasions, one of which was the laying of the corner-stone of the Washington Monument July 4, 1848.

GEORGE LEWIS PRENTISS, an American minister and author, born at Gorham, Me., May 12, 1816.

He was an eminent scholar, and during the civil war an ardent advocate of Union principles. His wife, Elizabeth P. Prentiss, is author of the well-known book "Stepping Heavenward."

JOHN RUSSELL HIND, an eminent English astronomer, born at Nottingham, England, May 12, 1823.

He discovered besides several comets, ten new asteroids between the years 1847–54. Was author of several astronomical works.

May 13.

MARIA THERESA, Empress of Germany, born May 13, 1717. Died Nov., 1780. She was crowned Queen of Hungary 1741. In 1745 her husband Francis, Duke of Lorraine, was elected to the dignity of Emperor Francis I. of Germany. He died in 1765, and Maria Theresa retained the administration of the government until her death.

CHARLES WATSON WENTWORTH, Marquis of Rockingham, a British statesman, born in England, May 13, 1730. Died at Wimbleton, July 1, 1782. He was Premier during the repeal of the "Stamp Act," for which his ministry were driven from power. But at the close of the American Revolution, when Lord North resigned in disgust, Rockingham was again called to the ministry.

JOHN SULLIVAN DWIGHT, a musical composer and critic, born in Boston, Mass., May 13, 1813.

He established "Dwight's Musical Journal" in 1852, and is author of "God Save the State."

ALEXANDER WILDER, M.D., an American editor and journalist, born at Verona, Oneida Co., N. Y., May 13, 1823.

He has edited the "Syracuse Star and Journal," "New York Teacher," and has been staff contributor to several other leading periodicals, also president of the Eclectic Medical College.

ARTHUR SEYMOUR SULLIVAN, a popular English musician, born in London, May 13, 1842.

He has written a large number of songs, cantatas, oratorios, etc., but is best known as the composer of "Pinafore" and "The Mikado," which have gained a popularity in English-speaking countries surpassing everything of the kind ever written. It is said that "The Mikado" was produced four thousand times in England, Australia, Canada and the United States, within one year of its appearance. But the success of his opera is greatly enhanced by his collaborator, William Gilbert, who is one of the most brilliant and wittiest of poets.

May 14.

ALIGHIERI DANTE, an illustrious Italian poet, born in Florence, Italy, May 14, 1265. Died at Ravenna, Sept. 14, 1321. He is regarded as the greatest poetical genius that flourished between the Augustan and the Elizabethan age. His great work the "Divina Commedia," is supposed to have been written while he was in exile from his native city, through the distracting feuds of the Guelphs and the Ghibelines.

GABRIEL DANIEL FAHRENHEIT, an eminent German natural philosopher and maker of philosophical instruments, born at Dantzic, May 14, 1686. Died 1736. He invented the thermometer which bears his name, and is said to have been the first who used mercury in the construction of thermometers. Fixing the zero of his scale at the point to which the thermometer sank in 1709, he reproduced the same degree of cold, with a mixture of sal-ammoniac, common salt and snow.

TIMOTHY DWIGHT, D.D., LL.D., an eminent divine and scholar, born at Northampton, Mass., May 14, 1752. Died at New Haven, Conn., Jan. 11, 1817. He was chosen president of Yale College, where he presided until his death, and rendered important service as a teacher of youth for which he was eminently qualified. His mother, a daughter of Jonathan Edwards, was a woman of talent and rare worth.

DR. CHARLES CALDWELL, an American physician and professor, born in Caswell Co., N. C., May 14, 1772. Died July 9, 1853. He became a student of phrenology under Drs. Gall and Spurzheim in Paris, and adopting their views, was the first to bring the new science into the United States.

James Donald Cameron, an American statesman, born at Harrisburg, Pa., May 14, 1830.

He was Secretary of War in Grant's administration, and was president of the North Central R. R., of Pennsylvania previous to the position being taken by the Hon. Thomas A. Scott.

May 15.

Prince von Metternich Clemens Wenzel, an eminent Austrian statesman and diplomatist, born at Coblentz, May 15, 1773. Died in 1859. He was appointed chancellor and minister of foreign affairs in October, 1809, and for more than thirty years had the chief direction of affairs in Austria, and experienced great influence in European politics. It was said that he always comprehended his position and never lost an opportunity. His conduct was always politic, but never precipitate. He was driven from power into exile, by the revolution of 1848.

James Gadsden, an American statesman and soldier, born at Charleston, S. C., May 15, 1788. Died there Dec. 26, 1858. When minister to Mexico, in 1853, he arranged the boundary line between the United States and Mexico, purchased the land south of the Gila River in Arizona, known as the "Gadsden Purchase," for which Mexico received $10,000,000.

May 16.

Sir William Petty, ancestor of the noble house of Lansdown, born in Hampshire, Eng., May 16, 1623. Died at Westminster, Dec. 16, 1687. He was one of the founders of the Royal Society, and made several philosophical discoveries; was inventor of a "pentagraph " or copying machine, and has the reputation of being the principal founder in England of the science of political economy.

SIR ISAAC COFFIN, an English officer during the Revolution, born in Boston, Mass., May 16, 1759. Died July 23, 1839. He was founder of the Coffin School in Nantucket.

WILLIAM HENRY SEWARD, LL.D., an eminent American statesman, born in the town of Florida, Orange Co., N. Y., May 16, 1801. Died at Auburn, Oct. 10, 1872. Early a lawyer, he was prominent in the councils which framed the policy of his State, and later the nation, when he was appointed Secretary of State during Lincoln's administration. He was selected as a victim when Lincoln fell at the hands of the assassin, but recovered from his wounds. One of the greatest events of his diplomacy was the purchase of Alaska from Russia, in 1867, for which the United States paid $7,200,000 in gold. This was considered a worthless addition of territory, but statistics prove that it has already paid for itself in seal skins.

LEVI PARSON MORTON, the Republican nominee for vice-president in the campaign of 1888, born at Shoreham, Vt., May 16, 1824.

He was for many years financier and banker, and entered political life by being elected to Congress in 1878. He accepted from Garfield the appointment of minister to France, which position he filled with great tact and popularity, and his philanthropic spirit mani_fested on several occasions, will be remembered with gratitude by his countrymen. Mr. Morton hammered the first nail in the construction of the Bartholdi Statue of Liberty, and delivered a speech, June 15, 1884, accepting the statue in behalf of the American Government.

May 17.

John Penn, an American patriot and signer to the "Declaration of Independence," born in Carolina county, Va., May 17, 1741.   Died 1788.

Seth Warner, an American patriot, born at Roxbury, Conn., May 17, 1743.   Died there Dec. 26, 1784. He settled in Vermont in 1765, and was the leader of the "Green Mountain Boys" during their conflict with the New York authorities, and was second in command to Ethan Allen at the capture of Ticonderoga and Crown Point in 1775.

Edward Jenner, M.D., celebrated for having introduced the practice of vaccination, as prevention of smallpox, born at Berkeley, Gloucester, Eng., May 17, 1749.   Died there Jan. 26, 1823.   His attention was first called to the subject by hearing a country woman say that she could not take the smallpox, because she had had the cow-pox.   After nearly twenty years of experiments he announced his discovery in 1798, and received £30,000 from Parliament in money and grants.

Anna Isabella Millbanks, "Lady Byron," born in England, May 17, 1792.   Died May 16, 1860.   She married the celebrated poet, Jan. 2, 1815, but soon separated, and devoted her large income to charitable purposes, and inherited the title of Baroness Wentworth.

Joseph N. Lockyer, an eminent astronomer, and author of astronomical works, born at Rugby, Eng., May 17, 1836.

May 18.

Richard Taylor, an English printer and journalist,

born at Norwich, Eng., May 18, 1781.   Died near London, 1858.   He was associate editor of the "Philosophical Magazine," and in 1838 founded the "Annals of Natural History."

May 19.

Sir George Prevost, an English general, born in New York, May 19, 1767.   Died Jan. 5, 1816.   He was governor-general and lieutenant-general of the British Provinces of North America at the opening of the war of 1812 ; but after being defeated at Plattsburg was recalled.

John Wilson, " Christopher North," a celebrated Scottish writer, critic and poet, born at Paisley, Scotland, May 19, 1785.   Died in Edinburgh, April 3, 1854. He was one of the first contributors to Blackwood's Magazine, which was founded in 1817, and which derived and retained its popularity from the brilliant contributions of " Christopher North."

Anna Jameson, an eminent author, born in Dublin, Ireland, May 19, 1797.   Died March 17, 1860.   She was an earnest laborer for the mental development of the women of England, and is considered the most celebrated female art critic of this century.

May 20.

Henry Percy, " Hotspur," son of the first earl of Northumberland, born in England, May 20, 1364.   He rebelled against Henry IV., and was killed at the battle of Shrewsbury, July 21, 1403.   He is immortalized in Shakespeare's Henry IV.

Dorothy P. Madison, wife of President Madison, was born in North Carolina, May 20, 1772.   Died July 12, 1849.   During the war of 1812, when the Capitol, the White House and other public buildings were burned by the British, Mrs. Madison assisted in saving valuable national documents, and under her own supervision the magnificent portrait of General Washington was taken down and carried to a place of safety.

DAVID DUDLEY FIELD, SEN., D.D., an American clergyman, father of the noted Field family, born at East Guilford, Conn. May 20, 1781. Died at Stockbridge, Mass., April 15, 1867.

JOHN STUART MILL, an eminent English philosopher and economist, born in London, May 20, 1806. Died May 8, 1873. He was for some time editor of the "Westminster Review," and acquired a high reputation by his "Principles of Political Economy." He was one of the few English writers who defended the cause of the North during the civil war in America, and was also an earnest advocate of the rights of women.

REV. ANTOINETTE BROWN BLACKWELL, the first woman regularly ordained by public services in America, and perhaps in the world, born at Henrietta, Monroe county, N. Y., May 20, 1825.

She took a three years' course in theology in Oberlin college, omitting no part of any class exercise, yet was not counted as a theological graduate "because she was a woman." Her ordination services took place in South Butler, N. Y., Sept. 15, 1853, but she had preached regular sermons for years previously.

ROSE HAWTHORNE LATHROP, an American author and artist, born in Lenox, Mass., May 20, 1831.

She studied painting in Dresden, Germany, but her taste for authorship developing in early years, has led her to devote her attention mainly to writing for the periodical magazines of the day. She is the second daughter, and youngest child of Nathaniel Hawthorne.

May 21.

PHILIP II., of Spain, son of the Emperor Charles V. of Spain, born at Valladolid, May 21, 1527. Died Sept. 13, 1598. He came into power when Spain was the empire "on which the sun never set," although his marriage with Mary I. of England, failed to add Great Britain to his territories. He also attempted the invasion of England thirty years afterwards, but the "Invincible Armada" also failed of its purpose.

ELIZABETH FRY, an eminent Quaker philanthropist, born in Norwich, Eng., May 21, 1780. Died at Ramsgate, Oct. 12, 1845. She renounced the gay amusements of city life, and devoted herself to the reformation of female prisoners in Newgate, and other prisons of London ; and yet found time to train with care a large family of her own.

JAMES BATES THOMSON, LL.D., an American mathematician, author and educator, born in Springfield, Vt., May 21, 1803.

He was an instructor in mathematics in the first "Teachers' Institute" and assisted in the organization of the New York State Teachers Association in 1845, and in 1864 became its president.

NELSON SIZER, phrenological examiner in the office of Fowler & Wells Co., born in Chester, Hampden Co., Mass., May 21, 1812.

He began his work as a phrenologist in 1839, and in 1849 was invited to take his present position. He has been associate editor and editor of the "Phrenological Journal," vice-president of the firm, and President of and teacher in the American Institute of Phrenology. As an author he has published books of great value, such as "Forty Years in Phrenology," "Choice of Pursuits," "How to Teach," which serve especially to bring the science of human nature home to practical uses in every-day life. He has made upward of 250,000 professional examinations, and by his advice has guided thousands to the best use of their powers, and saved other thousands from mental and moral wreck.

May 22.

ALEXANDER POPE, "the Bard of Twickenham," a popular English poet and critic, born in London, May 22, 1688. Died at Twickenham, May 30, 1744. The "Essay on Criticism" is among his earliest productions, but "The Essay on Man" is his most popular. "Pope's epistolary excellence," says Dr. Johnson, "had an open field ; he had no English rival, living or dead." Being noted for invective and sarcasm, he was sometimes called "The Wasp of Twickenham."

ARTHUR TAPPAN, an American merchant, born at Northampton, Mass., May 22, 1786. Died at New Haven, July 23, 1865. He was one of the founders of the "American Tract Society," "New York Journal of Commerce," and of Oberlin College, Ohio, and first president of the American Anti-Slavery Society at Philadelphia.

GIULIA GRISI, " Madame Melcy," a celebrated Italian vocalist, born at Milan, May 22, 1812. Died at Berlin, Nov. 29, 1869. She acquired great popularity as a singer in Italy, France, England and the United States.

WILHELM RICHARD WAGNER, a distinguished German composer, born at Leipsic, May 22, 1813. Died at

Vienna, Feb. 13, 1883. He is considered the greatest composer of music since Beethoven. His interest in the cause of human rights made him consent to write the "Centennial March," performed on the day in which the Philadelphia Exposition was opened, for which the United States government paid him $5,000.

RICHARD GRANT WHITE, an eminent American scholar and author, born in New York City, May 22, 1822. Died there 1885. He was for a time associate editor of the "Courier and Enquirer." He has been contributor to the leading literary periodicals of the day, besides author of many scholarly works. He was writing a series of papers on the English Language, for the "Chautauquan," at the time of his death.

May 23.

FREDERICK ANTON MESMER, founder of the doctrine of mesmerism, or animal magnetism, born in Suabia, May 23, 1733. Died at Meersburg, Germany, March 15, 1815. He made his doctrine known in 1775, and soon after established a hospital at Vienna for the perfection of his theory.

CHARLES EDWARD DUDLEY, United States Senator, born in Staffordshire, Eng., May 23, 1780. Died Jan. 23, 1841. He was at one time mayor of Albany, and erected the Dudley Observatory, to which his widow gave $70,000.

THOMAS HOOD, a famous English humorist, editor and author, born in London, May 23, 1798. Died there May 3, 1845. "The Bridge of Sighs" and "Song of a Shirt" are among his most popular poems.

SARAH MARGARET FULLER OSSOLI, an American scholar and author, born at Cambridgeport, Mass., May

23, 1810.   She received a classic education in early life, and at twenty-five became a teacher of languages in Boston.   In 1840 became editor of the "Dial," the organ of transcendentalism in America.   In this capacity she was associated with Emerson, Thoreau, Hawthorne and W. E. Channing, the great "Concord writers."   She married the Marquis Ossoli at Rome in 1847, and when returning to America in 1850, was shipwrecked on Fire Island Beach on the morning of July 16.   Among those who perished were the Marquis and Marchioness Ossoli and their child.

May 24.

EDWARD HITCHCOCK, D.D., LL.D., an eminent American geologist and author, born in Deerfield, Mass., May 24, 1793.   Died Feb. 27, 1864.   He was one of the originators and founders of Mount Holyoke Seminary, and of the Massachusetts Agricultural College. He is also among the pioneers of American geology.

SILAS WRIGHT, an American statesman, born at Amherst Mass., May 24, 1795.   Died in August, 1847.   He served in an official capacity for more than twenty years, yet declined being Vice-President and Secretary of the State under Polk, and would not accept a foreign mission.

EMANUEL LEUTZE, a distinguished historical painter, born in Wurtemberg, Germany, May 24, 1816.   Died in Washington, D. C., July, 1868.   Being obliged to leave Germany on account of political opinions, he made Philadelphia his home.   His "Western Emigration" is conspicuous in the National Capitol, and "Washington Crossing the Delaware" is everywhere familiar through engravings.

VICTORIA, Queen of Great Britain, and Empress of India, born at Kensington, May 24, 1819.

. She succeeded to the throne June 20, 1837, and was crowned June, 1838, and assumed the title of Empress of India in 1876. In 1887 she celebrated her jubilee, or reign as sovereign for fifty years over an empire on which now "the sun never sets." There has been but one instance of the kind before in English history. Henry III, reigned from 1216–1272. Edward III. only reached his fiftieth year as sovereign, and George III. was nominally king for sixty years, but the last ten he was an imbecile and his son reigned in his stead.

May 25.

CHARLES COOK, an eminent Wesleyan divine, born in London, May 25, 1787. Died in 1858. He was the chief founder of Methodism in France, and was to France and Switzerland, what Wesley was to England in his day.

RALPH WALDO EMERSON, LL.D., "the Concord Sage," born in Boston, Mass., May 25, 1803. Died April 27, 1882. He was chief of the "Concord writers" and the prophet of transcendentalism. As a poet his merits were of the highest order, yet he is better appreciated as an essayist and lecturer, wherein he could embrace almost every variety of subject with equal interest. His "Representative Men" published in 1850 is his most important publication and upon which his permanent reputation as a thinker will principally rest.

May 26.

JOHN ZEPHANIAH HOLWELL, member of the council at Calcutta, in the early establishment of the English government there, born in Dublin, May 26, 1711.

Died in 1798. He was one who survived the confinement in the " Black Hole," of which he wrote a narrative.

JOSEPH STEVENS BUCKMINSTER, D.D., an eloquent Unitarian minister, born in Portsmouth, N. H., May 26, 1784. Died June 9, 1812. In 1804 he became pastor of the Brattle Street Church in Boston, one of the largest and most intelligent congregations in New England. He acquired a high reputation as a preacher and scholar.

May 27.

JOHN WINSLOW, a descendant of Governor Winslow, of " Pilgrim " fame, born at Marshfield, Mass., May 27, 1702. Died at Hingham, Mass., April 17, 1774. He was founder of the town of Winslow, in Maine, and principal actor in the expulsion of the Acadians from their homes in 1755.

NATHANIEL GREENE, a distinguished American general of the Revolution, born at Warwick, R. I., May 27, 1742. Died near Savannah, June 19, 1786. He never gained a decided victory, yet his " retreats," for which he is noted, had the effect of successes. Congress voted him the highest honors, and he was considered next to Washington, the greatest general of the Revolution.

COM. CORNELIUS VANDERBILT, an enterprising American navigator and " railroad king," born on Staten Island, N. Y., May 27, 1794. Died at New York, Jan. 4, 1877. Originally a poor boy, he began business as master of a small sail-boat, which, by enterprise, grew into lines of improved steamboats and steamships ; one of which he started in 1851, between New York and California, *via* Nicaragua, and another in 1855, between New York and Havre. In 1862 he presented to the Federal government his finest steamer, worth

$800,000. He founded the Vanderbilt University at Nashville, Tenn., for the education of youth of the Methodist Episcopal Church. He was president of the Harlem, the Hudson River, and Central R. R. of New York, up to his eighty-second year, and "his enterprise, genius and success," says the "Merchants' Magazine," "are known and felt the world over."

JOHN DUDLEY PHILBRICK, LL.D., an American teacher and pioneer educator, born in Deerfield, N. H., May 27, 1818. Died 1866. He was principal of Connecticut State Normal School, Superintendent of Public Schools of Boston, and was Educational Commissioner of Massachusetts to the Vienna Exposition. He was also a prolific writer.

JULIA WARD HOWE, an American author, poetess and popular lecturer, born in New York, May 27, 1819.

Her poems possess merit of the highest order, and win for her the title of the "Browning of America." "Passion Flowers" and "Words for the Hour" are among her most important works. She is author of the deservedly-popular hymn, "The Battle Hymn of the Republic."

May 28.

GEORGE I., King, of Great Britain, belonging to the German branch of the House of Stuart, born at Osnaburgh, May 28, 1660. Died there while on a visit to his fatherland, June 10, 1727. In the reign of William III. a law was passed which rendered it impossible for none but a Protestant to be King of England, consequently George, Elector of Hanover, a descendant of James I., was preferred to the son of James II., who was a Catholic.

JOHN SMEATON, an eminent English civil engineer,

born near Leeds, Eng., May 28, 1724. Died at Aus.
thorpe, Oct. 28, 1792. He constructed Ramsgate
harbor, and was engineer of the great canal of Scotland
from the Clyde to the Forth, but his greatest work is
the Eddystone Lighthouse, finished in 1759.

JOSEPH IGNACE GUILLOTINE, a French physician,
born at Sainter, May 28, 1738. Died in 1814. He
was one of the founders of the Academy of Medicine
in Paris; but authority declares him *not* to be the inventor of the instrument called by his name. When
deputy to the States-General in 1789, he proposed de-
capitation as a humane measure, in preference to other
modes of punishment, and this may have given rise to
the name.

WILLIAM PITT, Jr., generally called "Younger Pitt,"
a celebrated statesman and debator, born at Hayes, in
Kent, May 28, 1759. He was appointed prime minister
in 1784, when only twenty-five years old. "A chip of
the old block," said Burke, when declaring the young
Pitt's resemblance to his worthy father. Being strongly
sustained by the favor of the court and the nation, he
became at this early age the most powerful subject of
Europe. He died Jan. 23, 1806, of vexation, at the
failure of England and her allies in the battle of
Austerlitz.

THOMAS MOORE, a celebrated Irish poet, born at
Dublin, May 28, 1779. Died Feb. 25, 1852. As a lyric
poet, Moore is said to be without a rival in the English
language. His "Lalla Rookh" and "Irish Melodies"
enjoy the highest reputation. Hazlitt says, "His is the
poetry of the toilette, of the salon, of the fashionable
world; not the poetry of nature, of the heart, or of
human life."

Bernhard Severin Ingemann, one of the most distinguished poets and novelists of Denmark, born on the Island of Falster, May 28, 1789. Died May 24, 1862. Like Walter Scott, he is the romantic historian of his country, and there perhaps, exists no Dane who has not read his series of romances.

Louis Agassiz, a Swiss naturalist of great eminence, born near Lake Neufchatel, May 28, 1807. Died Dec. 14, 1873. His visit to the United States in 1846 gave a decided impulse to the study of the natural sciences in America. He founded the great Museum of Natural History in Harvard University by contributing his valuable collection and arranging all the specimens. He was for many years a professor in that institution. When he made his famous South American scientific tour in 1865 he discovered 1,800 new species of fish in the region of the Lower Amazon and its tributaries.

James B. Eads, an American civil engineer, born at Lawrenceburg, Ind., May 28, 1820. Died March 8, 1887. Besides many inventions, he was the constructor of the Illinois and St. Louis bridge over the Mississippi at St. Louis, and of the famous jetties at the mouth of the Mississippi. Both Eads and De Lesseps have struggled for the rare honor of joining at the Isthmus of Panama the waters of the great Atlantic and Pacific.

May 29.

Charles II. of England, 1660–1685, born May 29, 1630. Died Feb. 6, 1685. He was son of Charles I., and when that king lost his throne, little Charles went with his mother to France. After the death of Cromwell, whose son did not wish to be Protector, Charles was called to the throne, which period was called the Restoration. He married Catherine, daughter of the

King of Portugal, and his father gave as a wedding gift the Isle of Bombay in East Indies. This was among the first places England possessed in that part of the world where her empire is so extensive now. About this time the words Whig and Tory originated, and were applied respectively to the opponents and partisans of the court. The great plague, followed by the great fire of London, occurred during Charles II.'s reign.

PATRICK HENRY, a celebrated American orator and patriot, born at Studley, Hanover Co., Virginia, May 29, 1736. Died in Virginia, June 6, 1799. In 1774 he was chosen a delegate to the Continental Congress, and among his great triumphs of unrivaled eloquence, was his speech delivered March, 1775, closing with the noted words, "Give me liberty, or give me death!"

GERALD MASSEY, an English poet, born in Hertfordshire, May 29, 1828.

He is a frequent contributor to periodical literature, and is a popular lecturer. He belongs to the asthetic school.

May 30.

COTTON TUFTS, M.D., an American physician and patriot, born in Medford, Mass., May 30, 1734. Died at Weymouth, Mass., Dec. 8, 1815. He was one of the founders of the American Academy of Arts and Sciences, and of the Massachusetts Medical Society, of which he was president for some time.

DR. HANNAH E. LONGSHORE, an American physician, born in Maryland, May 30, 1819.

She was the first woman to put up a professional "sign" in Philadelphia, and one of the ten members who composed the first graduating class of the Woman's Medical College in Pennsylvania.

May 31.

ALEXANDER CRUDEN, author of "Cruden's Concordance," an eccentric Scottish bookseller, born in Aberdeen, Scotland, May 31, 1700. Died at Islington, Nov. 1, 1770. His "Concordance," the result of his own unassisted industry, was the best which had then appeared, and is still considered indispensable to Biblical scholars.

HORATIO SEYMOUR, LL.D., an American politician, born at Pompey, Onondaga Co., N. Y., May 31, 1810. Died 1886. He was twice governor of New York, and in 1868 was an unsuccessful candidate for the presidency in opposition to Grant.

JOHN ALBION ANDREWS, an American statesman, born at Windham, Me., May 31, 1818. He was five times elected governor of Massachusetts, and in answer to Lincoln's call for 75,000 troops, April 15, 1861, he sent five regiments within a week. His death, Oct. 30, 1867, was deeply lamented, as his reputation had become national, and the highest honors of the country were hoped for him.

"WALT" WHITMAN, an American poet of rare talent, born at West Hills, L. I., May 31, 1819.

"My Captain," written after the assassination of President Lincoln, is his most popular poem.

June 1.

BRIGHAM YOUNG, high priest of the Mormons, born at Whitingham, Vt., June 1, 1801. He was founder of Salt Lake City, and leader of the Mormons from the death of Joseph Smith in 1844 until his own, Aug. 29, 1877.

FRANCIS PONSARD, a French dramatic poet, born at Vienne, France, June 1, 1814. Died at Paris, July 13,

1869. Standing at the head of classical literature in France, he was the rival of Victor Hugo. Among his most popular works is a comedy, "Honor and Money," which opened to him the French Academy.

June 2.

JOHN RANDOLPH, of Roanoke, an American orator and statesman, born in Chesterfield Co., Va., June 2, 1773. Died of consumption, June 24, 1833. He was a man of decided genius, distinguished for his ready wit, which joined to his mastery of sarcasm and invective, rendered him a formidable opponent in debate. He claimed to be a descendant of the Indian princess Pocahontas.

JOHN GODFRY SAXE, LL.D., an American humorous poet, born at Highgate, Franklin Co., Vt., June 2, 1816. Died March 31, 1887. He was for a time editor and proprietor of the "Burlington Sentinel," and for years editor of the "Albany Evening Journal." His poems rank among the most successful of their kind, and have obtained extensive popularity.

June 3.

SYDNEY SMITH, a celebrated English divine and writer, born at Woodworth, Essexfield, Eng., June 3, 1771. Died in London, Feb. 22, 1845. He, with Brougham, Jeffrey and other brilliant young men, founded the "Edinburgh Review" in 1802, and he was its first editor. Smith greatly promoted the cause of Catholic emancipation by an anonymous work, entitled "Letters on the subject of the Catholics to my Brother Abraham, by Peter Plymley."

NATHANIEL P. ROGERS, an American author, born at Plymouth, N. H., June 3, 1794. Died at Concord, Oct. 18, 1846. He established at Concord, N. H., the

" Herald of Freedom " in 1838, one of the pioneer anti-slavery papers in the United States. He wrote for the " New York Tribune " over the signature " The Old Man of the Mountains."

RICHARD COBDEN, an eminent English Liberal statesman and economist, born at Dumford, in Sussex, June 3, 1804. Died April 2, 1865. His untiring energy as a prominent advocate of the free importation of breadstuffs, which resulted in the repeal of the Corn Laws, June, 1846, won for him the title of " The Apostle of Free Trade." He was one of the few British statesmen who favored the cause of liberty and humanity in the United States during the civil war.

JEFFERSON DAVIS, an American statesman and military leader, born in Christian Co., Ky., June 3, 1808.

He served in the Black Hawk war of 1831–32, at which time Lincoln was captain and Davis lieutenant ; also in the Mexican war. He was elected to Congress in 1847, where he was an advocate of slavery and State rights. Having taken a prominent part in the secession movement of 1860–61, he resigned his seat in the Senate, and was elected President of the Confederate States, being inauguarated Feb. 22, 1862. At the close of the war he fled into southern Georgia, but was captured and confined in Fortress Monroe for two years. He was included in the general amnesty of Dec. 25, 1868.

June 4.

GEORGE III., King of Great Britain, 1760–1820, born in London, June 4, 1738. Died Jan. 29, 1820. The noted events of this reign were the gain of an empire in the East Indies—and the loss of one in the West—the United States, which latter was separated from the mother country by the blind obstinacy of the King and the over-reaching craft of the ministry. His reign was the longest known in English history. Sixty years a king ! yet the last ten years were clouded by a mental malady, and his son George ruled as regent.

ALTA Q. HULETT, the eminent lady lawyer of Chicago, born near Rockford, Ill., June 4, 1854. Died March 27, 1877. She graduated at the Rockford High School at the age of sixteen and took up the study of law, and for three years knocked incessantly at the doors of the Legislature of her native State and the Supreme Court of the United States for permission to practice in a profession which had been her earliest inspiration. After a severe examination, she stood at the head of a class of twenty-eight, all gentlemen her seniors, and at the age of nineteen, began to practice law in Chicago on an equal footing with her brother lawyers. Says the Rev. Phebe A. Hanaford: "Chicago is proud of its first lady lawyer, and like its famous water-crib, grain elevators, etc., she was regarded as one of its distinctive institutions."

June 5.

SOCRATES, the illustrious founder of Grecian philosophy, born at Athens, June 5, 470 B. C. Drank the fatal cup of poison, 400 B. C. He committed nothing to writing, and all that is known of his philosophical views is derived from the works of his disciples, Plato and Xenophon.

ADAM SMITH, a celebrated Scottish philosopher and political economist, born in Kirkaldy, Fifeshire, Scotland, June 5, 1723. Died July, 1790. His great work, "The Wealth of Nations," on which he worked many years, will continue to be, as it has been, a standard of reference on almost all branches of the science of legislation ; and it has won for him the title of "The Father of Political Economy."

LYMAN SPALDING, originator of the Pharmacopœia of the United States, born at Cornish, N. H., June 5, 1775. Died Oct. 31, 1821. He delivered the first course of lectures on chemistry in Dartmouth College.

June 6.

PIERRE CORNEILLE, a celebrated French dramatic author, and "founder of the French drama," born at Rouen, June 6, 1606. Died at Paris, Oct. 1, 1684. As a writer, he has perhaps contributed more to the national genius than any other author, and his productions gave a new tone and dignity to French tragedy, and eclipsed everything that had heretofore appeared on the French stage.

NATHAN HALE, an American patriot, born in Coventry, Conn., June 6, 1755. He was sent by Washington, after the battle of Long Island, to ascertain the strength and position of the enemy, and was captured and hanged as a spy, Sept. 22, 1776. His last words were, "I only regret that I have but one life to lose for my country."

JOHN TRUMBULL, an eminent American historical painter, son of Jonathan Trumbull, colonial governor of Connecticut, born in Lebanon, Conn., June 6, 1756. Died at New York, 1843. His "Battle of Bunker Hill," and "Death of Montgomery before Quebec," are well known through engravings. Four of the colossal pictures in the rotunda of the Capitol at Washington, viz., "Surrender of Cornwallis," "Resignation of Washington," "Declaration of Independence," and "Surrender of Burgoyne," are his.

NATHANIEL WILLIS, an eminent American journalist, born at Boston, June 6, 1780. Died there May 26,

1870. He established the " Eastern Argus " at Portland, Me., in 1803, the " Boston Recorder " in 1816, which was the first religious newspaper in America, and the " Youth's Companion " in 1827, the first American juvenile paper.

June 7.

SIR JOHN RENNIE, SEN., a distinguished British civil engineer, architect and mechanician, born in Haddingtonshire, Scotland, June 7, 1761. Died 1821. He removed to London in 1782, and was employed in the fabrication of steam-engines, etc. His first bridge was erected at Kelso, after which he was employed as engineer of public works, among which are the Kennet and Avon Canal, the Southwark Bridge over the Thames, the London Docks, the pier at Holyhead, and the Waterloo Bridge, which is considered his best work of that class. It was finished in 1817.

ELIJAH HEDDING, D.D., an American divine, born in Pine Plains, Dutchess county, N. Y., June 7, 1780. Died April 9, 1852. He began to preach in the Methodist Church in 1800. At the general Conference in 1824 he was elevated to the office of Bishop of the Methodist Episcopal Church. During the first eight years of his Episcopal life, he presided over fifty conferences, extending over the whole Union.

June 8.

THOMAS D. WHITAKER, LL.D., an English divine and writer, born in Rainham, Norfolk, England, June 8, 1759. Died at Blackburn, Dec. 18, 1821. Dr. Whitaker was one of the most popular of English topographers.

ROBERT STEVENSON, a Scottish engineer, born at Glasgow, Scotland, June 8, 1772. Died at Edinburgh,

July 12, 1850. During the time he was engineer to the board of commissioners for northern lighthouses, he erected twenty-three, the most celebrated of which was that on Bell Rock in the German Ocean, on the east coast of Scotland.

CHARLES READE, D.C.L., a distinguished English novelist, born June 8, 1814. Died April 11, 1884. He established his reputation by "Peg Woffington" in 1852, which was followed by many other novels. "Never too Late to Mend," "White Lies," "Put Yourself in His Place," etc., made him, after the death of Dickens, the most popular Bri ish novelist.

SAMUEL WHITE BAKER, K.C.B., a celebrated explorer of Africa, born in England, June 8, 1821.

He discovered the Albert Nyanza lake in Africa, and published an interesting account of his explorations.

JOHN EVERETT MILLAIS, an eminent English painter, born at Southampton, June 8, 1829.

He, with William Holman Hunt and Rosetti, inaugurated the "pre-Raphaelite school" of art.

June 9.

SAMUEL SLATER, an English artisan and mechanic, born in Derbyshire, Eng., June 9, 1768. Died 1835. He was instrumental in erecting the first cotton factories in the U. S., at Pawtucket, R. I. He also by his factories formed the nucleus of the prosperous village of Slaterville.

GEORGE STEPHENSON, "father of railways," an eminent English engineer, and inventor of the locomotive engine, born at Wylam, Northumberland, Eng., June 9, 1781. Died Aug. 12, 1848. The first railway was opened in 1822, and was eight miles long, but the first for public use, was from Stockton to Darlington, opened in 1825.

John Howard Payne, author of "Home, Sweet Home," an American actor and dramatic poet, born in New York, June 9, 1792. Died at Tunis, Africa, 1852, where for the second term he was consul. His "Home, Sweet Home," was written for one of his dramas "Clari, or the Maid of Milan."

June 10.

Peter I., "the Great," Czar of Russia, born at Moscow, June 10, 1672. Died Feb. 8, 1725. He founded St. Petersburg, and made it his capital in preference to Moscow. By his energy and enterprise he raised his country from semi-barbarism to civilization, and being the first Russian to take the title of Emperor, was really the founder of the Empire.

Jonathan Trumbull, LL.D., governor of Connecticut throughout the Revolution, born at Lebanon, Conn., June 10, 1710. Died there Aug. 17, 1785. He was considered a leader of the "Whigs" in New England, and "Brother Jonathan," the name applied as the personification of the United States, originated from Washington's habit of thus addressing him.

Samuel Bayard Woodward, M.D., an American physician, born at Torringford, Conn., June 10, 1787. Died Jan. 3, 1850. He was one of the founders of the "Hartford Retreat for the Insane," and assisted to establish other philanthropic institutions.

Edwin Arnold, an English author, born June 10, 1831.

He has been president of the Sanskrit college at Poonah, India, a journalist of London, and has published several volumes, but is best known by his "Light of Asia," a poem on Buddha, published in 1879.

June 11.

BENJAMIN JONSON, "Ben Jonson," one of the most celebrated English poets and dramatists, born at Westminster, June 11, 1574. Died Aug. 6, 1637.

In 1598 he produced "Every Man in his Humor," which at once brought him into notice. In 1619, James I. created him poet-laureate, with an annual pension of £100, and a tierce of Spanish wine. Dryden calls him "the Virgil of dramatic poets." He was buried at Westminster Abbey, where his tombstone bears the inscription, "O rare Ben Jonson."

JOSEPH WARREN, a distinguished American general and patriot, born at Roxbury, Mass., June 11, 1741. He possessed in perfection the gift of eloquence, and a speech delivered in March, 1772, on the anniversary of the Boston massacre, carried him at once to the helm, and for the brief period of his subsequent life he was one of the most prominent men in New England. He was elected major-general, June 14, 1775, and fell at the battle of Bunker Hill, June 17, 1775. The Bunker Hill Monument now stands near the spot where he fell.

June 12.

HARRIET MARTINEAU, an eminent English author, born at Norwich, Eng., June 12, 1802. Died June 27, 1876. Her tales illustrating political economy have been translated into French and German. She was a contributor to the "Westminster Review" and other periodicals.

JOHN A. ROEBLING, a celebrated engineer, born at Mülhausen, Prussia, June 12, 1806. At the age of twenty-five he emigrated to the United States, and devoting his talents to his adopted country, he has left monuments to his skill, in the elegant bridge at Pittsburg, over the

Alleghany, one over the Ohio at Cincinnati, the great suspension bridge at Niagara; but the grandest of all is the East River bridge connecting New York and Brooklyn, which, however, he never saw completed. He contracted lockjaw from an injury to his foot, and died in Brooklyn, July 22, 1869.

LEWIS GAYLORD CLARK AND WILLIS GAYLORD CLARK (twin brothers), American poets, authors and journalists, born June 12, 1810. Lewis became editor of the "Knickerbocker Magazine," in 1834, which he conducted many years with ability and success. Willis was associate editor of the "Columbia Star," and editor and proprietor of the "Philadelphia Gazette." He died in 1841, but his brother Lewis lived many years afterward, and died Oct. 3, 1873.

REV. CHARLES KINGSLEY, a popular English writer, born at Holne, Devonshire, England, June 12, 1819. Died Jan. 24, 1875. For his devotion to the improvement of the working classes, he has been styled "the Chartist parson." "Westward Ho" is among his many works, but he is best known by "Alton Lock, Tailor and Poet," written to illustrate the trials of the working classes in large towns. His philosophical romance "Hypatia," is considered his most powerful work.

June 13.

FRANCIS DANA, LL. D., an eminent American statesman and patriot, born at Charlestown, Mass., June 13, 1743. Died April 25, 1811. He was one of the patriot "Sons of Liberty," in the Revolutionary time, and served in the first provincial Congress of Massachusetts in 1774, and from that time forth he stood with the founders and supporters of the Federal Constitution. He was the father of Richard H. Dana, the poet.

Winfield Scott, one of the most distinguished of American generals, born near Petersburg, Va., June 13, 1786. Died May 29, 1866. He was voted a gold medal for his service in the war of 1812, and with Taylor was noted as the hero of the Mexican war. He was an unsuccessful candidate for the Presidency in 1852.

Thomas Arnold, D.D., of Rugby, an English historian and teacher of great merit, born on the Isle of Wight, June 13, 1795. Died June 12, 1842. As a teacher he found exercise for his rare qualifications while headmaster of the school at Rugby, and he raised the character of that school by the influence of his Christian principles enforced by his example. As a historian he is noted for his love of truth and conscientious judgment of political transactions.

June 14.

Robert Anderson, an American officer, born in Louisville, Ky., June 14, 1805. Died at Nice, France, Oct. 26, 1871. He was commander of Fort Sumter when it was forced to surrender to the first bombardment of the civil war, April 12, 1861.

Fernando Wood, an American politician, born at Philadelphia, June 14, 1812. Died Feb., 1881. He was Mayor of New York at the commencement of the civil war, and for recommending the city to secede and become a free city, he became the butt of much political sarcasm.

Harriet Beecher Stowe, one of the most distinguished of American authors, born at Litchfield, Conn., June 14, 1812.

It is said of "Uncle Tom's Cabin" that no book, save the Bible and "Imitation of Christ," has had so wide a circulation. The success of this work is without a parallel in the history of literature. Half a million copies have been sold in the United States, and more than that in Europe ; and it has been translated into all the European and into several of the Asiatic languages.

Charles Lanman, an American writer and editor, born in Monroe, Mich., June 14, 1819.

He was for some time librarian of the several departments of the government. and private secretary to Daniel Webster.

June 15.

Edward, "The Black Prince," so called from the color of his armor, eldest son of Edward III., born at Woodstock, June 15, 1330. Died June 8, 1376, leaving a son who became king as Richard II. He commanded the main body of the English at the victorious battle of Crecy, and there adopted the crest of ostrich feathers, and the motto "Ich dien " (I serve), since borne by his successors.

June 16.

Edward I., surnamed "Longshanks," King of England, 1272–1307, was eldest son of Henry III. He was born at Westminster, June 16, 1239. Died July 7, 1307, while on his march against Robert Bruce of Scotland. His reign is memorable by the confirmation of the Great Charter, the institution of the House of Commons, and great improvement in the common law.

William Jay, an American philanthropist, born in New York, June 16, 1789. Died at Bedford, N. Y., 1858. He was son of Chief-Justice Jay, and from early life exerted himself in behalf of social and religious reforms. He was for several years president of the

American Peace Society, and one of the founders of the American Bible Society.

June 17.

JOHN WESLEY, a distinguished religious reformer, the founder of the Society of Methodists, born at Epworth, Lincolnshire, Eng., June 17, 1703. Died in London, March, 1791. Influenced by his mother to make religion the study of his life, and becoming impressed by Jeremy Taylor's "Holy Living and Dying," the result was that since the days of the apostles, very few religious teachers have effected more good than John Wesley. Coming to America in 1736, he preached for a short time in the infant colony at Georgia. He returned to England in 1738, and following the example of Whitefield, preached in the open air at Bristol, where the foundations of the Society of Methodists, as an independent sect, were laid.

MARY ELLET, who has been termed the "Cornelia of America," born in Philadelphia, June 17, 1779.

She won the name by her heroic reply to one who sympathized with her in the loss of sons and grandsons during the civil war.

CHARLES FELIX GOUNOD, a popular French composer and musician, born in Paris, June 17, 1818.

He gained the grand prize for composition in 1839.

June 18.

RICHARD CARY MORSE, brother of the celebrated S. F. B. Morse, born in Charlestown, Mass., June 18, 1795. Died in Germany, 1868. He, with his brother Sidney, established the "New York Observer," and for thirty-five years was its proprietor and associate editor.

Robert Walter Weir, an American painter, born at New Rochelle, June 18, 1803.

Among his well known paintings is "The Embarkment of the Pilgrims" in the rotunda of the Capitol at Washington.

Frances Sargent Osgood, an American poetess, born in Boston, June 18, 1811. Died at Hingham, Mass., May 12, 1850. "A Wreath of Wild Flowers from New England," her best known collection of poems, was published in 1839, while residing in London with her husband, Mr. S. S. Osgood, a distinguished artist.

Samuel Longfellow, an American minister and poet, born in Portland, Me., June 18, 1819.

He was a brother of the "sweet poet" Longfellow, and like him a poet of the heart, as his many hymns prove.

Sir William Palliser, a British inventor, born in Dublin, Ireland, June 18, 1830.

He is inventor of the Palliser projectiles, and has made great improvements in the construction of ordnance. He was Knighted by the Queen, Jan. 21, 1873.

June 19.

Confucius, the most illustrious of Chinese philosophers, born in the kingdom of Loo, June 19, 551 B. C. Died 478 B. C. He came forward as a teacher when about twenty-two, and the excellence of his teachings has exerted an influence for good over nearly one-third of the human race.

St. Boniface, "The Apostle of Germany," born in Devonshire, England, June 19, 680. He distinguished himself by his zeal in converting the Germans to Christianity, and resided among them for thirty years, founding schools, cathedrals and monasteries. He was assassinated in 755 with a number of his companions, by an armed troop of pagans.

JAMES I. of England and VI. of Scotland, only son of Mary, Queen of Scots, born at Edinburgh Castle, June 19, 1566, succeeded to the throne of England, 1603, and died March 27, 1625. His reign is distinguished by the discovery of the "Gunpowder Plot," the brilliant career of Shakespeare and Ben Jonson, the colonization of Virginia and New England, and the translation of the English Bible.

BLAISE PASCAL, a celebrated French philosopher, mathematician and author, born in Auvergne, June 19, 1623. Died Aug. 19, 1662. In 1656 he produced his "Provincial Letters," which did more to show up the errors of the Jesuit monasteries than all the controversies of Protestantism or denunciations of courts. As a mathematician, he wrote a treatise on Conic Sections, and invented an ingenious calculating machine before he was twenty, and as a philosopher established the theory of atmospheric pressure.

RAPHAEL SANZIO MORGHEN, an eminent Italian engraver, born at Florence, Italy, June 19, 1758. Died in 1833. The "Transfiguration" and "The Last Supper" are among his master-pieces.

CHARLES HADDON SPURGEON, a popular and eloquent English Baptist preacher and author, born at Kelvedon, Essex, June 19, 1834.

He took charge of a small congregation at the age of eighteen, and in a few years his popularity was so great that his followers built for him the immense "Tabernacle," in which, since 1861, he has preached every week to thousands of hearers. "John Ploughman's Talk" is one of his many books, and he has edited "The Sword and Trowel," a monthly magazine since 1861.

June 20.

SALVATOR ROSA, a famous Italian painter of history, landscapes and battles, born near Naples, June 20, 1615. Died at Rome, 1673. The "Conspiracy of Cataline" is considered his masterpiece.

ANNA LETITIA BARBAULD, an English author, born in Leistershire, England, June 20, 1743. Died March 9, 1825. Her books for children are among the most useful of their kind, and all her writings are characterized by the elevated morality and deep devotional feeling which were so conspicuous in her life.

RICHARD COLLEY WELLESLEY, Marquis, an able statesman, brother to the Duke of Wellington, born in Dublin, Ireland, June 20, 1760. Died in London, Sept. 26, 1842. He was governor-general of India, 1793–1805, after which he was lord lieutenant of Ireland, and was a zealous friend of Catholic Emancipation, but this office he resigned in 1828, when the Duke of Wellington became prime minister, because the duke opposed the Catholic claims.

June 21.

ANTHONY COLLINS, an English writer on theology, born in Middlesex, Eng., June 21, 1676. Died Dec. 13, 1729. He gave great offence to the orthodox clergy of his day, by his independence of thought and investigation of religious ideas. Was an intimate friend of John Locke.

DANIEL D. TOMPKINS, an American statesman, born at Scarsdale, Westchester Co., N. Y., June 21,

1774. Died on Staten Island, June 11, 1825. He was governor of New York ten years, and twice elected as Vice-President of the United States.

ELIZA METEYARD, "Silverpen," an English writer, born in Liverpool, Eng., June 21, 1822.

She became known by her contributions to the magazines edited by Hood, Eliza Cook, and Douglass Jerrold.

June 22.

KARL WILHELM VON HUMBOLDT, a celebrated German philologist and statesman, born at Potsdam, June 22, 1767. Died April 8, 1835. He was one of the greatest philosophers and critics of his time, and has been called "the creator of comparative philology."

GIUSEPPE MAZZINI, a distinguished Italian patriot and writer, born at Genoa, Italy, June 22, 1808. Died March 10, 1872. Mazzini, Pope Pius IX., Count Cavour, Garibaldi and Victor Emanuel, were the five noted characters in the development of United Italy.

ROBERT SHELTON MACKENZIE, D.C.L., a British writer and journalist of much ability, born in Ireland, June 22, 1809. Died November 21, 1881. He was for some time foreign and literary editor of the Philadelphia "Press," and was a biographer of note.

A. B. CUMMINGS, U. S. N., a naval commander in the civil war, born in Pennsylvania, June 22, 1830. Died during the engagement of the batteries at Port Hudson, March 14, 1863. His self-forgetfulness after falling mortally wounded, was nearly equal to that of the noted Sir Philip Sidney.

JULIAN HAWTHORNE, the athlete and author, son of Nathaniel Hawthorne, born in Boston, Mass., June 22, 1846.

He is author of many works and also contributor to periodical literature.

June 23.

RUBEN DIMOND MUSSEY, M.D., LL.D., an eminent physician, born at Pelham, N. H., June 23, 1780. Died in Boston, June 28, 1866. He was the first to tie both common carotids, and successfully removed an entire scapula and clavicle, the first operation of the kind ever performed.

JOHN JAY, an eminent American lawyer, grandson of Chief-Justice Jay, born in New York, June 23, 1817.

He distinguished himself as an opponent of slavery, and was counsel for several fugitive slaves in the courts. In 1869 was sent as United States minister to Austria. He was thrice chosen president of the Union League of New York.

HENRY P. GRAY, an American painter, born in New York, June 23, 1819. Died Nov. 12, 1877. His reputation rests mainly on his composition pictures, the subjects of which are Biblical, classical and romantic. He was for several years president of the National Academy of Design.

FELIX O. C. DARLEY, an eminent American designer, born in Philadelphia, June 23, 1822.

He has illustrated Irving's " Sketch Book, " "Knickbocker's New York," "Rip van Winkle" and other humorous works, also J. F. Cooper's and Dickens' works.

June 24.

JEAN BAPTISTE MASSILLON, a French pulpit orator of great celebrity, born June 24, 1663. Died 1742. In 1699, he preached the " Advent " at Versailles before Louis XIV., and received the celebrated compliment from that potentate: "I have heard many great orators and been pleased with them, but after hearing you I am displeased with myself." After the death of Bossuet and Bourdaloue, he was at the head of French pulpit orators, and in 1715 pronounced the funeral oration of Louis XIV., beginning with "God only is great!" which simple exordium, so absolutely appropriate, brought his whole audience, by instantaneous impulse, to their feet.

WILLIAM HULL, an American officer of the Revolution, born at Derby, Conn., June 24, 1753. Died at Newton, Mass., 1825. He was governor of the territory of Michigan, at the opening of the war 1812, and his cowardly surrender of Detroit caused him to be tried by court-martial and he was sentenced to be shot; but for his age and former services he was reprieved.

JOSEPHINE, Empress of France, first wife of Napoleon I., born in Martinique, West Indies, June 24, 1763. Died May 29, 1814. Napoleon's ambition to form an imperial line caused his divorce in 1809.

SIR JOHN ROSS, a famous Arctic explorer, born at Balsarroch, Wigtonshire, Scotland, June 24, 1777. Died in London, August 30, 1856. In 1818 he was appointed commander of the first expedition sent to search for a northwest passage. In 1829 he made another voyage for the same purpose, but the party became ice-bound in the Arctic seas nearly four years. In 1831 he discovered a point which he believed to be the Northern Magnetic Pole.

MOST REV. JOHN HUGHES, an eminent Roman Catholic prelate, born at Annaloghan, Ireland, June 24, 1797. Died January 3, 1864. He was archbishop of New York fourteen years.

HENRY WARD BEECHER, a distinguished American
minister and writer, born in Litchfield, Conn., June 24,
1813. Died March 8, 1887. He was one of the originators of "The Independent," a weekly religious paper
published in New York, which acquired a wide popularity through his contributions. His articles sent to
the paper were signed with an asterisk, and these articles collected and published in book form, comprise
his noted "Star Papers." While in Amherst College in
1833, he was chosen to debate *against* Phrenology, a subject then recently introduced to public notice by the
visit and death of Dr. Spurzheim. To prepare himself,
he read the works of Spurzheim and Combe, and the
result was, the most able speech of his life up to that
time in *favor* of the science. This debate was the introduction of the brothers Fowler to Phrenology. As a
reformer in the cause of temperance and anti-slavery,
Beecher stood in the foremost rank, and was one of the
most successful lecturers in America. As a pulpit orator
he gathered around him the largest audiences in the
United States.

June 25.

JOHN HORNE TOOK, a celebrated English philologist and politician, born at Westminster, England,
June 25, 1736. Died March 18, 1812. During the
Revolutionary war in America, he was fined £200, and
imprisoned a year, for starting a subscription for the
benefit of the families of those whom " the King's
troops murdered at Lexington and Concord." He was
distinguished for his conversational powers.

ELIPHALET NOTT, D.D., LL.D., an American divine and scholar, born at Ashford, Conn., June 25,
1773. Died January 29, 1866. He became president

of Union College, Schenectady, and filled this post for nearly sixty years. As a pulpit orator he will retain his celebrity by his sermon on the death of Alexander Hamilton.

June 26.

SIR SAMUEL MORELAND, an English mechanician, inventor and writer, born in Berkshire, England, June 26, 1625. Died 1695. He invented the speaking trumpet, an arithmetical machine, and made great improvements on the fire-engine and steam-engine.

CHARLES XII., of Sweden, sometimes called "The Alexander of the North," a celebrated conqueror and military genius, born at Stockholm, June 26, 1682. He succeeded to the throne in 1697, and shortly after three kings, Peter I., of Russia, Frederick IV., of Denmark, and Augustus, King of Poland, taking advantage of his youth, formed a league to partition his dominions among themselves. This aroused the intrepid Charles to action, and in May, 1700, he left his capital with a well disciplined army, and within a year all the three kings were glad to sue for peace. Success emboldened him, and he continued his wars in Europe amid triumphs and defeats, until he was killed at the siege of Frederickshall, in Norway, Dec. 11, 1718.

PHILIP DODDRIDGE, an eminent English preacher and author, born in London, June 26, 1702. Died in Lisbon, Oct. 26, 1761. His work on the "Evidence of Christianity" has long been a text-book at Cambridge, Eng., but his most important work is "The Rise and Progress of Religion in the Soul." He is said to be the author of three hundred and seventy-five hymns.

June 27.

PHILLIP EMANUEL VON FELLENBURG, a Swiss philanthropist and writer, and a descendant of Admirable Van Tromp, born in Berne, Switzerland, June 27, 1771. Died there, Nov. 21, 1844. In 1799 he founded his famous educational and manual labor school, in Berne, which before his death contained ten distinct departments of education.

JOSEPH H. SCRANTON, an American manufacturer, born at Madison, Conn., June 27, 1813. Died at Baden-Baden, Germany, 1872. He, with his brother George, settled in the coal region of Lackawanna valley and founded the flourishing city of Pennsylvania which bears his name.

June 28.

HENRY VIII., King of England, 1509–1547, born at Greenwich, June 28, 1491. Died at Westminster, Jan. 28, 1547. Some of the events of his reign are the battle of "Flodden Field," so disastrous to the Scotch, but after which there was a peace between the two countries ; the "Battle of the Spurs," between England and France, so called because the French soldiers made more use of their spurs in fleeing, than their swords in fighting. In his reign we find "The Field of the Cloth of Gold," where Henry and Francis I., the young king of France, met to display their finery and amuse themselves. Henry wrote a book to defend the Pope against Martin Luther, and thus won the name of the "Defender of the Faith," but later when the Pope would not sign his divorce from Catherine of Arragon, he joined the Protestants against the Pope, and made himself "The Supreme Head of the English Church."

JEAN JACQUES ROUSSEAU, a celebrated Swiss philosopher and eloquent writer, born in Geneva, June 28, 1712. Died July 3, 1778. He stands in the front rank of classic writers of France. One of his political works became the catechism of the French Revolution. He has been styled the "father of modern democracy."

RICHARD HILDRETH, an American journalist and historian, born in Deerfield, Mass., June 28, 1807. Died at Florence, Italy, July 11, 1865. He is author of many works, but is best known by his "History of the United States," which is classed among the stand-ard histories of our country.

ROBERT SEARS, an American publisher and compiler of illustrated works, born at St. John, New Brunswick, June 28, 1810.

His books were among the first of the now well-known class of books sold exclusively by subscription.

COL. EDMOND RICHARDSON, the "Cotton King of the World," born in Caswell Co., N. C., June 28, 1818. Died at Jackson, Miss. He was owner and manager of forty cotton plantations in the Gulf States, marketing at an average 15,000 bales annually. Was also owner of the largest cotton factory in the southwest.

June 29.

PETER PAUL RUBENS, the most celebrated of the Flemish painters, born at Liegen, Westphalia, June 29, 1577. Died at Antwerp, May 30, 1640. Aided by his pupils, he left over 1,800 pictures. His master-pieces are the "Descent from the Cross" and "Elevation of the Cross."

BARON JOHN DEKALB, a German general, born in Alsace, June 29, 1732. He came to the United States with Lafayette to assist in the American Revolution, and was mortally wounded at the battle of Camden, S. C., and died August 19, 1780.

CELIA THAXTER, an American poet, born in Portsmouth, N. H., June 29, 1835.

She passed much of her early life upon the "Isle of Shoals," and her verses have the very swing of the sea. It is said that Lieutenant Greeley was so cheered by some of her poems during his dreary stay in Arctic winter, that when introduced to her on his return, he dropped on his knee in reverence.

STEPHEN H. TYNG, JR., an American divine, born at Philadelphia, June 29, 1839.

He was one of the founders of the "Christian at Work," and editor of the "Working Church," and is noted for his liberal fellowship with other denominations.

June 30.

HORACE VERNET, a celebrated French painter of battles, born in Paris, June 30, 1789. Died there Jan. 17, 1863. At the Exposition of 1855, a jury of painters from various nations, awarded him the grand medal of honor.

WILLIAM A. WHEELER, Vice-President of the United States in Hayes' administration, born in Malone, Franklin Co., N. Y., June 30, 1819. Died June 4, 1885. He was elected to the 37th, 41st, 42d, 43d and 44th Congresses, and during the last term adjusted difficulties existing in Louisiana, on the basis of what is known as "the Wheeler compromise."

WILLIAM HEPWORTH DIXON, an able and popular English writer and critic, born in Yorkshire, England, June 30, 1821. Died Dec. 27, 1879. Besides his many volumes of history, travels, etc., he was editor of the "Athenæum" for sixteen years.

July 1.

JEAN BAPTISTE DE ROCHAMBEAU, a French marshal, born at Vendome, France, July 1, 1725. Died May 10, 1807. During the American Revolution he commanded an army of six thousand sent by the French government to America, and contributed to the victory at Yorktown.

GIDEON WELLES, an American politician, born at Glastonbury, Conn., July 1, 1802. Died Feb. 11, 1878. He was editor of the "Hartford Times," 1826–37, and an original member of the Republican party, separating from the Democrats on account of the extension of slavery. He was Secretary of the Navy during the administrations of Lincoln and Johnson.

AMANTINE LUCILE AURORE DUPIN, "George Sand," a celebrated French novelist, born in Paris, July 1, 1804. Died June 8, 1876. She had the original merit to perceive and express the poetry of the landscapes of France. It is by her style more than by the subject of her writing that she especially excels.

July 2.

THOMAS CRANMER, Archbishop of Canterbury, an English statesman, divine and reformer, born in Nottinghamshire, Eng., July 2, 1489. Being prime minister to Henry VIII. he adopted the views of the Protestants, and was ready to go as far as any Swiss or Scottish Reformer; but when Mary I. became queen, he was accused of heresy, and in hopes of saving his life he recanted. But his enemies were anxious for his execution, and he was burned at the stake, March 21, 1556.

FRIEDRICH GOTTLIEB KLOPSTOCK, a celebrated German poet, born in Quedlinburg, Prussian Saxony, July 2, 1724. Died in Hamburg, March 14, 1803. He is considered "the father of German poetry," since he wrote the first great epic poem, "the Messiah," which was written in the German language.

FRANCOIS HUBER, a Swiss naturalist, born at Geneva, Switzerland, July 2, 1750. Died Dec. 22, 1831. Although he began to lose his eyesight at fifteen, and in a few years was totally blind, he devoted his life to the study of bees, and by the aid of his wife, son, and a faithful servant, added more to the knowledge of that science than has any other naturalist before or since.

July 3.

JOHN SINGLETON COPLEY, an historical and portrait painter, born at Boston, Mass., July 3, 1737. Died Sept. 25, 1815. He is said to have been the only native painter of real skill which the New World could boast before the Revolution, and to possess one of his portraits is America's best title to nobility. "The Death of Lord Chatham" is his masterpiece.

GABRIEL R. DERZHAVIN, a celebrated Russian lyric poet, born at Kazan, July 3, 1743. Died July 6, 1816. His most popular poem is an "Ode to Deity," commencing "O, Thou Eternal One."

HENRY GRATTAN, an eminent Irish statesman, born at Dublin, July 3, 1746. Died in London, May 14, 1820. In 1780 he brought forward and secured the passage of the famous "Bill of Rights," asserting the right of Ireland to self-government. Sir James Mackintosh says of him : "The purity of his life was the brightness of his glory."

July 4.

NATHANIEL HAWTHORNE, a distinguished American author, born at Salem, Mass., July 4, 1804. Died May 19,

1864. His place in American literature is a prominent one, being one of the noted "Concord writers" with Emerson, Thoreau, and William Ellery Channing. The "Old Manse," his home for a time, he immortalized in the work "Mosses from Old Manse." The "Scarlet Letter" raised its author at once to the first rank among American writers of fiction ; but his "Marble Faun" is regarded by some to be his best work.

GEN. GIUSEPPE GARIBALDI, a celebrated Italian patriot and general, born at Nice, July 4, 1807. Died June 2, 1882. He was the general, famous in the successful struggles of Italy to become a united nation.

DAVID P. PAGE, an eminent American educator, born at Epping, N. H., July 4, 1810. Died 1848. He was for many years principal of the State Normal School at Albany, and author of the valuable work, "The Theory and Practice of Teaching," and of an "Elementary Chart of Vocal Sounds," which was the first attempt of the kind in the English language.

July 5.

SARAH SIDDONS, a celebrated English tragic actress, born in Brecon, South Wales, July 5, 1755. Died in London, June 8, 1831. For thirty years she was the queen of the English stage, and by general consent is admitted to have been the greatest actress that England has produced.

DAVID GLASGOW FARRAGUT, America's "Great Admiral," born at Campbell's Station, East Tennessee, July 5, 1801. Died at Portsmouth, N. H., Aug. 14, 1870. His capture of New Orleans and Mobile during the civil war, created for him a name equal in fearless bravery to Nelson, and in grandeur of character, to the illustrious Collingwood.

Phineas Taylor Barnum, a famous American show-man and lecturer, born in Bethel, Conn., July 5, 1810.

He is noted for his energy and enterprise, rallying so quickly after his many severe losses by fire.

W. J. Macquorn Rankins, F.R.S., a British civil engineer, born at Edinburgh, July 5, 1820. Died at Glasgow, Dec. 24, 1872. He is distinguished as a writer on heat, electricity, and mechanics. Although noted as a philosopher, he had so keen a relish for music and literature, that he was as noted in the social circle as in the halls of philosophy.

July 6.

John Paul Jones, a famous naval officer, born at Arbigland, Scotland, July 6, 1747. Died in Paris, July 18, 1792. He is noted for the victory of the Bonhomme Richard over the Serapis, Sept. 23, 1779, for which he received a gold medal from Congress.

John Flaxman, the most poetical sculptor England has ever produced, born in the city of York, Eng., July 6, 1755. Died in 1826. "He was never happier," says Cunningham, "than when working in bas-relief, for which he had a genius all his own." The "Shield of Achilles" is one of the most beautiful and characteristic of his productions.

Ferdinand Joseph Maxmilian, Archduke of Austria, and for a brief period Emperor of Mexico, born at Vienna, July 6, 1832. In 1863 he was tempted by Napoleon III. to act the part of Emperor of Mexico, but after four years' struggle to gain a foothold, on the withdrawal of the French troops, the empire collapsed, and Maximilian was shot, June 18, 1867.

July 7.

Joseph Marie Jacquard, a French inventor, born at Lyons, France, July 7, 1752. Died Aug. 7, 1834. He is distinguished for the invention of a loom for weaving figured cloth, now called the Jacquard loom. He also invented a machine for weaving nets, by which he won the gold medal from the inspectors of Paris. In 1840 a public statue was erected to his memory in Lyons.

Philip Sing Physick, one of the most eminent of American surgeons, born in Philadelphia, July 7, 1768. Died Dec. 15, 1837. He was a student of the celebrated John Hunter, and distinguished himself by his faithful attention to his professional duties, during the frightful mortality caused by the yellow fever in Philadelphia, 1793, when not only citizens, but even physicians, fled from the city. In 1825 he was elected a member of the French Royal Academy of Medicine, and is said to be the first American who received this honor.

Nicholas I., Emperor of Russia, 1825–1855, born at St. Petersburg, July 7, 1796. Died March 2, 1855. He was noted for his ambition and despotism which in-volved him in wars to add to his territory. The long and famous seige of Sevastopol was an event of the closing years of his reign.

Sarah Payson Willis Parton, "Fanny Fern," born at Portland, Me., July 7, 1811. Died Oct. 10, 1872. Her works have obtained great popularity in America, and have been republished in England. She was sister to the noted author, N. P. Willis, and wife of the able and popular writer, James Parton.

July 8.

FitzGreene Halleck, a distinguished American poet, born at Guilford, Conn., 1790. Died there Nov. 19,

1867.   Among his well known poems are " Marco Bozzaris," and his poem on the death of his friend, J. R. Drake, in which occurred the well known couplet :

> " None knew him but to love him,
> None named him but to praise."

FREDERICK W. SEWARD, author, editor and statesman, born at Auburn, N. Y., July 8, 1830.

He is son of W. H. Seward, and was for several years assistant Secretary of State.

July 9.

ANNA WARD RADCLIFFE, a popular English novelist, born in London, July 9, 1764. Died there Feb. 7, 1823. Her writings had so much influence upon the literature of the time, that even Byron was among her imitators.

JACOB PERKINS, an American mechanician and inventor, born at Newburyport, Mass., July 9, 1766. Died in London, July 30, 1849. Among his inventions is a machine for cutting and heading nails at a single operation. He was the originator of using steel, instead of copper plates, for engraving banknotes.

ELIAS HOWE, inventor of the sewing machine, born at Spencer, Mass., July 9, 1819. Died Oct. 3, 1867. He obtained a patent for his machine in 1846, but in consequence of the infringement on his patents, he did not realize the benefit of his invention until 1854. During the civil war he raised and equipped a regiment at his own expense, and served as a private.

PHILIP PAUL BLISS, an American singing evangelist, born in Clearfield Co., Pa., July 9, 1838. He was killed by a railroad disaster at Ashtabula, Ohio, Dec. 30, 1876. He was associated with Moody in his noted evangelical tours, was composer and singer of many of the sweet inspirational hymns which vivified their meetings.

July 10.

CHRISTOPHER COLUMBUS, the most illustrious of navigators and discoverers, born at Genoa, Italy, July 10, 1436. Died May 20, 1506, at Valladolid, Spain. The period of his four voyages, 1492, 1493, 1498, 1502, is the most important decade in the earth's history, and "though," says Irving. "his discovery burst with such sudden splendor upon the world as to dazzle envy itself, he died ignorant of its grandeur."

JOHN CALVIN, after Luther, the greatest of the Protestant Reformers, born at Noyon, Picardy, July 10, 1509. Died in 1564. Being obliged to flee from France, and afterwards from Italy on account of his adhesion to the Protestant faith, he was induced by Farel, the Swiss reformer, to join him at Geneva in 1536, where he spent the remainder of his life—with the exception of a short exile in Strasburg—in founding the Genevese church, endeavoring to make it a model for all other Protestant churches.

SIR WILLIAM BLACKSTONE, an English jurist and eminent commentator on law, born in London, July 10, 1723. Died Feb. 14, 1780. His reputation is founded on his "Commentaries on the Laws of England," contained in four volumes, which passed through several editions and is extensively used by students of law.

GEORGE M. DALLAS, an American statesman, Vice-President with James K. Polk, born in Philadelphia, July 10, 1792. Died Dec. 31, 1864.

ROBERT CHAMBERS, LL.D., a well known Scottish writer and publisher, born at Peebles, Scotland, July 10,

1802.   Died in 1871.   Associated with his brother William, they published several popular works on Scottish history; afterwards published the "Edinburgh Journal." Their "Information for the People" had a sale of nearly two hundred thousand copies.   Robert was principal editor of "Chambers' Cyclopedia of English Literature," which is the best known of his works.

July 11.

GEORGE FOX, the founder of the Society of Friends, or Quakers, born at Drayton-in-the-Clay, Leicestershire, Eng., July 11, 1624.   Died in London, 1690.   He was early inclined to religious thoughtfulness, and at the age of twenty-three began to preach, believing that he was called by heaven to awaken men from lifeless forms and dogmas to an inward living spiritual religion.   The *thee* and *thou* he adopted from principles of truth and simplicity ; and to doff the hat in honor to any but the Creator, he considered inconsistent with the practice of the primitive Christians.   His followers were called Quakers by Justice Bennet, of Derby, because he bade the magistrates " tremble at the word of God."

JOHN QUINCY ADAMS, the "old man eloquent," an American statesman, orator and diplomatist, the sixth President of the United States, born at Braintree, Mass., July 11, 1767.   Died Feb. 23, 1848, being struck with paralysis two days before while in his seat in the Senate. His last words were, "This is the last of earth! I am content!" As early as 1793 he wrote several articles, which afterwards gave him the honor of publicly advocating the United States neutrality between England and France, which became a settled principle of American government.   Elected to the Senate in 1803, during the remainder of his long and useful life was prominent as a statesman and particularly as a diplomatist. His influence at St. Petersburg laid the foundations of that friendly relation ever existing between Russia and America, and he, with Clay, Gallatin and Russell, negotiated the treaty of peace at Ghent in 1814.

REUBEN E. FENTON, American legislator, born at Carroll, Chautauqua Co., N. Y., July 11, 1819. Died Aug., 1885. He was governor of New York for two terms, and in 1869 was elected U. S. Senator.

July 12.

JULIUS CÆSAR, the noted Roman general, and one of the most remarkable men that ever lived, born July 12, 100 B. C. Elected quæster at the age of thirty-two, he rapidly passed through all the Roman offices, reaching the consulship with his colleague Bibulus, at the age of forty-one. Shortly after, Cæsar, Pompey, and Crassus, formed an alliance known as the first "Triumvirate." Transalpine Gaul being given to him as his part of the government for a period of five years, he commenced that series of conquests of the German tribes which he described in his famous "Commentaries." Before his two terms as Governor of Gaul were ended his ambition caused him to "cross the Rubicon," subdue Pompey, his only remaining rival, and make himself master of Rome. This accomplished he extended his conquests to foreign countries and was soon undisputed master of the world. It was concerning his famous victory over Pharnaces, King of Pontus, that he sent his noted letter of three words to the Roman senate : "Veni, vidi, vici," "I came, I saw, I conquered." He did not long enjoy his triumph, for the Romans fearing he would convert the republic to a kingdom, assassinated him March

15, 44 B. C.   The improved method of computing time, introduced by him, has with slight modifications become the standard rule of civilized nations, and his name is immortalized in the name of the month July, and the phrases "Julian year," "Julian period," etc.

JOSIAH WEDGEWOOD, F.R.S., a celebrated English artisan, born at Burslem, Staffordshire, Eng., July 12, 1730.   Died at Etruria, Jan. 3, 1795.   He was inventor of several kinds of earthenware, chief among which are "Egyptian," "tortoise shell," "jasper," and "queen's ware."   The latter, a beautiful cream-colored ware, now goes by his name.

THOMAS GUTHRIE, a Scottish divine, born in Forfarshire, Scotland, July 12, 1803.   Died at Fifeshire, Feb. 24, 1873.   He was a social reformer and a brilliant orator.   Among his humanitarian efforts is the founding of the "Ragged or Industrial Schools" in 1847, which idea he took from John Pounds, a poor cobbler of London.

HENRY DAVID THOREAU, the "poet naturalist," an American poet, born in Concord, Mass., July 12, 1817. Died there May 6, 1862.   He lived a simple retired life, and "dedicated his genius with such entire love to the fields, hills, and waters of his native town, that he made them known and interesting to all his readers."   His home on the shore of Walden Pond near Concord, he has celebrated by his book, "Walden, or Life in the Woods."

July 13.

JOHN DEE, a famous astrologer and mathematician, born in London, July 13, 1527.   Died 1608.   He was remarkable for his versatile talents and learning, and in the reign of Mary I. was imprisoned for magic ; but was patronized by Elizabeth who employed him as her "intelligencer."

FRIEDRICH ADOLPH KRUMMACHER, a distinguished German theologian and writer, born in Westphalia, July 13, 1768. Died at Bremen, April 14, 1845. His "Parables" became a very popular book, and ran through several editions, and was translated into other languages.

July 14.

JULES MAZARIN, a celebrated courtier and prime minister of France, born in Italy, 1602. Died at Vincennes, March 9, 1661. It was during his reign as prime minister that the famous treaty of Westphalia with the German Emperor, ceded to France the province of Alsace, since the bone of contention between those two countries.

ISAAC WATTS, D.D., an eminent English divine and sacred poet, born at Southampton, England, July 14, 1674. Died Nov. 25, 1748. Although an author of many works, he is best remembered by his "Psalms and Hymns," " and is," says Montgomery, "almost the inventor of the hymns of our language."

JOHN HUNTER, F.R.S., an eminent British anatomist and surgeon, born near Glasgow, Scotland, July 14, 1728. Died Oct. 16, 1793. He is admitted to be the greatest British anatomist of the eighteenth century, and one of the fathers of zoological science.

WILLIAM ROBERT GROVE, F.R.S., an eminent English electrician and natural philosopher, born at Swansea, July 14, 1811.

Among his important inventions is the nitric-acid battery which bears his name.

July 15.

PAUL HARMONS REMBRANDT, a celebrated Dutch painter of history and portraits, born at Leyden, July 15, 1607. Died Oct. 8, 1669. He was recognized as the first master of the Dutch school of art, and as an engraver in aquafortis has never been surpassed.

CLEMENT CLARK MOORE, LL.D., an American scholar, author and poet, born at New York, July 15, 1779. Died at Newport, R. I., July 10, 1863. His well-known ballad "The Night before Christmas," will last as long as that joy-bearing season exists.

CHARLES EDWARD LESTER, an American journalist, lecturer and scholar, born at New London, Conn., July 15, 1815.

Among his many works are "Life of Charles Sumner," "Our First Hundred Years." He was a descendant of Jonathan Edwards.

July 16.

SIR JOSHUA REYNOLDS, the most celebrated portrait painter that England ever produced, born at Plympton, Devonshire, July 16, 1723. Died in February, 1792. He is considered as the head or founder of the British school of painting. Says Ruskin: "Reynolds, swiftest of painters, was gentlest of companions."

LADY CAROLINE OLIPHANT NAIRNE, a Scottish authoress, born in Perthshire, Scotland, July 16, 1766. Died Oct. 27, 1845. Her poetical productions were prompted by her desire to supplant the coarse, rough words of the popular songs, by putting new words to the beautiful tunes. She accomplished her design.

EMILY RUGGLES, a successful lady merchant of Reading, Mass., born in Dorchester, July 16, 1827.

She is a descendant of Peregrine White, the first child born among the Pilgrims of Massachusetts. Being deeply interested in the reforms of the day, she was one of the first women in Massachusetts elected to the office of School Committee.

EBEN E. REXFORD, an American author and poet, born in Johnsburg, N. Y., July 16, 1848.

He has gained a reputation in the literary world, by his regular contributions to the best magazines of the age, and to him the music-loving world owes some of its most popular songs, "Silver Threads among the Gold," and "Only a Pansy Blossom" being among them.

July 17.

TIMOTHY PICKERING, LL.D., an American statesman, born at Salem, Mass., July 17, 1745. Died there Jan. 29, 1829. He occupied three different positions in the cabinet during Washington's administration.

JOHN JACOB ASTOR, an eminent New York merchant and millionaire, born in Germany, July 17, 1763. Died March 29, 1848. He founded the city of Astoria, Oregon, in 1811. The Astor Library of New York was also founded by his bequest of $400,000. As much more has since been added to it by his son.

PAUL DELAROCHE, a French historical painter, born in Paris, July 17, 1797. Died Nov. 4, 1856. Among his noted pictures is "The Princes in the Tower," which greatly increased his reputation.

MARTIN F. TUPPER, a popular English poet and novelist, born in London, July 17, 1810.

He is best known by his "Proverbial Philosophy." In 1875, he wrote a drama in honor of American Independence.

July 18.

GILBERT WHITE, an eminent English naturalist and divine, born in Hampshire, Eng., July 18, 1720. Died at Selborne, June 26, 1793. His works on natural history have taken high rank among the English classics.

KARL VON ROTTECK, an eminent German historian, statesman and jurist, born at Freiburg, Baden, July 18, 1775. Died Nov. 26, 1840. Rotteck's "Universal History" is perhaps the most popular work of the kind that had yet appeared and, in 1841, had reached fifteen editions.

WILLIAM M. THACKERAY, an eminent English novelist, born in Calcutta—where his father held a position in the East India Company—July 18, 1811. Died in Kensington, Eng., Dec. 24, 1863. He was first recognized as a literary celebrity, upon the publication of " Vanity Fair," in 1847, after which followed " Pendennis," " Henry Esmond," " The Newcomes," and " The Virginians," which constitute his five greatest novels. Thackeray and Dickens were considered rivals without enmity for the first place in modern English fiction. Thackeray wrote of high life, Dickens of the lower classes; and in their chosen subjects, stood even in the balance.

July 19.

JOHN GIBSON, one of the most eminent sculptors of recent times, born in Conway, Wales, July 19, 1790. Died in Rome, Jan. 27, 1866. He studied under Canova and Thorwaldsen, and some of his productions are considered models of classic art.

ROBERT J. WALKER, a distinguished American writer on political economy, born in Northumberland, Pa., July 19, 1801. Died in Washington, D. C., Nov.

11, 1869. He was in the U. S. senate for several years, and was appointed Secretary of the Treasury under Polk.

AGNES STRICKLAND, an English historical writer, born in Suffolk, Eng., July 19, 1806. Died July 13, 1874. She has written numerous historical works, which have acquired an extensive popularity both in Great Britain and America.

SAMUEL COLT, an American inventor, born at Hartford, Conn., July 19, 1814. Died in 1862. He took out the patent for the revolver which bear his name, in 1835, and in 1848 began the manufacture of them in Hartford, where he built one of the most extensive armories in the world.

July 20.

FRANCESCO PETRARCH, a celebrated Italian poet, born in Tuscany, Italy, July 20, 1304. Died July 19, 1374. To him is due the preservation of many Latin authors, which were buried in the dust of monastic libraries. He founded the library of St. Mark, at Venice, and was one of the principal revivers of classical literature in Italy. The laurel crown of both Rome and Paris were offered him on the same day.

THOMAS BRUCE, Earl of Elgin, born in Scotland, July 20, 1777. Died Nov. 14, 1841. When appointed envoy extraordinary to Constantinople, he availed himself of the opportunity to procure with great labor and expense, a large collection of statues, bas reliefs, medals, monuments, and other remains of ancient art, at Athens, which were purchased by the British government, and now form part of the British Museum under the name of the "Elgin Marbles." For removing them he was severely satirized by Lord Byron.

July 21.

MATHEW PRIOR, an English poet and diplomatist, born in Dorsetshire, Eng., July 21, 1664. Died in Cambridgeshire, Sept. 18, 1721. He, with Charles Montagu, wrote the poem, "The City Mouse and the Country Mouse," in ridicule of Dryden's "Hind and Panther."

CHARLES TRISTAN MONTHOLON, a French general, born in Paris, July 21, 1782. Died in 1853. He served with distinguished bravery under Napoleon, during all his campaigns, and shared his exile at St. Helena, and was appointed executor of his will. After the emperor's death, he returned to France and published "The History of France under Napoleon, dictated by himself at St. Helena." He also wrote an "Account of the Captivity of Napoleon at St. Helena."

July 22.

ANTHONY ASHLEY COOPER, first earl of Shaftsbury, born in Dorsetshire, Eng., July 22, 1621. Died Jan. 22, 1683. He was a member of both the "Long" and "Short" Parliament; afterward he changed his party, and was member of "Barebones'" Parliament. He prepared with John Locke, his private secretary, the famous aristocratic constitution for the Carolinas, which proved such a failure. Ashley and Cooper rivers in South Carolina were named for him.

FREDERIC I., the first king of Prussia, born at Königsberg, July 22, 1657. Died at Berlin, Feb. 25, 1713. Previous to his reign, Prussia was only an electorate, but he purchased from the Pope the title of "King." He was father to "Frederic the Great."

FRIEDRICH WILHELM BESSEL, one of the greatest of modern astronomers, born at Minden, Prussia, July 22,

1784. Died in March, 1846. In 1811 he became director of a new observatory at Königsberg, built under his direction, and no observatory has contributed more during the present century to the improvement of every branch of astronomy than that of Königsberg.

July 23.

CHARLOTTE CUSHMAN, a distinguished American actress, born in Boston, July 23, 1816. Died Feb. 18, 1876. She is generally admitted to be the greatest of American actresses and readers, and by her stainless life, worked for the elevation of the stage. Her farewell to the stage was a great ovation, and she received from the noble and venerable poet Bryant, a laurel crown. She was a descendant of Robert Cushman, one of the founders of the Plymouth colony, who preached, in Dec., 1621, the first sermon in America that appeared in print.

July 24.

BENNING WENTWORTH, an American statesman and philanthropist, born in Portsmouth, N. H., July 24, 1696. Died Oct. 14, 1770. He was governor of New Hampshire for twenty years, and gave five hundred acres of land for the founding of Dartmouth College. The town of Bennington, Vt., was named in his honor.

JOHN PHILPOT CURRAN, a famous Irish orator and barrister, born near Cork, July 24, 1750. Died Oct. 14, 1817. His eloquence, humor, and mastery of sarcasm, procured him a large practice at the bar. In 1783 he entered Parliament, where he worked with Grattan, who was a leader of the opposition party.

JOHN ADAMS DIX, an American general and statesman, born at Boscawen, N. H., July 24, 1798. Died

April 21, 1879. He was elected to the Senate of the U. S. and was for a brief period Secretary of the Treasury. Was an efficient general during the civil war, and was afterwards governor of New York.

ALEXANDER DUMAS, a celebrated French novelist and dramatist, born in France, July 24, 1803. Died Dec. 5, 1870. His facial characteristics bore testimony to his African origin. "The Count of Monte Cristo" is his greatest work.

JOSIAH GILBERT HOLLAND, "Timothy Titcomb," a popular American author, born at Belchertown, Mass., July 24, 1819. Died Oct. 12, 1881. Among his well-known works are, " Bitter Sweet," "Gold Foil," "Letters to the Joneses," etc. In the latter is found a pleasant rebuke to every egotistic folly of human nature.

DONA MARTINA CASTELLS Y BALLESPI, a female M. D. of the Madrid University, born in Lerida, July 24, 1855. She graduated academically in 1874, and in June the same year received the degree of bachelor of Arts ; and when she won her licentiate's degree, the occasion was one of significance and importance, and all Spain wished health, long life and success to their plucky lady doctor.

July 25.

HENRY KNOX, an able American statesman and general of the Revolution, born at Boston, July 25, 1750. Died at Thomastown, Me., Oct. 1806. He took an active part in the battle of Bunker Hill, and served under Washington in most of his principal battles, enjoying in a high degree the esteem and confidence of his chief, which was manifest by his appointment in 1789, as the first Secretary of War of the United States of America.

SIMON BOLIVAR, the liberator of South America from

the Spanish domination, often called "The Washington of South America," born at Caracas, July 25, 1783. Died Dec. 17, 1830. The result of his military services was the independence of New Granada (now called United States of Columbia), Venezuela, Peru, and Bolivia, of which he was made President and dictator.

GEORGE H. PENDLETON, an American politician, born at Cincinnati, Ohio, July 25, 1825.

He was candidate for Vice President in 1864, and nominated by the democratic convention as candidate for President in 1868. He has of late been U. S. minister to Austria.

July 26.

GEORGE CLINTON, American patriot and statesman, born in Ulster Co., N. Y., July 26, 1730. Died April 20, 1812. Chosen governor of New York at the first election under the State Constitution of 1777, he held the office by successive re-elections for eighteen years. In 1804 he was elected Vice President for Jefferson's second term, and was re-elected for Madison's first term.

ROBERT FULTON, a celebrated American engineer and inventor, born in Lancaster Co., Pa., July 26, 1765. Died in the height of his popularity in New York, Feb. 21, 1815. He invented a machine for spinning flax, another for making ropes, and was proprietor of the first panorama exhibited in Paris. Though others had previously conceived the idea of steam navigation, Fulton was the first who successfully realized it. The "Clermont," sometimes called "Fulton's Folly," launched in 1807, was the first steamboat on the Hudson river.

ORANGE JUDD, an eminent American journalist and editor, born near Niagara Falls, N. Y., July 26, 1822.

The "American Agriculturist," under his supervision, is in the foremost rank of agricultural journals. He was publisher of the "Hearth and Home," and agricultural editor of the "New York Times."

July 27.

THOMAS CAMPBELL, a popular British poet, born in Glasgow, Scotland, July 27, 1777. Died June 15, 1844, and was buried in Westminster Abbey. His " Pleasures of Hope," written when only twenty-two, was considered by Byron " one of the most beautiful didactic poems in the English language," and his " Hohenlinden" is said to be the purest Saxon poem in literature.

THOMAS SAY, an American naturalist, born at Philadelphia, July 27, 1787. Died at New Harmony, Oct. 10, 1834. He was one of the founders of the Philadelphia Academy of Natural Sciences, and " has done more to make known the zoology of his country than any other man."

July 28.

COL. JOSEPH HABERSHAM, an American patriot and soldier, born at Savannah, Ga., July 28, 1751. Died there Nov. 17, 1815. He was postmaster-general under Washington.

MARIE ANNE CHARLOTTE DE CORDAY D'ARMANS, " Charlotte Corday," a French patriot and descendant of the illustrious Corneille, born in Normandy, July 28, 1768. She adopted with enthusiasm the principles of the Girondists during the French Revolution. The infamous Marat being then at the zenith of his influence, she resolved to sacrifice herself for the good of her country, and seeking a private interview with him, stabbed him to the heart. She was executed in July, 1793, a few days after the death of Marat.

WILLIAM MATHEWS, LL.D., an American author and editor of note, born at Waterville, Me., July 28, 1818. He is author of " Getting on in the World," " Words, their Use and Abuse," " Hours with Men and Books."

July 29.

JAMES WADDELL, D.D., an American divine, celebrated for his eloquence, born July 29, 1739. Died in Virginia, Sept. 17, 1805. He was blind, and the original subject of William Wirt's beautiful sketch of " The Blind Preacher."

REV. MOSES WADDELL, D.D., an eminent American educator, born in North Carolina, July 29, 1770. Died July 21, 1840. As an instructor of boys, he had few superiors in the United States, and ranks with Dr. Nott, of Union College, and Dr. Witherspoon, of Princeton. From his boarding-school at Wellington, S. C., were sent forth many prominent jurists, legislators, and divines.

HIRAM POWERS, an eminent American sculptor, born at Woodstock, Vt., July 29, 1805. Died June 27, 1873. Among his many works is his " Greek Slave," which became widely celebrated, and placed the artist in the first rank of sculptors.

EASTMAN JOHNSON, an American painter of portraits, born in Lovell, Me., July 29, 1824.

As a painter of common life, Mr. Johnson stands foremost among American artists. His picture " The Old Kentucky Home," was sent to the Paris Exhibition in 1867.

July 30.

SAMUEL ROGERS, the " banker poet," an eminent English banker and poet, born near London, July 30,

1763.   Died at London, Dec. 18, 1855.   He retired from business in the prime of life with an ample fortune, which he gave liberally to artists and literary men in pecuniary distress.   His "Pleasures of Memory" is considered his best poem, but "Italy" is his most extensive work.   It is stated that he spent £10,000 in illustrating this poem with engravings after Prout and Turner.

WILLIAM T. ADAMS, "Oliver Optic," a popular American writer, born in Medway, Mass., July 30, 1822. He has written much for youth and children, and founded the journal "Our Boys and Girls" in 1867.

July 31.

JOHN ERICSSON, an illustrious engineer and inventor, born in Sweden, July 31, 1803.

To this skilled inventor belongs much of the success of the late civil war, by the building of his iron-clad turret, the "Monitor," just in time to defeat the "Merrimac," and thus save the ports of the North from Southern or from foreign invasion.

GEN. GEORGE HENRY THOMAS, the "slow but sure" general of the American civil war, born in Southampton Co., Va., July 31, 1816. Died March 28, 1870. His wonderful skill exercised at the battle of Chickamauga, furnishes one of the most remarkable pages in the history of the war, and won for him the title of "The Rock of Chickamauga."

Z. K. PANGBORN, an American editor, born in Peacham, Vt., July 31, 1829.

He has been editor of several papers, some of which he established himself.

August 1.

WILLIAM CLARKE, an American general and explorer,

born in Virginia, Aug. 1, 1770. Died Sept. 1, 1838. He was associated with Lewis, and conducted the first exploring expedition across the American continent to the Columbia river, and gave the names of Lewis and Clarke to the two tributaries of that river.

FRANCIS SCOTT KEY, an American jurist and poet, born in Frederick Co., Md., Aug. 1, 1779. Died in Baltimore, Jan. 11, 1843. He is remembered as the author of the popular national song, "The Star-Spangled Banner," composed while a prisoner in the British fleet, during the bombardment of Fort McHenry near Baltimore, in the war of 1812.

GEORGE TICKNOR, a distinguished American scholar and writer, born at Boston, Aug. 1, 1791. Died 1871. His "History of Spanish Literature," in 1847, established the reputation of the author, and his "Life of William Prescott" is said to be one of the most interesting biographies in the language.

RICHARD HENRY DANA, JR., an eminent American lawyer and author, born at Cambridge, Mass., Aug. 1, 1815. Died Jan. 7, 1882. Being obliged, on account of his eyes, to suspend his studies at the age of nineteen, he took a voyage to California as common sailor, a narrative of which he gave in his popular book, "Two Years before the Mast." He was one of the founders of the "Free Soil" party in 1848.

MARIA MITCHELL, a distinguished American astronomer, born on the Island of Nantucket, Aug. 1, 1815.

In 1847, she received a gold medal from the King of Denmark, for the discovery of a new comet. She was appointed Professor of Astronomy at Vassar College soon after the opening of that institution in 1865, which position she has filled with honor, until her resignation in tne summer of the present year (1888).

PETER BONNETT WIGHT, an American architect, born in New York City, Aug. 1, 1838.

He drew the plan for the "New York Academy of Design," the "Yale School of Fine Arts" in New Haven, and the "Mercantile Library Building" in Brooklyn.

August 2.

WILLIAM II. of England, Rufus "the red-haired," born in Normandy, Aug. 2, 1056. He was accidentally shot by Walter Tyrrel, while hunting in the "New Forest," Aug. 2, 1100. He built London Bridge, and completed London Tower and Westminster Hall.

ROBERT RICHFORD ROBERTS, called by the Indians "the grandfather of all the missionaries," born in Frederick Co., Md., Aug. 2, 1776. His history is identified with the early Methodist church in the then "far west," occupying in the capacity of exhorter and minister from a "stalwart youth" to his death, March 26, 1843. He was mourned throughout the nation.

JOSEPH STURGE, an English philanthropist, born at Elberton, Gloucestershire, Aug. 2, 1793. Died in 1859. He was one of the first in England to advocate the immediate abolition of slavery, and co-operated with Cobden and Bright in the anti-corn-law movement.

REV. ADA C. BOWLES, an American minister, born in Gloucester, Mass., Aug. 2, 1836.

She is a successful pastor of a church in Easton, Penn., though she resides in Philadelphia, where her husband, Rev. B. F. Bowles, is pastor of a flourishing church.

August 3.

JAMES WYATT, an English architect of high reputation, born in Staffordshire, Eng., Aug. 3, 1746. Died Sept. 5, 1813. Among the many monuments to his skill is the famous Pantheon on Oxford street, London, and the House of Lords, which he designed in 1800.

SARAH PLATT DOREMUS, an eminent American philanthropist, born in New York, Aug. 3, 1802. Died Feb. 5, 1877. In 1842, she, with Miss Catherine Sedgwick, established a home for women from prison, now called the " Isaac T. Hopper Home." She was also one of the founders of the " House and School of Industry," which is but a fraction of her beneficent labors. She was considered one of the most remarkable women of her time.

SIR JOSEPH PAXTON, an English architect and landscape gardener, born in Bedfordshire, Eng., Aug. 3, 1803. Died June 8, 1865. " The Crystal Palace " built for the " World's Fair " of 1851, was designed and superintended by Mr. Paxton, who was knighted for this service.

HAMILTON FISH, LL.D. an American statesman, born in New York, Aug. 3, 1808.

He was appointed Secretary of State in Grant's cabinet, and suggested the " Joint High Commission " between the United States and Great Britain, to settle the various difficulties between the two nations including the famous " Alabama claim."

CHRISTINE NILSSON, COUNTESS MARANZI, a celebrated singer, born in Smaland, Sweden, Aug. 3, 1843.

She made her debut in Paris, 1864, appeared in London 1867, and in 1870–71 visited the United States.

August 4.

PERCY BYSSHE SHELLEY, an eminent English poet, born near Horsham, Surrey, Eng., Aug. 4, 1792. He left England in 1818, and took up his residence in Italy, and was intimate with Leigh Hunt, Byron, and Keats. He was drowned off the coast of Italy, July 8, 1822, and was buried in the Protestant burying-ground at Rome, near the grave of his friend Keats, who had died of consumption the previous year. Standing by the grave of his friend one day, he remarked that "it was enough to make one in love with death, to lie in so beautiful a spot," little thinking the privilege would so soon be his. Shelley has been styled by some "the poet of poets," and is regarded by critics as "the greatest English poet since Shakespeare."

August 5.

THOMAS LYNCH, JR., one of the signers of the "Declaration of Independence," born in Prince George parish, S. C., Aug. 5, 1749. In 1779 he sailed for the West Indies, on account of his health, but the ship was never again heard from.

COM. FOXHALL A. PARKER, an American naval commander and writer, born in New York, Aug. 5, 1821. Died 1879. He was one of the founders of the U. S. Naval Institute at Annapolis, in 1873, and for many years contributed to the Knickerbocker Magazine.

August 6.

FRANCOIS SALIGNAC DE LA MOTTE FENELON, Archbishop of Cambray, an illustrious French prelate and author, born in France, Aug. 6, 1651. Died at Cambray, Jan. 7, 1715. He ranks among the most excellent masters of graceful and eloquent diction that France ever produced.

WILLIAM HYDE WOLLASTON, an eminent English chemist and natural philosopher, born in London, Aug. 6, 1766. Died there Dec. 22. 1828. His many inventions and discoveries in the interest of chemistry have given him the name of "the founder of modern British chemistry."

DANIEL O'CONNELL, a famous Irish orator and political agitator, born in Kerry Co., Aug. 6, 1775. Died at Genoa, Italy, May 15, 1847. He was pre-eminent as the advocate of Catholic emancipation, and in 1823 founded the Catholic Association. He was elected to Parliament in 1828, and refusing to take the oath designed expressly to exclude Roman Catholics from the House, caused a violent excitement which resulted in the passage of the bill for Catholic Emancipation, i. e. they were relieved from the political disabilities under which they had suffered for more than a century.

WILLIAM A. ALCOTT, an American reformer and educational writer, born at Wolcott, Conn., Aug. 6, 1798. Died March 29, 1859. He labored earnestly in the cause of educational and hygienic reforms, being associated with Sylvester Graham in his dietetic and vegetarian principles. Besides editing and contributing to various journals, he published many volumes on educational and kindred matters.

August 7.

JOSEPH RODMAN DRAKE, an American poet, born in New York, Aug. 7, 1795. Died Sept. 21, 1820. Although but twenty-five at his death he left an impress on his country by the beautiful poem "The American Flag." "The Culprit Fay" is also a noted poem.

JOSEPH P. THOMPSON, D.D., an American divine, born in Philadelphia, Aug. 7, 1819. Died 1879. He was one of the founders of the " Independent," at Brooklyn, and the " New Englander ;" was also author of many theological works.

August 8.

James Bowdoin, LL.D., an American statesman, born at Boston, Mass., Aug. 8, 1727. Died Nov. 6, 1790. He was president of the convention which in 1778 formed the Constitution of Massachusetts, and was twice governor of that state. Bowdoin College, at Brunswick, Me., founded in 1802, was named in his honor, but endowed by his son James Bowdoin.

Benjamin Silliman, M.D., LL.D., an eminent American naturalist and professor, born in Trumbull, Conn., Aug. 8, 1779. Died at New Haven, Nov. 24, 1864. He founded the " Journal of Science and Art " in 1818, which was recognized in America and Europe as the chief repository of American science. He was considered by the country at large as the " Nestor of American Science."

Charles Anderson Dana, a noted American journalist, born at Hinsdale, N. H., Aug. 8, 1819. In 1847, he became city editor of the " Tribune," and two years later, Greeley's principal assistant. In 1865 was editor-in-chief of the " Republican," at Chicago. He formed the " New York Sun " association, and took charge of the paper Jan. 1, 1868, since which time he has made the " Sun " a power in the land.

August 9.

John Dryden, a celebrated English poet, born at Aldwinkle, Northamptonshire, Eng., Aug. 9, 1631. Died May 1, 1700, and was buried at Westminster Abbey.

He succeeded Davenant as poet-laureate in 1668, and by his "Essay on Dramatic Poesy" won the title from Dr. Johnson of "the father of English criticism." In 1686 he avowed himself a Catholic, which was the religion then favored at court, and wrote "The Hind and the Panther," an allegory in verse. The subject was a discussion between the two churches. His "Ode for St. Cecelia's Day" is pronounced his greatest work, and some critics consider it "the finest ode in the language." His "Translation of Virgil," says Pope, is the most noble and spirited translation in any language; and Brougham speaks of his prose as "the matchless prose of Dryden."

ADONIRAM JUDSON, D.D., an eminent Baptist and missionary, born at Malden, Mass., Aug. 9, 1788. Died at sea, April 12, 1850. He was forty years a missionary to Burmah, learned the language, translated both the Old and the New Testaments into Burmese; also wrote a dictionary of that language.

August 10.

LOUIS JACQUES MANDE DAGUERRE, an eminent French artist, whose name has been rendered memorable by the invention of the daguerrotype, born at Cormeilles, Aug. 10, 1789. Died July 12, 1851. When his invention was announced by Arago, in the Academy of Science, in 1839, it produced a profound sensation.

August 11.

JEAN VICTOR MOREAU, one of the most eminent generals of France, born at Morlaix, Bretagne, Aug. 11, 1763. He was the hero of the battle of Hohenlinden, won by the French over the Austrians, Dec. 3, 1800, which excited the enmity of Napoleon, his rival in generalship.

Being one of the party opposed to Napoleon as the "Emperor of the French," he was banished to the United States, and resided in Morristown, Pa., until invited to return to Europe by the Czar of Russia. He fell mortally wounded at the battle of Dresden, and died Sept. 2, 1813.

ROWLAND HILL, Viscount, an English general, nephew of the great preacher of the same name, born in Shropshire, Aug. 11, 1772. Died near Shrewsbury, Dec. 10, 1842. Hill was called the "right arm of Wellington," and was the most popular general in the British army.

JEFFRIES WYMAN, M.D., an American anatomist, born at Chelmsford, Mass., Aug. 11, 1814. Died at Bethlehem, N. H., Sept. 4, 1874. He is regarded as among the first of American comparative anatomists.

ANDREW JACKSON DAVIS, a clairvoyant and eminent spiritualist, born at Blooming Grove, Orange Co., N. Y., Aug. 11, 1826.

He is the author of many works on spiritualism, among which is "The Great Harmonia."

ROBERT GREEN INGERSOLL, a noted American lawyer, orator and author, born in Dresden, N. Y., Aug. 11, 1833.

He has taken part in numerous noted law-suits, in all parts of the country; was counsel for the so-called star-route conspirators, whose trial ended in acquittal, 1883. His services as a campaign orator are in demand throughout the country. He is well known by his books, pamphlets, and speeches, considered to be directed against the Christian religion.

August 12.

GEORGE IV., of England, grandfather of Queen

Victoria, born Aug. 12, 1762. Died June 26, 1830. He reigned ten years as regent during the inability of his father, George III., and became king at the death of his father in 1820.

Robert Southey, an eminent English poet and author, born at Bristol, Eng.. Aug. 12, 1774. Died March 21, 1843. In 1803 he settled in the lake region in the north of England, and with Wordsworth and Coleridge formed the "Lake Poets." He was appointed poet-laureate in 1813.

Elizabeth Oakes Smith, an American poet and miscellaneous writer, born at Cumberland, Me., Aug. 12, 1806.

She was the wife of Seba Smith, "Major Jack Downing," and has been a prominent advocate of the rights of women, both as a writer and lecturer.

August 13.

Antoine Laurent Lavoisier, an illustrious French chemical philosopher, born at Paris, Aug. 13, 1743. He discovered the composition of water in 1783, and was the principal inventor of the system of chemical nomenclature; and was thus styled "one of the fathers of modern chemistry." He was guillotined during the "Reign of Terror" in France, May 8, 1794.

Rev. Rowland Hill, an eccentric yet popular preacher, born at Hawkstone, Eng., Aug. 13, 1744. Died in London, April 11, 1833. In 1783 he built Surrey Chapel, London, in which he preached fifty years. He was a disciple of the eloquent Whitfield.

Elizabeth Stuart Phelps, Sen., an American writer, born at Andover, Mass., Aug. 13, 1815. Died there Nov. 30, 1852. She wrote many popular tales for the young under the name of "H. Trusta."

ARTHUR SHERBURNE HARDY, M.A., Ph.D., an American scholar and author, born at Andover, Mass., Aug. 13, 1847.

As a mathematician he holds a position among the brightest lights in that department, and is an authority in all the higher branches of the art. He has published several mathematical works, but is best known to the reading public by his novel "But yet a Woman," of which 20,000 copies have been sold in this country, besides the four editions issued in England. As a book it is equal to Longfellow's "Hyperion" in its wealth of pithy, felicitous expression, easily passed into proverbs.

August 14.

HANS CHRISTIAN OERSTED, a celebrated Danish natural philosopher, the founder of the science of electro-magnetism, born on the Island of Langeland, Aug. 14, 1777. Died March 9, 1851. He announced his great discovery of the relation between magnetism and electricity in 1820, and the electric telegraph is one of the most direct practical results of that discovery. He also made many discoveries in chemistry, and wrote a number of works on that science. At the close of 1850, a national jubilee was held in honor of the fiftieth anniversary of his connection with the University of Copenhagen, a festival he did not long survive.

JOHN H. GRISCOM, a lecturer, physician, and author, born in New York, Aug. 14, 1809. Died 1874. Author of "Uses and Abuses of Air" and other works.

CHARLOTTE FOWLER WELLS, an American phrenologist, born at Cohocton, Steuben Co., N.Y., Aug. 14, 1814.

She is a sister of the Fowlers, and was wife of S. R.

Wells, of the publishing house of "Fowler & Wells." She early became interested in the study of phrenology and is considered the pioneer woman in this field, having been for more than fifty years actively engaged in the work. On the death of her husband in 1875 she became owner and director of the establishment, together with the widely known "Phrenological Journal," and is the president of the Fowler & Wells Co. She was one of the incorporators of the New York Medical College for Women, and has been an active trustee since 1863.

August 15.

EDWARD PREBLE, a celebrated American Commodore, born in Portland, Me., Aug, 15, 1761. Died there Aug. 21, 1807. He is famous for the success of his squadron, under his flagship the "Constitution," sent against Tripoli in 1803. For these services he received a gold medal from Congress.

NAPOLEON BONAPARTE, Napoleon I., Emperor of the French, and the greatest general of modern times, born at Ajaccio, in Corsica, Aug. 15, 1769. Tired of anarchy and confusion produced by the "Reign of Terror" and subsequent wars, the French gladly accepted Napoleon as First Consul, Jan., 1800. In Dec., 1804, he crowned himself Emperor of France. His well-known career in his attempt to make all Europe, France, was terminated at the battle of Waterloo, June 18, 1815, and he died an English prisoner on the island of St. Helena, May 5, 1821.

SIR WALTER SCOTT, a celebrated Scottish novelist and poet, born in Edinburgh, Aug. 15, 1771. Died Sept. 21, 1832. The first of his three great poems, the "Lay of the Last Minstrel," appeared in Jan., 1805, and at once gave its author a place among the most distinguished poets of the age. "Marmion" was published in Feb., 1808, and the "Lady of the Lake" in May, 1810. According to Lockhart, "the Lay" is considered the most natural and original, "Marmion" the most powerful and splendid, and the "Lady of the Lake" the most interesting and graceful. In July, 1814, appeared "Waverley, or 'Tis Sixty Years Since," the first of that series of novels which formed a new era in the history of romance, and placed the name of Scott on the highest pinnacle of fame. When the Waverly novels appeared anonymously, the author was popularly styled "The Great Unknown," and on account of his marvelous power of creating illusions, was called "The Great Enchanter."

THOMAS DE QUINCEY, an eminent English author, born in Manchester, Eng., Aug. 15, 1785. Died in Edinburgh, Dec. 8, 1859. He early began to use opium to alleviate the pains of rheumatism, and contracted the habit of an excessive use of that drug; but in the prime of life, through severe struggle, reformed, and afterwards wrote his noted "Confessions of au Opium Eater." He was one of the most brilliant magazine writers of his time.

FRANCOIS P. JULES GREVY, a French politician and statesman, born in Jura, Aug. 15, 1813.

He was elected President of the Republic of France, Jan. 1879, which place he filled with the respect and confidence of all parties until his resignation, 1887.

CHARLES G. LELAND, an American author and humorist, born at Philadelphia, Aug. 15, 1824.

He first addressed himself to the public through the magazines, and has officiated as editor of some of the periodicals of the day, but has achieved his greatest popularity by productions of a humorous or burlesque character. As a writer of dialect poetry, Mr. Leland has shown a considerable mastery of the quaint speech of the "Pennsylvania Dutch," and his ballads are as highly appreciated in England as in America.

August 16.

GEORGE TAYLOR, one of the signers to the "Declaration of Independence," born in Ireland, Aug. 16, 1716. Died at Easton, Pa., Feb. 23, 1781. He came to America as a "redemptioner" in 1736.

NATHAN HALE, a journalist and lawyer, born at Westhampton, Mass., Aug. 16, 1784. Died in 1863. He conducted for many years the "Boston Daily Advis. er," the pioneer daily of New England, and was one of the founders of the "North American Review." He was nephew of the Revolutionary martyr patriot, Nathan Hale, and father of Rev. Edward Everett Hale.

ISAAC TAYLOR, JR., LL.D., an eminent English writer, born in Suffolk, Aug. 16, 1787. Died at Stanford Rivers, June 28, 1865. He published a number of moral, philosophical and theological works of a high character.

JEAN H. M. D'AUBIGNE, a Swiss divine and popular historian, born at Geneva, Switzerland, Aug. 16, 1794. Died Oct. 21, 1872. In 1835 he published the first volume of his capital work a "History of the Reformation," which obtained great popularity especially in England and the United States.

August 17.

FRANCOIS MANSARD, a celebrated French architect, born at Paris, Aug. 17, 1598. Died there 1666. He erected several chateaus and churches in Paris, and his designs were remarkable for nobleness and majesty. He was the inventor of the curb-roof which bears his name.

Fredrika Bremer, a celebrated Swedish novelist, born at Abo, Finland, Aug. 17, 1801. Died Dec. 31, 1866. Her works have been translated into several of the European languages and have enjoyed great popularity. She visited the United States in 1850, and afterwards wrote "The Homes of the New World."

John F. Hurst, D.D., an American Bishop of the M. E. Church and a noted author, born near Salem, Md., Aug. 17, 1834.

His writings consist of theological and historical works, the most important of which is a "History of the Church," covering the whole period from its earliest institution down to the present time.

August 18.

Meriwether Lewis, an enterprising American traveler and explorer, born near Charlotteville, Va., Aug. 18, 1774. Died in Tenn., Oct. 11, 1809. He was appointed by the United States government conjointly with Capt. Clarke, to explore the northwest part of the American continent. They gave the names of Jefferson, Gallatin, and Madison, to the three streams which form the Missouri, and the principal affluents of the Columbia were named Lewis and Clarke.

Charles Francis Adams, an American diplomatist and statesman, born in Boston, Aug. 18, 1807. Died 1886. One of the most noted events of his life was his appointment as minister to England during the civil war in America, and though encountering the most bitter social hostility in England, he maintained the right of his country, and "exercised the grandest qualities of true statesmanship just where and when they were of priceless value." His grandfather, John Adams, occupied an equally trying diplomatic position as minister to England in 1785.

HERVEY BACHUS WILBUR, M.D. an American physician and philanthropist, born at Wendell, Mass., Aug. 18, 1820.

He was founder of the schools for idiots in the United States, the first fully organized one being at Syracuse, N. Y., 1854, of which he was appointed superintendent.

FRANZ JOSEPH, the present emperor of the Austro-Hungarian monarchy. Born Aug. 18, 1830.

He ascended to the Austrian throne Dec. 2, 1848, upon the abdication of his uncle, the emperor Ferdinand. One of the first acts of his reign was the subjugation of Hungary. The famed house of Hapsburg has lost much territory in Europe since the beginning of offensive wars in 1859, and has been excluded from the German Confederation, but since the constitutional autonomy of Hungary was restored in 1867, the subjects of Francis Joseph have acquired an increase of civil and religious liberty.

August 19.

JOHN WOOLMAN, an American Quaker preacher and eminent philanthropist, born in Northampton, N. J., Aug. 19, 1720. Died at York, Eng., 1773. His influence contributed more than that of any other individual towards inducing the Society of Friends to pass regulations forbidding their members to hold slaves, and his writings have attracted the admiration of those not endorsing his Quaker views. Charles Lamb says: "Get the writings of John Woolman by heart, and love the early Quakers."

Samuel Griswold Goodrich, the famous " Peter Parley," born at Ridgefield, Conn., Aug. 19, 1793. Died in New York, May 9, 1860. His popularity as a writer for children consisted in writing history, geography, travels and stories, in a way to instruct as well as amuse, and which supplanted the idle tales of fiction which previously had been the only reading for children. Among his numerous works are "Recollections of a Lifetime," and " Illustrated Natural History of the Animal Kingdom."

Elisha Mitchel, D.D., an American chemist and divine, born in Washington county, Conn., August 19, 1793. Being appointed State surveyor of North Carolina, he was the first to discover that the mountains of that State were the highest east of the " Rockies." He lost his life upon the " Black Dome," June 27, 1857, which has since been called Mount Mitchel.

William H. Vanderbilt, son of Cornelius Vanderbilt, born in New Jersey, Aug. 19, 1821. Died Dec. 7, 1885. He inherited a large part of his father's immense fortune, and was a successful manager of his father's stupendous enterprises.

August 20

Robert Herrick, an English poet and clergyman, born in London, Aug. 20, 1591. Died at Devon, Oct., 1674. He was one of the best of English lyric and song writers.

Louis Bourdaloue, an eminent French pulpit orator, born at Bourges, Aug. 20, 1632. Died 1704. He was a man of spotless fame, yet he had so fearless a tact in the pulpit, that he retained his position as chosen preacher to the vilest yet most powerful court in the world, that of Louis XIV. longer than any other pulpit orator was ever tolerated.   He was styled by his countrymen, "The king of preachers and the preacher of kings."

JOHANN JAKOB BERZELIUS, M.D., F.R.S., a distinguished Swedish chemist, born at East Gothland, Sweden, Aug. 20, 1779.   Died Aug. 7, 1848.   He was the author of the symbols used as abridgements of the chemical nomenclature, also the discoverer of several chemical elements.

VALENTINE MOTT, a famous American surgeon, born at Glen Cove, L. I., Aug. 20, 1785.   Died in New York, April 26, 1865.   He was a brilliant and able lecturer and acquired a celebrity by his skill in the original operations which he performed.   Sir Ashley Cooper said that Dr. Mott had performed more of the great operations than any man living.   He was one of the founders of Rutgers Medical College.

JOHN MILTON NILES, an American journalist and statesman, born at Windsor, Conn., Aug. 20, 1787. Died at Hartford, May 31, 1856.   He was founder of the "Hartford Times," for which he wrote thirty years, also author of many works.

JAMES JARVIS, an American writer and traveler, born in Boston, Mass., Aug. 20, 1818.

He resided for some time in the Sandwich Islands, and published the "Polynesian," the first newspaper published there.

BENJAMIN HARRISON, the successful Republican nominee for President in the campaign of 1888, born at North Bend, Ohio, Aug. 20, 1833.

He is great-grandson of Benjamin Harrison, one of the signers of the Declaration, and grandson of Gen. William

H. Harrison, of Tippecanoe fame, afterward President of the United States, but for one month, being the first President who died in office. Mr. Harrison has been for many years an able lawyer of Indiana, leaving his profession in 1862 to take a position in the army, and again in 1881, when elected to the Senate. Said a noted lecturer, "whether he wins the Presidential chair or not, Mr. Harrison's campaign will be a clean one."

August 21.

JAMES CRICHTON, "The admirable Crichton," a Scottish prodigy, born in Perthshire, Aug. 21, 1560. When he was twenty he had run through the circle of the sciences, and could speak ten languages, after which he traveled over Europe and challenged all the learned doctors in a disputation in any of the tongues. Died at the hands of his pupil Vincentio, a dissolute youth, in 1583.

SIR BANASTRE TARLETON, an English officer of the American Revolution, born in Liverpool, Aug. 21, 1794. Died Jan. 23, 1833. He served under Cornwallis, and was the notorious antagonist of Marion and Sumpter, in the skirmishes of the Carolinas, and to this day "Tarleton's quarter" is a synonym for cruelty.

JOHN TYNDALL, LL. D., F.R.S., a distinguished British physicist and author, born near Carlow, Ireland, Aug. 21, 1820.

Prof. Tyndall has probably done more than any other writer to make known the great scientific truth of the mutual convertibility of heat and motion.

RICHARD S. STORRS, an American Congregational divine, born at Braintree, Mass., Aug. 21, 1821. Died, 1873. He was for several years one of the editors of the "Independent," contributing largely to other literature,

August 22.

JAMES K. PAULDING, a popular American novelist and miscellaneous writer, born in Pleasant Valley, Dutchess county, N. Y., Aug. 22, 1779. Died at Hyde Park, N. Y., April 6, 1860. He was associated with Washington Irving in the authorship of "Salmagundi." "The Diverting History of John Bull and Brother Jonathan," "The Dutchman's Fireside," and "Merry Tales of the Three Wise Men of Gotham," are among his many works. He was appointed Secretary of the Navy in 1837, by President Van Buren.

JOHN B. GOUGH, a reformed inebriate and celebrated lecturer on temperance, born at Sandgate, Kent, Eng., Aug. 22, 1817. Died 1886. For more than forty years he devoted himself to the temperance reform, combining in a remarkable degree the qualities of actor with those of an orator. It is said he spoke one hundred times on temperance in Exeter Hall, London.

EMILY JUDSON, "Fanny Forester," an American authoress, born at Eaton, N. Y., Aug. 22, 1817. Died at Hamilton, N. Y., 1854. She was the third wife of the missionary Judson, and accompanied him to Burmah, where she wrote some of her best poems.

LAURA C. HOLLOWAY, a distinguished American authoress, born at Nashville, Tenn., Aug. 22, 1848.

She began, to contribute to Southern periodicals at the age of eleven, and in 1870, when but twenty-two, while a guest at the White House, wrote her famous work, "The Ladies of the White House, or the Home of the Presidents," of which 140,000 copies have been sold in America, besides 25,000 in foreign lands. Besides her many other popular works, she was for twelve years associate editor of the "Brooklyn Eagle." Her lecture,

" The Perils of the Hour, or Woman's Place," delivered in all the large cities of America, was declared by Henry Ward Beecher to be " the most eloquent lecture ever delivered to the women of America."   Her recent lecture before the Women's International Convention in Washington, D. C., entitled " Women in Journalism," was telegraphed all over the country at the time.

August 23.

JEDEDIAH MORSE, an American geographer and divine, born at Woodstock, Conn., Aug. 23, 1761. Died in 1826.   He is principally known by his geographical works, the first of the kind published in America. He is the father of S. F. B. Morse.

SIR ASTLEY PASTON COOPER, F.R.S., LL.D., etc., an eminent English surgeon, born at Brooke, Norfolk, Eng., Aug. 23, 1768.   Died Feb. 12, 1841.   He acquired so extended a practice, that his income is said to have been £21,000 annually.   He was appointed surgeon to the king in 1828.

BARON GEORGE C. L. F. D. CUVIER, an illustrious philosopher, statesman and author, and one of the greatest naturalists of modern times, born in Wurtemburg, Aug. 23, 1769.   Died May 13, 1832.   In 1817 he produced his celebrated " Animal Kingdom," which immediately took the highest rank among the books of the kind, and became the guide to zoological studies throughout Europe.   He is considered the founder of comparative anatomy, in which he attained such skill that with a small fragment of a characteristic part of an animal, he could determine the class, order and even genus to which it belonged.

Com. Oliver Hazard Perry, a distinguished American officer, born at South Kingston, R. I., Aug. 23, 1785. Died on his birthday, on the Island of Trinidad, in 1819. "Perry's victory" in the battle of Lake Erie, Sept. 10, 1813, with his laconic dispatch to Gen. Harrison, "We have met the enemy and they are ours," makes his name one to glitter on the page of American history.

August 24.

Letitia Ramoline Bonaparte, the mother of Napoleon I., born in Corsica, Aug. 24, 1750. Died Feb. 2, 1836. She was celebrated for her beauty, amiable character and good sense. Napoleon once said: "It is to my mother and her good principles, that I owe my fortune and all the good that I have ever done."

William Wilberforce, an illustrious English philanthropist and statesman, born at Hull, Eng., Aug. 24, 1759. Died July 29, 1833. His whole life was spent in philanthropic enterprises, one of which was the abolition of slavery in the British dominion, which he lived to see accomplished.

James W. Wallack, an English actor, born in London, Aug. 24, 1795. Died in New York, Dec. 25, 1864. He settled in New York, in 1851, and founded the theater on Broadway called by his name.

Theodore Parker, a distinguished American scholar and rationalistic theologian, born at Lexington, Mass., Aug. 24, 1810. Died in Florence, Italy, May 10, 1860. He gave offence to the conservative Unitarians, by assuming the absolute humanity of Christ. Besides his ministerial duties, his labors extended intellectually into nearly every department of human knowledge on which he gave numerous lectures. But the question which seemed to have enlisted all his faculties, was Southern slavery and its attendant iniquities.

ELIZA JANE THOMPSON, an eminent worker in the temperance cause, born in Hillsboro, Highland Co., Ohio, Aug. 24, 1816.

She was the leader of the first "Woman's Crusade" band in the temperance cause in Hillsboro, Ohio, Dec. 24, 1873.   This novel plan of inducing druggists, dealers and saloon-keepers to stop their deadly traffic, was suggested by Dr. Dio Lewis in a temperance lecture, Dec. 23, 1873.

August 25.

JOHANN GOTTFRIED VON HERDER, one of the most remarkable and gifted writers that Germany has produced, was born at Mohrungen, East Prussia, Aug. 25, 1744.   Died at Weimar, Dec. 18, 1803.   He was an eloquent preacher, a zealous friend of education, and an encourager of rising talent; and though among his many writings there is hardly a complete work, yet he is admitted to have exercised a most important influence on German literature.   "The Philosophy of History" is his greatest work.

SAMUEL CHESTER RIED, an American naval officer, born at Norwich, Conn., Aug. 25, 1783.   Died in New York, Jan. 28, 1861.   He was in active service during the war of 1812, and regulated the pilot-boats and signals at the Battery and the Narrows.   He was also designer of the present U. S. flag.

JAMES LICK, an American philanthropist, born at Fredericksburg, Lebanon Co., Pa., Aug. 25, 1796.   Died 1876.   He was one of the earliest settlers in San Francisco, in 1847, and invested in real estate, which made him exceedingly wealthy.   In 1874 he placed his entire property in the hands of seven trustees, to be devoted to public and charitable purposes, one of which was to build an observatory, and erect a telescope more powerful than any made before. Since its erection on Mount Hamilton, Cal., it has been called by his name.

FRANCIS BRET HARTE, an American author born at Albany, N. Y., Aug. 25, 1839.

His theme for writing has been the life of California miners, but his popularity culminated with the publication of " The Heathen Chinee."

August 26.

SIR ROBERT WALPOLE, Earl of Orford, a celebrated English statesman, born in Norfolk Co., Eng., Aug. 26, 1676. Died in London, March 18, 1745. He was at the head of affairs in England more than twenty years, and resigned in 1742, after a spirited contest with the opposing party, composed of Tories and disaffected Whigs, during which contest occurred the famed orations of Walpole and Pitt.

PRINCE ALBERT, or more fully, Albert Francis Augustus Charles Emanuel, Consort of Queen Victoria of Great Britain, born near Coburg, Aug. 26, 1819. Died Dec. 14, 1861. He married Victoria Feb., 1840, and merited the confidence of the queen by his excellent qualifications, which rendered him her best adviser. His death was regarded as an irreparable loss not merely to the queen, but to the nation of which he had been king in all but in name.

August 27.

WILLIAM WOOLLETT, an eminent English engraver, born at Maidstone Kent, Eng., Aug. 27, 1735. Died in London, May 23, 1785, and a monument was erected to him in Westminster Abbey. His landscapes, both etched and engraved by a style of his own, are ranked among the most exquisite works of the kind.

BARTHOLD GEORGE NIEBUHR, a celebrated German historian and critic, born at Copenhagen, Aug. 27, 1776. Died Jan. 2, 1831. His "History of Rome" is considered the most original and profound work on ancient history which any modern writer has produced.

August 28.

JOHN STARKE, an American general of the Revolution, born at Londonderry, N. H., Aug. 28, 1728. Died at Manchester, N. H., May 8, 1832. He is a conspicuous figure in American history, by his victory over the British at Bennington, Aug. 16, 1777, and by his words before going into battle: "There are the red coats; we must beat them to-day, or Molly Starke is a widow!"

JOHANN WOLFGANG VON GOETHE, the most illustrious name in German literature, and one of the great poets of the world, born at Frankfort-on-the-Main, Aug. 28, 1749. Died at Weimar, March 22, 1832. Among his many works "Faust" is considered the great work of Goethe's life.

GEN. ORMSBY MCKNIGHT MITCHEL, LL.D., an eminent American astronomer, born in Union county, Ky., Aug. 28, 1810. He offered his services to his country in 1861, and died of yellow fever at Beaufort, S. C., Oct. 30, 1862. The direct cause of the establishment of the observatories at Albany, Clinton, Allegheny City, Cincinnati, Washington and Cambridge, is due to the impetus given to that study by his popular lectures.

COUNT LEO TOLSTOI, a celebrated Russian nobleman, author and poet, born Aug. 28, 1828.

His early life found him a soldier at Sevastopol, after which he became famous as a novelist, but becoming convinced that as a man, he ought to have a nobler object in life than amusing people, he turned his attention to instructive writing, and to solve the problem of true happiness. This he found to consist in the pure religion of the gospel of Jesus, as taught in the Testament; since which he has written many worthy works, one of which "My Religion," is one of the most practical works on Christianity ever published. Count Tolstoi is at the present time the most generally talked of and widely read author in Russia.

IRA DAVID SANKEY, an eminent American musical evangelist and co-laborer of D. L. Moody, born in Edinburgh, Lawrence county, Pa., Aug. 28, 1840.

He is the author of several popular hymns, and is one of the compilers of the revival hymn books entitled "Gospel Songs."

August 29.

JOHN LOCKE, a celebrated English philosopher and philanthropist, born at Wrington, Somersetshire, Aug. 29, 1632. Died Oct. 28, 1704. Locke's great work, an "Essay on the Human Understanding," was written upon, during an interval of more than twenty years. He was private secretary to the Earl of Shaftesbury, and assisted him in drawing up the noted aristocratic Constitution of the Carolinas, which proved such a failure.

CHARLES TOWNSHEND, an English statesman and orator, born in England, Aug. 29, 1725. Died in September, 1767. He supported the Stamp Act, so obnoxious to the American colonies, procured the passage of the bill which imposed a tax on tea, and other articles, and provoked the colonies into a revolt. "Townshend," says Macauley, "a man of splendid talents, lax principles, and of boundless vanity and presumption, would submit to no control, and when Pitt, of whom he stood in awe, resigned, he broke from all restraint."

WILLIAM G. BROWNLOW, "Parson Brownlow," an American divine and politician, born in Wythe county, Va., Aug. 29, 1805. Died April 28, 1877. Though residing in Tennessee, at the crisis of 1861, he proved himself a strong adherent to the Union, for which he was persecuted and imprisoned by the secessionists during the early part of the war. In 1867 he was chosen Senator of the United States.

OLIVER WENDELL HOLMES, M.D., "the Autocrat," a distinguished American author, wit and poet, born at Cambridge, Mass., Aug. 29, 1809.

He has been professor of anatomy and physiology in Dartmouth and Harvard Colleges, and has written ably on various subjects connected with his profession, yet his busy life in this direction is perhaps covered by his fame as a poet. As a lyric poet he has few if any superiors in America. His "Autocrat of the Breakfast Table," published in 1857–58, has given him his name.

ABBY HUTCHINSON, one of the remarkable Hutchinson family of singers, born at Milford, N. H., Aug. 29, 1829.

She, in company with her three brothers, attained a popularity unknown before in the Northern States, by the harmony and sentiment of their songs.

August 30.

SIR JOHN RENNIE, a distinguished British civil engineer, architect and mechanician, born in London, Aug. 30, 1794. Died Sept. 3, 1874. He was architect of the London Bridge, finished in 1831, for which he was knighted.

SAMUEL OSGOOD, D.D., an American Unitarian divine and author, born at Charlestown, Mass., Aug. 30, 1812. Died April, 1880. "Studies in Christian Biography," "Milestones on our Life-Journey," are among his theological works, and he was also a contributor to some of the prominent magazines.

August 31.

PROF. JAMES FERGUSON, an eminent American civil engineer and astronomer, born in Perthshire, Scotland, August 31, 1797. Died Sept. 26, 1867. He has been a valued contributor to discoveries in astronomy and an assistant in determining the boundary of the United States.

ELIZABETH STUART PHELPS, JR., an American authoress, born at Andover, Mass., Aug. 31, 1844.

Among her many works is "Gates Ajar," which attained such a popularity that it passed through more than twenty editions in less than a year.

September 1.

LYDIA H. SIGOURNEY, "the Hemans of America," an American poetess and miscellaneous writer, born in Norwich, Conn., Sept. 1, 1791. Died at Hartford, June 10, 1865. She published fifty-nine volumes of poems, essays, and letters, chiefly on moral and religious themes, and through a long life was one of the most popular of American poets.

CHESTER HARDING, an American portrait painter, born in Conway, Mass., Sept. 1, 1793. Died in Boston April 1, 1866. Among the eminent men who sat to him in England, were the Dukes of Sussex, Hamilton.

and Norfolk, the historian Alison, and the poet Rogers. In America, were Presidents Madison, Monroe, and J. Q. Adams; Chief Justice Marshall, Webster, Clay, and Calhoun.

JAMES GORDON BENNETT, an eminent American journalist, born in Banffshire, Scotland, Sept. 1, 1795. Died in New York, June 1, 1872. He emigrated to the United States in 1819, and in 1835 founded the " New York Herald," the first newspaper that published a daily money article and stock lists. He was its editor and proprietor for nearly forty years.

September 2.

JOHN HARVARD, an English divine, born in England Sept. 2, 1608. Died Sept. 14, 1638. After being ordained he emigrated to Massachusetts, and officiated a short time at Charlestown. At his death he left a legacy of £799 to endow a school at Cambridge, and is thus memorable as the founder of the university which bears his name.

JOHN HOWARD, F.R.S., a celebrated English philanthropist, born at Hackney, near London, Sept. 2, 1726. Died at Kherson, Russia, Jan. 20, 1790. His interest in the much needed prison reforms was awakened by his being taken by a French privateer, while on his way to Lisbon, to relieve the misery caused by the earthquake of 1775, and detained in prison long enough to see the abuses of the prisoners.

WILLARD PARKER, M.D., LL.D., an eminent American physician, born in Lydeborough, N. H., Sept. 2, 1800. Died 1884. He has made many important discoveries in practical surgery, and was for thirty years professor of surgery in the New York College of Physicians and Surgeons.

HARVEY NEWCOMB, D.D., an American author and editor, born at Thetford, Va., Sept. 2, 1803. Died at Brooklyn, Aug. 30, 1863. He was at different times editor of five different papers, besides contributing to several others.

HENRY GEORGE, now recognized as one of the foremost thinkers of the age, born in Philadelphia, Sept. 2, 1839.

September 3.

HEINRICH CHRISTIAN SCHUMACHER, an able Danish astronomer, born at Branstedt, Holstein, Sept. 3, 1780. Died Dec. 28, 1850. He was long the professor of astronomy at the University of Copenhagen, and by his observations, formed the basis of the Danish scale of measure.

JOHN HUMPHREY NOYES, founder of the sect called Perfectionists, which finally culminated in the Oneida Community, of which he was the leader, born at Brattleboro, Vt., Sept. 3, 1811. Died April 13, 1886.

CAROLINA A. SOULE, an eminent American lecturer, writer and journalist, born in Albany, N. Y., Sept. 3, 1824.

SARAH ORNE JEWETT, an American author, born in South Berwick, Me., Sep. 3, 1849.

She has traveled extensively in Europe, Canada and the United States, and in addition to valuable contributions to periodicals, is author of many books.

September 4.

THOMAS U. WALTER, an eminent American architect, born at Philadelphia, Sept. 4, 1804.

Among the many monuments of his skill, as designer

and architect, are the Girard College, perhaps the finest specimen of classical architecture in America ; the iron dome and extension of the Capitol at Washington, east and west wings of the Patent Office, extension of the General Post Office ; he also designed the new treasury building, and government hospital for the insane.

HAMILTON STEWART, one of the most noted men of Texas, born in Kentucky, Sept. 4, 1813.

He has resided in Galveston, Texas, from the foundation of the city, has been repeatedly its mayor, also editor of its chief paper, " The Galveston News."

PHEBE CARY, the younger sister of Alice Cary, both talented American poets and prose writers, born near Cincinnati, Ohio, Sept. 4, 1824. Died July 31, 1871. " One sweetly solemn thought " is one of her earliest productions, written at the age of seventeen.

September 5.

ARMAND JEAN De RICHELIEU, " Cardinal Richelieu," a celebrated and ambitious French statesman, born in Paris, Sept. 5, 1585. Died in his palace at Paris, Dec. 4, 1642. His reign as prime minister to Louis XIII., was one of tyranny and oppression. The destruction of the Huguenots and their stronghold La Rochelle, is one of the memorable events in the history of France. He built the Palais Royal, and gave substantial encouragement to literature and art.

CHRISTOPHER MARTIN WIELAND, " the German Voltaire," a celebrated German poet, born in Wurtemberg, Sept. 5, 1733. Died near Weimar, Jan., 1813. " Oberon," which is his most celebrated poetical production, was considered by Goethe to be a master-piece. Wieland, Goethe, Schiller and Herder, were intimate and by their association benefited one another, and made Weimar the literary center of Germany.

JOHN DALTON, F.R.S., a noted English chemical philosopher, born at Eaglesfield, in Cockermouth, Eng., Sept. 5, 1766. Died July 27, 1844. In 1803 he began to develop the most important and fundamental principles of chemistry, which resulted in the "atomic theory," of which he is the author. He had a singular defect of vision, in consequence of which, red, blue, and green all looked alike to him, and this peculiar vision has since been called "Daltonism." He was a member of the Society of Friends and maintained an excellent moral character.

JEAN PIERRE ABEL REMUSAT, an eminent French Orientalist, born at Paris, Sept. 5, 1788. Died there June 4, 1832. His interest in the Tartar language, caused him to leave the medical profession, and it is said that he learned the Chinese language without a teacher. He founded the Asiatic Society of Paris, in 1822, and his important works on the eastern languages, leave monuments to his reputation.

GIACOMO MEYERBEER, an eminent German musical composer of Jewish extraction, born in Berlin, Sept. 5, 1794. Died in Paris, May 2, 1864. At nine years old, he was regarded as the best pianist in Berlin. Among his many compositions was "The Huguenots," which was the first of the "historical lyric drama," and added new laurels to Meyerbeer's fame and made an epoch in operatic art.

HON. JOHN CARLISLE, Speaker of the House of Representatives for the Forty-eighth, Forty-ninth and Fiftieth Congress, born in Campbell Co., Ky., Sept. 5, 1835.

September 6.

Marie Paul Jean Roche Yver Gilbert Motier La Fayette, a French statesman and patriot, born in Auvergne, Sept. 6, 1757. Died in Paris, May 20, 1834. His valuable service, so unselfishly given to the American cause during the Revolution, and his triumphant visit to the United States in 1824-25, are events in his history which seemingly overshadow even a busier political life in his own country.

Frances D'Arusmont, better known as "Fanny Wright," a distinguished reformer and writer, born in Dundee, Scotland, Sept. 6, 1795. Died at Cincinnati, Ohio, Dec. 14, 1852. She was really the leader of the "Woman's Rights" movement, which cause she awakened as early as 1820 by her lectures in the United States. She was associated with Robert Owen, and his son, Robert Dale Owen, in their reform ideas.

Catherine Esther Beecher, an American writer, sister of Henry Ward Beecher, born at East Hampton, Long Island, Sept. 6, 1800. Died May 12, 1878. She was principal of a female seminary in Hartford, Conn., and author of works among which are those pertaining to domestic economy.

Horatio Greenough, an eminent American sculptor, born in Boston, Mass., Sept. 6, 1805. Died in Somerville, near Boston, Dec. 18, 1852. His "Chanting Cherubs" was the first group in marble executed by an American sculptor. He executed the colossal statue of Washington in front of the National Capitol, for which Congress paid $20,000, and a group entitled "The Rescue," on the steps leading to the rotunda of the same building.

WILLIAM L. ROSECRANS, an American general of the civil war, born in Kingston, Ohio, Sept. 6, 1819.

He was the victorious general at the battles of Rich Mountain, Corinth and Murfreesboro, but was defeated at Chickamauga.

September 7.

QUEEN ELIZABETH, of England, daughter of Henry VIII. and Anne Boleyn, born at Greenwich, Sept. 7, 1533. Died 1603. She became queen on the death of her sister Mary, Nov. 17, 1558, and her reign was considered eminently beneficial and glorious to the nation. The great events of her reign were her rivalry with her cousin, Mary, Queen of Scots, who was executed in 1587, and the attempt of Philip of Spain to subjugate England by means of the "Invincible Armada," which proved a failure. The "Elizabethan Age" of literature, was created by such men as Spenser, Shakespeare, Sidney, Bacon and Raleigh. Her faults as a woman have been covered by her ability as a ruler.

GEORGE LOUIS BUFFON, a celebrated French naturalist and philosopher, born in Burgundy, Sept. 7, 1707. Died in Paris, April 16, 1788. He achieved his fame by his great work "Epochs of Nature," and was the writer of thirty-six volumes of Natural History. Besides these, he left an unfinished "Dissertation on Style," in which occurs the celebrated phrase, "Le style est de l'homme."

SAMUEL WILBERFORCE, "Slippery Sam," a brother of the noted philanthropist, William Wilberforce, born at Clapham, England, Sept. 7, 1805. Died near Dorking, Surrey, Eng., July 19, 1873. He was a leader of the High Church party, and was skilled as a debater in the House of Lords, and for his versatility of opinion received his well known sobriquet.

Hon. Thomas A. Hendricks, an American lawyer and statesman, born at Zanesville, Ohio, Sept. 7, 1819. Died 1885. He was an able and experienced leader of the Democratic party, but was a defeated candidate for the Vice-Presidency on the ticket with Tilden. Was again nominated in 1884, with Cleveland, but died in office.

September 8.

Lodovico Ariosto, a celebrated Italian poet, born at Reggio, near Modena, Sept. 8, 1474. Died June 6, 1533. He has been considered, after Homer, the favorite poet of Europe, and yields to only three of his predecessors, Homer, Virgil and Dante.

Pietro Martire Vermigle, "Peter Martyr," an eminent Protestant theologian, born at Florence, Italy, September 8, 1500. Died Nov. 12, 1562. He was considered one of the most learned theologians of his age, and as a Protestant writer, was second only to Calvin.

Joseph Story, LL.D., an eminent American jurist, born at Marblehead, Mass., Sept. 8, 1779. Died at Cambridge, Mass., Sept. 10, 1845. He was appointed a justice of the supreme court of the United States by President Madison, when only thirty-two years of age. So young a man had never, in the history of England or America, been appointed to so high a judicial position. He occupied that place for thirty-four years, and his judgments in the supreme court form an important part of thirty-four volumes.

William Cranch Bond, an American astronomer, born at Portland, Me., Sept. 8, 1789. Died Jan. 29, 1859. He distinguished himself by his observations on

Saturn and celestial photography. He, with his son, discovered a satellite of Neptune and the eighth satellite of Saturn.

Francis Bowen, an American scholar and author, born at Charlestown, Mass., Sept. 8, 1811.

He was for eleven years editor of the "North American Review," was also professor in Harvard University, and author of many works.

Clarence C. Cook, an American journalist and art critic, born in Dorchester, Mass., Sept. 8, 1828.

Emilio Castelar, an eminent Spanish orator and Republican statesman, born in Spain, Sept. 8, 1832.

He is a brilliant writer, and is considered the most eloquent political orator in Spain; and from Sept., 1873, to Jan. 3, 1874, was President of the Spanish Republic.

Richard Morris, LL.D., an eminent English author and poet, born in Southwark, England, Sept. 8, 1833.

September 9.

Edmund Pendleton, an eminent American statesman and judge, born in Carolina Co., Va., Sept. 9, 1712. Died in Richmond, Va., Oct. 23, 1803. He was president of the Virginia Convention in 1776, and again in 1788, when the Convention met to consider the new Constitution of the United States.

Alvisio Galvani, an eminent Italian physician and physiologist, born at Bologna, Sept. 9, 1737. Died there Dec. 4, 1798. His durable reputation is founded on the accidental discovery of the phenomena since called by his name "Galvanism."

Thomas Coke, D.D., LL.D., the first bishop of the Methodist Episcopal Church, born in Brecon, Wales, Sept. 9, 1747. Died May 2, 1814, on a voyage to India, and was buried at sea. He founded the Wesleyan mission in the East and West Indies, at the expense of nearly his entire fortune.

RICHARD C. TRENCH, D.D., an eminent English ecclesiastic and philologist, born Sept. 9, 1807. Died 1886.

He was appointed Archbishop of Dublin in 1863, and his many valuable works are standards among ecclesiastical scholars.

September 10.

MUNGO PARK, an eminent and enterprising explorer of Africa, born near Selkirk, Scotland, Sept. 10, 1771. He perished in the Niger River, in 1805, while attempting to escape, by swimming, from an attack by the natives.

ROBERT TURNBULL, D.D., a Baptist divine and author, born in Scotland, Sept. 10, 1809. Died Nov. 20, 1877. Author of "Christ in History, or the Central Power," and other works.

September 11.

JAMES THOMSON, a celebrated Scottish poet, born in Roxburghshire, Scotland, Sept. 11, 1700. Died at Kew Lane, near Richmond, Aug. 27, 1748. "The Castle of Indolence," considered his best work, is far less known than "The Seasons," which is still one of the most popular poems in the language.

DANIEL S. DICKENSON, an American lawyer and statesman, born in Goshen, Conn., Sept. 11, 1800. Died Apr. 12, 1866. He was remarkable for his memory and literary attainments, and became so distinguished for his Biblical knowledge and apt quotations from the Scripture in his speeches in senate and court, that his friends familiarly applied to him the sobriquet of "Scripture Dick."

September 12.

FRANCIS I., King of France, from 1515–1547, born at Cognac, Sept. 12, 1494. Died at Rambouillet, March 31, 1547. Some of the noted events of his reign are the great battle of Marignano, called " the Battle of the Giants," Sept. 14-15, 1515 ; the meeting with Henry VIII. of England, on "the field of the cloth of gold," in June, 1520, and his great defeat in 1524, when the famous Chevalier Bayard fell, and his own defeat and capture at the battle of Pavia, 1525, at which time he is said to have written to his mother these noted words : " Madame, all is lost except our honor."

ALEXANDER CAMPBELL, D.D., founder of the religious sect known as the " Disciples of Christ," born in the county of Antrim, Ireland, Sept. 12, 1788. Died in 1866. Not finding among the Christian sects any whose system he could sincerely adopt, he declared against all human creeds, and formed religious associations with the Bible as the only rule of faith. In 1841 Dr. Campbell founded Bethany College in Virginia, and was long its president.

RICHARD MARCH HOE, an eminent American inventor, born in New York, Sept. 12, 1812. Died at Florence, Italy, 1886. He was one of three sons of the original founder of the house of Robert Hoe. These three sons, with Richard as head of the firm, in 1847 gave to the world the first rotary printing press, and later the web perfecting printing machines which have made the cheap newspaper a possibility, and completely revolutionized the world of printing.

RICHARD JORDAN GATLING, an American inventor, born in Hertford Co., N. C., Sept. 12, 1818.

Among his many inventions, is a machine for sowing

wheat in drills, which is very popular in the large wheat farms of the west. But his greatest invention is the repeating machine-gun, known as the Gatling gun, which can be made to fire four hundred shots per minute. It has been adopted by Russia, Great Britain and other nations.

CHARLES DUDLEY WARNER, a popular American author and humorist, born at Plainfield, Mass., Sept. 12, 1829.

He is contributor and correspondent to several magazines, besides his many other works. Also joint author with Samuel L. Clemens, of "The Gilded Age."

CHARLES VALENTINE RILEY, an eminent entomologist, born in London, Sept. 12, 1843.

In 1860 he came to the United States, and has rendered valuable service to science and to agriculture by his study of insects injurious to vegetation, such as the Colorado potato beetle (as a destroyer of which he introduced using Paris green), the cotton worm, "the seventeen-year locust," the yucca moth, and the insects injuring grape culture. For his services rendered to the French, in this last named industry, he received from their government a gold medal.

September 13.

RICHARD I., "the lion-hearted" king of England, 1189-1199, born at Oxford, Sept. 13, 1157, and was killed in battle, April 6, 1199. He was one of the sovereigns of Europe who enlisted in the Crusades.

ANDREW PICKENS, a distinguished American general of the Revolution, born at Paxton, Bucks Co., Pa., Sept. 13, 1739. Died at Hopewell, Aug. 17, 1817. He shared with Marion and Sumter the honor of the heroic defence of South Carolina, when it was overrun by the British and Tory forces.

CASPER WISTAR, M.D., a distinguished American physician, born at Philadelphia, Sept. 13, 1761. Died Jan. 22, 1818. He was highly distinguished in his profession and conferred great luster upon the Philadelphia Medical School. The wistaria, one of our beautiful spring flowering climbers, was named in his honor.

ALICE HAVEN, an American author, born at Hudson, N. Y., Sept. 13, 1825. Died Aug. 23, 1863. She produced many excellent juvenile stories over the signature of "Cousin Alice."

September 14.

FRANCOIS AUGUSTE CHATEAUBRIAND, the most celebrated of French authors, who wrote during the first empire, born at St. Malo, Sept. 14, 1768. Died July 4, 1848. In 1791, he made a visit to America, and gathered the gems of his romance "Atala," a picture of aboriginal American life, which won from Europe a general exclamation of surprise and admiration. "The Martyrs; or, the Triumph of the Christian Religion," appeared in 1809, after his tour through Greece, Asia Minor, Palestine, and Spain. These brilliant works made a revolution in French literature, and caused him to be recognized as the literary glory of his age.

FREDERICK H. ALEXANDER, VON HUMBOLDT, an illustrious German savant and traveler, born at Berlin, Sept. 14, 1769. Died May 6, 1859. He was fitted out in 1799, by the Spanish government, for an extended tour through the Spanish colonies of Central and South America, and returned in 1804 with an immense store of scientific knowledge, which he afterward printed in twenty-nine volumes. In 1829 he was fitted out by the Russian government for a tour through Asia. The greatest literary work of his life was the publication of his "Kosmos" in four volumes.

Seba Smith, "Jack Downing" an American writer, born at Buckfield, Me., Sept. 14, 1792. Died at Patch-ogue, L. I., July 29, 1868. He won a wide reputation as a humorist by his series of political letters by "Major Jack Downing."

September 15.

Gotthold Ephraim Lessing, an eminent German author, born at Kamentz, in Upper Lusatia, Sept. 15, 1729. Died at Brunswick, 1781. The efforts of Lessing to build up a national literature caused him to be regarded as the "father of the new era of German literature." His "Emilia Galotti" has been styled "the masterpiece of German tragedy," the "Laocoon," "the masterpiece of German criticism," and "Minna von Barnhelm" is regarded as the most perfect of his comedies. The noble and prominent character in "Nathan the Wise," his last important work, was in imitation of his intimate friend, Moses Mendelssohn, grandfather of the noted composer, Felix Mendelssohn.

Jean Sylvain Bailly, an eminent French astronomer, philosopher and eloquent writer, born in Paris, Sept. 15, 1736. He, with Lafayette, endeavored to maintain order and moderate the violence of the "Reign of Terror," but was unsuccessful. He was executed Nov. 12, 1793. "The name of Bailly," says Lamartine, " was an inscription on the frontispiece of the Revolution."

James Fenimore Cooper, a popular American novelist, born at Burlington, N. J., Sept. 15, 1789. Died at Cooperstown, Sept. 14, 1851. In his second novel, "The Spy," a tale of the Revolution, he laid the foundations of the American romance. Says W. H. Prescott: "No one has succeeded like Cooper in the portraiture of American character, or has given such truthful and glowing pictures of American scenery; yet, whatever opinion may be entertained of his success in these respects, all will agree that his most triumphant march is on the ocean wave;" and "the empire of the sea," has been accorded to him by acclamation. His father founded Cooperstown on Otsego lake in New York.

JAMES G. PERCIVAL, an eminent American poet and scholar, born at Berlin, Conn., Sept. 15, 1795. Died at Hazel Green, Wis., May 2, 1857. In 1827 he was appointed by Dr. Webster to revise the manuscript of his large dictionary. In 1835 he was appointed to make a geological survey of Connecticut, and at his death, was state geologist of Wisconsin.

ADELINE D. T. WHITNEY, a popular American writer, born in Boston, Sept. 15, 1824.

Among her many works are "Faith Gartney's Girlhood," "We Girls," "Sights and Insights," "Real Folks," etc., which reviewers have decided "will carry her name to latest American journalists."

September 16.

LOUIS XIV., "the Great," king of France, 1643-1715, born Sept. 16, 1638. Died Sept. 1, 1715. The great but unpopular Mazarin was prime minister during the early part of his reign, after whose death his ambition was to make the monarchy absolute, and he became his own prime minister. In 1685 he revoked the edict of Nantes which had secured the religious liberty of the

Protestants. His attempt to restore James II. to the throne of England, created a general war in which Spain, Austria and England were leagued against him. This was extended to the American colonies, known as King William's war, 1789-97, and was suspended by the treaty of Ryswick. The war of the Spanish succession, in which occurred the noted battle of Blenheim, won by the English and Austrians under Marlborough and Eugene, and which was ended by the treaty of Utrecht, 1713, was an event of his reign. The age of Louis was considered the most brilliant in the literary history of France, and France itself was then without doubt the greatest and most compact power of Europe; and although his internal administration was bad, and the military triumphs not achieved by himself, while his later years were crowned with defeats, still he was so consummate a master of "king-craft," that he succeeded in passing himself off on his people as a being above humanity.

WILLIAM AUGUSTUS MUHLENBERG, D.D., an American philanthropist and poet, born in Philadelphia, Sept. 16, 1796. Died 1877. St. Paul's College in Flushing, L. I., and St. Luke's Hospital, New York, owe their existence to him. But he will best be remembered by his hymns, one of which is "I would not live alway."

FRANCIS PARKMAN, JR., an American author, born in Boston, Sept. 16, 1823.

He is author of several historical works of great value.

HENRY S. DRAYTON, LL.B., M.D., present editor of the "*Phrenological Journal and Science of Health*," born in New Jersey, Sept. 16, 1840.

After graduating from the University of the city of

New York, he studied law and was connected with an office. But literature and science being more to his taste, he entered the office of Fowler & Wells, in 1865, and by rapid steps passed from reporter and assistant editor to his present position. Besides his editorial work that would fill volumes, he is author of several books, among them," Light in Dark Places," " Brain and Mind," etc., the latter of which he is joint author with Mr. James McNeal, has obtained a wide circulation in America and Europe, and is considered one of the best textbooks for the student in mental science. After several years of study and research in physiology, he received the degree of M.D., from a New York medical college, and has since been interested in the study and treatment of brain and nerve diseases.

September 17.

John Foster, an English essayist and moralist of great merit, born at Halifax, Sept. 17, 1770. Died Oct 15, 1843. His reputation is founded on his essays, which are the productions of a profound and liberal thinker, and class him as one of the most eloquent writers that England has produced.

Samuel Hopkins, D.D., an American divine, born at Waterbury, Conn., Sept. 17, 1721. Died at Newport, Dec. 20, 1803. It was in consequence of his labors that Rhode Island freed all her slaves born after March, 1784. He is one of the prominent characters in Mrs. Stowe's novel, "The Minister's Wooing."

Dr. Mercy B. Jackson, an eminent physician of Boston, born in Hardwick, Mass., Sept. 17, 1802. Died in Boston, Dec. 13, 1877. She was one of the pioneers in all the reforms of female education, proving by example that woman's sphere can be complete, and yet rounded out beyond the limits of housekeeping.

ALPHONSO WOOD, an American scholar and botanist, born at Chesterfield, N. H., Sept. 17, 1810. Died in 1880. His popular "Class Book of Botany" has gone through more than fifty editions. He has also several other valuable works on this study.

September 18.

SAMUEL JOHNSON, one of the most eminent writers of the eighteenth century, called by Smollett, the "Great Cham of Literature," born at Litchfield, Eng., Sept. 18, 1709. Died at London, Dec. 13, 1784. His "Rasselas" was written in a single week to pay the funeral expenses of his mother. His "Dictionary of the English Language" is considered the most remarkable work of the kind ever produced by a single person. "Lives of the British Poets" was his last work.

GEORGE READ, an American patriot, born in Cecil county, Maryland, Sept. 18, 1733. Died Sept. 21, 1798. He was a member of the Continental Congress, and a signer of the "Declaration of Independence."

OLIVER HOLDEN, one of the earliest American composers, born at Shirley, Mass., Sept. 18, 1763. Died at Charlestown, Mass., 1831. He will always be remembered by his world-wide regal hymn, "Coronation."

JOHN TOWNSEND TROWBRIDGE, an eminent American writer and editor, born at Ogden, N. Y., Sept. 18, 1827.

Besides being the author of many novels, he is a writer for some of the leading magazines of the day. Many of his popular tales are written over the signature of "Paul Creyton."

September 19.

JEAN BAPTIST JOSEPH DELAMBRE, an eminent French astronomer and author, born at Amiens, Sept. 19, 1749. Died August 19, 1822. Between 1792–99, he published his "Basis of the Decimal System of Measure," and on presenting this to Napoleon, the latter said, "Conquests pass away, but these operations remain." After the immense labors of thirty years devoted to observations and calculations, he wrote his five volumes of the "History of Astronomy from the Earliest Times."

LORD HENRY BROUGHAM, an eminent and learned British orator, lawyer and writer, born in Edinburgh, Sept. 19, 1779. Died at Cannes, France, May 9, 1868. As a parliamentary debater he occupied the first rank, and for many years found no equal in the House of Commons, except Canning, who was his political adversary. As chancellor and legislator he manifested prodigious activity in the performance of his duties, promoting the abolition of slavery in the colonies, and other reforms. He, with Francis Jeffrey and Sydney Smith, founded the "Edinburgh Review."

ABSALOM PETERS, D.D., an American editor and author, born at Wentworth, N. H., Sept. 19, 1793. Died in New York, May 18, 1869. He originated the "American Eclectic Review," and "American Journal of Education."

CHRISTIAN HENRY FREDERICK PETERS, Ph.D., an eminent astronomer, born in Germany, Sept. 19, 1813.

He has discovered more than twenty asteroids, catalogued 16,000 zodiacal stars, and recorded 20,000 solar spots. He was sent by the United States government to New Zealand to observe the transit of Venus, Dec. 9,

1874, and was the only observer on the island who had complete success.

September 20.

Robert Emmet, an Irish patriot and author, born in Cork, Sept. 20, 1780. In his efforts with the "United Irishmen" to free his country from British domination, he was arrested and tried for treason. His speech, in which he defended himself, is preserved as a model of eloquence. He was executed Sept. 20, 1803.

David Ross Locke, "Petroleum V. Nasby" born at Vestal, Broome Co., N. Y., Sept. 20, 1833. Died Feb. 15, 1888. He was successful as an editor, publisher and writer. In 1860, he began to publish his "Nasby" letters, a series of political satires, which were widely popular, and have appeared in book form.

September 21.

Francis Hopkinson, an American author, wit, patriot and judge, born in Philadelphia, Sept. 21, 1737. Died May 9, 1791. His humorous writings, the best known of which is "The Battle of Kegs," did much to foment the spirit of freedom. He represented New Jersey in the Continental Congress, and was a signer of the "Declaration of Independence."

John Loudon Macadam, a Scottish engineer, born at Ayre, Scotland, Sept. 21, 1756. Died at Moffat, Dumfrieshire, Nov. 26, 1836. During the American Revolution he was agent for the sale of prizes in the port of New York, but at the peace of 1783, he, with other loyalists, were obliged to return to England. He was engaged for several years traveling at his own expense through Great Britain to examine the condition of the roads. In 1816 he commenced the system of roadmaking called by his name ; and within a few years personally supervised the roadmaking of twenty-eight counties of England. He solicited no patent for his system, and asked no remuneration, beyond the payment of the expenses of his personal supervision.

September 22.

Philip Dormer Stanhope, Earl of "Chesterfield," English author and courtier, born in London, Sept. 22, 1694. Died March 24, 1773. He was distinguished for his wit and politeness, and was the oracle of taste. His reputation as an author is chiefly founded on his "Letters to his Son."

Philip Milledoler, D.D., an American divine, born at Farmington, Conn., Sept. 22, 1775. Died on Staten Island, Sept. 22, 1852. He was for several years presiden of Rutgers College, N. J., and was one of the founders of the American Bible Society.

Michael Faraday, F.R.S., an English chemist and natural philosopher of great eminence, born near London, Sept. 22, 1791. Died in August, 1867. The celebrity of Faraday is chiefly founded on his discoveries in electricity and electro-magnetism. He was one of the eight foreign members of the Academy of Science in Paris, an honor reserved exclusively for savants of the highest rank and merit.

September 23.

Jane Taylor, a meritorious and popular English writer, born in London, Sept. 23, 1763. Died at Ongar, Essexshire, April 12, 1824. She was a popular writer for children, and her works generally ran through several editions. "The Discontented Pendulum" and "The Philosopher's Scales" are among her moral teaching productions.

JOHANN FRANZ ENCKE, a German astronomer, born at Hamburg, Sept. 23, 1791. Died May 26, 1865. He gained distinction by his determination of the orbit of 1680, and of the distance of the earth from the sun. He afterwards made important and successful investigations concerning the comet since known as Encke's comet.

AUGUSTUS CÆSAR, first Emperor of Rome, and second of the noted rulers of that name, born near Rome, Sept. 23, 63 B.C. Died in August A.D. 14. He was adopted as son and heir by his uncle Julius Cæsar, and at the assassination of the latter, claimed his inheritance. Finding in Mark Antony a dangerous rival, he won him over by political intrigue and with him and Lepidus formed the second triumvirate. But Augustus and Antony soon quarreled, and a civil war ensued which terminated in the naval battle of Actium, 31 B.C., and rendered Augustus sole master of the Roman empire. He was elected consul several times, and in 27 B.C. received the name of Augustus. He had previously borne the name of Octavius. In the year 23 B.C., he accepted the power of absolute ruler of the empire for life. His reign was very beneficial to Rome, and he boasted that he found the city brick and left it marble.

ELIHU BENJAMIN WASHBURNE, an eminent American statesman, born at Livermore, Me., Sept. 23, 1816. Died Oct. 22, 1887. He was a member of Congress from 1852–69, and when he retired was, in Congressional parlance, "father of the House." He was sent by Grant as minister to France, and remained at his post during the siege of Paris and the terrible reign of the Commune, when all other foreign ministers left; and will long be remembered by his protection to those foreigners in Paris who were unprotected by their own governments.

September 24.

AULUS VITELLIUS, the ninth Cæsar, Emperor of Rome, born in Rome, Sept. 24, 15 A.D. He is noted only for his notorious gluttony, for which he spent fabulous sums. He met the fate of most crowned heads of those days; was killed by the partisans of his successor, Dec. 21, 69 A.D., after reigning only a few months.

JOHN MARSHALL, LL.D., an eminent American jurist and statesman, born at Germantown, Va., Sept. 24, 1755. Died at Philadelphia, July 6, 1835. He was appointed Chief Justice of the United States by President Adams in 1801, which office he filled for thirty-four years, and his fame as a solid reasoner, a just judge, and a profound jurist is world-wide.

ZACHARY TAYLOR, "Old Rough and Ready," twelfth President of the United States, born in Orange Co., Va., Sept. 24, 1784. His successes in the Mexican War won for him the Presidency. He was inaugurated March 4, 1849, and died July 9, 1850.

RICHARD HENRY WILDE, an author and lawyer, born in Dublin, Ireland, Sept. 24, 1789. Died of yellow fever in New Orleans, Sept. 10, 1847. He was an able lawyer and member of Congress, taking rank with the most accomplished orators of the day; but will longest be remembered by his famous lyric, "My life is like a summer rose," and his "Life of Tasso."

JAMES AUGUSTUS ST. JOHN, a distinguished editor, writer and traveler, born in Wales, Sept. 24, 1801,

Died Sept., 22, 1875.   He founded the "London Weekly Review," in 1827, and added much to the knowledge of the physical geography of upper Africa by his extensive travels and elaborately written works.

September 25.

OLE ROMER, a Danish astronomer, born at Aarhuns, Jutland, Sept. 25, 1644.   Died, 1710.   He invented the transit instrument, and determined the velocity of light by observations of the eclipses of Jupiter's satellites.   He also regulated the weights and measures of Denmark.

ABRAHAM GOTTLOB WERNER, an eminent German geologist and mineralogist, born in Upper Lusatia, Sept. 25, 1750.   Died at Dresden, June, 1817.   He rendered a service to mineralogy analogous to that rendered to botany by Linnæus, in proposing a methodical and precise language to express all the sensible qualities of minerals.   "He was the first," says Cuvier, "that raised the theory of the earth to the rank of a positive science by divesting it of the fantastic systems, of which it was for a long time composed."

FELICIA DOROTHEA HEMANS, an amiable and excellent English poet, born in Liverpool, Eng., Sept. 25, 1794.   Died near Dublin, May 12, 1835.   She is said to be the most touching and accomplished writer of occasional verses that our literature has yet to boast of.

WILLIAM H. RINEHART, an eminent American sculptor, born in Frederick Co., Md., Sept. 25, 1825.   Died at Rome, Oct. 28, 1874.   He was commissioned to finish the modeling of the bronze doors of the Capitol at Washington, which Crawford had left unfinished at his death. Copies of several of his noted pieces, are in the Corçoran Gallery of Art, in Washington, D. C.

JAMES MONTGOMERY BAILY, the "Danbury News Man," born in Albany, N. Y., Sept. 25, 1841.

He is a well known American humorous journalist, editor of the "Danbury News."

September 26.

LORD CUTHBERT H. COLLINGWOOD, an eminent English admiral, born in Newcastle-upon-Tyne, Sept. 26, 1750. Died at sea, near Minorca, March 7, 1810. He was an intimate friend of Lord Nelson, and was second in command, at the battle of Trafalgar, Oct., 1805, and when Nelson fell, succeeded to the chief command. For his part in this victory he was raised to the peerage.

CHARLES BRADLAUGH, an English atheist and republican, born in Hoxton, London, Sept. 26, 1833.

September 27.

JACQUES BENIGNE BOSSUET, a celebrated French divine, one of the great pulpit orators of France, born at Dijon, Sept. 27, 1627. Died in Paris April 12, 1704. He has been styled by different commentators, a "Father of the Church," "The Corneille of the pulpit" and "the eagle of Meaux." Bossuet's individual distinction is, that he was a great man, as well as a great orator. His funeral orations are generally esteemed the masterpieces of his eloquence. He had great occasions, and he was great to match them.

SAMUEL ADAMS, a celebrated American patriot and orator, born in Boston, Sept. 27, 1722. Died in Oct., 1803. He was a member of the first Continental Congress, and "signer" to the "Declaration of Independence." So ardent was his patriotism, that he was one of the three leaders who were to be exempt from the pardon offered in 1775.

Joseph Green Cogswell, LL.D. an American scholar and author, born at Ipswich, Mass., Sept. 27, 1786. Died Nov. 26, 1871. He, with the historian Bancroft, founded the celebrated "Round Hill School" at Northampton, Mass.

Raphael Semmes, an American naval officer and author, born in Charles Co., Md., Sept. 27, 1809.

At the beginning of the civil war he entered the Confederate navy and obtained notoriety as the commander of the Alabama, which was so ruinous to the commerce of the Federal States. Sixty-five ships and $6,000,000 were destroyed by this one vessel, which was at last sunk in the battle with the Kearsarge off the coast of France.

Epes Sargent, an American journalist and miscellaneous writer, born at Gloucester, Mass., Sept. 27, 1812. Died Dec. 30, 1880. He was an author of excellent educational works, and editor of the New York "Mirror," and the Boston "Evening Transcript." Several of his poems have been set to music and are favorites.

Thomas Nast, an American caricaturist, born in Bavaria, Sept. 27, 1840.

When fifteen years old he began to furnish illustrations for the papers, and during the war began his long series of effective political caricatures in "Harper's Weekly." It is said that Thomas Nast did more by his caricatures to deprive Horace Greeley of the Presidency than any other man or party.

September 28.

George Cruikshank, an English caricaturist and painter, born in London, Sept. 28, 1792. Died Feb. 1,

1878. His series of plates called "The Bottle," in which he illustrated the miseries of intemperance, had great success.

ARNOLD HENRY GUYOT, LL. D., a meritorious writer on physical geography, born in Switzerland, Sept. 28, 1807. Died 1884. His glacial studies and discoveries have added greatly to the knowledge of those erratic wanderers. He came to the United States in 1848, and was employed for six years by the Massachusetts Board of Education to lecture on physical geography, which inaugurated a reform in geographical teaching.

SARA CLARKE LIPPINCOTT, "Grace Greenwood," a popular American writer, born at Pompey, Onondaga Co., N. Y., Sept. 28, 1823.

She is a great grand-daughter of Jonathan Edwards; author of many volumes, and a frequent contributor to the leading New York papers. She is also noted as a lecturer in the various reform movements.

FRANCES E. WILLARD, president of the Women's Christian Temperance Union, born near Rochester, N. Y., Sept. 28, 1839.

In 1871 she was elected president of Evanston College, the first institution of high grade in which every department was successfully administered by women. She is endowed with a most varied talent; educator, writer and speaker. "Nature meant her for a journalist, but thwarted her own designs by giving her the heart of a philanthropist."

September 29.

ROBERT CLIVE, founder of the British empire in India, born in Shropshire, Sept. 29, 1725. His

success at the battle of Plassey, 1757, raised him to
the office of governor of Bengal.   Like Warren Hastings, his successor, he was arraigned by Parliament for
riches obtained by tyrannical use of power, but was
acquitted.   He became a slave of opium, and committed suicide in London, Nov. 22, 1794.

HORATIO NELSON, a British naval hero and admiral
of the first rank, born at Burnham Thorp, Norfolk,
Eng., Sept. 29, 1758.   Died Oct. 21, 1805, at the battle
of Trafalgar, at the moment of victory.   It was just
before this battle that he gave the famous signal,
"England expects every man to do his duty."

September 30.

POMPEY THE GREAT, a famous Roman general and
triumvir, born Sept. 30, 106 B.C.   He, with Cæsar and
Crassus, formed the first triumvirate; but the jealousy
of Cæsar caused a rival war, and Pompey being defeated in the battle of Pharsalia, August, 48 B.C., fled
into Africa, where he was treacherously stabbed by his
own soldiers.

SARGENT SMITH PRENTISS, an American orator, born
in Portland, Me., Sept. 30, 1808.   Died near Natchez,
Miss., July 1, 1850.   He was one of the most gifted men
this country has produced.

EDWARD SHEPHERD CREASY, an English historian
and lawyer, born at Bixley in Kent, Sept. 30, 1812.
Died Jan. 27, 1878.   His "Fifteen Decisive Battles of
the World" has passed through nine editions.   In
1860 he was appointed Chief-Justice of Ceylon.

HON. S. S. COX, an American statesman and author,
born in Zanesville, Ohio, Sept. 30, 1824.

He has been an extensive traveler, each trip having its

book as a grand finale. Thus, "The Buckeye Abroad," "A Search for Winter Sunbeams," "Arctic Sunbeams," are all accounts of his travels. "Eight years in Congress," and "Three Decades of Federal Legislation" are his reminiscences and observations as a statesman.

October 1.

HENRY ST. JOHN BOLINGBROKE, an eminent English author, orator and politician, born at Battersea, Surrey, Oct. 1, 1678. Died Dec. 15, 1751. He was for a time Prime Minister to Queen Anna, and the principal English negotiator of the treaty of Utrecht, April, 1713, which ended the long war of the Spanish succession.

CAPTAIN JAMES LAWRENCE, an American naval officer of distinguished bravery, born at Burlington, N. J., Oct. 1, 1781. He was mortally wounded in the memorable battle between the English frigate Shannon and the American frigate Chesapeake, and died July 5, 1813. It was, as he was carried below after he fell, that he utterred those memorable words, "Don't give up the ship."

RUFUS CHOATE, LL.D., one of the most eminent advocates and orators America ever produced, born in Ipswich, now Essex, Mass., Oct. 1, 1799. Died in Halifax while on his way to Europe for his health, July 13, 1859. When Webster accepted the office of Secretary of State under Harrison in 1841, Mr. Choate was chosen Senator in his place, and after the death of Webster, he was the acknowledged leader of the Massachusetts bar.

October 2.

RICHARD III., the last king of England of the Plantaganet line, born at Fotheringay Castle, Oct. 2, 1452.

He was killed in the battle of Bosworth, Aug. 21, 1485, after reigning only two years. On the death of Henry VI. he became regent for Edward V., who was a minor, but his unrestrained ambition coveted the throne, which he usurped by causing the death of the young king and his brother in the Tower.

ELIZABETH R. MONTAGUE, a celebrated English lady, born in Yorkshire, England, Oct. 2, 1720. Died in London, Aug. 25, 1800. Her "Essay on the Genius and writings of Shakespeare," won her a wide reputation. She is said to have been the founder of the literary society called the "Blue Stocking Club."

THEODORE TILTON, an American journalist, publisher, lecturer and author, born in New York, Oct. 2, 1835.

He was for a time connected with the "Independent," was editor of the "Brooklyn Union," and established "The Golden Age."

October 3.

RICHARD BOYLE, founder of the house of Cork and Orrery, and styled "the Great Earl of Cork," born at Canterbury, Oct. 3, 1566. Died Sept. 15, 1644.

GEORGE BANCROFT, Ph.D., LL.D., etc., an eminent American historian and statesman, born at Worcester, Mass., Oct. 3, 1800.

He was Secretary of the Navy under President Polk, and has been minister to England and Germany. He established the naval school at Annapolis, and improved the Observatory at Washington. But the great monument of his life is his voluminous work on "American History," the first volume of which appeared in 1834.

George Ripley, LL.D., an American editor and scholar, born at Greenfield, Mass., Oct. 3, 1802. Died July 4, 1880. He was associated with Emerson and Margaret Fuller in conducting the "Dial," was the chief promoter of the socialistic experiment at Brook Farm, Roxbury, Mass., has been literary editor of the New York "Tribune," and edited with Charles A. Dana, Appleton's "New American Cyclopedia."

Harriet Hosmer, an eminent American sculptor, born at Watertown, Mass., Oct. 3, 1831.

To prepare herself for her chosen career, she studied anatomy with her father, also at the medical college in St. Louis. She modeled her first work in 1851, after which she was sent to Rome and became the pupil of Gibson. Her much admired statute of Beatrice Cenci was made for the mercantile library of St. Louis. Her most ambitious work is a colossal statute of "Zenobia in Chains." The "Sleeping Faun" is one of her best works.

October 4.

Francois Pierre Guillaume Guizot, a distinguished French statesman and historian, born at Nêmes, Oct. 4, 1787. Died near Paris, Sept. 13, 1874. As a statesman Guizot is ranked among the great and good men of France, but is generally considered to be even more successful as a historian, and has shown himself to be an effective and imposing parliamentary orator.

Rutherford B. Hayes, nineteenth President of the United States, born at Delaware, Ohio, Oct. 4, 1822.

He was in active service during the entire civil war, and was afterward governor of Ohio for three terms, an honor never before conferred on a citizen of that State.

He was nominated as candidate for President, June 16, 1876, and inaugurated March 4, 1877, after one of the most bitter and exciting elections known in our national history. His administration should ever be held as a model of excellence, in consequence of the banishment of wine from the State dinners.

October 5.

JONATHAN EDWARDS, a celebrated American divine and metaphysician, born at East Windsor, Conn., Oct. 5, 1703. Died March 22, 1758. He began his duties as minister before he had completed his nineteenth year, and spent many years of conscientious and faithful labor in his chosen field. But his faith and virtue were destined to undergo the great trial of being driven from his church, because he sought to reform the lax custom of admitting members into the church without regard to the consistency of their life and character. He was author of many works, but his most celebrated production was "The Freedom of the Will," in which he exhibits a power of close and subtle reasoning which has never been equaled by any other writer.

EBENEZER PORTER, D.D., an American divine and scholar, born at Cornwall, Conn., Oct. 5, 1772. Died at Andover, April 8, 1834. He was compiler of the noted "Rhetorical Reader," of which more than three hundred editions were issued.

WILLIAM SCORESBY, D.D., F.R.S., an Arctic navigator, minister and author, born at Cropton, England, Oct. 5, 1790. Died at Torquay, March 21, 1857. In May, 1806, while chief mate of his father's ship, they reached the highest northern latitude that had then been attained, 81° 12'. Scoresby's Sound, near Greenland, was named in his honor.

CHESTER A. ARTHUR, twenty-first President of the United States, born in Franklin Co., Vt. Oct. 5, 1830. Died Nov. 18, 1886. He was elected Vice-President in 1880, and at the death of Garfield, Sept. 19, 1881, he succeeded to the Presidency.

October 6.

FERDINAND HASSLER, a Swiss mathematician, born in Switzerland, Oct. 6, 1770. Died at Philadelphia, Nov. 20, 1843. He was the first superintendent of the United States Coast Survey; and the Hassler Expedition of 1871–72, fitted out for scientific purposes under the direction of eminent scholars, one of whom was Prof. Agassiz, was named in his honor.

JENNY LIND GOLDSCHMIDT, a celebrated Swedish vocalist, the "Swedish Nightingale," born in Stockholm, Oct. 6, 1821. Died Nov. 2, 1887. She was the first great public singer that visited America, where she arrived September, 1850, and under the direction of P. T. Barnum, gave one hundred and fifty concerts. When she returned to Europe in 1852, she had won all hearts by the sweetness of her voice, the versatility of her dramatic power, and the excellence of her character, in which simplicity and benevolence were the guiding powers.

October 7.

WILLIAM LAUD, a celebrated archbishop of Canterbury, born at Reading, Berkshire, Oct. 7, 1573. He became the chief minister and favorite of Charles I. in 1628, and disgraced himself by his persecutions of the Puritans. He made several attempts to compel both Scotland and England to conform to the Established Church, which resulted in rebellion. The Long Parliament accused him of treason, and he was executed after three years' imprisonment, June 10, 1644. -

KASPER HAUSER, the celebrated Nuremberg foundling, born at some unknown place, Oct. 7, 1812. In May, 1828, he was first seen in the streets of Nuremberg, with every evidence that he had been confined from infancy in a dark subterranean prison, provided only with bread and water, and kept in childish ignorance of the most common things of life. He was placed under good care, and his education rapidly progressing when he was stabbed by an unknown person, Dec. 17, 1833. Although full accounts of the above foundling may now be seen in old English magazines, printed at the time of its occurrence, late investigations declare the whole thing a farce.

WILLIAM BILLINGS, an early American musical composer, born in Boston, Oct. 7, 1746. Died there Sept. 26, 1800. He was the first one in America to evince any real musical talent; he was self taught, and compiled several collections of hymns.

October 8.

JOHN WALTER, an English journalist, born in London, 1739. Died 1812. He was founder of "The London Times," the first number of which appeared in 1788 He was also inventor of logography or the art of printing with entire words or syllables. His son, of the same name, born in 1784, became in 1803 exclusive manager of "The Times," which, under his direction, became the most able and influential journal of Europe. Dying in 1847, his son, John, born Oct. 8. 1818, succeeded to the proprietorship. Thus for one hundred years one of the leading journals of the world has been under the management of a John Walter.

CHARLES A. JOY, Ph.D., an American editor, scholar and chemist, born at Ludlowville, Tompkins Co., N. Y., Oct. 8, 1823.

He has made many contributions to chemistry by his scientific researches ; was for two years editor of the "Scientific American," also editor of all chemical articles in Appleton's "New American Cyclopedia," besides being president of various scientific associations.

EDMUND CLARENCE STEDMAN, an American author and poet, born at Hartford, Conn., Oct. 8, 1833.

He has been editor of and contributor to prominent papers, but is best known by his poems, one of which, "Gettysburg," he delivered at the meeting of the Army of the Potomac in 1872.

October 9.

SAAVEDRA CERVANTES, a celebrated Spanish author born in Alcala de Henares, Oct. 9, 1547. Died on the same day as Shakespeare, April 23, 1616. He is author of "Don Quixote," almost the only book in the Spanish language said to possess much of a European reputation. Numerous translations and countless editions in every language bespeak its adaptation to mankind. "By the streets of By and By, one arrives at the house of Never," a quotation from Don Quixote, is the one warning which should be emblazoned on every moral guide-board.

LEWIS CASS, LL.D., an American general and statesman, born at Exeter, N. H., Oct. 9, 1782. Died June 17, 1866. He was Secretary of War in Jackson's administration, and afterwards ambassador to France. He is said to be the first clear enunciator of the doctrine called "squatter sovereignty;" and was a defeated candidate for the Presidency when Taylor was elected.

JOHN TODD, D.D., an American divine and author, born at Rutland, Vt., Oct. 9, 1800. Died in Pittsfield, Mass., Aug. 24, 1873. He was pastor of the First Congregational church in Philadelphia, 1836–42, and of the First Church in Pittsfield Mass., 1842-72, and was one of the founders of Mt. Holyoke Female Seminary. His " Lectures to Children " are among the best works of their kind, and his " Students' Manual " has had an immense circulation and exerted great influence both in the United States and Europe.

GIUSEPPE VERDI, one of the most eminent Italian composers, born in Parma, Oct. 9, 1814.

Verdi's genius and character are highly appreciated all over the world, but in his own country are cherished with a peculiar affection by all classes.

ELIZABETH AKERS ALLEN, " Florence Percy," a sweet poet of America, born in Strong, Franklin Co., Me., Oct. 9, 1832.

ELAINE GOODALE, one of the "sweet children poets," born at " Sky Farm," Mt. Washington, Berkshire Co., Mass., Oct. 9, 1863.

She and her sister, Dora Read Goodale, three years younger, by their precocity as poets have won the above endearing name in literature. Elaine, at the age of eight, began the publication of a little paper, " Sky Farm Life," in which their poems appeared from month to month. In 1877 their productions appeared in the St. Nicholas, since which they have been frequent contributors to the leading magazines of the day. Their poems have been published in three volumes ; "Apple Blossoms" in 1878, and since that time, "In Berkshire with the Wild Flowers," and "All Round the Year."

October 10.

Henry Cavendish, an eminent English chemist and natural philosopher, born at Nice, Oct. 10, 1731. Died Feb. 24, 1810. He was a profound mathematician, and ranks among the first of chemical philosophers. He discovered the distinctive properties of hydrogen gas, and demonstrated the proportion of oxygen and nitrogen in common air (1783).

Benjamin West, the eminent American Quaker artist and painter, born in Springfield, Delaware Co., Pa., Oct. 10, 1738. Died in London, March 11, 1820. Early in life he took up his residence in London, and was patronized as an artist by George III. Some of his finest pictures are in the Academy of Fine Arts, Philadelphia. He succeeded Sir Joshua Reynolds as president of the Royal Academy in 1792.

Daniel Treadway, an American mechanician, born at Ipswich, Mass., Oct. 10, 1791. Died Feb. 27, 1872. He invented a machine for spinning hemp for cordage, and a cannon which bears his name.

Harriet A. Newel, one of the first female missionaries from the United States, born in Haverhill, Mass., Oct. 10, 1793. Died on the Isle of France, Nov. 30, 1812.

David Scott, a celebrated Scottish artist, engraver and painter, born in Edinburgh, Oct. 10, 1806. Died there March 5, 1849. His works were mostly imaginative, among which is " The Genius of Discord."

George P. Morris, an American journalist and poet, born in Philadelphia, Oct. 10, 1802. Died in New

York, July 6, 1864. He assisted in founding the "New York Mirror," and "Home Journal," and was author of a number of beautiful and popular poems, among which are "My Mother's Bible" and "Woodman, Spare that Tree."

Hugh Miller, the eminent Scottish mason, geologist and author, born at Cromarty, on the east coast of Scotland, Oct. 10, 1802. Died by his own hand at Portobello, near Edinburgh, Dec. 26, 1856. Besides the labor spent as a geologist, he was editor of the "Witness" for sixteen years, which he rendered popular and influential. As an author his "Old Red Sandstone," "Footprints of the Creator," and "My School and Schoolmasters," secure for him the lasting admiration of his countrymen, and mark an important epoch in the progress of geology.

Michael Munkacsy, an eminent artist, born in a small town in Austro-Hungary, at the foot of the Carpathian Mountains, Oct. 10, 1844.

Among his many pictures are "Milton dictating his Paradise Lost," now in the Lenox Library, New York city, "The Last Day of a Condemned Man," owned by a lady of Philadelphia, and "Christ before Pilate," which has been the object of much interest in New York.

October 11.

Orson Squire Fowler, one of the founders of the firm of "Fowler & Wells," born in Cohocton, Steuben Co., N. Y., Oct. 11, 1809. Died Aug. 18, 1887. He graduated at Amherst College, and after a course of study on Phrenology, engaged at once in lecturing and writing on that subject. In connection with his brother, L. N. Fowler, he conducted the "*Phrenological Journal.*"

Thomas Osmond Summers, an American divine, scholar and editor, born near Dorsetshire, Eng., Oct. 11, 1812.

He was one of the nine members to constitute the first conference of Texas, also assisted in organizing the Methodist Episcopal Church in the South.

October 12.

Lyman Beecher, D.D., father of the noted Beecher family, born in New Haven, Conn., Oct. 12, 1775. Died in Brooklyn, N. Y., Jan. 10, 1863. He was distinguished for the boldness and energy of his character. His sermons on temperance have had an immense circulation and have been translated into several different languages.

Jesse Olney, A.M. an eminent American educator, born at Union, Tolland Co., Conn., Oct. 12, 1798. Died at Stratford, July 30, 1872. He was the first American teacher to separate geography from astronomy, and to begin the former study through the localities of home. His Geography and Atlas, issued in 1828, sold by the million, and his " National Preceptor," a reading manual, was far superior to any of its predecessors.

George Washington Cable, an American author, born in New Orleans, La., Oct. 12, 1844.

He began his literary career writing for the New Orleans " Picayune," under the pen-name of " Drop Shot;" and his subsequent sketches of Creole life, written for Scribner's Monthly (now the Century), were so successful that he determined to devote all his time to literature. His rendering of the Creole dialect, with its French and Spanish varients, is full of originality. He has also successfully entered the lecture field, reading selections from his own writings, and singing to northern audiences the strange wild melodies, current among the French-speaking negroes of the southern Mississippi.

October 13.

Joseph Reddeford Walker, a noted American traveler, born at Knoxville, Tenn., Oct. 13, 1798. Died Oct. 27, 1876. He was guide to Bonnevill's expedition to the Rocky Mountains in 1832, and conducted the party from Great Salt Lake to California, which discovered the beautiful Yosemite valley. Walker's river, lake and pass, discovered by this expedition, were named for him.

William Motherwell, a Scottish poet and editor, born in Glasgow, Scotland, Oct. 13, 1798. Died there Nov. 1, 1835. He edited successfully three different periodicals, and his " Poems, Narrative and Lyrical," published in 1833, are remarkable for their pathos and earnestness of feeling.

October 14.

William Penn, the founder of Pennsylvania, born in London, Oct. 14, 1644. Died at Ruscombe, Berkshire, Eng., July 30, 1718. Penn is considered one of the most illustrious of Christian philanthropists, and spent his entire life for the service of others. As a courtier he exerted his utmost ability for civil and religious liberty in England; but as he lost hope in this, he turned his attention to establish a more liberal commonwealth in America. Accordingly he obtained from the king, Charles II., a tract of land west of the Delaware, and north of Maryland, in payment for a claim against the government which he inherited from his father. He sailed from England, Sept., 1682, and in November of the same year, held the famous treaty with the Indians which was the only league between the aborigines and the Christians which was never sworn to, and the only one never broken.

SAMUEL JOHNSON, D.D., an American clergyman and author, born in Guilford, Conn., Oct. 14, 1696. Died in Stratford, Conn., Jan. 6, 1772. He was first president of King's, now Columbia, College in New York, and author of " System of Morality " and other works.

FRANCIS LIGHTFOOT LEE, an American statesman and patriot, born at Stratford, Westmoreland Co., Va., Oct. 14, 1734. Died in Richmond, 1797. He was elected to the General Congress in 1775, and signed the " Declaration of Independence."

October 15.

VIRGIL, the most illustrious of Latin poets, born at Andes near Mantua, Oct. 15, 70 B.C. Died at Brundusium, Sept. 22, 19 B.C. He was author of the " Æneid," the great national Latin epic poem; also of several other noted works. The most popular English translation of Virgil is that of Dryden.

JAMES II., of Great Britain, 1685–88, born at the palace of St. James, London, Oct. 15, 1633. Died at St. Germain, France, Sept. 16, 1701. He was the Duke of York and Albany when the English took possession of the Dutch settlements on the Hudson, and New York and Albany were named in his honor. He was deposed from the throne of England by stratagem, and the endeavor by Louis XIV. of France to restore him, caused the war between England and France, which extending to the American colonies, is known as King William's war.

IDA PFEIFFER, the eminent German traveler, born in Vienna, Oct. 15, 1797. Died there Oct. 27, 1858. In 1842 she traveled through Asia Minor. In 1845 she made the tour of Sweden, Norway and Iceland, after which she accomplished two journeys around the world and wrote accounts of both.

IRWIN McDOWELL, an American general, born at Franklin Co., Ohio, Oct. 15, 1818. Died May 4, 1885. In May, 1861, he was appointed brigadier-general of the army of the Potomac, and commanded the Union forces at the battle of Bull Run.

October 16.

NOAH WEBSTER, an eminent American philologist and lexicographer, born in West Hartford, Conn., Oct. 16, 1758. Died in New Haven, May 28, 1843. He expended the labor of many years on a " Dictionary of the English Language," published in 1828, which has run through several editions, and is considered the standard authority of the English language. His world renowned " Speller," up to 1876, had reached a sale of 70,000,000 copies.

LORENZO DOW, an eccentric American Methodist preacher, born in Coventry, Conn., Oct. 16, 1777. Died at Washington, D. C., Feb. 2, 1834. He was noted for his earnestness and courage, as well as for some singularity in dress and expression. He left a journal of his life and travels.

October 17.

JEAN BAPTISTE REGNAULT, a French painter of history, born in Paris, Oct 17, 1754. Died there Nov.,

1829.　Among his best works are a "Descent from the Cross," and the "Education of Achilles."

Sir John Bowring, LL.D., an English statesman, linguist and author, born at Exeter, Eng., Oct. 17, 1792. Died Nov. 23, 1872. As a linguist he is noted for his attainments in the Sclavonic languages, and as an author he published specimens of the poetry of these languages. In 1825 he was editor of the "Westminster Review," and in 1835 was elected to Parliament, where he remained until 1849, when he was appointed British Consul at Hong-Kong and superintendent of trade in China, and was afterward governor of Hong Kong. In addition to all this we find him author of such priceless hymns as "God is love, His mercy brightens," "In the Cross of Christ I glory," "Watchman, tell us of the Night."

John Wilkes, an eminent English politician, born in London, Oct. 17, 1727. Died there, Dec. 27, 1797. Although of an erratic character, he was a strenuous opponent of the American taxation. The town of Wilkesbarre in Pennsylvania, was named in honor of him and Col. Isaac Barre, another firm friend of the Colonies.

October 18.

Giovanni Battista Marini, an Italian poet, born at Naples, Oct. 18, 1569. Died there, March 25, 1625. Many of his sonnets are among the most beautiful in the Italian literature, and the Marinists, a literary school of which he was the head, enjoyed a great reputation in the seventeenth century.

Richard Nash, "Beau Nash," born at Swansea, Wales, Oct. 18, 1674. Died Feb. 3, 1761. He distinguished himself as a man of fashion, and though coarse and ungainly in his person, was master of the science of gentility. He converted the city of Bath from a vulgar and mismanaged watering-place into an elegant place of resort, for which he was also styled, "king of Bath."

EMANUEL GEIBEL, a celebrated German poet, born at Lubeck, Oct. 18, 1815.

He ranks among the most popular German poets of the age.

FREDERICK WILLIAM, who succeeded to the throne of his venerable and illustrious father, March 9, 1888, under the title of Frederick III., Emperor of Germany and King of Prussia, was born Oct. 18, 1831. Died April, 1888, after a reign of only fifty days. "Unser Fritz," as he was familiarly known in Prussia, distinguished himself both in the Austrian and French wars and the two decisive battles of each were directly due to him. He was a great favorite with the German people and his death was mourned among all civilized nations.

HELEN HUNT JACKSON, "H. H.," an eminent American author, born at Amherst, Mass., Oct. 18, 1831. Died in San Francisco, Aug. 12, 1885. Her public literary career began in 1866, after a sorrowful retirement from the world, occasioned by the death of her first husband and cherished son. She was a valued contributor to the "Independent," "Hearth and Home," "Atlantic Monthly" and "The Century," besides being author of several volumes. It was at one time proposed by the editors of the "Century" to let her varied contributions accumulate sufficiently to fill one number of that periodical; and though the plan was dismissed, not from a doubt of its practicability, it was probably

the greatest compliment ever paid by editors to the resources of a single contributor.

October 19.

ELISHA WHITTLESEY, an American politician and
statesman, born at Washington, Conn., Oct. 19, 1783.
Died at Washington, D. C., Jan. 7, 1863. He was one
of the founders of the Whig party, and was a conspicuous example of integrity, in a long and arduous
public service.

JAMES HENRY LEIGH HUNT, an English author and
poet, born in Southgate, Middlesex, Eng., Oct. 19,
1784. Died at Putney, Aug. 28, 1859. He was contemporary with Byron, Moore, Lamb, Shelley and Keats,
and resided for a time in Italy with Byron and Shelley.

BENJAMIN H. WRIGHT, an American engineer, born
in New York, Oct. 19, 1801.

By his personal efforts, railroads were introduced into
the island of Cuba, and the first road was made under
his superintendence.

CASSIUS M. CLAY, an American politician and statesman, born in Madison Co., Ky., Oct. 19, 1810.

He was an ardent advocate of anti-slavery principles,
and when editor of "The True American," an anti-
slavery paper, published at Lexington, Ky., met with
a violent and abusive opposition. In 1862 he was appointed minister to Russia, which place he occupied
until 1869.

October 20.

CHRISTOPHER WREN, an eminent English architect,
born in Wiltshire, Eng., Oct. 20, 1632. Died at Hampton Court, Feb. 25, 1723. He was designer of many

of the public buildings of London, after the great fire of 1666, prominent among which were St. Paul's Cathedral and Westminster Abbey.

THOMAS HUGHES, an English author, social economist and barrister, born in Newbury, near Berkshire, Eng., Oct. 20, 1823.

He acquired celebrity by his "Tom Brown at Rugby," 1857, which quickly passed through several editions, and was soon followed by "Tom Brown at Oxford." In 1881 he came to America with a colony of farmers to settle a tract of country in the mountains of Tennessee, which place they named Rugby.

October 21.

SAMUEL TAYLOR COLERIDGE, an eminent English poet and critic, born at Ottery, in Devonshire, Oct. 21, 1772. Died at Highgate, London, July 25, 1834. He formed with Southey the idea of founding a pantisocracy on the Susquehanna river in Pennsylvania, but like other Utopian plans it failed. He with Southey and Wordsworth, were the "Lake Poets" of the Lake district in the north of England. The "Ancient Mariner" is one of his well known works.

GEORGE COMBE, an eminent Scottish phrenologist and lecturer, born in Edinburgh, Oct. 21, 1788. Died at Moor Park, Eng., Aug. 14, 1858. He became a believer in Phrenology on hearing Spurzheim lecture in 1816, after which he wrote many works on Phrenology, the most prominent of which is the "Constitution of Man," which passed through several editions. He visited the United States in 1838, and was considered the ablest writer and lecturer who had advocated this science.

ALPHONSO DE LAMARTINE, a French poet, orator and historian of great celebrity, born at Macon, France, Oct. 21, 1792. Died in February, 1869. He was a master spirit and moderator of the French Revolution of 1848. His harangue to the infuriated mobs, Feb. 25, 1847, was one of the most remarkable triumphs of eloquence recorded in history.

JOHN J. G. C. BRAINARD, an American poet, born at New London, Conn., Oct. 21, 1796. Died there Sept. 26, 1828. He was for a time editor of "The Connecticut Mirror," and produced a volume of poems. His "Falls of Niagara," written while the printer's boy was waiting for his regular contribution to the paper, is generally considered the best short poem written on that subject, and is one of the "gems" of American literature.

October 22.

JAMES NORTHCOTE, an English artist, celebrated as a portrait painter, born at Plymouth, Eng., Oct. 22, 1746. Died July 13, 1831. He was also author of "Northcote's Fables" and other works.

FRANZ LISZT, a Hungarian musician and one of the most celebrated pianists of modern times, born at Raiding, Oct. 22, 1811. Died July 30, 1886. Hearing Paganini, the great violinist, perform in Paris, he resolved to obtain the same mastery over the piano which that great musician had gained over the violin, and it is allowed that he succeeded. In 1848 he was appointed leader of the imperial orchestra at Weimar.

October 23.

EMMANUEL DE GROUCHY, a celebrated French general, born in Paris, Oct. 23, 1766. Died in St. Etienne,

May 29, 1847. He assisted in gaining the battle of Hohenlinden, Dec. 3, 1800, and was conspicuous for his skill and courage. Napoleon gave signal proof of his confidence in Grouchy by placing him at the head of his "Sacred Battalion." Some historians attribute him to be the indirect cause of the defeat of the French at Waterloo, by his failing to appear at the appointed time; others say he had no order from the emperor to do so.

FRANCIS JEFFREY, a distinguished Scottish critic and essayist, born in Edinburgh, Oct. 23, 1773. Died at Craigerook, Jan. 26, 1850. He was for twenty-six years editor of the "Edinburgh Review," of which he was one of the projectors, and which is said to have formed a new era in English literature, and completely changed the style of the popular magazines. His contributions to the "Review" extended over a period of nearly fifty years. As a lawyer his fluency and eloquence had no equal at the Scottish bar. So rapid was his enunciation that it was once declared by an opposing counsel "that by calculation with his watch, that man had actually spoken the English language twice over in three hours." In 1830 he was elected to the Parliament of William IV. and afterward received an appointment to a Scottish judgeship with the honorary title of Lord.

October 24.

EDMUND QUINCY, an American statesman in the colonial times, born at Braintree, now Quincy, Mass., Oct. 24, 1681. Died in London, Feb. 23, 1738. He was the ancestor of a very distinguished line of Massachusetts statesmen.

SIR JAMES MACKINTOSH, an illustrious British author, orator and statesman, born near Inverness, Oct. 24, 1765.

Died May 1832. "It would be difficult," says Mr. Whipple, " to mention any writer in the literary journals of the nineteenth century who has carried into the task of criticism so much fairness and moderation as Mackintosh; and the beauty of his character will long continue to exert an influence in moulding the minds of scholars and statesmen.

THADDEUS OSGOOD, an American minister and missionary, born at Methuen, Mass., Oct. 24, 1775. Died at Glasgow, Scotland, Jan. 19, 1852. He organized the first church at Buffalo, N. Y., and established Sunday and day schools and Bible societies at many places in Canada.

SIR MOSES MONTEFIORE, an English Jew noted for his philanthropy, born in London, Oct. 24, 1784. Died July 28, 1885. His ancestors for several generations were successful bankers, in which business this distinguished Jew made an honest fortune, which he devoted to philanthropic measures in behalf of his people in all parts of Europe. His last act of business, although a centenarian, was to draw a check for the Princess Beatrice of England, and to dictate a tasteful letter of presentation.

BELVA A. LOCKWOOD, the woman lawyer of Washington, D. C., born at Royalton, N. Y., Oct. 24, 1830.

She early signalized herself by her executive abilities, and during the civil war was efficient in organizing hundreds of young women into committees for clothing the soldiers. She prepared herself, and applied in vain to be appointed as consul to Ghent, also to enter Columbia College as a student. But when the National University Law Class was opened, she was one of the fifteen ladies who entered their names. She afterward graduated and was admitted to the bar.

October 25.

JAMES BEATTIE, a Scottish poet and philosophical writer, born in Kincardine, Oct. 25, 1735. Died in 1803. His greatest works were his " Essay on Truth," written to refute the doctrine of Hume, and "The Minstrel." Cowper pronounced Beattie "the most agreeable and amiable writer he ever met with."

JOEL JONES, LL.D., an American lawyer and judge, born at Coventry, Conn., Oct. 25, 1795. Died in Philadelphia, Feb. 1860. He was the first president of Girard College, and was perfectly familiar with several modern and dead languages.

THOMAS BABINGTON MACAULAY, an eminent English scholar, critic and historian, born at Rothley Temple, in Leicestershire, Oct. 25, 1800. Died at Kensington, London, Dec. 28, 1859, and was buried in Westminster. Although a member of Parliament and of the supreme council of India, yet his fame rests not upon his ability as a statesman, but upon his merits as an essayist and historian. He had the remarkable faculty of assimulating printed matter at first sight, and at one period of his life was known to say that if every copy of " Paradise Lost " and " Pilgrim's Progress " were destroyed, he would undertake to reproduce them both from recollection. In 1842 he published his "Lays of Ancient Rome." His "History of England," though unfinished, met with almost unparalleled popularity, and was soon translated into twelve languages. His works will be read and admired as long as the English language is the dominant tongue.

October 26.

EDMUND HALLEY, an eminent English astronomer and mathematician, born in a suburb of London, Oct. 26,

1656. Died Jan., 1742. He was the first who successfully predicted the return of a comet, and his observations on a remarkable comet caused it to be named in his honor. He appears to have been the first to discover the proper motion of the fixed stars, also to catalogue the southern stars. He was intimate with Newton, and persuaded him to publish his "Principia."

Charles Sprague, an American poet, born in Boston, Oct. 26, 1791. Died there Jan. 14, 1875. His "Ode" in honor of Shakespeare is considered one of the most beautiful lyrics in the English language. His most extensive work is "Curiosity," a satirical poem. "The Winged Worshipers," "Art" and "The Family Meeting," are among his short poems.

Helmuth Karl Bernard von Moltke, a Prussian general, or *the* great general of Germany, born at Parchim, Mecklenburg, Oct. 26, 1800.

He became major-general in 1856, and lieutenant-general in 1859. He planned the campaign which resulted in the great and decisive victory of Sadowa, July 3, 1866, and directed in person the armies which gained in France, in 1870, a series of great and memorable victories.

Elizabeth P. Prentiss, an American author, born in Maine, Oct. 26, 1818. Died in 1788. She has written several interesting books for youth and children, among which is "Stepping Heavenward."

October 27.

James Cook, a celebrated English navigator and discoverer, born at Marston, Yorkshire, Eng., Oct. 27, 1728. He was killed by the natives at the Sandwich Islands, Feb. 14, 1779. He twice circumnavigated the globe, discovering New Caledonia, and started on the third, in which he discovered the Sandwich Islands, where he lost his life.

JOANNA BAILLIE, one of the most eminent British female poets, born at Bothwell, near Glasgow, Scotland, Oct. 27, 1762. Died at Hempstead, near London, Feb. 23, 1851. Her great work "Plays on the Passions," was considered a noble monument to the powerful mind and the pure and elevated imagination of its author.

BENJAMAN FRANKLIN WADE, an eminent American statesman, born in Springfield, Mass., Oct. 27, 1800. Died March 2, 1878. He was distinguished as a zealous advocate of the anti-slavery question, and for his resolute character and inflexible fidelity to the cause of liberty, was chosen president of the Senate after the assassination of Lincoln.

ALEXANDER T. STEWART, a merchant prince of New York, and considered the greatest merchant in the world, born near Belfast, Ireland, Oct. 27, 1802. Died April 13, 1876. He is said to have made his immense fortune by attending to details, and following closely the "one priced" system of merchandizing of which he was the father. He built some magnificent houses in New York and in Garden City, L. I.

WHITELAW REID, an American journalist, born at Xenia, Ohio, Oct. 27, 1837.

He early began to edit papers with great success, and his abilities as a war correspondent, during the civil war, gave him great distinction. In 1869 he became managing editor of the New York "Tribune," and upon the death of Horace Greeley, became proprietor as well as editor.

October 28.

ERASTUS FAIRBANKS, LL.D., an American manufacturer, born at Brimfield, Mass., Oct. 28, 1792. Died at St. Johnsbury, Vt., Nov. 30, 1864.   In 1825, he with his brother, formed a partnership for the manufacturing of his scales which have a world-wide reputation.   He was twice elected governor of the State of Vermont.

HENRIETTA SHUCK, the first American woman missionary to China, born in Kilmarnock, Va., Oct. 28, 1817.   Died in China, Nov. 27, 1847.

ANNA ELIZABETH DICKENSON, an American lecturer and author, born in Philadelphia, Oct. 28, 1842.

She gained great distinction during the civil war by her public speeches against slavery, and has been considered one of the most popular lecturers of the United States.

October 29.

JAMES BOSWELL, the biographer of Samuel Johnson, born in Edinburgh, Oct. 29, 1740.   Died in London, June 19, 1795.   His "Life of Johnson" is considered to be the best biography in universal literature.

JOHN KEATS, a celebrated English poet, born in London, Oct. 29, 1795.   Died in Rome, Feb. 27, 1821. His celebrity is perhaps to be attributed as much to the circumstances of his early death, as to his poetical ability.   His "Endymion" being severely criticised by the "Edinburgh Review," is thought to have aggravated the disease under which he was suffering, and contributed to his early death.

THOMAS FRANCIS BAYARD, an American statesman, born at Wilmington, Del., Oct. 29, 1828.

He was appointed Secretary of State in President Cleveland's Cabinet, and was for many years previous U. S. Senator.

October 30.

JOHN ADAMS, an American statesman and patriot, second President of the United States, born in Braintree, Mass., Oct. 30, 1735. Died there (though by that time it had changed to Quincy), July 4, 1826. He was an ardent advocate of American Independence from his college days, and when the real " Declaration of Independence" was laid upon the table, he as much as any one man secured its adoption, by his eloquent debates during the four days' session of the General Congress, previous to its being signed. He, of course, was one of the "signers," and after the war was the first American minister to England, and first Vice-President. It was during his administration that the capital was removed to Washington. His support of the "Alien and Sedition Laws " lost for him a second term.

ANDREW JACKSON DOWNING, an American landscape gardener and author, born in Newburg, N. Y., Oct. 30, 1815. He was lost on the *Henry Clay*, a North River steamboat, July 28, 1852. He was editor of " The Horticulturist " for six years previous to his death ; and his " Fruits and Fruit-Trees of America" has passed through several editions. He probably had few superiors as a landscape-gardener, even in Europe.

ADELAIDE ANNE PROCTOR, an English poetess, born in London, Oct. 30, 1825. Died there Feb. 2, 1864. Her short poems are among the choicest in English literature.

ROSCOE CONKLING, an American senator and lawyer, born at Albany, N. Y., Oct. 30, 1828. Died April 17, 1888. He was elected to Congress in 1858, and from that time was a recognized leader of the Republican party, which place he won by his remarkable gift of oratory.

John Rogers, an American sculptor, born in Salem, Mass., Oct. 30, 1829.

He is modeler of the famed "Rogers' groups," which he began as illustrations of the civil war.

October 31.

Richard Brinsley B. Sheridan, a celebrated Irish orator and dramatist, born at Dublin, Oct. 31, 1751. Died in London, July 7, 1816. As an orator his celebrated Begum speech on the trial of Warren Hastings, in 1787, is still regarded as one of the most splendid displays of eloquence in ancient or modern times. His "School for Scandal," published in 1777, established his reputation as a dramatic genius of the highest order, and is considered "if not the most original, perhaps the most finished and faultless comedy of the language." He has been called a dramatic star of the first magnitude.

Theodore Dwight Woolsey, D. D., LL. D., an eminent American scholar, born in New York, Oct. 31, 1801.

He was president of Yale College for twenty-five years, 1846–71, and as an author is celebrated for his series of text-books of Greek classics.

William Cowper Prime, an American journalist and author, born at Cambridge, N. Y., Oct. 31, 1825.

In 1861 he took the editorship of "The Journal of Commerce," and has traveled extensively and written many works.

Gen. Joseph R. Hawley, an American editor,

lawyer, general and legislator, born in Stewartsville, N. C., Oct. 31, 1826.

He was president of the Centennial Exposition in 1876, and is said to be the first volunteer that offered his services in the civil war.

BENJAMIN W. RICHARDSON, an English physician, born at Leicestershire, Eng., Oct. 31, 1828.

He was the first to employ ether spray for local pain.

November 1.

SIR MATHEW HALE, an eminent English judge, born at Alderley, Gloucestershire, Eng., Nov. 1, 1609. Died there Dec. 25, 1676. He was appointed by Cromwell, in 1653, judge of the common bench, and twice elected to Parliament. Charles II. appointed him chief baron of the exchequer, and afterward lord chief justice of England. He is regarded as one of the greatest, wisest and best judges that ever attained this dignity.

NICHOLAS BOILEAU, an eminent French poet and satirist, born in Paris, Nov. 1, 1636. Died there March 1711. "Boileau," says Hallam, "is the analogue of Pope in French literature; 'The Art of Poetry' has been the model of the 'Essay on Criticism.'" He has the honor of having effected a revolution in the poetical taste of the French; his poems containing no line that would offend the strictest moralist.

ANTONIO CANOVA, a celebrated Italian sculptor, born at Possagno, in Venitia, Nov. 1, 1757. Died in Venice, Oct. 13, 1822. When twelve years old, he made a lion of butter for a grand dinner, which started him on the road to fame. His admirable statue of Napoleon afterward came into the possession of the Duke of Wellington, and his statue of Washington is not unworthy of his fame.   He produced fifty statues, as many busts, cenotaphs and groups, and has the reputation of the greatest sculptor of his age.

Stephen Van Rensselaer, LL.D., known as "the Patroon," a distinguished American statesman and soldier, born in New York, Nov. 1, 1764. Died in Albany, Jan. 26, 1839. He was for six years Lieutenant-Governor of New York State, and commanded the New York militia in the war of 1812. He founded the Rensselaer Polytechnic School at Troy, in 1824.

November 2.

Maria Antoinette, fifth daughter of Maria Theresa and Francis I. of Austria, born at Vienna, Nov. 2, 1755. She was the ill-fated Queen of France, wife of Louis XVI., during the French Revolution and after the fall of the Girondists, they were condemned to death by the Jacobins, and were excuted Oct. 16, 1793.

James Knox Polk, eleventh President of the United States, born in Mecklenberg Co., N. C., Nov. 2, 1795. Died in Nashville, Tenn., June 15, 1849, about three months after his retirement from office. The Mexican war, the agitation caused by the "Wilmot Proviso," and the discovery of gold in California, were events of his administration.

November 3.

Marcus Annæus Lucan, a Roman epic poet, born at Cordova, Spain, Nov. 3, 38 A.D., was a nephew of the philosopher Seneca. He was for a time a favorite of Nero, who invested him with office in the government. But the notorious tyrant, fearing him as his literary rival, forbade Lucan any more public audiences, which resulted in a plot to take Nero's life. This being detected, the poet was put to death 65 A.D. Lucan's fame rests on a poem entitled " Pharsalia," which treats of the civil war between Cæsar and Pompey.

WILLIAM CULLEN BRYANT, the great American " poet of Nature," born at Cummington, Mass., Nov. 3, 1794. Died in New York, June 12, 1878. His earliest poems, " The Embargo" and " The Spanish Revolution," were printed in 1808, and " Thanatopsis," by many regarded as his finest poem, was published in 1816. In 1826 he became editor of the " Evening Post," which position he filled for more than forty years. " No poet," says Griswold, " has described with more fidelity the beauties of the creation, nor sung with nobler song the greatness of the Creator. He is the translator of the silent language of the universe to the world."

JAMES MURRAY MASON, an American lawyer and politician, born in Fairfax Co., Va., Nov. 3, 1798. Died near Alexandria, Va., April 28, 1871. He was the author of the " Fugitive Slave Law," and as a member of the Confederate Congress, was sent as commissioner with John Slidell to England and France, in the Autumn of 1861. He, with Slidell, was taken from the British steamer Nov. 8, 1861, and confined in Fort Warren near Boston, but they were released on the demand of the British government.

DANIEL G. CROLY, an American journalist and author, born in New York, Nov. 3, 1829.

He has been employed on the " Evening Post," " New York Herald," editor of the " Rockford Daily News," city editor of the " New York World," and managing editor of " The Graphic." He is husband of " Jennie June," also an eminent journalist.

Isabella Alden, " Pansy," an American author, born in New York, Nov. 3, 1841.

She is author of a popular juvenile series called " Pansy Books," embracing nearly sixty titles, most of which are adapted to the use of Sunday school libraries. Mrs. Alden has from the beginning been identified with the Chautauqua system of instruction, and also edits " Pansy," a juvenile publication.

November 4.

Edward V., of England, of the York branch of the Plantagenets, born at Westminster Abbey, Nov. 4, 1470. He was the elder of the two princes who were put to death in the tower of London, by order of their uncle, the Duke of Gloucester, the young king's regent, who then usurped the throne under the title of Richard III.

James Montgomery, a distinguished British poet, born in Ayrshire, Scotland, Nov. 4, 1771. Died near Sheffield, April 30, 1854. His poems are distinguished for depth and tenderness of feeling, elevated moral sentiment, and graceful description.

Samuel Ireneus Prime, an American divine, editor and author, born at Ballston, N. Y., Nov. 4, 1812. Died 1885. He was for a time editor of the " New York Observer," and published several works; was also an interested worker in the temperance cause.

November 5.

Hans Sachs, a popular German poet, born in Nuremberg, Nov. 5, 1494. Died Jan., 1576. He produced, it is said, 6,000 poems of all kinds, but only one-fourth are in print,

WASHINGTON ALLSTON, one of the most eminent of American artists, born at Waccamaw, S. C., Nov. 5, 1779. Died in Cambridge, Mass., July 9, 1843. He was the foremost of American painters in his delineations of sacred history. "Jacob's Dream," "Elijah in the Desert," and "Belshazzar's Feast," the latter on which he was at work when he died, are among his sacred historical paintings. He also possessed poetic talent of a high order. Said Washington Irving: "The memory of Allston I hold in reverence and affection, as one of the purest, noblest, and most intellectual beings that ever honored me with his friendship."

SIR JOHN RICHARDSON, a British naturalist, Arctic explorer and author, born in Dumfries, Scotland, Nov. 5, 1787. Died near Grasmere, June 5, 1865. He assisted Sir John Franklin in two of his Arctic expeditions, 1819, 1825, and in 1848 conducted an expedition to search for the lost explorers. Was author of "Zoology of the Northern Parts of British America," and a "Boat-Voyage to the Arctic Sea."

BENJAMIN F. BUTLER, an American politician and general, born at Deerfield, N. H., Nov. 5, 1818.

He was an efficient general during the civil war, and his decisive measures in New Orleans, in the summer of 1862, restored the city to order, and preserved it from its annual pest, the yellow fever. While in charge of Fortress Monroe, three slaves coming there for protection, Butler applied to them the famous phrase, "contraband of war," "an epigram," said Theodore Winthrop, "which abolished slavery in the United States." Since the war he has been U. S. Senator and Governor of Massachusetts.

November 6.

James Gregory, a celebrated Scottish geometer, astronomer and mathematician, born in Aberdeen, Nov. 6, 1638. Died in Edinburgh, Oct., 1675. He was the most eminent of a family which, during several successive generations, has been distinguished for profound attainments in the sciences. Sixteen of the family have held professorships in British colleges and schools. One of the most important of his inventions is the concave burning mirror.

Sarah Moore Grimke, a noted lecturer on anti-slavery and the equality of the sexes, born in Charleston, S. C., Nov. 6, 1792. Died at Hyde Park, Mass., Dec. 23, 1873.

Cornelius C. Felton, a distinguished American scholar and author, born at West Newbury, Mass., Nov. 6, 1807. Died in 1862. Being a professor of Greek literature in Harvard College, he is mostly noted for his translations of the classics, many of which have passed through several editions and have been reprinted in England.

November 7.

Platt R. Spencer, the originator of the Spencerian method of penmanship, born in East Fishkill, N. Y., Nov. 7, 1800. Died May 16, 1864. Mr. Spencer, who had given penmanship much attention from early youth, was led to perfect his semi-angular system, by seeing the necessity of a more rapid execution than the old round Roman method, and a more legible hand than the angular or German system.

Robert Dale Owen, a distinguished political and miscellaneous writer, born at New Lanark, Scotland,

Nov. 7, 1801. Died June 24, 1877. Among his many works are "Footfalls on the Boundaries of another World" and "Beyond the Breakers." He introduced the bill into Congress organizing the Smithsonian Institute, and was chairman of its building committee.

November 8.

EDWARD POCOCK, an eminent English divine and Orientalist, born at Oxford, Nov. 8, 1604. Died there Sept. 10, 1691. He is said to have been the best Arabic scholar of his time, and in 1636 became the first professor of Arabic in Oxford.

WILLIAM WIRT, an eloquent American lawyer and author, born at Bladensburg, Md., Nov. 8, 1772. Died in Washington, D. C., Feb. 18, 1834. He distinguished himself at the trial of Aaron Burr, as one of the counsel for the prosecution. He was attorney-general of the United States from 1817 to March, 1829. As an author, his "Letters of a British Spy" and "Life of Patrick Henry" attained great popularity.

November 9.

MARK AKENSIDE, an English physician and poet, born at Newcastle-on-Tyne, Nov. 9, 1721. Died in London, June 23, 1770. His principal poem, "The Pleasures of the Imagination," written in blank verse, appeared in 1744, and had great success. Addison's essays on the "Pleasures of the Imagination" formed the groundwork of this poem.

DR. HARRIET K. HUNT, the first woman physician in America, born in Boston, Nov. 9, 1805. Died there Jan. 2, 1875. She acquired quite a fortune in her profession, and every year, when she paid her taxes, she filed her protest against "taxation without representation." This she followed for twenty-five years.

John A. Winslow, an American naval officer, born in Wilmington, N. C., Nov. 9, 1811. Died in Boston, Sept. 29, 1873. He was commander of the "Kearsarge," which on June 19, 1864, encountered and sunk the confederate cruiser "Alabama," off the coast of France.

Albert Edward, Prince of Wales, eldest son of Queen Victoria, and heir-apparent to the British throne, born in Buckingham Palace, London, Nov. 9, 1841.

November 10.

Martin Luther, the great leader of the Reformation in Germany, born at Eisleben, now in Prussian Saxony, Nov. 10, 1483. Died there Feb. 18, 1546. He entered an Augustine convent in 1505, but in 1517, began to protest by his celebrated ninety-five propositions, against the pernicious doctrine of the sale of indulgences, which terminated, as all the world knows, in the separation of Luther from the Catholic church, and the inauguration of the Reformation. His noted trial at the "Diet of Worms," through which he came out unscathed, commenced April 17, 1521. Beside his renowned work as reformer, he stands in the front rank as German author. His translation of the Bible into German is his greatest work, but his "Table Talk," a collection of anecdotes, letters and conversations, published by his friends after his death, is the most interesting of his works.

Robert Devereux, second Earl of Essex, born at Netherwood, Nov. 10, 1567. Was convicted of treason and executed in 1601. He was at one time a special favorite of Queen Elizabeth, to whom she gave a ring, with injunctions to send it to her should his life ever be in danger ; and when finding that her displeasure was proving fatal, he sent the ring, but the treacherous messenger failed to present it, and she signed the death warrant. But learning too late the state of affairs, she became inconsolable at his loss, and never recovered from the shock.

OLIVER GOLDSMITH, an eminent British author and poet, born at Pallas, Longford Co., Ireland, Nov. 10, 1728. Died in London, April 4, 1774. Of his many works, "She Stoops to Conquer," a comedy, "The Deserted Village," a poem, and the "Vicar of Wakefield," are perhaps the best known. The last named work was written while under arrest for debt, from which he was released by Dr. Johnson, who obtained from a bookseller £60 for the work. Dr. Primrose is said to portray "the most amiable, humane and pious soul in English literature."

GRANVILLE SHARP, an English philanthropist, distinguished by his earnest opposition to negro slavery, born in Durham, Eng., Nov. 10, 1734. Died in London, July 6, 1813. He was one of the originators of the "Association for the Abolition of Negro Slavery," and took a prominent part in founding the colony of Sierra Leone, in Africa.

JOHANN CHRISTOPH FRIEDRICH VON SCHILLER, the great national poet of Germany, born at Marbach, Nov. 10, 1759. Died in Weimar, May 9, 1805. Among his minor poems, "The Song of the Bell" may claim the first place. Nothing more admirable in its way has ever been written, and had the author composed but this single poem, it would have secured him a lasting fame. His "History of the Thirty Years' War" was pronounced by Carlyle to be the best historical performance of which Germany could boast. "Wallenstein," his greatest work, is regarded by many as the finest tragedy in the German language.

DR. SAMUEL G. HOWE, an eminent American philanthropist, born in Boston, Nov. 10, 1801. Died Jan. 9, 1876. He visited Europe, in 1831, to obtain information in regard to educating the blind, and on his return to Boston opened the "Perkins Institute for the Blind." His success in the case of Laura Bridgeman, a deaf, blind mute, whom he taught to read, write and instruct in religion, has immortalized his name. His noted wife, Julia Ward Howe, was his assistant in his philanthropic labor.

JAMES BROOKS, an American journalist and politician, born in Portland, Me., Nov. 10, 1810. Died in Washington, D. C., April 30, 1873. He, with his brother Erastus, founded "The New York Express" in 1836.

CINCINNATUS HEINE MILLER, "Joaquin Miller," an American author, born in the Wabash district, Ind., Nov. 10, 1841.

He was one of the main newspaper correspondents of the New Orleans Exposition, and is author of several successful volumes.

November 11.

BERNARDO TASSO, an Italian poet, born at Bergamo, Nov. 11, 1493. Died in Ostiglia, Sept., 1569. He composed numerous sonnets, hymns, eclogues and lyrics, but was eclipsed by his son, the celebrated Torquato Tasso.

WILLIAM EDWARDS, an American inventor, born Nov. 11, 1770. Died in Brooklyn, N. Y., Dec. 1, 1851. To Edwards belongs the honor of the success in the

United States of the manufacture of leather, both by his method and the improved machinery. His first tannery was built at Northampton, Mass. He was grandson of the Rev. Jonathan Edwards.

MARIE FRANCOIS XAVIER BICHAT, a French physiologist and anatomist of great eminence, born at Thoiretta, in Jura, Nov. 11, 1771. Died prematurely of overwork, July, 1802. He was the first who reduced the organs of the body to their elementary tissues, and explained the chemical, physical and vital properties of each primitive tissue. He also ascertained so many other important facts in physiology, that it was said of him, that " No one has done so much and so well in so short a time."

THOMAS BAILEY ALDRICH, an American poet, novelist and journalist, born in Portsmouth, N. H., Nov. 11, 1836.

He entered the literary world through his connection as assistant editor with Willis and Morris, of the " Home Journal." Although he composed one of his best poems when only eighteen, " Baby Bell," at once marked its author as one of rare skill. " Peck's Bad Boy " is largely autobiographical, and, though extremely popular, it carries the anathema of many an anxious parent.

November 12.

RICHARD BAXTER, an English non-conformist divine and theological writer, born at Rowdon, Shropshire, Eng., Nov. 12, 1615. Died Dec. 8, 1691. "Saints' Everlasting Rest" and " Call to the Unconverted," his best known works, are generally and justly admired. Of the latter, about twenty thousand copies were sold in one year. He was the founder of a new school of theology which bears his name. "Baxter's life of himself," says Coleridge, "is an inestimable work ; there is no substitute for it, in a course of study for a clergyman or a public man." Doddridge styles Baxter the "English Demosthenes."

JACQUES ALEXANDRE CÆSAR CHARLES, a French physicist and chemist, born at Beaugency, Nov. 12, 1746 Died at Paris, April 7, 1823. He is noted for his experiments in electricity and ballooning, and made great improvements in the balloon which Montgolfier invented, by substituting hydrogen gas for heated air. He and M. Robert were the first persons who ventured to ascend in a balloon, Aug. 2, 1783.

AMELIA OPIE, a popular English writer, born at Norwich, Eng., Nov. 12, 1769. Died in 1853. Among her many works is "Illustrations of Lying," by which she will long be remembered, and which should be placed in the library of every young person in the formative period of their character.

REV. DR. RAY PALMER, an American author and poet, born at Little Compton, R. I., Nov. 12, 1808. Died March 29, 1887. He was a poet from early youth and author of many sacred lyrics. His best known hymn, "My faith looks up to Thee," was written when he was but twenty-two. Dr. Lowell Mason, who arranged the music, foretold its popularity at the time in these prophetic words : "Mr. Palmer," said he earnestly, "you many live many years, and do many things, but you will always be best known as the writer of this hymn."

ELIZABETH CADY STANTON, an eminent American

lecturer and advocate of woman's rights, born at Johnstown, N. Y., Nov. 12, 1815.

The first woman's rights convention met at her place of residence, July 19–20, 1848.

November 13.

St. Augustine, the greatest of the Latin fathers, born at Tagaste, Numidia, Nov. 13, 354. Died Aug. 28, 430. He was baptized into the Christian faith, April 25, 387. His "Confessions," written in 397, consisted of thirteen books, and is a deep, earnest and sacred autobiography of one of the greatest intellects the world has ever known.

Valentine Harvy, a French philanthropist, born at St. Just, Nov. 13, 1745. Died at Paris, June 3, 1822. He invented the art of printing with raised letters for the blind, and is universally recognized as "the apostle of the blind."

Sir John Moore, a British general, born in Glasgow, Nov. 13, 1761. Fell in battle at Corunna, in Spain, Jan. 16, 1809. The memory of his death is well preserved in "The Burial of Sir John Moore," written by Charles Wolfe, which Byron pronounced "the most perfect ode in the English language."

Joseph Hooker, an American soldier and Union general in the civil war, born at Hadley, Mass., Nov. 13, 1815. Died 1879. He succeeded Burnside as commander of the army of the Potomac, in Jan., 1863, and for his bravery was called "Fighting Joe Hooker," an epithet he was never well pleased with.

Robert Louis Stevenson, a popular British author, born at Edinburgh, Scotland, Nov. 13, 1850.

He is the son of the distinguished engineer, Thomas

Stevenson, who has been called "the Nestor of light-house illumination." His grandfather, Robert Stevenson, constructed the famous Bell Rock light-house, and invented the "intermittent" and "flashing" lights. Robert's father intended that he should follow the family calling, but he took no interest in engineering and cared only for literature. Though an author of but few years' publicity, he has produced twenty volumes.

November 14.

ALEXEL PETROVITCH SUMAROKOFF, a Russian dramatist, born at Moscow, Nov. 14, 1727. Died there Oct. 1777. He was founder of the first national theater at St. Petersburg.

JOHN CASPAR LAVATER, a celebrated Protestant minister and writer on physiognomy, born at Zurich, Switzerland, Nov. 14, 1741. He was author of many noted theological works, but signalized himself by his celebrated "Physiognomic Fragments," the result of multiplied and curious observations. He was shot by a soldier, Sept., 1799, in the streets of Zurich, at the capture of that city by the French, and died of the wound in 1801, more than a year afterward.

SIR CHARLES LYELL, F.R.S., an eminent British geologist, born at Kinnordy, in Forfarshire, Scotland, Nov. 14, 1797. Died in London, Feb. 22, 1875. His "Principles of Geology" has become a standard work on the subject.

REV. JACOB ABBOTT, a popular American author, born at Hallowell, Maine, Nov. 14, 1803. Died Dec., 1879. Few writers have given to the public a greater number of volumes. He has addressed himself principally to the young, with whom his works have been exceedingly popular. Nearly all of his books have been republished in England, and many have been translated into the various European and Asiatic languages. The twenty-eight volumes of "Rollo Books" are perhaps his best known.

ANSON BURLINGAME, an American statesman and diplomatist, born in New Berlin, Chenango Co., N. Y., Nov. 14, 1822. Died at St. Petersburg, Russia, Feb. 23, 1870. In 1861 he was sent as minister to China, and in 1867 was appointed ambassador from China to the United States and the great powers of Europe.

WILLIAM A. WHEELER, M.A., American editor and author, born at Leicester, Mass., Nov. 14, 1833. Died Oct. 28, 1875. He assisted Dr. Worcester in the preparation of his quarto Dictionary, and in 1861 was employed by Messrs. G. & C. Merriam as one of the editors of the new edition of Webster's quarto Dictionary. He is author of valuable books of reference, such as "Dictionary of the noted names of Fiction," "Who Wrote It," etc., which idea was original with him.

November 15.

WILLIAM PITT, first Earl of Chatham, "the great commoner," an illustrious English statesman and orator, born at Boconnoc, in Cornwall, Nov. 15, 1708. He was seized with an apoplectic fit, as he rose to speak in the House of Lords, and died May, 1778. He commenced his public life as an opponent of the Walpole ministry, and addressed the House for the first time in April, 1736, and from this time until his death, his life was interwoven with his country's history, and he was almost idolized by the people, who regarded him as the foremost Englishman of his time. He was a great friend of the American colonies, and condemned with all his eloquence, every measure of the British ministry which oppressed them.

FREDERIC WILLIAM AUGUSTUS STEUBEN, a distinguished Prussian general, born in Magdeburg, Prussia, Nov. 15, 1730. Died near Utica, N. Y., Nov. 28, 1794. He volunteered to assist the Americans in the war of the Revolution, and received the township of Steuben, near Utica, N. Y., in acknowledgment of his services.

SIR WILLIAM HERSCHEL, the eminent English astronomer and astronomical discoverer, born in Hanover, Nov. 15, 1738. Died at Slough, near Windsor, Aug. 23, 1822. He commenced his life as a musician, and when about thirty years of age directed his talents to the study which has given him his renown. The price of telescopes at that time exceeding his resources, after many attempts he constructed one of his own, and encouraged by this success, continued his exertions until he obtained one of twenty feet focal length, through which he discovered a new primary planet, March, 1781, which in honor of the king he named Georgium Sidus. It has sometimes been called by his name, but late astronomers have named it Uranus. Continuing his observations, and increasing the size of his telescopes until he produced his gigantic instrument of forty feet, he discovered two new satellites of Saturn and six of Uranus. In 1803 he ascertained the motion of the double stars around each other, thus attesting the universal influence of that attractive force which binds the members of the solar system. His discoveries had so little resemblance to those of his predecessors, that he may be said to have ushered in a new era in astronomy.

RICHARD HENRY DANA, an American poet and essayist, born in Cambridge, Mass., Nov. 15, 1787. Died Feb. 2, 1879. He was associate editor of the "North American Review," also author of many poems, chief among which is "The Dying Raven" and "The Buccaneer," the last of which was considered at the time by far the most powerful and original of American poetical compositions.

Eliza Leslie, an American authoress, born in Philadelphia, Nov. 15, 1787. Died in Gloucester, N. J., Jan. 2, 1857. She produced numerous tales and sketches referring to home life and manners, which acquired extensive popularity.

Thurlow Weed, an eminent American journalist and politician, born at Cairo, Greene Co., N. Y., Nov. 15, 1797. Died Nov. 22, 1882. His first effort in journalism, the great work of his life, was to establish a paper called the "Agriculturist," after which he edited various newspapers, until in 1830 he became editor of the "Albany Evening Journal," which position he occupied until 1865, and acquired great distinction and influence as a party manager for the Whigs and Republicans. Being the father of so many newspapers he is sometimes called "The Priam of the Press."

November 16.

Tiberius, the third Cæsar, Emperor of Rome, born 42 b.c. Died 37 a.d. He became Emperor in 14 a.d., and was the Cæsar to whom the Jews paid tribute during Jesus' ministration as related in the Gospels.

Jean D'Alembert, an eminent French geometer and philosopher, born in Paris, Nov. 16, 1717. Died there Oct. 29, 1783. His celebrated "Treatise on Dynamics" initiated a revolution in physico-mathematical sciences, and made him one of the most popular men of Europe. He was offered positions by "Frederic the Great" of Prussia, and Catherine II. of Russia, both of which he declined. He associated with Diderot, as joint editor of the famous "Encyclopedia."

ROBERT B. MINTURN, an American shipping merchant and philanthropist, born in New York, Nov. 16, 1805. Died Jan. 9, 1866. By his energy and ability, the shipping house of "Grinnell, Minturn & Co.," in which he achieved fortune and reputation, became one of the great shipping houses of the world.

JOHN BRIGHT, a celebrated English orator and radical statesman, born at Greenbank, near Rochdale, Lancashire, Nov. 16, 1811.

He is a member of the Society of Friends, which with his intimacy with Richard Cobden, made him a strong advocate of the "Anti-Corn-Law League." As a consistent friend of liberty and equal rights, he testified his sympathy with the American Republicans during the civil war by several eloquent speeches. He is not identified with either of the great political parties, but is an advocate of reform in the elections, and non-intervention in.foreign wars. In 1868 he became President of the Board of Trade, being the first Quaker who had ever had a seat in the British Cabinet, and his eloquent speech on Ireland, in March of that year, did more to draw the noblest men of all parties together than long years of discussion had effected before.

MANTON MARBLE, an American editor and journalist, born at Worcester, Mass., Nov. 16, 1835.

He was one of the founders of the "New York World."

November 17.

JULIAN, "the Apostate," Roman Emperor, 361–363, born at Constantinople, Nov. 17, 331 A.D., was mortally wounded in battle, and died June 26, 363. He was educated as a Christian, yet after being crowned emperor, avowed himself a pagan, hence his name. He did not persecute the Christians but tolerated all sects; at the same time he favored paganism by his edicts, and closed the Christian schools.

FRIEDRICH CHRISTOPH SCHLOSSER, a celebrated German historian, born at Jever, Nov. 17, 1776. Died in Heidelberg, Sept. 23, 1861. He occupied a high rank as historian, and has acquired extensive popularity.

SIR SAMUEL CUNARD, head of the extensive firm of steamship owners, Cunard & Co., born in Halifax, Nova Scotia, Nov. 17, 1787. Died April 28, 1865.

GEORGE GROTE, an English politician and historian, born at Clay Hill, Beckenham, Kent, Nov. 17, 1794. Died in London, June 18, 1871. His great work, "The History of Greece" in twelve volumes, is pronounced "the most important contribution to historical literature in modern times," and is considered the best history of that country ever written.

ELIZA FARNHAM, an American authoress and philanthropist, born in Rensselaerville, N. Y., Nov. 17, 1815. Died Dec. 15, 1864. She was for four years matron of the female department of the State prison at Sing Sing, and was highly successful in her efforts to govern by kindness. She was also author of many popular volumes.

November 18.

WILLIAM TULLY, an American physician, born at Saybrook, Conn., Nov. 18, 1785. Died in Springfield,

Mass., Feb. 28, 1859. He was a professor in the medical department at Yale College, and an author of medical works.

Sir David Wilkie, an eminent Scottish painter, born in Fifeshire, Nov. 18, 1785. Died at sea near Gibraltar, June 1, 1841. "Distraining for Rent," "The Sheep Washing," "The Reading of the Will," "Sir Walter Scott and his Family," and "Chelsea Pensioners listening to the News of Waterloo," are among his familiar pieces.

Asa Gray, an eminent American botanist, born at Paris, Oneida Co., N. Y., Nov. 18, 1810. Died Jan. 30, 1888. He was appointed, in 1842, professor of natural history in Harvard College, and was at the time of his death one of the faculty at the Smithsonian Institute, at Washington, D. C. He has received a just meed of praise from foreign botanists, and stood at the head of the science in our own country. Yet with all his many duties of high order, he still found time to write two works for the young, and the best of their kind.

Franz Siegel, a general, born in Baden, Germany, Nov. 18, 1824.

He emigrated to the United States in 1850 and enlisted as colonel in the civil war, and was prominent in several engagements.

November 19.

Albert Bertel Thorwaldsen, one of the most eminent of modern sculptors, born Nov. 19, 1770, on the sea between Denmark and Iceland. Died in Copenhagen, March 24, 1844. Among his noted works are "The Triumphal March of Alexander," executed for the emperor Napoleon, "Christ and the twelve Apostles," and statues of Schiller, Galileo, and Copernicus. But the most remarkable of his productions is the image of a wounded and dying lion of colossal size, near Lucerne, Switzerland, designed to commemorate the heroic fidelity of the Swiss guards who fell Aug. 10, 1792.

FERDINAND DE LESSEPS, a French diplomatist and celebrated engineer, born in Versailles, Nov. 19, 1805. As a diplomatist he was in early life an attache to the consulate at Lisbon, Tunis, Alexandria and Barcelona. During the last days of Louis Phillipe, he was French minister to Madrid, and afterward sent to Rome to negotiate a peace between the French soldiers and the republicans there. But his greatest fame rests on his wonderful achievement as an engineer in building the Suez canal. He first opened the project in 1853, but so many delays occurred in obtaining commissions from the different governments, that the work was not commenced until 1859. Steamboats were floated on it in August, 1865, and by March, 1867, schooners and small ships could pass into it. August 15, 1869, the waters of the Mediterranean mingled with those of the Red Sea, and on Nov. 19, the canal was formally opened at Port Said. The canal is about one hundred miles long, and cost $60,000,000. De Lesseps of late years has turned his attention to other equally gigantic schemes, a central Asian railroad, the Panama railroad, and the flooding of the Sahara Desert.

JAMES A. GARFIELD, an American statesman and general, twentieth President of the United States, born in Cuyahoga Co., Ohio, Nov. 19, 1831. Died at Long Branch, N. J., Sept. 19, 1881, from a shot wound given him by Charles A. Guiteau, July 2, of the same year. He was promoted to Major-General during the civil war, and being elected to Congress, proved himself a wise and prudent legislator, and was soon recognized as the leader of his party in the House. In 1880 he was chosen Senator from Ohio, but before he could take his place, was nominated for the presidency. He was inaugurated March 4, 1881, but his anticipated administration was cut short by the assassin's hand.

November 20.

PHILIP SCHUYLER, an able American general and senator, born in Albany, N. Y., Nov. 20, 1733. Died there Nov. 18, 1804. He served in the French and Indian war, in 1756, and in the Revolution took command of an army in New York, but was superseded by Gates, in 1777, in consequence of unreasonable jealousy ; yet he still rendered important service in military affairs. He was a member of the General Congress from 1778–1781, and in 1789 was elected a Senator of the United States from New York.

THOMAS CHATTERTON, an English poet, celebrated for his genius, precocity and literature impostures, born in Bristol, Nov. 20, 1752. Died by poison, Aug. 24, 1770. He was very fond of antiquarian literature, and wrote poems which he professed to derive from ancient manuscripts, and which deceived even the most learned men. No English poet ever equaled him at the same age.

November 21.

BRYAN WALLER PROCTOR, " Barry Cornwall," an English poet, born in London, Nov. 21, 1790. Died there Oct. 5, 1874. He acquired distinction by a volume entitled " Dramatic Scenes and other Poems."

Among his other works are " The Flood of Thessaly," " Essays and Tales in Prose." His songs have obtained much popularity. He is the father of Adelaide A. Proctor.

WALTER WILLIAM SKEAT, an eminent English philologist and author, born in London, Nov. 21, 1835.

He is a member of the " Early English Text Societies," and editor of corrected editions of English classics.

November 22.

OTHO, " the Great," a German emperor, born Nov. 22, 912. Died at Memleben, Thuringia, May 7, 973. He was crowned emperor at Rome by Pope John XII. in 962, and assumed the title of Cæsar. Some historians think he deserves more than Charlemagne, the name of " Great," because his reign had a much more salutary influence on the nations whom he subjected.

DUGALD STEWART, an eminent Scottish professor of moral philosophy, born in Edinburgh, Nov. 22, 1753. Died there June, 1828. He was the author of many works, among which is his noted " Elements of the Philosophy of the Human Mind," which enjoyed a great popularity. As a professor of moral philosophy in the University of Edinburgh, he promoted the opinions of liberality in politics, by his influence over such men as Lord Brougham, Lord Jeffrey and Lord John Russell, who were his pupils.

ANDREAS HOFER, a celebrated Tyrolese patriot, born at St. Leonard, in the Passeyr valley, Tyrol, Nov. 22, 1767. The Tyrolese, assisted by the Austrians, rose against the French and Bavarian government to whom Tyrol was subject; and after many triumphs, was at last defeated. He took refuge in the mountains, but was betrayed by a former friend, and shot by order of Napoleon, Feb. 20, 1810.

LIONEL NATHAN ROTHSCHILD, grandson of the founder of that celebrated family of bankers, born Nov. 22, 1808.

He was repeatedly elected to Parliament, but could not take his seat until 1858, when the "act for removing the disabilities of the Jews" was passed, he being the first Jew admitted to Parliament.

MARIAN EVANS LEWES CROSSE, "George Eliot," a celebrated English novelist, born in Warwickshire, Nov. 22, 1820. Died Dec. 22, 1880. She had acquired a reputation in the literary circles of London, before she became known as the author of the remarkable series of fiction with which her name is popularly associated. "Adam Bede," the first of this series, appeared in 1858; the next year followed "The Mill on the Floss," "Romola" in 1863, "Middlemarch" in 1872, and "Daniel Deronda" later. It is said that she read one thousand books in preparing to write the last named volume, and the work of preparing "Romola" was equally immense.

November 23.

ST. CLEMENT, a bishop of Rome, born Nov. 23, 67 A.D. He is the patron saint of hatmakers, from the supposition that he discovered the art of making felt by putting wool between his feet and sandals, when on a pilgrimage, and it matted into felt. The 23d of November is observed as his day.

EDWARD RUTLEDGE, an American jurist and patriot, born at Charleston, S. C., Nov. 23, 1749. Died there Jan. 23, 1800. He was a member of the first Continental Congress, a "signer" of the Declaration of Independence, and one of the committee to draft General Washington's commission. He was a U. S. Senator, and Governor of South Carolina.

FRANKLIN PIERCE, fourteenth President of the United States, born in Hillsborough, N. II., Nov. 23, 1804. Died in Concord, N. II., Oct. 8, 1869. Among the important events of his administration were the repeal of the "Missouri Compromise" and "Kansas-Nebraska" Bill. Every measure of his administration favored slavery.

November 24.

BENEDICT SPINOZA, a celebrated Dutch pantheistical philosopher, born in Amsterdam, Nov. 24, 1632. Died at the Hague, Feb. 21, 1677. His parents were Portuguese Jews, but he early announced heretical opinions, for which he was excommunicated from the Jewish church, and narrowly escaped with his life. The anathemas under which he lived, rested upon him for more than a century after his death. But when biographers, studying into his quiet, sequestered, frugal life, found that he was a calm, reflective, diligent scholar, a good citizen, a sympathizing neighbor, and a peaceable domestic man, a reaction followed and he became a favorite with the leading minds of Germany. "They seemed to have forgotten," said Goethe, in speaking of his accusers, "the words of the gospel 'By their fruits ye shall know them.'" His main writings were on ethics and geometry.

LAURENCE STERNE, a celebrated English author and humorist, born in Clonmel, Ireland, Nov. 24, 1713. Died in London, March 18, 1768. His noted works, "Tristram Shandy" and a "Sentimental Journey," made him popular as an author; but we forget that his levity and dissipation as a preacher often stigmatize him, when we remember him as the author of "Go tempers the wind to the shorn lamb."

GRACE DARLING, an English heroine, born at Bamborough, on the coast of Northumberland, Nov. 24, 1815 Died Oct. 20, 1842. She was the daughter of the light-house keeper of Longstone, on one of the Farne Islands, and won her fame by rescuing, at the imminent peril of her life, nine persons who were clinging to a rock, Sept. 6, 1838.

November 25.

FELIX LOPE DE VEGA, a celebrated Spanish poet and dramatist, born in Madrid, Nov. 25, 1562. Died there Aug. 26, 1635. He possessed in a remarkable degree such a fertile and rapid invention, that it required only a single day to compose a versified drama ; and this astonishing faculty enabled him to produce nearly two thousand original plays, which were performed with such immense applause that his name became a synonym for the superlative degree. He was called the "Center of Fame," the "Darling of Fortune," the "Phœnix of Ages."

HENRY SARGENT, an eminent American artist, born at Gloucester, Mass., Nov. 25, 1770. Died Feb. 21, 1845. He is widely known through his engraving, "The Landing of the Pilgrims."

HENRY MAYHEW, a distinguished English scholar, author and journalist, born in London, Nov. 25, 1812. Died 1876. He was one of the founders of the periodical entitled "Figaro in London," and the first editor of "Punch." Among his many works are "What to Teach, and How to Teach it," "London Labor," "London Poor," and "The Wonders of Science."

November 26.

Oliver Wolcott, an American patriot and statesman born in Windsor, Conn., Nov. 26, 1726. Died in Litchfield, Dec. 1, 1797. He was a member of Congress in 1776, signed the "Declaration of Independence," and in 1796 became Governor of Connecticut.

William Cowper, one of the most eminent and popular of English poets, born in Hertfordshire, Eng., Nov. 26, 1731. Died April 25, 1800. Though, as expressed by himself, "he was encompassed by the midnight of absolute despair, when he commenced as an author," his are some of the most brilliant pages in the great tome of English literature, and no English poet, except Shakespeare, is more frequently quoted. "His familiar letters sparkling with playful humor, the most genial ever written, are the finest specimen of the epistolary style in our language." Of his short poems, "John Gilpin" and "Lines on his Mother's Portrait" are world-renowned. His "Task" was the most popular poem of its length in the language, and his version of Homer, considered with respect to fidelity to the original, is perhaps the best in the language.

Octavius Brooks Frothingham, a Unitarian divine and eloquent rationalistic theologian, born in Boston, Mass., Nov. 26, 1822.

November 27.

Robert R. Livingston, an American statesman and jurist, born in the city of New York, Nov. 27, 1746. Died Feb. 26, 1813. As a member of the Congress of 1776, he was appointed one of the committee to draw up the "Declaration of Independence." He was chancellor of the State of New York, secretary of foreign affairs, and in 1801 was sent as minister to France, where he assisted in the negotiation for the purchase of Louisiana ; he afterward aided Fulton in the introduction of steam navigation. He was a descendant of Robert Livingston, the first possessor of the Livingstone Manor, New York.

HENRY WHEATON, an American jurist, civilian and diplomatist, born in Providence, R. I., Nov. 27, 1785. Died in Dorchester, Mass., March 11, 1848. He was editor of the " National Advocate," and as an author, his " Elements of International Law " is his most important work, and is esteemed as a standard authority.

FRANCES ANNA KEMBLE, Mrs. Butler, best known as Fanny Kemble, a popular English actress and writer, born in London, Nov. 27, 1811.

She has performed both tragedy and comedy with equal success, and is author of several works.

November 28.

WILLIAM BLAKE, a singular gifted English artist and poet, born in London, Nov. 28, 1757. Died there Aug. 12, 1827. His "Songs of Innocence and Experience," published in 1789, contained etched illustrations of great beauty. Subsequently he illustrated Young's " Night Thoughts," Hayley's " Life of Cowper," and Blair's "Grave." His entire devotion to his art compensated him for the privations to which his poverty subjected him.

ALPHONSO FRANCISCO, known as Alphonso XII. of Spain, born Nov. 28, 1857. He was crowned in 1875, and died Nov. 25, 1885.

November 29.

SIR PHILIP SIDNEY, an English statesman, soldier and author, born at Penshurst, in Kent, Nov. 29, 1554.

In the literary world he was called " the father of poetic prose," and as a statesman was considered "one of the ripest and greatest councillors of State in that day." He was mortally wounded on the field of Zutphen, and died Oct. 7, 1586. His self-forgetful expression, "Thy necessity is greater than mine," as he passed the water proffered him to a dying soldier, as they both lay on the field at Zutphen, has more than anything else immortalized his name.

CHARLES THOMSON, LL.D., an American patriot, born in Ireland, Nov. 29, 1729. Died near Philadelphia, Aug. 16, 1824. He was secretary of the first Continental Congress, from 1774–1789, and was the one chosen to inform Washington of his election.

AMOS BRONSON ALCOTT, an American philosopher and educator, born at Wolcott, Conn., Nov. 29, 1799. Died March 4, 1888. In early life he gave his attention to reforms in theology, education, diet and social institutions, and came to be known as one of the leading transcendentalists. He, with two English friends, endeavored to found a new community at Harvard, Mass., which scheme failed. He was noted as a brilliant conversationalist, by which method he usually lectured, and his personal worth and originality of thought always secured him a respectful hearing. He was the father of Louisa May Alcott.

WENDELL PHILLIPS, an American reformer and eminent anti-slavery orator, born in Boston, Nov. 29, 1811. Died 1884. In 1836 he joined the abolitionists, and in 1837 addressed a vast assembly at Faneuil Hall, many of whom were strong for slavery, with an indignation and eloquence which Dr. Channing often alluded to as " morally sublime." Believing that the constitution of the

United States was a compact between freedom and slavery, he relinquished the practice of law, because he was unwilling to act under an oath to it, and for the same reason refused to recognize its authority by voting. He succeeded Mr. Garrison as President of the American Anti-slavery Society until it was dissolved, April 9, 1870.

LOUISA MAY ALCOTT, sometimes styled "the most successful woman author of America," born in Germantown, Pa., Nov. 29, 1833. Died March 6, 1888. She lent her assistance as a nurse during the civil war, which was the origin of her "Hospital Sketches." "Little Women," her most popular book, was written by an earnest request for a "book for girls." In it is woven many an instance of her own life. "Little Men," "Under the Lilacs," "The Eight Cousins," "Rose in Bloom," and numerous others, will long live a delight to the young, as well as to those whose interest it is to watch the progress of life's unfoldment.

November 30.

JONATHAN SWIFT, known as "Dean Swift," a celebrated humorist and satirist, born in Dublin, Ireland, Nov. 30, 1667. Died there Oct. 19, 1745. In 1704 he produced his "Tale of a Tub," in which he exposed religious abuses, especially those of the Romish church; and shortly after the "Battle of the Books" appeared, a satire in allusion to a controversy of that day, regarding the respective merits of ancient and modern learning. "His "Gulliver's Travels," a series of satires on human nature and society, is the most original and extraordinary of all his productions, and by which he will be known while language lasts.

THEODORE MOMMSEN, a German jurist and historian, born at Garding, in Schleswig-Holstein, Nov. 30, 1817.

His "Roman History" is regarded as one of the authorities on that subject. He is an associate of the French Institute, and a member of other foreign academies.

Cyrus West Field, an American merchant and capitalist, distinguished as the projector of the Atlantic cable, born at Stockbridge, Mass., Nov. 30, 1819.

He organized his first "Atlantic Telegraph Company" in 1856, and in 1857 and 1858, after repeated trials and failures, was successful, and a message was sent from the Queen and a reply transmitted from the President. The event was celebrated Sept. 1, 1858, but on that· day it ceased to work. Undismayed, he revived the company, and in 1865, the Great Eastern started with another cable, to again meet failure; it parted in mid-ocean. A new company was now formed, a third cable made, and again the Great Eastern sailed, in June, 1866, with its 1,866 miles of wire cable, and this time was successful. It is said that if the single wire of which the cable is made, was in one extended line, it would reach from the earth to the moon.

Anton Rubenstein, a noted Russian musician, born in a village of Bessarabia, Russia, Nov. 30, 1830.

He founded the conservatory of music in St. Petersburg, and as a pianist, is said to have no superior now in public. The "Ocean Symphony" is one of his masterpieces.

Samuel Langhorne Clemens, "Mark Twain," an American humorous author, born at Florida, Monroe Co., Mo., Nov. 30, 1830.

"Innocents Abroad," "Roughing It," "The Gilded Age," "Life on the Mississippi," are among his numerous and popular books. He took his "nom de plume"

from the leadsmen's call, while pilot on a Mississippi
steamer.

December 1.

MARTIN HEINRICH, an eminent German analytical
chemist and mineralogist, born at Wernigerode, in
Prussian Saxony, Dec. 1, 1743. Died in Berlin, Jan. 1,
1817. He was the discoverer of five mineral elements,
and of other facts of this science; was a professor of chemistry in Berlin, and an associate of the French Institute,
which latter honor is a synonym for a chemist of the
first rank.

CLARK MILLS, a distinguished American sculptor, born
in Onondaga Co., N. Y., Dec. 1, 1815. Died Jan. 12,
1883. He was the designer of the equestrian statue of
Gen. Jackson, in Lafayette Square, Washington, D. C.
It was cast from the brass guns and mortars captured by
Jackson. The horse is poised upon his hind feet, and
balanced by the laws of gravity. It is probably the only
instance of the kind in the world. The equestrian statue
of Washington, in Washington Circle of the same city, is
also his work. It was cast from guns donated by Congress, and represents Washington at the crisis of the
battle of Princeton. The colossal statue of Freedom,
eighteen feet high and weighing fifteen tons, crowning
the dome of the national Capitol, though designed by
Crawford, was cast in bronze by Mr. Mills, at Bladensburg.

ALEXANDRA, Princess of Wales at the present time,
born in Denmark, Dec. 1, 1844.

She was married March 10, 1863, and is the eldest
daughter of Christian IX. of Denmark, sister of the
empress Dagmar of Russia, and of George I., king of
Greece.

December 2.

RICHARD MONTGOMERY, a distinguished general, born near Raphoe, Ireland, Dec. 2, 1736. He fell while fighting in the colonial cause at the attack of Quebec, Dec. 31, 1775.

SIR JAMES EDWARD SMITH, an English physician and botanist, born at Norwich, Eng., Dec. 2, 1759. Died there March 17, 1828. He was founder and first president of the Linnaean Society in 1788, and author of several noted works on botany.

PEDRO II., de Alcantara, the present emperor of Brazil, born at Rio Janeiro, Dec. 2, 1825.

He began to act as emperor July 23, 1840, although his father had abdicated in his favor nine years before. His reign has been marked by the exercise of wisdom and good judgment. In 1871 he issued a decree authorizing the gradual abolition of slavery. In 1876 he visited the United States and on May 10, assisted President Grant in the formal opening of the Centennial Exhibition at Philadelphia.

LAURA BRIDGEMAN, the celebrated blind deaf-mute, born at Hanover, N. II., Dec. 2, 1829.

She was born with the enjoyment of all her faculties, but at two years old lost her sight, hearing, smell, and partially her taste by a severe fit of sickness. At eight years old she was placed under the care of Dr. S. G. Howe, in the Perkins Institute for the Blind in Boston, with what results every one knows. Can read from raised letters, write, and skillfully play the piano, make fine crochet-work, and select colors all by the sense of touch; being the first person so afflicted who was educated.

December 3.

SAMUEL CROMPTON, an English inventor and artisan, born near Bolton, Lancashire, Eng., Dec. 3, 1753. Died June 26, 1827. He was the inventor of the spinning jenny or mule, which came into use about 1778.

ISAAC T. HOPPER, a benevolent Hicksite Quaker and philanthropist, born near Woodbury, N. J., Dec. 3, 1771. Died in New Jersey, May 7, 1852. He was a successful merchant of New York, a prominent abolitionist, and devoted a large part of his lifetime to works of benevolence.

HENRY A. WISE, a distinguished American politician, born in Accomac Co., Va., Dec. 3, 1806. Died Sept. 12, 1876. He represented Virginia in Congress for several years, and was also minister to Brazil under Tyler. When governor of Virginia in 1856, he declared that if Fremont was elected President, he would march with 20,000 men and take Washington. He was the governor who sanctioned the execution of John Brown.

MARY LOWELL PUTNAM, an American authoress and linguist, born in Boston, Dec. 3, 1810.

She is a sister of James Russell Lowell, and was early distinguished for her extraordinary attainments in languages, ancient and modern. She has contributed largely to periodical literature.

GENERAL GEORGE B. McCLELLAN, an American engineer, soldier and general, born in Philadelphia, Dec. 3, 1826. Died February, 1886. In July, 1861, at the resignation of General Scott, he was appointed General-in-Chief of all the armies of the United States, and after McDowell's disaster at Bull Run, was appointed to the command of the army of the Potomac, but not being considered successful was removed, Nov. 5, 1862.

He was in 1864 a defeated candidate for the Presidency.

December 4.

PERSIUS, a celebrated Roman satirical poet, born at Etruria, Dec. 4, 34 A.D. Died Nov., 62 A.D. Being a stoic, the object of his satires was to inculcate the morality of that sect; and the moral beauty of his satires have made them popular in ancient, mediæval and modern times.

JOHN COTTON, a learned English Puritan minister, born at Derby, England, Dec. 4, 1585. Died 1652. He emigrated to Massachusetts in 1633, and preached in Boston, where he acquired great influence, and was the antagonist of Roger Williams.

JEANNE F. J. A. RECAMIER, a beautiful and accomplished French lady, born in Lyons, Dec. 4, 1777. Died in Paris, May 11, 1849. She was an intimate friend of Madame De Stael, for which cause she was banished from Paris by Napoleon in 1811, as an enemy to the Empire. After her return to Paris she was an intimate friend of Chateaubriand, the great French author, and her salon was the most celebrated in France. Every art, trade and profession found in her a friend.

THOMAS CARLYLE, an eminent British essayist, historian and speculative philosopher, born at Ecclefechan, Scotland, Dec. 4, 1795. Died Feb. 5, 1881. His most noted work, "Sartor Resartus," was published anonymously in 1834. He was noted for his critical essays, and biographical scketches, and for his German translations. Though much criticised as a man and as an author, it is said that no author of this century has exerted a greater influence upon the mind and literature of England than Carlyle.

CHARLES F. DEEMS, D.D., an American divine and scholar, born in Baltimore, Md., Dec. 4, 1820. He was president of several different colleges in the South, and in 1865 came to New York, where he aided .in founding the "Church of the Strangers" and edited Frank Leslie's "Sunday Magazine."

December 5.

HUGH WILLIAMSON, an American physician and patriot, born in West Nottingham, Pa., Dec. 5, 1735, Died in New York, May 22, 1819. He was a noted surgeon during the Revolution, and a member of the convention that framed the Federal Constitution.

MARTIN VAN BUREN, eighth President of the United .States, born at Kinderhook, N. Y., Dec. 5, 1782. Died there July 24, 1862. The chief event of his reign was the terrible financial crisis of 1837, when, owing to improvident measures of President Jackson and the government, not only individuals, but States and even the National government became insolvent. His political intrigues won for him the name of "The Fox," also of "Little Magician." After his term of office closed, he separated himself from the Democratic party, because it favored the extension of slavery.

GEORGE A. CUSTER, an American general, born in Harrison Co., Ohio, Dec. 5, 1839. He served in many battles of the civil war, after which he was appointed to Western frontier duty, and lost his life in a skirmish with the Indians, June 25, 1876.

December 6.

JOHN PHILLIPS, LL.D., an American merchant, born at Andover, Mass., Dec. 6, 1719. Died in Exeter, N.

H., April 21, 1795. He founded an academy at Exeter, N. H., called by his name, and enriched Phillips Academy at Andover.

WARREN HASTINGS, the first Governor-General of British India, born in Worcestershire, Eng., Dec. 6, 1732. Died Aug. 22, 1818. In 1750 he obtained a clerkship at Calcutta in the service of the East India Company, and rising step by step was, in 1773, invested with the title of Governor-General. But his extortions of the rich native princes to supply the demands of the East India Company and his own treasury, drained by the Carnatic wars, caused his impeachment, and seven years' trial, noted more on account of the orations of Burke, Fox and Sheridan, than the termination thereof. He was acquitted, and before his death stood high in royal favor.

JOSEPH LOUIS GAY-LUSSAC, an eminent French chemist and natural philosopher, born at St. Leonard, France, Dec. 6, 1778. Died at Paris, May 9, 1850. In 1804 he, with M. M. Biot, made the first balloon ascent, for scientific purposes, reaching a height of thirteen thousand feet. He discovered the law by which air and gases are expanded uniformly by increase of temperature, and made important contributions to nearly every branch of chemical and physical science.

CAROLINE ANNE BOWLES SOUTHEY, born in Hampshire Co., England, Dec. 6, 1787. Died July 20, 1854. She was the second wife of Robert Southey, and like him an eminent author.

FRIEDRICH MAX MULLER, an eminent German Orientalist and scholar, born in Dessau, Germany, Dec. 6, 1823.

He is considered one of the greatest living Orientalists,

a distinguished author and lecturer. He is the son of William Muller, the poet, and is said to be one of the handsomest men seen in a hundred years.

December 7.

ABIGAIL HOPPER GIBBONS, an American philanthropist, born in Philadelphia, Dec. 7, 1801.

She was the daughter of Isaac T. Hopper, and like him has devoted her life in philanthropic services, visiting prisons and hospitals, and ameliorating the condition of the sick and unfortunate. She was one of the founders of the Isaac T. Hopper Home in New York.

GEORGE HOUSEMAN THOMAS, an eminent English painter, an illustrator of books and newspapers, born in London, Dec. 7, 1824. Died at Boulogne, France, July 21, 1868. He attracted the attention of Queen Victoria by his sketches of the siege of Rome, and was afterwards employed as painter to the Queen.

December 8.

HORACE, an eminent and popular Latin poet, born at Venusia, Apulia, in Italy, Dec. 8, 65 B.C. Died Nov-27, 8 B.C. He was introduced to the literary circles of Rome by the benevolent Maecenas, and his life was eminently prosperous and serene, preferring his independence as author to the tempting prizes of political ambition. His poems consist of odes, satires and epistles, the merits of which rendered him, next to Virgil, the most illustrious poet of ancient Rome.

MARY STUART, Queen of Scots, born in the palace of Linlithgow, Dec. 8, 1542. She was early married to the Dauphin, afterward Francis II. of France, and upon the death of Mary I. of England, they claimed the English throne, which was the cause of the life-long enmity of Queen Elizabeth. Mary spent twelve happy years in France, but upon the death of her husband, the king, in 1560, she went reluctantly back to Scotland, where she reigned as queen amid the checkered scenes attending royalty in those days, until 1568, when by her own misdemeanors she was obliged to fly for refuge to Queen Elizabeth, and was kept by her a prisoner, until she closed her eventful life upon the scaffold at Fotheringay Castle, Feb. 8, 1587.

ELI WHITNEY, an American inventor, born in Westborough, Mass., Dec. 8, 1765. Died in New Haven, Conn., Jan. 8, 1825. The first of his inventions was the cotton gin, which he was stimulated to devise by the widow of Nathaniel Green. He afterward reaped a fortune by his various improvements on fire-arms, the manufacturing of which became the origin of the flourishing village of Whitneyville, Conn.

ELIHU BURRITT, "the learned blacksmith," an American reformer and linguist, born at New Britain, Conn., Dec. 8, 1811. Died there March 7, 1879. He is noted for having learned in the intervals of labor as a blacksmith, several of the ancient and modern languages. As an author he published "Sparks from the Anvil," "Thoughts on Things Home and Abroad," etc. As a lecturer he was an advocate of temperance and other reforms.

ROBERT COLLYER, "the blacksmith preacher," an English Unitarian divine and lecturer, born at Keighley, Yorktown, Eng., Dec. 8, 1823.

By perseverance and study he rose from a blacksmith's apprentice to one of the most eloquent and distinguished men in the United States, to which country he emigrated in 1850.

JOEL CHANDLER HARRIS, " Uncle Remus," an American author, born at Eatonton, Ga., Dec. 8, 1848.

He has contributed in both prose and verse to current literature, but is noted for illustrating the " folk-lore " of the Southern negro. He was, in 1887, one of the editors of the Atlanta, Ga., " Constitution."

December 9.

JOHN MILTON, the " Homer of Britain," an immortal poet, and excepting Shakespeare, the most illustrious name in English literature, born in Bread street, London, Dec. 9, 1608.   Died in London, Nov. 8, 1674.   The last twenty years of his life he was totally blind, and it was during this sad period that he wrote his most famous works " Paradise Lost," " Paradise Regained," and " Samson Agonistes," selling the copy of " Paradise Lost " for the immediate sum of £5, and the promise of an equal amount after the sale of thirteen hundred copies of each edition.   When a youth at Cambridge, his beauty and innocence caused him to be styled " The Lady of Cambridge " for twenty years afterward.

ROBERT TREAT PAINE, JR., an American author, born in Taunton, Mass., Dec. 9, 1773.   Died in Boston, Nov. 13, 1811.   For his celebrated song of " Adams and Liberty " he is said to have received $11.00 a line.

EMMA A. ABBOTT, an American singer, born in Chicago, Dec. 9, 1849.

When very young she attracted the attention of Clara Louisa Kellogg, and was given a musical education in New York.   She was afterward sent to Europe to complete her course, at the expense of the members of Dr.

Chapin's church. She has since sung in most of the principal cities of Europe and America.

December 10.

JOHN WILLIAMS, an American divine, born in Roxbury, Mass., Dec. 10, 1644. Died in Deerfield, Mass., June 12, 1729. He is known as "the redeemed captive" from the fact that in 1704, he with his family were taken captive by the Indians, and afterwards redeemed ; and an account of his adventures he gave the above title.

GEN. HENRY LEAVENWORTH, an American general during the war of 1812, born in Conn., Dec. 10, 1783. Died at Cross Timbers, Indian Territory, July 21, 1834. He established several military posts on the Western frontier, one of which formed the nucleus of the present flourishing city of Leavenworth, Kansas.

THOMAS HOPKINS GALLAUDET, LL.D., an American scholar, author and philanthropist, born in Philadelphia, Dec. 10, 1788. Died at Hartford, Conn., Sept. 9, 1851. Becoming interested in deaf-mutes, he visited Europe to qualify himself for their tuition, and on his return in 1817 opened the Asylum for the Deaf and Dumb, at Hartford, the first institution of the kind in America.

DANIEL APPLETON, founder of the publishing house of D. Appleton & Co., New York, born in Haverhill, Mass., Dec. 10, 1785. Died in New York, March 27, 1849. He began life as a dry goods merchant of his native place, and removing to New York, in 1825, began the importation of books, in conjunction with his dry goods business, but soon abandoned the latter and gave entire attention to the importation and sale of books. His first publishing venture was a collection of religious tracts, from which has grown one of the most prosperous firms in America.   Appleton's " American Cyclopedia " is the largest and most widely circulated work of its kind.

EDWARD EGGLESTON, D.D., a distinguished American divine and author, born in Vevay, Ind., Dec. 10, 1837.

He began his literary career as editor of " The Little Corporal," and in 1870 became editor of the " Independent," and was for some time editor of " Hearth and Home," also contributor to " Scribner's Monthly." His " Hoosier Schoolmaster," which appeared in 1871, determined his rank as among the first of American novelists.

December 11.

SIR DAVID BREWSTER, an eminent British optician, experimental philosopher and author, born at Jedburgh, Scotland, Dec. 11, 1781.   Died near Melrose, Feb. 10, 1868.   He was editor of the " Edinburgh Encyclopædia " from its commencement in 1808, until its completion in 1829.   Was also one of the founders of the " Edinburgh Philosophical Journal," in 1819, and the "Edinburgh Journal of Science."   In 1816 he invented the kaleidoscope, and received from the French Institute one thousand five hundred francs, as an award for one of the two most important discoveries made in physical science in two years.   Among his chief titles to celebrity are his discovery of the law of the polarization of light by reflection, and his researches on double refraction.

December 12.

JOHN JAY, an illustrious American statesman, the first Chief Justice of the United States, born in New York, Dec. 12, 1745.   Died at Bedford, Westchester Co., N. Y., May 17, 1829.   He was elected in 1774 to the first Continental Congress, but being called to the Provincial Congress in New York, his name does not appear on the "Declaration of Independence." He associated with Adams and Franklin in negotiating the treaty of peace between the United States and Great Britain, and signed in Paris, Sept. 3, 1783. In 1789 he was offered by Washington the choice of office, and he accepted that of Chief Justice, which position he held for six years, being afterward minister to England and governor of New York. He was a second time nominated as Chief Justice but declined the honor.

WILLIAM LLOYD GARRISON, an American philanthropist and great leader of the modern anti-slavery movement of the United States, born in Newburyport, Mass., Dec. 12, 1804. Died May 24, 1879. In 1827 he became editor of the "National Philanthropist," the first journal in America devoted to the advocacy of the cause of "total abstinence." On Jan. 1, 1831, he began in Boston, the publication of the "Liberator," a decided uncompromising anti-slavery journal, taking for his motto, "My country is the world, my countrymen all mankind," which paper he edited until its necessity ceased, Dec., 1865, when he made his editorial farewell, saying, "My work is finished, and I am satisfied." He suffered much in the anti-slavery cause, both by mobs and imprisonment, when several times his life was in peril, but knowing he was right he had no fear, and was triumphant.

December 13.

JOHN BUTTERWORTH, author of "Butterworth's Concordance," born in Lancaster, England, Dec. 13, 1727. Died 1803.

REV. PHILLIPS BROOKS, a popular American clergyman, born in Boston, Dec. 13, 1835.

He is one of the most brilliant pulpit orators of the United States ; was ordained at Philadelphia in 1859, where he was for some time pastor until called to take charge of Trinity church in his native city.

ROBERT HENRY NEWELL, "Orpheus C. Kerr," an American humorist, born in New York, Dec. 13, 1836.

He has been literary editor of the New York "Mercury," one of the editors of the New York " World," and since editor of " Hearth and Home.'

December 14.

CHARLES WOLFE, a British clergyman and poet, born in Dublin, Ireland, Dec. 14, 1791. Died in Cork, Feb. 21, 1823. He was author of a collection of sermons, prose sketches, and lyric poems of great beauty. Among the last named is his " Burial of Sir John Moore," which is esteemed one of the finest productions of its kind in the language.

NOAH PORTER, D.D., an eminent American author and scholar, born in Farmington, Conn., Dec. 14, 1811.

He was appointed president of Yale College in 1871. Was the principal editor of the new edition of Webster's "Unabridged Dictionary," and the author of Human Intellect."

December 15.

NERO, the sixth emperor or Cæsar of Rome, born at Antium, on the coast of Latium, Dec. 15, 37 A. D. He was emperor from 54–68, and at last killed himself through fear of the prætorian guards, June 11, 68 A.D.

ISAAC WALTON, sometimes called " The Father of Angling," a celebrated English writer, born at Stafford, Eng., Dec. 15, 1593. Died 1683. He was author of several good biographies, but his principal work,

"The Complete Angler" is considered one of the best pastorals in the English language.

Francois La Rochefoucauld, born at Paris, Dec. 15, 1613. Died there March 17, 1680. As an author he is particularly noted for his "Reflexions" or "Maxims," which made a great sensation, both on account of its elegant style and accute observations, for which reasons it is still considered a classical work in France. These "Maxims" are about seven hundred in number, included in one small volume, the underlying tone of which is, "Self-love is the mainspring and motive of everything we do, say, feel or think."

Samuel B. Webb, an American patriot and soldier, born at Wethersfield, Conn., Dec. 15, 1753. Died at Claverack, N. Y., 1807. He held the Bible for Washington when he took his oath as first President of the United States.

December 16.

George Whitefield, an eminent and eloquent English preacher, born at Gloucester, Eng., Dec. 16, 1714. Died at Newburyport, Mass., Sept. 30, 1770. He was founder of the sect of Calvin Methodists, and beyond all natural endowments there was such a power of evangelical truth in his ministry, that even Hume said it was worth going twenty miles to hear him.

Gerald L. von Blucher, a celebrated Prussian field-marshal, born at Rostock, Dec. 16, 1742. Died Sept. 12, 1819. He was an ally of the English in their campaigns against the French, and his arrival on the field of Waterloo, on the evening of June 18, 1815, decided that memorable battle. It is said that Wellington, toward the close of that great struggle, fearing the fates were against him, cried out, " O, for sundown or Blucher!" He got Blucher and victory first, and sundown afterward.

MARY RUSSELL MILFORD, a charming English writer, born in Hampshire, Dec. 16, 1786. Died Jan. 10, 1855. She devoted herself to authorship at an early age, and the graceful simplicity and freshness of feeling displayed in her tales won the favor of all classes.

ABBOTT LAWRENCE, LL.D., an eminent American merchant and philanthropist, born at Groton, Mass., Dec. 16, 1792. Died at Boston, Aug. 18, 1855. He was one of the principal founders of the city of Lawrence, Mass., also founded the Lawrence Scientific School of Harvard University.

THOMAS STARR KING, an American Unitarian divine, born in New York, Dec. 16, 1824. Died in San Francisco. Cal., March 4, 1864. To his remarkable powers as a writer and speaker is ascribed the devoted loyalty of California during the civil war.

December 17.

PRINCE RUPERT, or Robert of Bavaria, grandson of James I. of England, born at Prague, Dec. 17, 1619. Died in London, Nov. 29, 1682. He united himself to the cause of his uncle Charles I., and was one of the founders of the Royal Society. He was the first governor of the Hudson Bay Co., in 1670, and spent much of his time in the interests of science, and is credited with the invention of mezzotint, " prince's metal," and the glass bubbles called " Rupert's drops."

NATHANIEL MACON, an American statesman, born in Warren Co., North Carolina, Dec. 17, 1757. Died June 29, 1837. His services in Congress for thirty-

seven years exceeds that of any other American statesman, and the cities, towns and counties in the Southern
and Western States which bear his name, show the ex-
tent of his popularity in his day.

Ludwig van Beethoven, a famous musical composer
of Dutch extraction, born at Bonn, in Prussia, Dec. 17,
1770. Died March, 1827. It is said that his compositions constitute a musical library by themselves ; but
his masterpieces are his celebrated symphony in honor
of Napoleon, which was the study of two years, and the
opera of " Leonore " or " Fidelio." He became deaf in
the prime of life, and consequently fell into the habit of
gloom and distrust.

Sir Humphrey Davy, one of the most celebrated
chemists that Great Britain has produced, born at Pe-
nanze, in Cornwall, Dec. 17, 1778. Died in Geneva,
May, 1829. As a chemist, lecturer and author, he gave
to the world many grand discoveries, which are considered second in importance only to those of Sir Isaac
Newton ; but he is best known by his important invention of the miner's safety lamp. He has been styled by
Dumas " the greatest chemical genius that ever appeared."

Joseph Henry, LL.D., an American scholar and
natural philosopher, born in Albany, N. Y., Dec. 17,
1797. Died May 13, 1878. He is said to have invented
the first machine moved by the agency of electro-magnetism. He was for many years one of the faculty of Smithsonian Institute, Washington, D. C.

John Greenleaf Whittier, a distinguished Ameri-
can poet and philanthropist, born at Haverhill, Mass.,
Dec. 17, 1808.
He was educated in the principles of the Quakers, with

whom he has always remained in connection. He early identified himself with the anti-slavery party, and was considered the poet of the cause, in the interest of which he edited the " Pennsylvania Freeman." Whittier has written no extended poem, but his beautiful lyrics will always live, the pride of the American people.

December 18.

CHARLES WESLEY, an English preacher and writer of poems, born at Epworth, Eng., Dec. 18, 1708. Died March 29, 1788. He was brother of and co-laborer with the celebrated John Wesley, but is chiefly known as "the poet of Methodism." The noted Dr. Watts said of Charles Wesley that his "Wrestling Jacob" was worth all the hymns he himself had written.

KARL MARIE FRIEDRICH ERNST VON WEBER, an eminent German composer and musician, born near Lubeck, Dec. 18, 1786. Died at London, June 5, 1826. His great object in music was to drive Italian opera out of Germany, which he succeeded in doing by the success of " Der Freischutz," his master-piece.

WILLIAM CHANNING WOODBRIDGE, an American educational writer, born at Medford, Mass., Dec. 18, 1794. Died at Boston, Nov. 9, 1845. He was an ardent advocate of the Pestalozzi system of education, and published in connection with Mrs. Emma Willard, his noted geographical text books for schools.

GEORGE D. PRENTISS, an American poet and journalist, born at Preston, Conn., Dec. 18, 1802. Died at Louisville, Ky., Jan. 22, 1870. As an editor of the " Louisville Journal " he acquired the reputation of one of the ablest and most brilliant journalists in the country. He was also author of several poems of rare beauty.

ALFRED B. STREET, an American poet and miscellaneous writer, born at Poughkeepsie, N. Y., Dec. 18, 1811.
Died June 2, 1881. His writings have done much to
familiarize the reading public with the history, woods,
and waters of Northern New York.

AUSTIN ABBOTT, LL.D., an American lawyer and
author, born in Boston, Mass., Dec. 18, 1831.

Individually he is a valued contributor to current literature, and with his brother Benjamin, has prepared
legal compilations of great value to the profession. He
is a son of the noted Jacob Abbott, and brother to the
Rev. Lyman Abbott.

REV. LYMAN ABBOTT, third son of Rev. Jacob Abbott,
born in Roxbury, Mass., Dec. 18, 1835.

As lawyer, minister, editor and author, his literary
career is a marked one. As co-editor of the "Christian
Union," and editor of the "Illustrated Christian Weekly," he is well known. The C.L.S.C. now claim him as
counselor, and he has been called to fill Plymouth pulpit, left vacant by the celebrated Rev. H. W. Beecher.

December 19.

THOMAS WILLING, an eminent American merchant
and statesman, born at Philadelphia, Dec. 19, 1731.
Died there Jan. 19, 1821. He was head of the great
mercantile house of Willing & Morris, at Philadelphia,
who were the agents of Congress during the Revolution
to supply naval and military stores, and besides filling
many other important offices, was president of the first
chartered bank in America.

CARL WILHELM SCHEELE, an eminent Swedish chemist, born at Stralsund, Dec. 19, 1742. Died at Koping,
May 21, 1786. He discovered tartaric acid, fluoric acid,

barytes, chlorine, the coloring matter of prussian blue, and the pigment called "Scheele's green," known in this country as Paris green. In 1788 Puymaurin presented to the French Academy of Sciences, a glass plate upon which there was a beautiful fluoric etching representing Chemistry and Genius weeping at the tomb of Scheele, who had contributed so much to the history of fluohydric acid. "This work was of interest to the Academy, on account of the fitness of the subject, as well as the elegance of its execution."

Sir William Edward Parry, an English navigator, born at Bath, Eng., Dec. 19, 1790. Died at Ems, Germany, July 8, 1856. In 1819–20, 21–23 and 26, he commanded expeditions which penetrated further west and north than any earlier navigator. Parry Isles were named in his honor.

Edwin M. Stanton, an American statesman and lawyer, born at Steubenville, O., Dec. 19, 1815. Died in Washington, D. C., Dec. 24, 1869. He was appointed Secretary of War by Lincoln, Jan., 1862, and by his indefatigable industry, courage and honesty, endeared his name to his country. For his support of the many important measures vetoed by President Johnson, the latter undertook to remove Stanton from office, without the consent of Congress, which, with other offences, brought on the great impeachment trial of the President; and when the one vote was lacking for his conviction, Mr. Stanton resigned, receiving a vote of thanks from Congress, for his great ability and fidelity to trusts.

Mary Ashton Livermore, an eminent American author and lecturer, born at Boston, Dec. 19, 1821.
She labored with much ability in behalf of the Sani-

tary Commission, during the civil war, and has been one
of the most successful of lecturers on woman's suffrage,
and other social and religious reforms.

December 20.

BENJAMIN YOUNG PRIME, M.D., an American poet
and physician, born at Huntington, L. I., Dec. 20, 1733.
Died at New York, Oct. 31, 1791. He wrote political
songs and ballads, which were widely circulated during
the Revolution ; and in 1791 wrote "Columbia's Glory,"
a poem on the Revolution.

LAURA SMITH HAVELAND, an American philanthropist, born at Ketley, Ont., Dec. 20, 1808.

She was instrumental in founding philanthropic insti-
tutes and asylums, and during the civil war was a
minister of aid and comfort to the suffering in hospitals
and camps.

JAMES HAMMOND TRUMBULL, an eminent American
philologist and scholar, born at Stonington, Conn.,
Dec. 20, 1821.

He was one of the founders of the American Philological Association, established in 1869. Has devoted much
time to the Indian languages, and prepared a glossary to
Eliot's Indian Bible, and is said to be the only American
scholar now able to read that work.

December 21.

JEAN BAPTISTE RACINE, an eminent French dramatic poet, born in France, Dec. 21, 1639. Died April 21,
1699. By even French critics, Racine is considered
next to Shakespeare as a tragedian, and as a poet second
only to Virgil.

RT. HON. BENJAMIN DISRAELI, Lord Beaconsfield,

the eminent English statesman of Jewish extraction, born in London, Dec. 21, 1805. Died April 19, 1881. He was twice prime minister of England, and an author of note. His "Endymion" is said to be the most successful political novel ever written.

Dr. Archibald Tait, an English archbishop, born in Edinburgh, Dec. 21, 1811. Died Dec. 3, 1882. In 1843, he succeeded Dr. Thomas Arnold as Head Master of Rugby, and in 1868 was appointed Archbishop of Canterbury.

December 22.

James Edward Oglethorp, an English general, born in London, Dec. 22, 1696. Died in Essex, July 1, 1785. In 1732 he obtained from Parliament the royal charter for founding a colony in North America for poor debtors, which he named Georgia in honor of the king. He founded Savannah in 1733.

John Strong Newberry, M.D., LL.D., an American scholar and explorer, born at Windsor, Conn., Dec. 22, 1822.

He was attached to the expedition under Lieut. J. C. Ives, which made the first exploration of the Colorado River, the most important of the surveys of our Western Territories. He was one of the original incorporators of the National Academy of Sciences.

Thomas Wentworth Higginson, an American author of note, born in Cambridge, Mass., Dec. 22, 1823.

He was a captain and colonel during the civil war, since which time he has devoted himself to literature and social reform, and has rendered efficient aid to the management of Harvard College. He is author of many volumes, besides various pamphlets and magazine articles; he is also a well known lyceum lecturer.

December 23.

ROBERT BARCLAY, an eminent writer and defender of the Society of Friends, born at Gordonstown, in Morayshire, Scotland, Dec. 23, 1648. Died at Ury in October, 1690. In 1667 he entered into a fellowship with the Friends, and defended their principles by a treatise entitled "Truth cleared of Calumnies." In 1677 he, in company with George Fox and William Penn, visited Germany on a religious mission. He was appointed governor of the province of East Jersey, but he sent a deputy and never himself visited America.

SIR RICHARD ARKWRIGHT, a noted English inventor, born at Preston, Lancashire, Eng., Dec. 23, 1732. Died August, 1792. He invented the spinning frame, and by his admirable talent for management, founded a factory system which, it is said, has never been greatly improved.

JEAN FRANCOIS CHAMPOLLION, a French savant and linguist, born at Figeac, Dec. 23, 1791. He is celebrated as interpreter, from the famous Rosetta stone, of the symbols by which ancient Egypt sought to eternize its annals and its institutions. He died in 1832, while preparing to publish the results of his researches in Egypt.

JOSEPH SMITH, founder of the Mormon sect, born in Sharon, Windsor Co., Vt., Dec. 23, 1805. (For facts concerning the "Book of Mormon," see Feb. 19.) Smith after failing to start a colony of his sect in Ohio and Missouri, at last settled at Nauvoo, Ill. But this failed as all others had, on account of the opposition of the people to the peculiar doctrines of the Mormons. Joseph and his brother being confined in jail, were surrounded by a mob and both killed, May 27, 1844.

December 24.

GALBA, a Roman Emperor, the seventh Cæsar, and the first of the noted twelve not of the Cæsar family, born near Terracina, Dec. 24, B.C. 3.   He succeeded Nero in 68 A.D., but his avarice and cruelty rendered him unpopular, and he was murdered by the prætorians, Jan., 15, 69.

BENJAMIN RUSH, an eminent American physician and philanthropist, born near Philadelphia, Dec. 24, 1745.   Died in that city April, 1813.   He was an active supporter of the popular cause during the Revolution, was a member of Congress in 1776, and signed the "Declaration of Independence."   In 1777 he was appointed physician and surgeon-general of the army and acquired distinction by his writings, and for his successful treatment of yellow fever.   He was treasurer of the Mint during the last fourteen years of his life, president of the society for the abolition of slavery, and vice-president of the Bible Society of Philadelphia, In 1811 the emperor of Russia sent him a diamond ring, as a testimonial of respect for his medical skill.

GEORGE CRABBE, a popular English poet, born at Aldborough, Suffolk, England, Dec. 24, 1754.   Died Feb., 1832.   His poem "The Village," published in 1783, at once confirmed his reputation as a powerful and original poet.

ELIZABETH M. CHANDLER, an American poetess and philanthropist, born near Wilmington, Del., Dec. 24, 1807.   Died in Michigan, 1834.   When only eighteen years old, she received a prize from the editor of "The Casket" for her poem, "The Slave-ship."

CHRISTOPHER CARSON, "Kit Carson," an American traveler, guide and trapper, born in Kentucky, Dec. 24,

1809. Died May, 1868. He rendered important services as guide to Fremont in his noted western explorations. Serving in the civil war, he received the title of brigadier-general.

MATTHEW ARNOLD, an English poet, born at Lalcham, Middlesex, Eng., Dec. 24, 1822. Died April 16, 1888. He was the eldest son of Dr. Thomas Arnold, the famous Rugby teacher, and has himself occupied the chair of Professor of Poetry at Oxford for ten years, was also the government inspector of schools, being considered as authority on all educational matters.

December 25.

SIR ISAAC NEWTON, an illustrious English philosopher and mathematician, born at Woolsthorpe, Lincolnshire, Eng., Dec. 25, 1642. Died March 20, 1727, and was buried at Westminster Abbey. Newton's acquisitions to mathematical astronomy place his name higher than any other in the annals of science, but his crowning glory is his magnificent theory of universal gravitation, given to the world in his "Principia," published in 1687. Near the close of his life he said : "I know not what I may appear to the world, but to myself I seem to have been only like a boy playing on the sea-shore, and diverting myself in now and then finding a smoother pebble, or a prettier shell than ordinary, whilst the great ocean of truth lay all undiscovered before me." Humility seems to be a prominent grace of most of the great astronomers, yet Newton's worth to the world is manifested by the inscription on his monument :

"Nature and Nature's laws lay hid in night,
God said, ' Let Newton be ' and all was light."

Patrick S. Gilmore, the world renowned band-master, born in Ireland, Dec. 25, 1830.

His first great feat as leader of a jubilee was on the fourth of March, 1864, after the restoration of New Orleans to the Union, when he collected ten thousand children and five hundred instruments, to inaugurate the first Union governor of Louisiana. He next conceived the idea of the great national peace jubilee of 1869, after which followed the great international jubilee of 1872, when a chorus of twenty thousand voices and an orchestra of two thousand instrumentalists occupied the great coliseum, besides the five noted bands from the musical centers of Europe.

December 26.

Thomas Gray, an eminent English poet, born in London, Dec. 26, 1716. Died in Cambridge, July 24, 1771. He was a fine scholar and lover of art ; but his fame rests almost entirely on his " Elegy written in a Country Churchyard," which has given him a high position in English literature. No poem, perhaps, was more universally admired, and it has been translated into all the principal languages of Europe.

Mary Somerville, F.R.S., an eminent astronomer and scientific writer, born at Jedburgh, Scotland, Dec. 26, 1780. Died at Naples, Nov. 29, 1872. She is considered one of the most remarkable women of the world. To her great gifts of intellect were added refined and beautiful taste, ability in music and painting, and the glory of womanhood—an executive ability to properly manage her home and conduct the education of her children.

Dion Boucicault, a noted dramatic author and actor, born in Dublin, Ireland, Dec. 26, 1822.

He has done much as a manager and reconstructor to elevate the stage, and has established several theaters himself. Through his influence, dramatic authorship was made remunerative in England.

December 27.

JOHANN KEPLER, a celebrated German astronomer, born in Würtemberg, Dec. 27, 1571. Died at Ratisbon, Nov. 15, 1630. Kepler's three great astronomical laws, were the result of seventeen years of careful study, " and comprise," says Sir John Herschell, " a compendium of the motion of all the planets, and assign their places in their orbits, at any instant of time, past or to come." He composed his own epitaph in the following words : " I have measured the heavens, I now measure the earth. The mind was of heavenly origin, only the shadow of the body lies here."

OLIVER JOHNSON, an eminent American editor, born at Peacham, Vt., Dec. 27, 1809.

He has been editor of the "Christian Soldier," "Weekly Tribune," and "Christian Union;" also managing editor of the "Independent."

December 28.

CATHERINE M. SEDGWICK, an eminent American writer and moralist, born at Stockbridge, Mass., Dec. 28, 1789. Died near Roxbury, Mass., July 31, 1867. "Redwood," published in 1824, was translated into several of the European languages, and her tales for the young are among the most valuable and attractive works of the kind.

CHARLES HODGE, D.D., an eminent American theologian, born at Philadelphia, Dec. 28, 1797. Died June 19, 1878. He was for fifty years, 1822–1872, professor of

Oriental and Biblical literature in Princeton Theological Seminary, and when he celebrated his semi-centennial anniversary in the college, it was the first of the kind in America.

December 29.

CHARLES GOODYEAR, an eminent American inventor, born at New Haven, Conn., Dec. 29, 1800. Died at New York, July 1, 1860. After five years spent in constant experiments, suffering from extreme destitution, he produced the vulcanized or ebonized India rubber, which immortalized his name, and he lived long enough to see his material applied to nearly five hundred uses.

ANDREW JOHNSON, seventeenth President of the United States, born at Raleigh, N. C., Dec. 29, 1808. Died July 31, 1875. He succeeded to the Presidency upon the assassination of Lincoln, and his administration is marked by his disagreement with his Cabinet and with Congress, on account of his too free use of the veto power. His subsequent impeachment failed of being carried into effect for the lack of one vote.

RT. HON. WILLIAM EWART GLADSTONE, an eminent English statesman, financier, orator and author, born in Liverpool, Dec. 29, 1809.

Although not the prime minister, he is the first man of England, and is called by his subjects "The Grand Old Man." He is considered the greatest living statesman, and as premier may be said to be one of the most popular and influential that ever ruled England.

December 30.

JOHN PHILIPS, an English poet, born at Bampton, Oxfordshire, Dec. 30, 1676. Died at Hereford, Feb. 15,

1708. Among his various productions is " Blenheim," in honor of Marlborough's victory.

Stephen H. Long, an American engineer and explorer, born at Hopkinton, N. H., Dec. 30, 1784. Died at Alton, Ill., Sept. 4, 1864. His five years' exploring expedition between the Mississippi river and the Rocky mountains, leaves its memento on one of the loftiest peaks of that chain, which bears his name. As an engineer he is noted as being the first in this country to apply the rectangular trussed frame, pure and simple, to bridges for railroads.

December 31.

Jacques (James) Cartier, a French navigator, born at St. Malo, Dec. 31, 1491. Died in 1554. He discovered the St. Lawrence river in 1534, and explored it as far as the present site of Montreal.

Herman Boerhaave, M.D., F.R.S., a Dutch physician and philosopher, born near Leyden, Dec. 31, 1668. Died Sept. 23, 1738. It is said that his fame has scarcely been equaled in modern times. It extended not only to every part of Christendom, but to the farthest bounds of Asia. A Chinese mandarin once addressed a letter to him with this superscription : " To Boerhaave, Physician in Europe," and the missive was duly received.

Charles Cornwallis, the ablest of the British generals serving in the American Revolution, born Dec. 31, 1738. Died in India, 1805. His surrender to Washington, at Yorktown, was the well known terminus to the Revolution. He was afterward appointed Governor-General of India.

John Gaspar Spurzheim, M.D., a German physician, the worthy coadjutor of Dr. Gall, the discoverer of Phrenology, born in Longwick, Prussia, Dec. 31, 1776. Died in Boston, Mass., Nov. 10, 1832. He lectured in Germany, France, England, Scotland, and the United States, and organized the great original principles discovered by Gall, renamed most of the organs, discovered several, and wrought out a beautiful system of Mental Philosophy. He is also said to be the discoverer of the fibrous structure of the brain.

General George Gordon Meade, a distinguished American general, born in Cadiz, Spain, Dec. 31, 1815. Died at Philadelphia, Nov. 6, 1872. Gen. Meade took an active part in many of the noted battles of the civil war, but his name will ever be identified with the great battle of Gettysburg, which he commanded on the first, second and third days of July, 1863, the victory of which produced such decided results.

James T. Fields, an American author, poet and publisher, born at Portsmouth, N. H., Dec. 31, 1817. Died April 24, 1881. He was a member of the publishing firm in which we find his name, for twenty-five years as third, second, and at last as first. He was editor of the "Atlantic Monthly," 1862–70, and was noted as a lecturer.

UNKNOWN DATES.

The following biographical briefs are, with few exceptions, of those the dates of whose birth we suppose have not been recorded, since by the most diligent search we have failed to ascertain the exact time.

Should any one reading these pages find that they possess the knowledge here wanting, it would add to their interest in the book, to insert the missing dates in their own copy, and forward the information for future use.

Many other names of those still living have been selected for the book, but are reluctantly omitted for the want of the date of birth, but these can be added when their place in the book is determined.

DANIEL DE FOE, an English writer, born in London, 1661. Died April 24, 1731. He produced many successful volumes, but his most popular work is "The Adventures of Robinson Crusoe," published in 1719.

REBECCA BREWTON MOTTE, an American patriot of the Revolution, born in South Carolina, 1740. Died 1815. Her fine mansion on the Congaree was taken by the British, and named Fort Motte, and when this was besieged by the Americans under Marion and Lee, she furnished the bow and arrows to shoot combustibles upon the roof, which caused the surrender of the British. The flames were afterward extinguished, and Mrs. Motte presided at a dinner to which the officers of both forces sat down.

SIR ALEXANDER MACKENZIE, an enterprising Scotchman, born at Inverness, 1755. Died in 1820. In his youth he emigrated to Canada in the service of the Northwest Fur Company. From 1781–89 he traded with the Indians at Lake Athabasca, and in the latter year discovered the river which bears his name, tracing it from its source to its entrance into the Arctic Ocean.

WILLIAM MORRISON, an American traveler and explorer, born at Montreal, Canada, 1785. Died on Morrison Island, Aug. 7, 1866. He made extensive explorations in the Northwest Territory while in charge of John Jacob Astor's fur trade in Canada. He rendered many important services to geography, and was the first white man who explored the sources of the Mississippi River.

WILLIAM MOULTRIE, a distinguished general of the American Revolution, born in South Carolina, 1731. Died in 1805. He is distinguished for his gallant defence of the fort on Sullivan's Island, which was named Fort Moultrie in his honor. He was appointed major-general in the army, and was afterwards elected governor of South Carolina.

STEPHEN F. AUSTIN, founder of the State of Texas, born 1790. Died Dec., 1836. In 1821 he conducted a party of emigrants from New Orleans to take possession of a tract of land granted to his father by the Mexican government, and they settled where the city of Austin now stands. In 1833 the Texas colonists formed a constitution, and applied for admission to the Mexican confederacy, but Mexico being in a state of anarchy, he failed to find recognition. In 1835 he went as commissioner to the United States, to promote the liberation of Texas from Mexico, but did not live to see it admitted into the Union.

STEPHEN ALLEN, a distinguished citizen of New York, born in that city, July , 1767. While commissioner for visiting prisons, he proposed the erection of the State prison at Sing Sing, and was one of the principal originators of the project for supplying New York city with water from the Croton river. He perished in the steamer Henry Clay, which was burned July , 1852.

DR. JOHN F. GRAY, M.D., born in Sherbourne, N.Y., Sept. , 1804. Died   He was the first physician in America who adopted homœopathy, or the medical system of Hahnemann.

FABIO COLONNA COLUMNA, one of the greatest botanists of his time, born in Naples,   1567. Died there in 1650. His first work, " Touchstone of Plants," was remarkable for the accuracy of the descriptions, and the correctness and beauty of the figures. He was the first to use copper plates to delineate plants.

JEAN ALTHEN, a native of Persia, born   1711. Died   1774. He was made captive in his youth by some Arabs, and sold as a slave at Smyrna, whence he escaped to Marseilles. He carried some seeds of madder with him, which was at that time forbidden exportation under penalty of death. These he cultivated in France, which was the beginning of that flourishing trade there.

LANCELOT ANDREWS, an English divine of great learning, born in London,   1555. Died Sept. 25, 1626.

He was one of the ten great divines selected to translate the Bible into English in the reign of James I.

Saint Vincent de Paul, a philanthropist and reformer, born near Dax, in the south of France, 1576. Died in Paris, 1660, and was canonized by Pope Clement XII. in 1737. He distinguished himself by his zeal to improve the moral and physical condition of the sick and poor by establishing and organizing philanthropic societies, the most widely known and useful of which was the "Sisters of Charity." His services during the civil war of his time in relieving the miseries of famine procured for him the title of "father of the country."

Caroline Elizabeth Sarah Norton, an eminent English writer, born 1808. Died June 15, 1877. Her novels and poems are remarkable for their fidelity to nature, pathos and intensity of feeling. She is described by Mrs. Sedgwick in her "Letters from Abroad," as the perfection of intellectual and physical beauty, uniting masculine force with feminine delicacy.

Alexander VI., Pope of Rome, born in Valencia, Spain, 1430. He was elected to the Pope's chair by bribery and intrigue Aug. 11, 1492, and his reign constituted the blackest page in the history of modern times, which entitles him to the name of "worst of all Popes." It is said he died by taking poisonous food, by mistake, which he had prepared for some of his guests, Aug. 18, 1503.

John Pounds, an English philanthropist, born at Portsmouth, Eng., 1766. Died in 1839. He was the originator of ragged schools, which institution he inaugurated by gathering poor children around him as he worked at his trade as shoemaker in his humble shanty. Dr. Thomas Guthrie, a Scottish divine, took the idea from this small beginning and the present model industrial schools are the result.

MARTIN HARPERTZOON TROMP, a celebrated Dutch admiral, born at Briel,   1597.   He is noted for his bravery during the naval hostilities between the English and Dutch, then the greatest naval powers of the world.   The victory oscillated from one side to the other at different encounters, and in Nov., 1652, when the Dutch were decidedly victorious, he immortalized his name by sailing up the channel with a broom at his masthead to denote that he had swept his foes from the seas.   But his victory was of short duration, for in two more obstinate battles the following year the Dutch were entirely defeated and Admiral Tromp was killed off the coast of Holland, July 31, 1653.

JOSEPH GILLOTT, the celebrated manufacturer of steel pens, born in Sheffield, Eng.,   1800.   Died Jan. 6, 1872.   His first effort in this direction was in a garret, and the result sold to small shopkeepers in Birmingham.   But his machines for turning the points out by thousands, in the time it formerly required a man to make one, brought him an almost unprecedented success.   Of late years the work of his manufactory has reached the enormous number of 150,000,000.

HENRY WHITFIELD, an English divine, born in England,   1597.   Died at Winchester, 1650.   During the persecution of the Puritans, which sect he favored, he came to America and was one of the founders of Guilford, Conn., 1639, where his house, one of the oldest in the United States, was in 1876 still standing, and by his liberal use of a handsome fortune, was esteemed one of the chief founders of the New Haven colony.   He afterward returned to England.

SIR THOMAS GRESHAM, a wealthy English merchant, born in London, 1519. Died Nov. 21, 1579, He was sent by Queen Elizabeth on several diplomatic missions, and was employed as her agent at Antwerp. In 1566 he built at his own expense the "Royal Exchange" in London, the first edifice of the kind in England; and also founded, in 1575, the college called by his name.

ROBERT POLLOCK, a British poet, born at Muirhouse, in Scotland, 1798. Died near Southampton, Sept., 1827. His reputation is founded on "The Course of Time," which, for so young a man, was considered a vast achievement. His "Providential Distinctions" and "Lord Byron" are among the gems of English literature.

ROBERT RAIKES, an English philanthropist, born at Gloucester, 1735. Died April 5, 1811. He was publisher and editor of the "Gloucester Journal," but his name is rendered immortal as being the founder of Sunday schools. Montgomery said of his work:

> "Once by the Severn's side
> A little fountain rose.
> Now, like the Severn's seaward tide,
> Round the whole world it flows."

THOMAS AUGUSTINE ARNE, an eminent English musician and composer, born in London, 1710. Died March 5, 1778. He composed the music for Addison's opera of "Rosamond" and Milton's "Comus," which established his reputation. The two principal national songs of England, "God Save the King," and "Rule Brittania," are claimed by many to owe their popularity chiefly to his music, though both have other claimants.

Samuel Richardson, an eminent English novelist, born in Derbyshire, 1689. Died July 4, 1761. His first novel, " Parmela," opened a new era in English romantic literature, and was burlesqued by Fieldings' "Joseph Andrews." Richardson's "Clarissa Harlowe," his capital work, 1748, acquired for him an European reputation. Dr. Johnson was his friend and warm admirer.

Thomas Wharton, an English politician, born 1645. Died April 12, 1715. He was known during life as the "greatest rake in England," and was author of "Lillibullero," a famous satirical ballad, written in ridicule of the Papists during the reign of James II., which " though slight and insignificant as it may now seem, had at that time a more powerful effect than either the philippics of Demosthenes or Cicero, and contributed not a little toward the revolution of 1688. The whole army and at last the people, both in city and country, were singing it continually. Never had so slight a thing so great an effect."

Pierre Du Terrail Bayard, ("Chevalier Bayard,") a heroic French knight, called "the knight without fear and without reproach," born at Castle Bayard, near Grenoble, 1475. He was remarkable for his modesty, piety, magnanimity, and his various accomplishments. He served under Charles VIII., Louis XII., and Francis I., and for his success against the invading army of Charles V. of Spain, was saluted as " the saviour of the country." He was killed in battle at the river Sesia, April 30, 1524, having won the reputation of being a model of nearly every virtue.

Arnold Hoogvliet, a popular Dutch poet, born at

Vlaardingen,   1687. Died 1763. He was author of a collection of poems on various subjects, but his reputation is founded on an epic poem entitled "Abraham, the Patriarch," which was received with extraordinary and durable favor; "no other book in Dutch literature is said to have been honored with a more decided national adoption."

JONAS HANWAY, an English traveler and philanthropist, born in Portsmouth, 1712. Died Sept. 5, 1786. His life was spent in the interest of doing good in the little things, which if done, seem not of much account, but if neglected create great wrong ; such as the care of parish infants, chimney sweeps, fitting poor boys and men for the navy, etc. But he is popularly remembered as the first Englishman to carry an umbrella in his native country.

THOMAS HATFIELD, an English divine, born Died   , 1381. He founded Trinity College, Oxford.

EDWARD YOUNG, an eminent English poet, born at Upham, in Hampshire, Eng.,   , 1684. Died at Welwyn, April 12, 1765. "Night Thoughts," the poem on which the reputation of Young is chiefly founded, enjoyed great popularity, and found admirers and imitators in Germany and France. He constantly sought preferment, but often in vain, and his disappointment shows itself by a scorn of royalty and fame, so often manifested in his writings.

THOMAS SULLY, an eminent painter, born in Lincolnshire, Eng., June   , 1783. Died Nov. 5, 1872. He emigrated to America in 1792, and studied for his profession in Charleston, S. C. He produced many full-length portraits of eminent men in America, and several

historical pictures, among which is " Washington crossing the Delaware."

JOHN ARBUTHNOT, a British author, satirist and physician, born at Arbuthnot, Scotland,   , 1675.
Died   , 1735.   He was celebrated for his wit,
genius and learning.   His "Tables of the Grecian,
Roman, and Jewish Weights, Measures and Coins" are
regarded as a standard.   In 1712 he produced the humorous "History of John Bull"—the origin of the
name—which Macaulay says is the most ingenious and
humorous satire extant in our language.

JAMES BRADLEY, pronounced by Sir Issac Newton,
"the best astronomer of Europe," born in Gloucestershire, Eng.,   , 1693.   Died at Chatford, July
   , 1762.   He discovered the cause of the phenomenon
called the "aberration of light," also the "nutation of
the earth's axis," which had the greatest influence on all
astronomy; accounting for many conflicting observations
which before were considered errors.   He left at his
death thirteen volumes of valuable observations, which
were considered "a monument of patience and fidelity."

JOSEPH LANCASTER, a popular English educator,
born in London, 1778.   Died in New York, 1838.
He was the founder of the "Lancastrian System of
Education," which was the outgrowth of that of Pes-
talozzi, his tutor and master.   He came to the United
States in 1818.

DINAH MARIA CRAIK, or "Miss Mulock," a popular
English writer, born in Staffordshire,   1826.
Died Oct. 14, 1887.   Among her many principal works
are "The Head of the Family," "John Halifax, Gentleman," "A Noble Life," etc.   She has written admir-
ably on a variety of subjects.

HARRIET LEE, an English writer of fiction, born in London, 1756. Died in 1851. Among her other productions as author are "The Canterbury Tales," in which she was assisted by her sister Sophia. These "Tales" bear no resemblance to the "Canterbury Tales" of Chaucer, written nearly four centuries before, except in being a collection of stories told by different persons.

HENRY WILD, sometimes called "the learned tailor," born in Norwich, Eng., 1684. Died 1730. He studied several of the Oriental languages, while working at his trade, and translated from the Arabic the legend of "Mohammed's Journey to Heaven."

SIR EDWIN LANDSEER, the most celebrated modern painter of animals, born in London, 1803. Died there Oct. 1, 1873. "The Old Shepherd's Chief Mourner," is considered by Ruskin one of the most perfect pictures which modern times has seen. Among his masterpieces are a portrait of a Newfoundland dog, styled "A Member of the Humane Society," "A Scene from the Midsummer Night's Dream," and "The Children of the Mist." The majority of his compositions have become popular engravings.

SYLVESTER GRAHAM, a noted American reformer and writer on dietetics, born in Suffield, Conn., 1794. Died in Northampton, Mass., Sept. 11, 1851. He early became a dyspeptic, and his great care to restore his health sufficiently to be of use, led him to advocate those principles of hygiene and diet by which others could escape what he had suffered. He was author of "Science of Human Life." The bread made of unbolted wheat, which he recommended, has taken his name.

JOHN BUNYAN, author of "Pilgrim's Progress,"

born near Bedford, Eng., 1628. Died Aug. 31, 1688. He wrote his great work while in jail, where he was confined twelve years for his religious teachings. Macaulay considered Bunyan "one of the two great creative minds of the latter half of the seventeenth century;" the other being Milton, author of "Paradise Lost."

JOHN HARRIS, the founder of Harrisburg, Pa., born in Pennsylvania, 1716. Died at Harrisburg. July 29, 1791. He was chosen by the Indians at one of the "council fires" held with the Indians of the Six Nations, to keep the store on the frontier, which was the nucleus of the present city named for him. His house, built in 1766, near Harrisburg, is still standing.

WILLIAM H. ASPINWALL, born in the city of New York, 1807. Died there Jan. 19, 1875. He was the chief promoter of the construction of the Panama Railroad, the eastern terminus of which is named for him.

BERNARD PALISSY, a celebrated French potter and enameler, born in the south of France, 1509. Died in the Bastile in 1589, where he was confined for his religious principles. He is noted for his discovery, after years of toil and privation, of the beautiful art of enameling stoneware and pottery, which bears his name.

HENRY BERGH, founder of the "Society for the Prevention of Cruelty to Animals," born in New York city, 1823. Died . Alone, in the face of indifference, opposition and ridicule, he began that reform which is now recognized as one of the beneficent monuments of the age. The legislature passed laws prepared by him, and on April 10, 1866, the society was legally organized with Mr. Bergh as president.

In 1874 he rescued a little girl from inhuman treatment, which led to a "Society for the Prevention of Cruelty to Children." He has written several plays, and is the author of a volume of tales and sketches entitled " The Streets of New York."

HENRY W. SHAW, "Josh Billings," an American humorist, born in Lanesborough, Mass.,   1818. Died Oct. 14, 1885. His first production in print appeared in 1863. His writings consist largely of quaint maxims in phonetic spelling. He has lectured extensively, and has published four volumes of his sketches besides his popular "Alminax."

JOHN FORBES, an English general during the French and Indian war, born at Fifeshire, Scotland, 1710. Died at Philadelphia, March 11, 1759. He was made brigadier-general in America, in 1757, and after taking Fort Du Quesne, named it Pittsburg, in compliment to the Prime Minister of England, William Pitt.

FRANCIS MARION, an American general during the Revolution, born in St. John's parish, near Georgetown, S. C., 1732. Died near Eutaw, Feb. 28, 1795. By his successful maneuvers in baffling the English in North Carolina, and still evading capture, he won the name of the " Swamp Fox."

ANTHONY TROLLOPE, an English novelist, born 1815. Died Dec. 6, 1882. He was the son of Frances Trollope the novelist, who visited the United States in 1829, and wrote so novel an account of domestic life in America.

MISCELLANY.

DATES THAT DIFFER.

In searching for dates we often find that biographers differ. In that case we have consulted several authorities, and preferred the majority. If there is a difference of eleven days in the dates of those born previous to the year 1752, when the " New Style " was inaugurated, we have followed the plan of the most reliable cyclopedias and taken the latter. The names here given are those whose dates are disturbed by some other cause than the "New Style."

GLUCK,	Feb. 14 and July 2.
WELBY, AMELIA B.,	Feb. 3 and May 3.
PETER THE GREAT,	June 10 and 12.
JONSON BEN,	Jan. 31 and June 11.
GARIBALDI,	July 4 and 22.
BROWNLOW, W.,	Aug. 5 and 29.
DAVIS, ANDREW J.,	Aug. 11 and 26.
LAVOISIER,	Aug. 13, 16 and 26.
WRIGHT, SILAS,	May 24 and Aug. 27.
" PETER MARTYR,"	Sept. 6 and 8.
BAXTER, RICHARD,	Oct. 12 and Nov. 12.
GAMBETTA, LEON,	Oct. 30 and April 2.
TAYLOR, ZACHARY,	Sept. 24, Oct. 24, Nov. 24.
MONROE, JAMES,	April 2 and 28.

Doré, P. G.	Jan. 6 and 7.
Dickens, Charles,	Jan. 7 and Feb. 7.
Putnam, Israel,	Jan. 7 and 10.
Kane, Elisha K.,	Feb. 3 and 20.
Queen Anna,	Feb. 4 and 6.
Napoleon I.,	Aug. 15 and Feb. 5.
Butler, Samuel,	Feb. 8 and 13.
Galileo,	July 15 and Feb. 15.
Poe, Edgar A.,	Jan. 19 and Feb. 19.
Farragut, David G.,	July 5 and March 7.
Klopstock,	July 2 and March 14.
Howe, Sir William,	Aug. 10 and March 2.

THE YEAR OF "GREAT BABIES."

The year 1769, called the year of "great babies," is noted for the birth of Napoleon, Wellington, Francis Accum, chemist; Bessières; duc d'Istria, one of Napoleon's best generals; Bourrienne, secretary and biographer of Napoleon; Brunel, architect of the Thames tunnel; Chateaubriand, author; Governor De Witt Clinton, of N. Y.; Cuvier, naturalist; Admiral Sir Thomas Hardy; Alexander Von Humboldt, Count Lavalette, Judge Lowell, founder of Boston Athenæum; Memed Ali, pasha of Egypt; Marshal Ney; William Owen, naturalist; Picard, French dramatist; Marshal Soult; Lord Castlereagh; Tallien, French statesman. These are twenty of the best names selected from a list of noted men born in this year.—From "Quizzism and Key" by Southwick.

ADAM'S BIRTHDAY.

By an act of the English Parliament, October 23, 4004 B.C., was declared the natal day of the earth.   As Adam was created on the fifth day after, he must have been born October 28, 4004 B.C.—FROM "QUIZZISM."

———

PECULIARITIES.

In compiling the foregoing work, several items of interest have presented themselves, among which are the following :

There are more surnames beginning with W than any other letter.

The winter, spring, and autumn months were much easier filled than those of summer ; the 7th of May and June being the last days represented, and the latter date only after extensive research.

It will be observed that in several instances, two of those born the same day of the month, are also born the same year.   Thus the natal day of Lincoln and Darwin, is Feb. 12, 1809.   That of Horace Mann and William H. Prescott, May 4, 1796.   Maria S. Cummins, author of "The Lamplighter," and Gen. Lewis Wallace, author of "Ben Hur," were born April 10, 1827.   Other instances of the kind will also be found in the book.

W. D. Howells and his friend John J. Piatt, joint author with him of "Poems by Two Friends," were born March 1, but in different years.   Elihu Burritt, "The Learned Blacksmith," and Robert Collyer, "The Blacksmith Preacher," were also born the same day (Dec. 8), though different years.

Certain days seem crowded with very eminent people, while for other days there are but few, and those not so prominent.

In several instances persons of a similar profession or notoriety are born in the same season of the year.

The arrangement of the names for each day, is according to age.

INDEX OF NOTED EXPRESSIONS.

" A chip of the old block."

Burke, on William Pitt, Jr.

" Always brave, but always the enemy of kings."

King of Poland, on Pulaski.

" An ambassador is an honest man sent abroad to lie for the good of his country."

Sir Henry Wotton.

" By the streets of By and By, one arrives at the house of Never."

Cervantes.

" Children, as soon as I am released, sing a psalm of praise to God."

Last words of Susannah Wesley.

" Conquests pass away, but these operations remain."

Napoleon to Delambre.

" Contraband of war."

Gen. B. F. Butler.

" Cotton is king."

James Hamilton Hammond.

" Don't give up the ship."

Capt. James Lawrence.

" England expects every man to do his duty."

Horatio Nelson.

"First in war, first in peace, and first in the hearts of his countrymen."

GEN. HENRY LEE, on Washington.

"Get the writings of John Woolman by heart and love the early Quakers."

CHARLES LAMB.

"Give me liberty or give me death."

PATRICK HENRY.

"God only is great."

MASSILLON, at the funeral of Louis XIV.

"God tempers the wind to the shorn lamb."

LAURENCE STERNE.

"Here lies a man who was in public service fifty years, and never attempted to deceive his countrymen."

J. C. BRECKENRIDGE, on Henry Clay.

"He smote the rock of the national resources, and abundant streams of revenue burst forth. He touched the corpse of public credit and it sprang upon its feet."

WEBSTER, on Hamilton.

"He wrested the thunderbolt from heaven and the scepter from the tyrants."

TURGOT, on Franklin.

"I awoke one morning and found myself famous."

LORD BYRON.

"I have heard many great orators, and been pleased with them, but after hearing you, I am displeased with myself."

LOUIS XIV., to Massillon.

"I have measured the heavens, I now measure the earth. The mind was of heavenly origin, only the shadow of the body lies here."

KEPLER'S EPITAPH, written by himself.

"I know not what I may appear to the world, but to myself I seem to have been only like a boy playing on the seashore and diverting myself in now and then finding a smoother pebble or a prettier shell than ordinary, whilst the great ocean of truth lay all undiscovered before me."

SIR ISAAC NEWTON.

"I'll try, sir."
JAMES MILLER, at the battle of Lundy's Lane.

"It is to my mother and her good principles that I owe my fortune, and all the good that I have done."
NAPOLEON BONAPARTE.

"I only regret that I have but one life to lose for my country."
NATHAN HALE.

"I would rather be right than President."
HENRY CLAY.

"Le style est de l'homme."
BUFFON.

"Liberty and Union, now and forever, one and inseparable."
DANIEL WEBSTER.

"Madame, all is lost except our honor."
FRANCIS I. of France.

"Millions for defense, but not one cent for tribute."
CHARLES C. PINCKNEY.

"My country is the world, my countrymen all mankind."
MOTTO OF THE "LIBERATOR."

"My work is finished and I am satisfied."
WILLIAM LLOYD GARRISON.

"Nature and Nature's laws lay hid in night
God said 'let Newton be!' and all was light."
NEWTON'S EPITAPH.

" None knew him but to love him
None named him but to praise."
FITZ-GREENE HALLECK, on J. R. Drake.

"No right without its duties—no duty without its rights."
FRANCIS LIEBER.

"O for sundown or Blucher."
DUKE OF WELLINGTON.

"O God ! it is all over !"
LORD NORTH.

"O Liberty ! what crimes are committed in thy name."
Last words of MADAME ROLAND.

"Once by the Severn's side
A little fountain rose,
Now, like the Severn's seaward tide
Round the whole world it flows."

MONTGOMERY, on Robert Raikes.

"Our Union—it must be preserved."

ANDREW JACKSON.

"Swiftest of painters, and gentlest of companions."

RUSKIN, on Reynolds.

"The firmest pillar of Washington's administration."

JOHN ADAMS, on Oliver Ellsworth.

"The greatest happiness of the greatest number."

PRIESTLY, on Jeremy Bentham.

"There are the red coats; we must beat them to-day, or Molly Starke is a widow."

GEN. JOHN STARKE.

"The United Colonies are and ought to be free and independent."

RICHARD H. LEE.

"This is the last of earth! I am content."

Last words of JOHN Q. ADAMS.

"Thy necessity is greater than mine."

SIR PHILIP SYDNEY.

"Turn, boys, we're going back."

GEN. PHIL. SHERIDAN.

"Veni, vidi, vici" (I came, I saw, I conquered.)

JULIUS CÆSAR.

"We have met the enemy and they are ours."

COM. O. H. PERRY.

"Westward the course of empire takes its way."

GEORGE BERKELEY.

"What hath God wrought?"

FIRST TELEGRAPHIC MESSAGE.

"What we know is but little, that which we know not is immense."

LAPLACE.

ANALYTICAL INDEX.

Authors.

Clergymen and Theologians.

Lawyers and Jurists.

Military and Naval.

Miscellaneous.

Musicians and Composers.

Patriots.

Philanthropists and Reformers.

Physicians and Surgeons.

Scientists.

Statesmen.

Travelers and Explorers.

Fowler & Wells Co.'s New Publications.

Physical Culture. For Home and School. Scientific and Practical. By D. L. Dowd, Professor of Physical Culture. 12mo, 322 pages, 80 illustrations, fine binding. $1.50.

The best work on the building up of Health and Strength by systematic exercise ever published. It will be called for by professional and all sedentary people, and all who do not have the necessary and proper exercise in their daily occupation ; it also tells how to work for health and strength.

A Practical Plan of Instruction in Shorthand. By Bates Torry. $1.

Consisting of a series of twenty lessons, in the form of Lesson leaves. Every teacher of shorthand will prize this, and those attempting self-instruction should use it.

Nervousness: Its Nature, Causes, Symptoms, and Treatment. By H. S. Drayton, M. D., Editor Phrenological Journal. 25 cents.

A practical treatise on this rapidly increasing malady.

Pope's Essay on Man. With responding Essay, Man Seen in the Deepening Dawn. By Dr. C. S. Weeks. Paper, 25c.

A unique and interesting volume giving Pope's Essay, and on the opposite pages parallel lines also parallel to and responding to the sentiments of Pope. All admirers of the Essay on Man will enjoy this.

How to Succeed as a Stenographer or Typewriter, should be in the hands of every shorthand writer and student, containing quiet hints and gentle advice by one who "Has Been There." A Handbook of miscellaneous information and suggestions for the young law reporter ; the Shorthand Student; the Typewriter operator; with rules for the proper use of capital letters and punctuation. Also some practical suggestions for the formation of a general American Association of Stenographers. By Arthur M. Baker. 25c.

Andrews' Chart of Comparative Phonography. Showing and comparing the principal features in the leading systems of Phonography of interest to all shorthand writers and students. 15 x 20 inches. Price, 25c. Mounted on muslin, 50c.

Horace Mann: A view of his life and its meaning ; a memorial address. By Rev. J. B. Weston, D.D. Paper, 10c.

A worthy tribute to this great man, it will prove to be of interest to every intelligent reader.

Men and Women Differ in Character.

[PORTRAITS FROM LIFE IN "HEADS AND FACES."]

No. 1	James Parton.	No. 5.	Emperor Paul of Russia.	No. 9.	General N...
No. 2.	A M Rice.	No. 6.	George Eliot.	No. 10.	Otho the G...
No. 3.	Wm M. Evarts	No 7.	King Frederick the Strong.	No. 11.	African.
No. 4.	General Winowell.	No. 8.	Prof. George Bush.		

IF YOU WANT SOMETHING

that will interest you more than anything you have ever read and ena...
you to understand all the differences in people at a glance, by the "Si...
of CHARACTER," send for a copy of

HEADS AND FACES; How to Study Them.

A new Manual of Character Reading for the people, by Prof. Nel...
Sizer, the Examiner in the phrenological office of Fowler & Wells (...
New York, and H. S. Drayton, M.D., Editor of the PHRENOLOGI...
JOURNAL. The authors know what they are writing about, Prof. S...
having devoted nearly fifty years almost exclusively to the readin...
character and he here lays down the rules employed by him in his ...
fessional work. It will show you how to read people as you wou...
book, and to see if they are inclined to be good, upright, honest, true, k...
charitable, loving, joyous, happy and trustworthy people, such as ...
would like to know.

A knowledge of Human Nature would save many disappointment...
social and business life.

This is the most comprehensive and popular work ever published...
the price, 25,000 copies having been sold the first year. Contains 200 l...
octavo pages and 250 portraits. Send for it and study the people you ...
and your own character. If you are not satisfied after examining ...
book, you may return it, in good condition, and money will be ...
turned to you.

We will send it carefully by mail, postpaid, on receipt of price, 40 c...
in paper, or $1 in cloth binding. Agents wanted. Address

FOWLER & WELLS CO., Publishers, 775 Broadway, New York.

A STORY WORTH READING.

ABOUT HUMAN NATURE.

We have recently published a volume containing a story of Human Nature which will be found of interest. It is called "The MAN WONDERFUL in the HOUSE BEAUTIFUL," and is an allegory, teaching the principles of Physiology and Hygiene, and the effects of Stimulants and Narcotics. The House is the Body, in which the Foundations are the Bones, the Walls are Muscles, the Skin and Hair the Siding and Shingles, the head an Observatory in which are found a pair of Telescopes, and radiating from it are the nerves which are compared to a Telegraph, while communications are kept up with the Kitchen, Dining-room, Pantry, Laundry, etc. The House is heated with a Furnace. There are also Mysterious Chambers, and the whole is protected by a Burglar Alarm. In studying the inhabitant of the House, the "Man Wonderful," we learn of his growth, development, and habits of the guests whom he introduces. He finds that some of them are friends, others are doubtful acquaintances, and some decidedly wicked. Under this form, we ascertain the effects of Food and Drink, Narcotics and Stimulants.

It is a wonderful book, and placed in the hands of children will lead them to the study of Physiology and Hygiene, and the Laws of Life and Health in a way that will never be forgotten. The book will prove of great interest even to adults and those familiar with the subject. The authors, Drs. C. B. and Mary A. Allen, are both regular physicians, and therefore the work is accurate and on a scientific basis. "Science in Story" has never been presented in a more attractive form. It is universally admitted that a large proportion of sickness comes from violations of the laws of Life and Health, and therefore it is important that this subject should be understood by all, as in this way we may become familiar with all the avoidable causes of disease. The reading of this book will very largely accomplish this end. It will be sent securely by mail, prepaid, on receipt of price, which is only $1.50. Address

Fowler & Wells Co., Publishers, 775 Broadway, New York.

Brain and Mind,

OR, MENTAL SCIENCE CONSIDERED IN ACCORDANCE WITH THE PRINCIPLES OF PHRENOLOGY AND IN RELATION TO MODERN PHILOSOPHY.

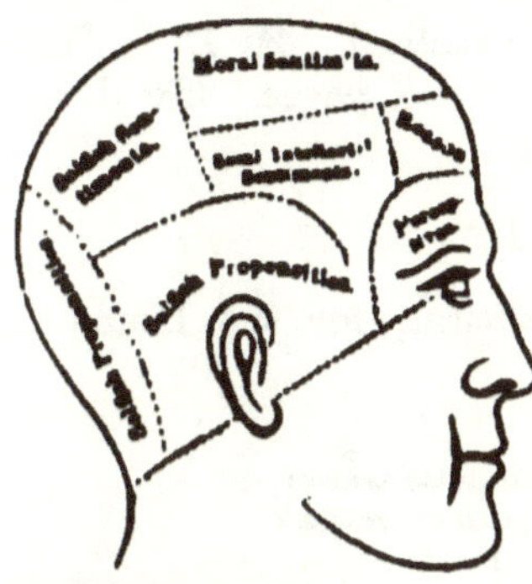

By H. S. Drayton, A.M., M.D., and James McNeill, A.B. Illustrated with over One Hundred Portraits and Diagrams. $1.50.

The authors state in their preface: "In preparing this volume it has been the aim to meet an existing want, viz: that of a treatise which not only gives the reader a complete view of the system of mental science known as Phrenology, but also exhibits its relation to Anatomy and Physiology, as those sciences are represented to-day by standard authority."

The following, from the Table of Contents, shows the scope and character of the work:

GENERAL PRINCIPLES.
THE TEMPERAMENTS.
STRUCTURE OF THE BRAIN AND SKULL.
CLASSIFICATION OF THE FACULTIES.
THE SELFISH ORGANS.
THE INTELLECT.
THE SEMI-INTELLECTUAL FACULTIES.
THE ORGANS OF THE SOCIAL FUNCTIONS.
THE SELFISH SENTIMENTS.
THE MORAL AND RELIGIOUS SENTIMENTS.

HOW TO EXAMINE HEADS.
HOW CHARACTER IS MANIFESTED.
THE ACTION OF THE FACULTIES.
THE RELATION OF PHRENOLOGY TO METAPHYSICS AND EDUCATION.
VALUE OF PHRENOLOGY AS AN ART.
PHRENOLOGY AND PHYSIOLOGY.
OBJECTIONS AND CONFIRMATIONS BY THE PHYSIOLOGISTS.
PHRENOLOGY IN GENERAL LITERATURE.

Notices of the Press.

Phrenology is no longer a thing laughed at. The scientific researches of the last twenty years have demonstrated the fearful and wonderful complication of matter, not only with mind, but with what we call moral qualities. Thereby, we believe, the divine origin of "our frame" has been newly illustrated, and the Scriptural psychology confirmed; and in the Phrenological Chart we are disposed to find a species of "urim and thummim," revealing, if not the Creator's will concerning us, at least His revelation of essential character. One thing is certain, that the discoveries of physical science must ere long force all men to the single alternative of Calvinism or Atheism. When they see that God has written Himself sovereign, absolute, and predestinating, on the records of His creation, they will be ready to find His writing as clearly in the Word; and the analogical argument, meeting the difficulties and the objections on the side of Faith by those admitted as existing on the side of Sight, will avail as well in one case as in the other. We will only add, the above work is, without doubt, the best popular presentation of the science which has yet been made. It confines itself strictly to facts, and is not written in the interest of any pet "theory." It is made very interesting by its copious illustrations, pictorial and narrative, and the whole is brought down to the latest information on this curious and suggestive department of knowledge.—*Christian Intelligencer.*

As far as a comprehensive view of the teachings of Combe can be embodied into a system that the popular mind can understand, this book is as satisfactory an exposition of its kind as has yet been published. The definitions are clear, exhaustive, and spirited.—*Philadelphia Enquirer.*

In style and treatment it is adapted to the general reader, abounds with valuable instruction expressed in clear, practical terms, and the work constitutes by far the best Text-book on Phrenology published, and is adapted to both private and class study.

The illustrations of the Special Organs and Faculties are for the most part from portraits of men and women whose characters are known, and great pains have been taken to exemplify with accuracy the significance of the text in each case. For the student of human nature and character the work is of the highest value.

It is printed on fine paper, and substantially bound in extra cloth, by mail, postpaid, on receipt of price, $1.50.   Address

FOWLER & WELLS CO., Publishers, 775 Broadway, New York.

PHYSICAL CULTURE.

For Home and School. Scientific and Practical. By D. L. Dowd, Professor of Physical Culture. 322 12mo. pages. 300 Illustrations. Fine Binding. Price $1.50.

CONTENTS.

Physical Culture, Scientific and Practical, for the Home and School. Pure Air and Foul Air.

Questions Constantly Being Asked:

No. 1. Does massage treatment strengthen muscular tissue?
No. 2. Are boat-racing and horseback-riding good exercises?
No. 3. Are athletic sports conducive to health?
No. 4. Why do you object to developing with heavy weights?
No. 5. How long a time will it take to reach the limit of development?
No. 6. Is there a limit to muscular development, and is it possible to gain an abnormal development?
No. 7. What is meant by being muscle bound?
No. 8. Why are some small men stronger than others of nearly double their size?
No. 9. Why is a person taller with less weight in the morning than in the evening?
No. 10. How should a person breathe while racing or walking up-stairs or up-hill?
No. 11. Is there any advantage gained by weighting the shoes of sprinters and horses?
No. 12. What kind of food is best for us to eat?
No. 13. What form of bathing is best?
No. 14. How can I best reduce my weight, or how increase it?
No. 15. Can you determine the size of one's lungs by blowing in a spirometer?

Personal Experience of the Author in Physical Training.
Physical Culture for the Voice. Practice of Deep Breathing.
Facial and Neck Development. A few Hints for the Complexion.
The Graceful and Ungraceful Figure, and Improvement of Deformities, such as Bow-Leg, Knock-Knee, Wry-Neck, Round Shoulders, Lateral Curvature of the Spine, etc.
A few Brief Rules. The Normal Man. Specific Exercises for the Development of Every Set of Muscles of the Body, Arms and Legs, also Exercises for Deepening and Broadening the Chest and Strengthening the Lungs.
These 34 Specific Exercises are each illustrated by a full length figure (taken from life) showing the set of muscles in contraction, which can be developed by each of them.] Dumb Bell Exercises.
Ten Appendices showing the relative gain of pupils from 9 years of age to 40.
All who value Health, Strength and Happiness should procure and read this work ; it will be found by far the best work ever written on this important subject. Sent by mail, postpaid, on receipt of price. $1.50.

Address, Fowler & Wells Co., Publishers, 775 Broadway, New York.

A Natural System of Elocution and Oratory.

Founded on an analysis of the Human Constitution, considered in its three-fold nature, Mental, Physiological, and Expressional. By Thos. Hyde and Wm. Hyde. Illustrated. 12mo. Extra Cloth, $ 2.00. Library, sprinkled edges, $2.50. Half Turkey Morocco, polished marbled edges, gilt back, $3.25.

We call the attention of Clergymen, Lawyers, Teachers and Scholars to this new book on Elocution and Oratory, as one of the most scholarly, original and inspiring books ever written on the subject of Eloquence. It begins a new era in oratorical Instruction, since it supplies what has long been needed, and the want of which has retarded up to the present moment the progress of oratorical Instruction, namely, a scientific exposition of the emotional and intellectual elements, which are at the base of persuasive oratory. It covers the entire field of the art of eloquence, and is so full and clear in its statements and definitions that students can master this noble art by its aid without a teacher. In truth, the book is so full of Instruction, thought and experience, that one can learn from reading it what it would cost him several hundred dollars to obtain through the channels of professional Instruction. And, besides, the book is original in its system, matter, and plan, what it contains can not be obtained from any one professor of the art. It is a book which ought to be in every one's possession and be studied slowly and carefully, for every perusal of it will reveal something new, and strengthen and improve the talents of speech. The authors have brought to bear ripe experience and zealous study in its production, and hence it is unsurpassed as an exhaustive, practical and comprehensive treatise. There are no superficial glimpses given of oratorical truths; no mere verbal enunciations of graceful positions of body, or tricks of voice Intonation, but the authors go to the root of the matter and unfold the germinal thought and oratorical passion; show how such thought expresses itself in look, voice and gesture, and how each may be cultivated. It teaches the clergyman how to improve the composition and delivery of his sermons; the lawyer, the most persuasive arrangement of the arguments and details of his plea, and the platform orator, how to make his discourse suit the needs of a popular assembly, and the teacher of elocution the method of Instruction best adapted to awaken and stimulate the natural endowments of his pupils. The book is invaluable to teachers in Public Schools, since it gives a careful, clear, and exhaustive analysis of every vocal element with its correct pronunciation. Such analysis, with the many other valuable suggestions it contains, will enable the teacher to drill his pupils successfully in articulation and pronunciation. The book, besides teaching in a thorough manner that is essential to oratory, unfolds in a practical way all that is embraced under the term elocution. Public readers and actors can learn from this book more about the natural training and developing of voice and character impersonation than from any book now before the public.

Sent by mail on receipt of price. Agents wanted.

Address, Fowler & Wells Co., Publishers, 775 Broadway, New York.

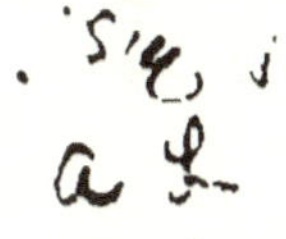